KT-418-238

IMAGES

IMAGES

ROSE DOYLE

POOLBEG

First Published 1993 by
Poolbeg Press Ltd.
123 Baldoyle Industrial Estate,
Dublin 13, Ireland
Email: poolbeg@poolbeg.com
www.poolbeg.com

Reissued 2001

© Rose Doyle 1993

Copyright for typesetting, layout, design
© Poolbeg Group Services Ltd.

The moral right of the author has been asserted

3 5 7 9 10 8 6 4 2

A catalogue record for this book is available from
the British Library.

ISBN 1 84223 014 X

All rights reserved. No part of this publication may be reproduced or
transmitted in any form or by any means, electronic or mechanical,
including photography, recording, or any information storage or
retrieval system, without permission in writing from the publisher. The
book is sold subject to the condition that it shall not, by way of trade or
otherwise, be lent, resold or otherwise circulated without the publisher's
prior consent in any form of binding or cover other than that in
which it is published and without a similar condition, including this
condition, being imposed on the subsequent purchaser.

Printed in the UK by Cox & Wyman Ltd,
Reading, Berkshire

For the friends and family who encouraged.
They know who they are.

A Note on the Author

Rose Doyle is a journalist and writer of fiction. She lives in Dublin. *Images* was her first novel for adults and has since been followed by five others. Her sixth novel will be published later this year.

Acknowledgements

Great thanks to Gerald Davis, painter, gallery owner and old friend, who painlessly and hilariously educated me as to the whys and wherefores of dishonest dealing in the art world. And of course Arthur and Lorna who also helped with research.

Great thanks too to Pat Fay, Counsellor with the Coolmine Therapeutic Community, for taking the time to fill me in on the chilling facts about drug addiction amongst the young in Dublin.

And eternal gratitude to Ella and Kate, who read the manuscript and assured me I'd written a book.

PROLOGUE

The road ahead streamed wet and muddy in the headlights. Rain, great torrents of it, beat on the roof of the car. She hadn't seen another moving thing since leaving the main road outside the village. Nor a glimmer of light. Nothing but blackness, wet and inky, everywhere beyond the car. She might have been swallowed into it.

There was a wind blowing up now, too. Not gale force but bad enough to shake the car. October was unpredictable. A mercurial month. She was driving faster than any rational person should on a narrow, windy road like this. But it cut cross country and would take miles off her journey. Time too, maybe as much as half an hour.

She prayed, the first time she had really prayed in years, that he wouldn't have gone by the time she got there. She had to see the proof for herself, the evidence of her gullibility. It wasn't enough that she knew, already, how she'd been used. She had to see as well.

She slowed down hardly at all as she hit a flooded patch of road. The water, a lot deeper than she'd anticipated, hit the car with a wallop. She caught her breath, put her foot down hard on the accelerator. The car cut through and away.

Then she was on a straight stretch of road again. The headlights picked up a set of cat's eyes along the centre.

Another pair, yellowly misleading, appeared by the side of the road. They stared, unblinking, as she passed. Country cats travelled far in search of whatever it was they hunted. Sex and companionship, she supposed. Primal instincts were the same, whatever the species.

Another two miles, according to the man in the pub, and there would be a sign for the cliff road. She rounded a corner and almost didn't see the cow until her huge head turned, staring at her in the headlights. A shuddering awareness of what could have happened made her slow down so that she didn't miss the small, obscure road sign when she came to it five hundred yards further on. From now on she knew there was nothing but stony, mountain land on her right, an almost sheer drop into the Atlantic on her left.

She drove for another ten minutes before she saw a light, another five before she got to the cottage. Heeding her instinct, bitterly regretting that she'd ignored it for months past, she drove on until she found a widening in the road and turned the car. Hands clenched hard on the wheel she drove back to the gate leading to the cottage and parked the car on the road. She would at least be ready for a quick getaway. If the need arose.

The wind almost knocked her off her feet as she got out of the car but once she was in the yard it was more sheltered. The man had been right: her shoes were sodden before she got to the door.

It was quite a big cottage, lights on in two of its rooms. A black Volvo, English registration, was parked in front. Voices came from inside. He was here then, and not alone. But then she hadn't expected that he would be.

She took a deep breath and knocked on the door, hard.

CHAPTER ONE

Bea Hennessy put her foot on the accelerator and speeded up.

It was Christmas Eve. The countryside flashed past: skeletal trees, frost-silver fields, neat bungalows, a still river, horses in a field. She opened the window. The sharp air was a jolt. It brought with it the smell of wood fires.

The dawn which had been threatening and overcast when she left Dublin had given way to a clear, bright morning when she was about forty-five minutes out of the city. The frost over the muddy grass of winter lent the fields a Christmas card look. Or maybe her imagination did that. It was, after all, the beginning of the season of tinsel and fantasy.

The season of peace too, and togetherness. Bea bit her lip, a childhood habit, and touched the wood of the dashboard for luck. "Please," she spoke aloud, "let this Christmas have those things as well. And let it be the Christmas my child and I become friends again."

She crossed her fingers. The thought of the family party planned for the evening ahead filled her with hope and dread in almost equal measure.

It was to be a double celebration this year since her

daughter Sinéad was bringing her new husband to meet the family. Bea pulled a rueful face. Given the family's track record in such things it could become more of a baptism by fire than a post-nuptial revel. She would have prayed for it to go well if she knew how, but she'd lost the habit. Wishing would have to do.

More bare, wintry trees flitted past. The underbelly of the earlier storm clouds filled the sky behind her but ahead it continued miraculously clear and blue. Bea, whose innate optimism had not been destroyed by a bad marriage, nor indeed by seventeen years in the art business, decided to take this as a good sign. There would be no sadness, no regretful memories, for her this Christmas. Let the season do its stuff, work its magic. Just this once.

Squinting into the winter sun, glaringly bright on the silver landscape, she searched the glove compartment for sunglasses. She was glad to be out of Dublin. She didn't get away often enough. Certainly not to Inverskena, the rambling old house she owned with her brother Charles. Pretty inexcusable, she thought, as her groping hand came in contact with the sunglasses, since it was less than an hour-and-a-half's drive from town. But having less time for herself was, she knew, the price she paid for the ever-increasing success of her art gallery.

Business had never been better, the artists she showed never more exciting. And now, with the possibility of showing Miroslav Capek on the horizon, it looked as if things were going to become more challenging still.

She slipped the sunglasses over the dark blue eyes which were such a stunning contrast to the auburn of her hair. At forty-one Bea was as beautiful as she'd ever been. And a lot more elegant. The years had toned and refined her looks, her high cheekbones coming into their own as her face thinned. Her eyes now looked on the world with a more penetrating and perceptive blue. Her hair, worn for years in a long, heavy plait, swung these days to her shoulders in a well-cut bob.

She checked the time and saw that it was just nine o'clock. Not bad. She'd be there by ten at this rate.

Unless she stopped. The tranquillity of the passing country scene beckoned. "There is a tide in the affairs of men, and women..." she murmured to herself, eyeing the quiet, empty fields. Now was the moment to grab a few breaths of clean, fresh air. There would be no time to spare later. Once she got to Inverskena the day would be devoured by a scramble of preparations for the party.

Bea bit her lip again. The day had begun, very early and badly, with her hurting a friend. The evening could well bring more pain. Might as well fortify herself with some bracing fresh air while she had the chance. She stopped the car, swung her long legs in their leather boots out onto the crackling frost of the verge. The air was bitingly cold, snapping at her nose and mouth as she took deep breaths. Closing her eyes she put her head back and faced into the whitish sun. Her mid-calf length cashmere coat hung well on her tall, slim body. A vivid, cerise scarf clashed wildly with her hair but looked superb. She had, after years in the art business and like Coco Chanel, learned discrimination from observing other people's bad taste. Her fine physical appearance apart, she had grace and intelligence.

And she had a will that life had hardened to iron.

She closed the door and had taken the first brisk steps towards a gate into a field when she heard the phone, faint and insistent, ring from inside the Audi.

She stopped. If it wasn't important they would ring off. But the faint sound persisted and, reluctantly, she retraced her steps.

"No peace for the wicked," she groaned, then clicked into brisk efficiency as she pressed the "on" switch. "Hello, Bea Hennessy here."

"Bea, is that you?" The voice sounded sleepy. Its owner yawned.

"Yes, Olivia, it's me. Why are you telephoning at this hour?" Bea, shorter than she meant to be with her sister, was instantly contrite.

"You *will* be down in time for the party, won't you?" She put as much enthusiasm as she could muster into the question. Apart from the considerable bond of family the sisters had little in common.

"Yes, of course I will." Olivia sounded impatient. "We'll all be there. As usual."

By all Olivia meant her husband, Albert D'Arcy, and grown children, Mark and Stephanie. Bea sighed to herself as she thought of Olivia.

Physically, the sisters resembled each other in height only. Olivia, who was a year younger than Bea, had a blonde, ice-cool beauty of which she took great care. Their personalities could not have been more different. Olivia, self-interested and manipulative, was an instinctive mischief-maker. Bea, fiercely independent and honest, almost feared her sister's capacity to make trouble. Had it not been for the ties of blood it was doubtful they'd have even tolerated one another.

"That's good," Bea said now. "We'll see you later then…" She looked longingly across the field she'd been hoping to walk. "But that's not why you rang, is it?" Olivia never did anything without a reason. She certainly never made pointless telephone calls.

"Only partly," Olivia yawned. Quite loudly this time. Bea, controlling her irritation, said nothing. Olivia's tactic of slowly releasing information was calculated to annoy. It took another long yawn before Olivia finally began to get to the point.

"Where exactly are you?" she asked. "I wondered if you were too far down the road to turn back...?"

"Much too far." Bea was firm. "What is it you want, Olivia?"

"God, but you're touchy, Bea. On Christmas Eve too. Not much affected by the season's goodwill, from the sound of things. But then you haven't had much to feel good about these last few weeks, have you? Christmas is definitely not your time of year, old dear..."

"Olivia!" Bea made the word a warning. "I don't have time for this!" But you're right, she thought. I'm *not* affected by seasonal goodwill. Too many memories, too many sad associations with these short, dark midwinter days. I don't feel much goodwill when it comes to you either, sister dear. Aloud she said, "Charles is waiting..."

"Let him wait!" Olivia snapped. "He doesn't have much else to do."

This was not true. Charles it was who, each year, put generous time and energy into preparing Inverskena for their coming. He decorated in advance, hewed logs for burning, made bedrooms comfortable and generally created a warmly traditional Christmas ambience. That family members did not always measure up with a generosity of mood, or contribute the general good nature required to make things perfect, did not bother him at all. While Bea had developed independence as a protection, Charles had become sanguine, with a remarkable detachment which kept him from becoming too involved in the pain of family matters.

Because he loved to cook he would make the dinner too, five courses with trimmings. All of it he saw as an annual duty to the family, a small price to pay for the pleasures of a peaceful January after they had all gone.

"I simply thought," Olivia was ice, "that you might collect Mark and take him down with you. He appears to be staying somewhere in Castleknock and that's an impossible place for me to get to from here..." Olivia lived, in some splendour, in leafy Foxrock. Mark was twenty and Bea was surprised to hear he was not living at home.

"It's not my side of town either," she pointed out.

She lived in Sandymount, in a flat occupying the entire top floor of an old house there. Her living room and bedroom views took in the entire sweep of Dublin Bay, from the Kish to Baily lighthouses. She loved Sandymount. It was real, had style as well as conviviality, a literary history, good village shopping. It was close enough to her business for her to walk to work, when she had the time. She could not imagine living anywhere else.

"I'm aware it's not your side of town." Olivia was getting tetchier all the time. "But since you insist on leaving pre-dawn I thought you could pop by wherever it is he's buried himself and pick him up. The traffic will be horrendous by the time Albert and I are ready to leave. Anyway, you've no one but yourself in the car. We've got Stephanie to think about as well as Mark. Plus all our luggage of course...."

Bea groaned, a long, inward groan. The luggage was, of course, the real problem. Even for a few days, Olivia,

Stephanie too, would pack bags and cases with designer gowns and tailored country wear. Paul Costello and Pat Crowley would lie in tissue with Fendi bags and Kelian pumps. Scent, toiletries and make-up would occupy further bags, Albert and Mark would fit their clothes in where they could.

But the groan was double-edged. Olivia was well aware that the Audi was packed to its grey-lined roof with fresh flowers, vegetables, fruit, drink and presents. They were the reason Bea had been abroad in pre-dawn Dublin, visiting the Smithfield fruit and vegetable market before 6.30am. They were a regular part of her contribution to the family Christmas. She'd been making it for all of the five years they'd been gathering as a clan at Inverskena.

"You know the car is crammed to the gills." Bea didn't pretend patience any more. "And I can't turn back now. I'm more than half-way there and Charles needs a hand. Why can't Mark get a taxi across town to meet you? Or a bus, for God's sake?"

"I don't know why. He says he can't. I don't think he wants to go to Inverskena for Christmas at all, as a matter of fact. At twenty he's quite entitled to make up his own mind, of course. But Albert's insisting that he come...I suppose I'll just have to collect him..."

"I suppose you will," Bea agreed. "Sinéad will be sorry if he doesn't come down..."

Sinéad and Mark had always been good friends but Bea knew, as soon as she mentioned her own daughter's name, that she'd made a mistake. It was tantamount to giving Olivia a big, fat cue to poke her most sensitive feelings. And Olivia never missed a cue, large or small.

"Oh? Sinéad's definitely expected then?" Olivia's voice took on an almost joyful malice.

"Of course she is." Bea kept her voice even. "You know the party's partially for her this year. She agreed..."

"Agreeing doesn't mean she'll turn up, does it? And are we to be allowed meet her new spouse? Has she agreed to bring him along?"

Bea clenched her teeth and silently and gently swore at her adored, only child for putting her in the position of defending her to Olivia. She thought about cutting her sister off, but immediately thought better of it. Better by far to deal with Olivia's bitching on the phone, now, than face a row in Inverskena when everybody was there. Taking a long breath, Bea decided to play for time. And to calm herself down a little.

"Olivia, can I ring you back?" She was quietly polite. "I'm turning to ice, sitting here in the car. I want to stretch my legs, get the circulation going again. Give me ten minutes..."

Ignoring Olivia's protests she ended the call. Pulling a face at the silent console she took a deep, calming breath and stepped once again into the sharp morning air outside.

The gate to the field was stiff but opened enough to allow her slip through and into the field. She walked quickly then, watching her breath make clouds in the cold air. God, but she needed this; the freedom of an open space, the invigoration of exercise. Walking, preferably alone, was the best therapy she knew.

She especially needed its calming effect after a conversation with Olivia. Bea had long given up hope of any kind of real friendship with her sister. They disagreed just as much now as they had when they were children. It wasn't just that their personalities were at odds either. To say that Jude, their mother, had discouraged affection or sharing was putting it mildly. An there was so much of Jude in Olivia...

I am not, Bea resolved, going to think about it now. I've got too many other things to think about...

She would, of course, have to ring Olivia back. If only for the sake of peace between them over Christmas.

But first she needed to figure out a way to handle things, to deal with any plans on Olivia's part to make mischief.

She would be unable to resist capitalising on the fact that her niece had married in secret three weeks before. Not even Bea, who had reared Sinéad with much difficulty on her own, had known. The news had come ten days ago, in a letter. Brief and to the point, it had been sent from the Hotel Cipriani in Venice where Sinéad and her husband were honeymooning.

She had been married, Sinéad had written, in the registry office in Kildare Street. A small affair, no fuss. They'd both wanted it that way. She was twenty-one, after all. She knew her own mind. It was her life.

The sentences, short and unapologetic, had stabbed at Bea as she read, each one a wound.

Sinéad's husband was someone she'd met six months before. They would live in Blackrock, where he owned a townhouse. His name was Daniel Kirwan and he was an accountant. She was not, the last line assured, pregnant.

For that much thank God, Bea had thought as she put the letter away. She is not, at least, repeating my mistake.

Three days before, within hours of returning from her honeymoon, Sinéad had telephoned Bea. Bea had been absurdly grateful. Feeling as though she were walking on eggs, careful not to push things, she had persuaded Sinéad to make the traditional Hennessy

Christmas Eve party a dual celebration this year.

"A sort of post-nuptial Yuletide bash, you mean?" Sinéad had sounded cautious.

"Yes, something like that. It'll give everyone a chance to meet your husband and...well, wish you luck..."

Bea, trying hard to prolong the first real conversation she'd had with her daughter in a long time, had found herself without anything to say. Time was when she and Sinéad had discussed everything, when evenings together were never long enough for all they had to tell each other. It had been like that until two years ago. It all seemed a very long time ago now.

"Okay." Sinéad had been grudging. "A combination party should keep things in proportion. We'll get there about seven on Christmas Eve. See you then..."

"Sinéad, wait..." Desperate, Bea couldn't prevent her voice from taking on a pleading quality. She knew she was risking accusations of moral blackmail from her daughter but she didn't care.

"Will you stay on after Christmas? We see so little of one another these days...And it would be nice to get to know your husband..."

"All right." Sinéad's voice had been politely agreeable, nothing more. "I think Daniel will like Charles anyway. And Mark too. Ciao then, as the Italians say."

And she was gone.

Bea stood for a long time looking at the phone. Nothing about him liking *me*, she thought, but immediately reproached herself for this self-pity. She felt sad, a little angry, but very relieved. She had been terribly afraid that Sinéad would stay away for Christmas. And that would have been unbearable.

Bea, reaching the end of the field and another stiff

gate, decided to turn back. The Audi, parked in the distance, brought Olivia to mind. Her sister could spoil the delicate balance at Inverskena. She had the capacity and she had the inclination. She had, Bea reflected, been in fine, provocative form when she'd paid a brief visit to the gallery a week before.

Elegantly swathed in musquash, hair a golden glow, Olivia had idly studied some pictures while Bea dealt with a customer. As he left the gallery she had, quite nakedly, studied the man. Her disdainful expression dismissed him as she turned to Bea.

"Was he really worth the time?" she asked.

Bea decided to ignore the question, replying instead with one of her own.

"How was the trip to Forest Mere?"

By getting onto the subject of Olivia's recent trip to the fashionable English health resort Bea hoped to make the cat in her sister purr. She was terribly tired of her claws.

"Wonderful!" Olivia did a reasonable imitation of contentment. "It was marvellously pampering. Just what I needed. I feel quite prepared for anything the Christmas shenanigans may throw my way. Quite fighting fit in fact!"

She laughed and Bea's heart sank. To Olivia conflict and discord were as milk and cream to a cat. Mere civility was not going to put her off. Bea decided to ignore the innuendo.

"What's the word on Miroslav Capek?" Immediately she asked the question she regretted it.

Olivia's eyes sharpened as she looked around the gallery.

"I hope you're planning to give him a good

showing..." Her tone implied it would need to be a lot
better than anything she saw in front of her. Bea counted
to five before she answered.

"Depends on what he comes up with by way of
pictures..."

"They'll be brilliant, naturally..." Olivia checked her
watch. "Must rush. Luncheon appointment. I'll be in
touch, about Christmas and all that..."

And she was gone, leaving Bea quietly fuming as she
got on with her day's work. Not for the first time she
regretted breaking her rule about not mixing family with
work. But her art dealing instinct, always sharp and nearly
always reliable, had made her unable to resist when Olivia
had come to her with the story of an acclaimed Romanian
painter working in seclusion in Ireland. She could, Olivia
had assured, get him to show at The Hennessy Gallery.
For a commission, of course.

Olivia had got the scent of a good investment at a
Dublin fine arts auction some months previously. A
Miroslav Capek picture, newly painted in Ireland, had
gone for three times the figure the auctioneer had
expected. The sale had made the columns of *The Irish
Times* next day and Olivia, curious and greedy, had vowed
to Bea that she would track the painter down.

She hadn't quite made it to Capek but she had tracked
down his patron. Which was, Olivia declared, even better.
Possessed of much charm when she chose to exert it,
Olivia had persuaded the patron that Bea's should be
the gallery to show Capek's new work.

From the patron, an art collector who wished to keep
his name out of things, Olivia had also learned the
outlines of the painter's story. After being freed from
one of Ceausescu's jails Capek had, for a while, painted

in New York. Unable to cope with that city he had come seeking, and found, isolated contentment somewhere in Ireland. His seclusion was so extreme that only his patron knew where he lived.

If everything went according to plan, Olivia's plan, then a first, small showing of his Irish pictures would take place in Bea's gallery at the end of January.

Bea had yet to see the pictures and meet the man. She was used to the eccentricities, the individuality of artists, but she still held that judgement of character was as important as judgement of art. She would not agree to show until she met the painter, reclusive or not. And time was running out. Olivia would have to set up a meeting early in the new year.

But the gallery was closed now, she was on holiday. She took a few last, deep breaths as she reached the car and got back inside. Her skin tingled, her head felt wonderfully cleared. She checked the car clock and saw that her walk had taken twenty minutes. Best to get back on the road. She would talk to Olivia as she drove— illegal, she knew, but the roads were practically empty and she would drive slowly.

She drove thoughtfully through a just-awakening village before, squaring her shoulders, she pressed the phone into action again.

Olivia answered almost immediately, but cautiously and as if she were sifting calls. Which of course she was. Olivia had a talent for complicating her life.

"You took your time," she became snappy once she'd established it was her sister.

"Sorry," Bea said agreeably. "The fresh air went to my head, I'm afraid. And I'm sorry too that I can't oblige about Mark."

A car passed, filled with a cheerful family. The children waved to her, bright Santa Claus hats on their heads. She grinned and waved back. She was feeling quite light-hearted as she asked Olivia what time she expected to arrive at Inverskena that evening.

"Depends on Mark really. But we will, naturally, try to get there before the guest of honour. Mustn't usurp the bride's prerogative to be late..."

Olivia's laugh tinkled down the line. In the fields Bea could see the frost white as ever. Perhaps it wasn't going to melt at all. Perhaps the day was going to get progressively colder.

"We're planning to get things started about eight o'clock," she said. "It would be nice if you could be there by then..."

Bea knew better than to suggest that Olivia arrive earlier and help with preparations. Olivia would simply suggest caterers which was not, as far as Bea and Charles were concerned, what Christmas entertaining was about.

Albert D'Arcy, Olivia's kindly and long-suffering husband, would fit himself to his wife's schedule.

Stephanie, who was eighteen and already in possession of much of her mother's cool, blonde beauty, had never been known to involve herself in any kind of practical activity.

"We'll try..." Olivia didn't like committing herself. "What time is Sinéad expected? I presume her husband is coming too—do you know yet who it is she's married to? Anybody we know? He *does* have a name, I suppose?"

"Yes, he's coming. His name is Daniel Kirwan."

"Kirwan? Never heard of him. What does he do?"

"He's an accountant. They'll be arriving about seven. See you about eight then, Olivia..."

"Wait!" A sudden urgency in Olivia's tone stopped Bea in the act of cutting off the call. "There's something else. We need to talk about Capek..."

"We don't. I'm on holiday, Olivia. The gallery's closed until the new year. We'll talk about it then..."

"We have to talk now!" Olivia paused dramatically. "He's agreed to meet you on Stephen's Day! He says he'll come to Dublin with a selection of pictures for you to see and..."

"Hold it right there, Olivia!"

In the confines of the car it seemed to Bea that she was yelling as she tried to get her sister to stop talking. What *could* Olivia have been thinking about, arranging a meeting right after Christmas?

She couldn't possibly go back to town; not now that she'd persuaded Sinéad to stay on.

"I would prefer," she went on more calmly, "if he came to see me early in the new year..."

"Well, *he'd* prefer to see you on Stephen's Day. And in the circumstances, given all he's been through, I think he's entitled to name the day. He says he wants to come to Dublin then because it'll be quiet. He still can't cope with throngs of people, apparently. Not surprising really. He'll be at the gallery at 9pm and he'll bring three pictures with him..."

Bea's mind raced, trying to figure a way out of the meeting. She was interested in showing the Romanian but knew she had to see him, as well as some recent work, before committing herself. If he was as good as reports and sales indicated then her gallery could be on the threshold of the international market. Even so...

"Look, Olivia, can't you make contact and put him off? Stephen's Day is very difficult..."

"You *know* I can't make contact. I've no idea where
he is—I simply got word through a third party..."

Bea groaned. Sinéad would be furious, and with
justification, if her mother abandoned the family holiday
to go back to Dublin the day after Christmas.

"Look, Olivia, you'll have to get word to him
somehow. Rearrange it for later in the week. Can't the
patron do something?"

"Can't be contacted either. He's gone to Mexico for
Christmas. Really, Bea, you're being terribly limp about
all of this. This is not one of your everyday painters
we're talking about..."

Bea boiled over.

"I don't show everyday painters! I show only the best
and I'm the one who will make the decision about
whether or not to show Miroslav Capek. They're my
walls and it's my gallery we're putting on the line. I'm
the one taking the risk. If he wants an exhibition then
he's going to have to meet me half-way..."

"Oh, come on Bea! You know there's no risk
involved!" Olivia was suddenly placatory. "He's going to
be *huge*—and you'll have made it possible. The meeting
has been arranged now and I really can't contact him to
cancel. Can't you simply nip back to town for a few
hours?"

"I suppose I could..."

Bea sighed. Olivia, she knew, saw a fat commission
in all of this. Money was magic to her. It also meant
power, which was something she was devoted to. Her
instinct about Miroslav Capek could very well be right—
even though she couldn't tell a work of art from a
donkey's ear.

"Fine. That's that then." Olivia sounded quite brisk.

Afraid I'll change my mind again, Bea thought ruefully.

"I've got a hairdresser's appointment so I'd better get up and dress." Olivia, successful in achieving at least part of the purpose of the call, became dismissive. "I hope Charles has already installed Jude at Inverskena?"

"He collected her from the nursing home yesterday." Bea was curt. How Olivia could imagine that their eighty-two-year-old mother would allow the slightest deviation from this tradition was beyond her.

"How is she?" Olivia sounded sublimely uninterested.

"Charles says she's in her usual form..."

Which was to say cantankerous and demanding, when she was *compos mentis*, which these days was only about seventy per cent of the time.

"That's good. Fine." Olivia really had lost interest. "Must rush. So much to do. I do hope the bride turns up! I've got a *lovely* surprise planned for her! For you, too!"

"Of course she'll turn up." Bea, furious at herself, heard the uncertainty in her own voice.

"I'm sure you're right. All that nasty business of rejecting you will end now. I have felt for you, Bea. Rejection must be so hard to take. I've no experience of it myself, of course, but you have, poor dear. First Sinéad's father, now this. Still, practice makes perfect, so they say. Can't natter any more now. Byeee...A happy Christmas and all that..."

Bea ground her teeth as the line went dead. Olivia and Jude were the only two people in the world who made her grind her teeth.

She had been driving slowly through open countryside for some time but now she speeded up. Maybe her sister didn't mean to be such a total bitch. A lot of it was Jude's fault. The basic ingredients had been

there—Olivia had been a precociously selfish child—but
Jude's woeful neglect had allowed the characteristics to
develop unfettered. Still, Bea firmly believed that when
the chips were down Olivia would be there to help.

The chips had been down a few times in Bea's life
already and Olivia's absence had been notable. Even so
Bea believed.

Approaching the small village of Conary, the other
side of which lay Inverskena, Bea wondered idly what
surprise her sister had in store for Sinéad. She hoped it
would be kind.

CHAPTER TWO

B ea drove slowly through the village, which was very quiet. Its jumble of houses, in three wan-dering uneven rows, was home to a population of just two hundred. But it served well the needs of the wider farming community of its meandering hinterland and some odd bods like herself and Charles. She was well aware that they were regarded locally as eccentrics but were liked, now they'd been around ten years.

As she passed the newsagent's a pale hand waved and Bea smiled, returned the salute. Agnes Walsh never missed a thing and was proud of her encyclopaedic knowledge of everybody's business. A little further on the small supermarket boasted a huge and brightly lit fire but the nearby Huntsman, larger of Conary's two pubs and which doubled as a Bed and Breakfast establishment, was miserably naked of any decoration.

"Probably take grant aid to encourage Larry Dowling to hang an extra bulb," Bea muttered drily.

Time was she had spent almost every weekend at Inverskena. But for almost a year now she hadn't been able to get down more than once a month, sometimes not even that often. She used the demands of the gallery, increased by its success, as an excuse when Charles gently asked why. The gallery was only partly to blame. James Harte was the real reason. Since meeting him two years ago he'd been taking up an increasing number of Bea's free weekends.

Or had, up to now. Events earlier that morning had probably changed all that. Bea, frowning, bit her lip. Time enough to think about James after Christmas. She had plenty to occupy her for the moment.

She left the village and drove slowly along the stretch of tree-lined road, which led to the turn for Inverskena. The air inside the car, warm after the journey, was an intoxicating blend of spices, celery, and flowers, especially carnations and the white chrysanthemums Charles liked so much. Bea, feeling adventurous, had splurged on armfuls of bright, daisy-like flowers, sprays of Dutch ilex for its red berries and some painted leaves all the way from Africa. She had avoided the ubiquitous poinsettia but had good-humouredly given way to a flowerseller's insistence that she buy mistletoe.

"We're selling condoms with it this year," he'd grinned as he'd taken her money. "Making sure of a safe Christmas! Want a packet?" She'd laughingly refused. James had laughed too, the only time that morning he'd done so.

Charles would have already got the holly and ivy and, though he swore every year that he wouldn't, a large Noblis fir for the hallway too. Presents, a drinks contribution of champagne and brandy and lots of Godiva chocolates took up the remaining space in the car. They would all have to be taken out immediately she got to the house or the berries would shrivel and the chocolates turn to curdled cream.

The sun's glare was less now so she took off the dark

glasses, put them on the seat beside her. Her hand brushed against the richly wrapped jeweller's box left there earlier by James.

"God, I wish he hadn't," Bea swore softly. "Expensive presents don't solve anything. I need space. What I said this morning needed to be said...It *had* to be said..."

Believing she was right didn't ease the feeling of guilt. Her timing had been wrong. Christmas Eve was probably not the best day in the year to make a decision about marriage.

On reflection, it definitely would have been better not to have allowed James to come to the market with her. Her instinct had said no, had advised her to slip from his bed early with a silent goodbye kiss. Words, and decision, could be saved for after Christmas, for the brisker, less sentimental mood of January.

But James had woken before her, forestalling her plan and insisting he wanted to go to the Smithfield too. He had looked strangely defenceless, but lovable too at that grey hour of the morning. Leaning over her in the bed he had smiled, taken a strand of her wayward hair and kissed it. "I adore you," he'd whispered as he'd begun gently to explore her body. Bea had known she should stop his hands and remind him that she had a busy day ahead, a great many things to do. But her arms and tongue had refused to obey. Soon the rest of her had given in, willingly.

Her delight in James's lovemaking was a source of great joy to Bea. It was a relief too, after years alone and almost celibate, to discover her responses undimmed. Even grown more insistent. Almost forgotten feelings, dormant for so long, had rapturously awoken to James's fine blend of passion and skill.

The night before had been a special pleasure. She should have left before morning, leaving its good taste between them for Christmas.

They'd had an early dinner at Patrick Guilbaud's and followed it with leisurely post-prandial brandies in the intimate luxury of James's study. Panelled in dark oak, filled with books and comfortable old leather, it had been just the place to dance to the smooth, seasonal velvet of Nat King Cole. They had gone to bed then and had made love slowly and for a long time. James, almost excessively sober in his everyday habits, was in bed transformed by his passion for Bea. When they came, together at last, it had been exquisitely satisfying for both of them.

That morning, in contrast to the night before, they had made love quickly. Afterwards, in the peace and contentment of spent passion, she had weakened in her resolve not to allow him to come to the market with her. Removing his arm from around her shoulder she left the bed, gave him a gentle shove, and said "Get dressed and come on then. But I know you won't like it..."

James had, of course, dressed appropriately. He always looked right, whatever the occasion. He was not a vain man but self-sufficiency was a matter of enormous pride to him. Clothing and personal fitness he saw as integral parts of this. For the trip to the market he wore chunky cords and a warm, crew-necked jumper. Over these he wore a lined Bugatti coat. He looked casually rich, which he was, and far too serious. His long face with its too firm mouth could be off-putting until you saw the laughter lines around the grey eyes. Bea liked to think she had added a few in the last couple of years.

James would have made them breakfast but Bea,

conscious of the already lightening sky outside, had
insisted that the market was the place for that. They had
travelled in tandem, Bea driving the Audi and James
following close behind in the old green Jaguar he was so
fond of. It was still quite dark when they crossed the
Liffey, went around the back of the Four Courts and
parked as close as they could to one of the high, arched
entrances to the market.

A damp cold came off the Liffey and James stamped
his feet to keep warm, eyeing his hand-sewn shoes. A
mistake, he said, annoyed with himself, not to have
worn boots.

The temperature inside the market was very little
higher than outside but the bustle of activity was
enormous, the indifference to the cold impressive.
"Sorry…" James's apology was irritable as the driver of
a loaded fork-lift impatiently yelled at him to get out of
the way. And that was the moment Bea knew, for certain,
that he wasn't going to enjoy the market. Knew positively
that letting him come along had been a *really* bad idea.
She became deliberately cheerful, catching him by the
arm.

"This way," she urged, "I'll get the vegetables first."

James trailed after her. It was not in his nature to
follow. He was too used to making decisions, to having
others follow him. His normal gait was a quick, businesslike stride. Now he was forced to a meandering pace as
Bea poked at fruit, examined vegetables.

Why, he demanded a little petulantly, couldn't she
have got someone to do this shopping for her? He could
have sent someone himself if she'd asked…When Bea
tried to explain the enjoyment she got from this yearly
expedition to the market he nodded, forbearing. He

understood, he said. Bea knew quite well that he did not.

"Anyway," she said, "you might as well make yourself useful now you're here."

Determined to keep the mood buoyant she piled his arms high with celery, chestnuts, garlic, and mandarin oranges. James tried to register enthusiasm but failed, looking instead bleakly resigned.

"You all right, love?" a fruitseller asked, sympathetically. James nodded, stiffly.

"You don't look too happy to me," the woman said with an accusing glare at Bea. James, for some unknown reason, brought out the mothering instinct in most women. For reasons just as mysterious the emotions he evoked in Bea had nothing at all motherly about them.

James was a widower. Had been for eight years. The death of his wife Ann had been slow and painful with James in constant attention through the last stages of her cancer. He had spoken of it only once to Bea. He spoke more often, with both humour and love, of their three children. They were grown now but he was still very close to all of them. Bea studied his face, inscrutable above the piled vegetables, as he purposefully made his way to the car. He planned to play Santa Claus that night to his two-year-old grandson. She shook her head. James the grandparent was something she found impossible to imagine. As for Bea the grandparent…she shook her head even harder, squaring her shoulders.

"Something wrong?" James looked concerned.

"Not a thing," Bea assured. "Shaking a few cobwebs out of the old brain, that's all…"

They put the fruit and vegetables into her Audi and went back inside. Bea, walking up and down the banks of flowers, sniffing the carnations, admiring the lilies, felt James's impatience grow. She was positive by now that her suspicions about his wanting to use the occasion for a "talk" had been right. Knowing him as well as she did she'd suspected that he would think the early morning, with its raw energy, a good time to discuss serious matters. And, for James, the question of whether or not they would marry had become a very serious matter indeed. Much in love as he was with her he was nevertheless a man used to having his own way. He could not understand her reluctance to commit herself.

Bea couldn't understand it herself. She liked most things about James and she loved being with him. She liked his dry sense of fun, his very real thoughtfulness. She even liked the wings of straight, iron-grey hair each side of his head. He was, to all intents and purposes, the perfect man for her.

And still she could not make up her mind to marry him.

She did not, on the other hand, want to lose him. She wanted things to stay the way they were, for them to remain good friends and sometime lovers. But James wanted her by his side all the time, as his wife. He was not prepared to settle for anything less.

"Now, what will I buy *you*?" she asked, playfully. "Something in a pot would be best, I think."

"Yes," James caught her hand. "Something in a pot. Then maybe we could have a drink in one of the pubs or something..."

"I'm here to do some serious buying, you know that. First things first..." Bea slipped her hand out of his, walked ahead. "I'll buy you a winter cherry," she said decisively. "Then I'd better start buying flowers for

Inverskena while stocks last. Things are shifting pretty fast around here..."

They were too. Mistletoe especially was in great demand, though not by the groups of efficient nuns selecting lilies and maiden's breath for their cribs and altars. The buyers from the flower shops and restaurants were scooping up the best of everything else. Taking a deep breath Bea waded in and, brow furrowed and biting her lip, bought enough flowers to fill most of the large old rooms in Inverskena.

"That's it," she said at last, flushed and pleased with herself. James, shaking a bemused head, smiled at the collected blooms.

"This calls for a coffee at least," he said, nodding at the steaming windows of Paddy's Place, the market café.

"It calls for breakfast!" Bea cried gaily, lighthearted now the buying was done. "*After* we've put these in the car."

The Audi packed, they sat on high stools in Paddy's Place and ordered. Bea, made ravenous by the cold air, had a bacon sandwich, hugely filling and hot. James averted his eyes from the eggs swimming in deep fat on the hotplate and ordered a coffee.

"Like a bit?" Bea held her sandwich up questioningly.

James shook his head, fingering the leaves of the winter cherry, between them on the long, bench table.

"It would be nice to have your answer for Christmas," he said. This is not fair, Bea thought and was surprised at her own anger. He's pushing me. Using the bloody Christmas thing as a lever. Making me responsible for his happiness.

"I can't give it to you, James."

"When, then? When will you give me an answer?"

James looked gently quizzical and Bea's anger dissolved. He had an amazingly open, straightforward manner. It was one of the things she loved about him. It was a reflection of how he ran his life, which was ordered and uncomplicated.

"Look, Bea." James fixed his eyes on the wall behind her head and looked suddenly bleak. "I'd prefer if you told me, once and for all, whether or not Walter Treacy is the reason you don't want to marry me."

Bea sighed. Playing for time she turned and followed his gaze to the fifties photographs of the market, framed on the wall behind her. The laughing black-and-white images created the impression of a simple, wonderful life back then. Her own memories of the fifties, her childhood years, were anything but wonderful. No wonder she had fallen into the arms of Walter Treacy a decade later, when she was nineteen.

The warmth and joy she'd found with Wally had been like a door to a new world. Within a year she'd been pregnant and, hastily, married. Two years later she was alone, a deserted wife and mother. Wally, handsome and larger than life, had disappeared on the dreg ends of the hippie trails to India. These days he lived in London and made contact about once a year, usually by telephone.

James didn't repeat the question and when Bea turned back to face him she found him waiting patiently. His eyes met hers. Still he said nothing.

"No," Bea said eventually. "Wally is not the reason. Not in the way you mean, anyway. I'm not emotionally involved with him. That ended years ago. You know that."

"In what way then?" James sounded perplexed.

"Well," Bea took a large final bite out of the bacon sandwich. "Sure you don't want to try it?" she asked, a little desperately.

"Bea..." James's voice held a warning note. He was not, Bea saw, going to be side-tracked. She took a deep, steadying breath. After having avoided this conversation for weeks, it seemed to her infinitely lousy timing to end up having it on Christmas Eve morning.

"Look, James," she began, "for me to marry will be a complicated business. You must realise that. Wally won't give me a divorce. I know he won't. It's not his style. What he owns, or thinks he owns, he holds on to."

"And I'm his insurance policy, his way of avoiding marriage to any of his London girlfriends. I'm the little wife at home in Ireland." She pulled a wry face. "I'm also his hedge against loneliness in old age. He seriously imagines he can come back to me in ten, fifteen years time. That we will spend our declining years reminiscing about the years apart. Wally," she spoke flatly, "has enormous confidence in his own charm."

"Sounds manic to me." James's voice was harsh. He covered her hand with his and beckoned for a second coffee. His face had hardened and Bea could see the decision-making business magnate taking over from the lover/friend of minutes before. The coffee came immediately and James rooted in a pocket for coins.

"Pay when you're finished," the girl said after a quick look at his set face.

"Treacy doesn't have to give you a divorce." James spoke quickly and urgently as the girl moved off. "You can divorce *him*. If you want to. It can all be set up, right here in Dublin, through a company I know which arranges foreign divorces. Once the paperwork's done we go to somewhere like the Dominican Republic, you and I together, and spend twenty-four hours there finalising things. Afterwards we can go wherever you like—New York, Mexico, anywhere—and get married. It's quite simple. I can manage everything once you agree."

Bea was quite sure he could, and would. James's organising abilities were legendary. So was his penchant for running things his way. She looked at her hand, trapped under his. She wasn't surprised by anything he'd said. In a way she'd known it was coming.

"Will you manage Sinéad too? How do I tell her that I'm divorcing her father, after all these years?"

"Sinéad's making her own life, Bea," James's tone was blunt. but not unkind. "She's twenty-one, she's a married woman. She doesn't need a father. Certainly not one who's never been around anyway. And she doesn't need a full-time mother any more either."

Bea closed her eyes against the pain. James didn't understand. Sinéad *did* need her. Not the way she had done as a child, of course, but she still needed her. They needed one another. She pulled her hand free.

"You're wrong," she whispered. "She does need me. And I don't want to alienate her any further..."

"You can't put your life on hold until Sinéad sorts herself out!" James tried to retrieve her hand but Bea placed it out of reach on her lap. "She'll come round. She's a bright girl. And you have to let her make her own way."

Feeling quite detached, Bea studied James's long, finely chiselled features. She reminded herself that he didn't mean to be unkind. That there was, in fact, a lot of truth in what he was saying. The pain became less, the aching loneliness for her daughter's company subsiding a little.

"What's it to be, then?" James pushed the coffee cup aside. He rested his elbows on the table and fixed her with his steady gaze. The gesture, Bea felt quite sure, was one he used in boardrooms. That concludes the argument, it said, and now I want a decision. Well, it might work in boardrooms. But this was her life he was dealing with.

"James." Bea rested her own elbows on the table and her chin on her cupped hands. She spoke firmly. "For weeks now you've talked about how good it would be to have me travelling with you, as your wife. You've told me that your house in Leopardstown needs a woman's touch. But what about what I need? What about my gallery? What do I do with my flat in Sandymount? How do we fit our lives together so that I keep my independence?" She stopped for breath and saw that James was faintly smiling.

"All of that can be arranged too," he said. For the second time that morning Bea felt angry. This time though it was a deep and primitive emotion, fuelled by her instinct for self-preservation. She was not going to have everything that she had worked a lifetime for dismissed as something to be "arranged" by James.

"All of that. What the hell do you mean by 'all of that?' It's my life and my business you're talking about, James!" Her eyes darkened to an almost gun-metal grey, her face had turned white except for two spots of red high on her cheekbones. She was shaking and completely unaware of the dramatic quality anger had given her beauty.

"You will not arrange my life, James. I will decide and I will arrange my life! I've been doing it for years

and I'm not going to be taken over at this point!" Pausing
for breath she saw that James's boardroom manner had
completely deserted him. His face had become quite
ashen and his usual calm was replaced by an agitated
concern Bea hadn't seen before.

"I'm not trying to take over your life! For God's sake
Bea, I want to marry you!"

His cry, she knew, came from the heart. He really did
want to marry her. Very much. But, whether he knew it
or not, he wanted to marry her on his terms. He hadn't
meant to negate everything she'd done. It was just that,
deep down, he didn't think it mattered. James was a
sophisticated and thoughtful companion. He was warmly
loving in bed. But he was a long way from being a New
Man.

"But on your terms." Bea finished the sentence for
him, tucking a wayward strand of hair behind her ear.

"No. We'll arrange things together. You can take on
someone to help you with the gallery. Give you more
free time."

"I don't want more free time. I want to spend time
at the gallery. There are lots of things I want to do with
it..."

"That's the real problem, isn't it Bea?" James, all at
once, seemed deflated. "The gallery means more to you
than I ever could." He made a wry grimace. "You were
right, earlier this morning. I should have left things until
after the holiday. Why don't you think it over while
you're away? We'll talk again when you get back."

"Okay." Bea drew another long, calming breath. She
touched his face briefly as she got down from the high
stool. "Let's go, partner. The horses are waiting!" She
smiled.

They were quite companionable as they strolled toward the market exit. James put an arm around her and Bea leaned, briefly, against him. Outside, the dome of the Four Courts still had its night-time lighting. It glowed, eerily orange, against the low clouds racing across the city sky.

By the car, James took Bea's face in his hands.

"It is so much easier to be loved than to love," he said sadly. "The loved one merely has to be kind. Think kind things about me, Bea." He kissed her, a gentle, undemanding kiss.

"I'd like some time," Bea said. "I need some time. I'll call you early in January. I'd like to be on my own for a while, to think things through."

"You'll have that time, at Inverskena. Call me when you get back? Please?"

He took the glitteringly wrapped present from his overcoat pocket, opened the car door and slipped it on the seat.

"That's so that you won't forget me when you're lost in that family of yours!" He pulled her close. "I'll expect to hear from you soon. You might even ring to let me know if you like the present." This time his kiss was demanding; rough too and with an edge of desperation about it.

"Yes, I will phone," Bea said when he let her go. She did not say when.

Driving away she could see him in the mirror, alone on the footpath. He was fingering the leaves of the winter cherry.

CHAPTER THREE

In the summertime Inverskena was hidden from view of the road by the great trees along its winding avenue. At this time of year, with only the occasional conifer providing cover, its modest splendour was visible from quite a distance across the flat countryside.

Bea was never sure which season she preferred to make the approach. In the growing time of the year she liked the drive through the leafy cover of the horse-chestnuts, white poplars and two giant oaks that lined the avenue. It was always a joy to emerge from their shade, round the last bend, and be faced with the tranquillity of Inverskena's grey, ivy-clad walls. Whatever the season Bea always felt she'd come home. Inverskena was her security, the place that had to take her in.

The original house had been built in the nineteenth century as a hunting lodge. The much grander house it had served had long since fallen prey to age, poverty and dry rot. But Inverskena, stoically accommodating the changing times, had survived. If local stories about its past were even half-true then it had, in its time, seen many a sad and sorry deed. Happy ones too, most likely, but no one seemed to know about them. Over the years it had grown bigger, more rambling. And more accommodating

Their conviction that it was a benign house had persuaded Bea and Charles to buy Inverskena. Ten years ago it had seemed the right thing to do with a sudden, unexpected inheritance.

Their father had died. It had been an undignified end, drink and a heart condition catching up with him at a public function. A bequest of money to each of his three children had astonished them as much as it had infuriated their mother. Given the quantities of Jameson whiskey Tom Hennessy had consumed during his lifetime it had been supposed that his assets had long since become liquid. But their father had been devious as well as a drinker, and keeping the profits from some of his more doubtful deals secret from his wife had given him no small satisfaction. Though Jude had always been independently wealthy (her adoring father had seen to that) she had also wanted control of her husband's money. Since the reading of his will Jude had not once mentioned his name. He might never have existed. She had let it be known that her own money would go to fund a poetry foundation in her memory.

Bea and Charles, for different reasons, had decided jointly to invest their inheritance in the security of property. Charles, after fifteen years in Paris, wanted somewhere to come home to. Bea, alone with a growing daughter, felt the need of a weekend place in the country. Inverskena, new to the property market, was going for a song. Along with the house they bought five acres— orchards, fields and their own small wood.

Neglected, rundown, Inverskena had taken several years of restoring, refurbishing and arguing to make of it a home that they were both happy with. But the result, a blend of elegance and eccentricity, suited the old house perfectly.

Charles, especially, had filled Inverskena with his own *objets d'art*. Many were unconventional but all were stylish.

Bea drove the last few hundred yards slowly. Even at this early hour there were lights in two of the long front windows. One, in an upstairs window, came from the room occupied by Jude.

Jude. Bea felt the familiar, quiet dread which, all her life, had preceded a meeting with her mother. She held her breath, willed the feeling to go away. It eased.

The other light, to the right of the front door, came from the dining room window. Charles was probably sorting out table arrangements. He worried a great deal about such things and spent a lot of time getting them right—usually to great effect.

As Bea came closer, a light went on over a large wreath on the front door. It picked up the blue ribbon twined through the holly and the ivy and she smiled, a fond smile. Blue, obviously, was Charles's theme colour this year. Last year it had been gold and the result had been an over-abundance of gilded cones. Blue would be more fun. She would have to work her flowers around it, somehow. Charles could be fussy about his Christmas theme colours.

The Audi crunched on to the gravel in front of the house. Before it had even stopped the door was thrown open, to reveal a tree ablaze with coloured lights in the hallway beyond. An aged Airedale wandered out, lolloped over to the car. He sniffed suspiciously and wetly at Bea's boots as she got out. When she stood on the gravel he gave a tired growl which she ignored. He growled again.

"Oh, shut up, Jake," she said, but half-heartedly. It didn't do to get on the wrong side of Jake. His loyalty to Charles was total, his irritability renowned. He had been known to kill cats but not, so far, to attack man, or woman. Even so, Bea bent down, gave him a conciliatory pat to the head.

"Good dog," she said. "Good old Jake."

The Airedale sniffed, then followed closely behind as she made for the house. Listening to his wheezing pant behind her a sudden thought became a silent prayer. Dear God, she prayed, if this dog chooses to bite someone this Christmas then please, dear God, let it be Olivia. She felt only slight guilt at the unseasonal wish. As a lapsed Catholic she was quite sure God would understand her weakness.

"What do you think? Is it vulgar enough to make everyone happy?" Charles, tall and every inch the country gent, stood in the doorway, an arm thrown dramatically in the direction of the huge, brightly lit tree.

"Oh, I think it'll do," Bea laughed, shielding her eyes as she looked past him. She kissed his cheek, a welcome he returned twofold, Paris habits dying slow. They hugged briefly, then stood back to consider one another.

"You look tired." Charles was the first to speak.

"I'm fine," Bea dismissed the concern in his eyes. "It's been a busy month. You've got thin."

"Fit," Charles defended himself as she passed on into the hall and stood looking at the hugeness of the Christmas tree. "I've become fit."

In another hallway it would have been ludicrous but in this one, designed to take hunting hordes, the tree seemed just about adequate. It had three sets of lights and Bea was touched to see that Charles had, once again, hung the decorations Sinéad had made the Christmas after they'd bought the house.

"It's perfect. Couldn't be more perfect…" She fingered an angel with red hair. Sinéad, aged eleven, had tried very hard to get the colour exactly like Bea's. Charles touched her arm.

"Come on," he said, "you need a coffee. Or maybe something stronger?"

He led the way across the hall to the drawing room, Jake grumbling in his wake. A fire had already been lit and Bea saw that she'd been right about the blue. Central to the decorations was a magnificent festive garland stretching the length of the marble mantelpiece. It was made from evergreen foliage and had a wide blue ribbon threaded through.

Two heavy blue candles at each end were reflected in the antique mirror over the chimney-piece. Elsewhere in the room evergreen with blue adorned pictures. Charles's gifts for everyone, piled on a small table, were blue wrapped. Bea clapped her hands and laughed.

"It works, Charles, it really does!"

"Glad you like it." Charles, deceptively nonchalant, gestured for her to sit down. Bea's opinion mattered to him.

"It's good to see you," he said laconically as he began to pour coffee from a thermos flask. "It may be the approach of premature senility but I find that I'm actually looking forward to being locked up with my family for a week or so. Or maybe it's just a craving for excitement."

He grinned as he passed her a cup of strong black coffee. It would, Bea knew, be excellent. Rich and tart, just the way she liked it. Jake, head on his paws, watched balefully. She drank, sinking with a sigh into the reliable comfort of a Chesterfield.

She loved this room. She loved the way light poured in from the two high windows overlooking the avenue and sweep of countryside beyond. They were hung with light muslin curtains—carefully conserved shutters made anything else unnecessary—and there were generous window seats in each. The walls were a dusty terracotta and the couple of creamy Chesterfields had cushions to match. Bea stretched a hand toward the heat from the burning logs in the original, restored fireplace.

Inverskena's epicentre was the great, square, reception hallway just outside this room. Once one came through the door everything seemed to open out from there. Facing the front of the house, and to right and left of the hallway, were this drawing room, a dining room and study. All of them were high-ceilinged and elegant. A wide corridor led to the back where the rooms were more rustic and had lower ceilings.

Bea and Charles had been able to save the mullioned windows and flagstone floors they'd found in the kitchen and had converted the large room next to it into an extraordinarily comfortable living room. They'd added a conservatory too, small but a miracle of green promise, and converted the several small rooms which had been the servants' quarters into a workroom for Charles.

From the hallway there ran a wide staircase which branched, pretty quickly, into a bewildering number of other steps and stairways. All of these led, sometimes miraculously it seemed, to seven bedrooms, two of which were in the attic. With their beamed ceilings and dormer windows, these too could have been part of another house, so different were they from the airy bedrooms on the return and first floors.

Leaning back in her seat by the fire Bea felt Inverskena's benign mood envelop her.

"It's great to be here." She spoke with feeling.

"No reason why you can't enjoy country comforts more often." Charles's tone was dry. "We're always here." He often used the Papal we to mean himself and Inverskena.

"Yes. I know. I shouldn't leave you carrying the can."

"That is not what I meant." Charles sounded sharp, his vague, good-humoured courtesy cracking momentarily. The essence of urbane detachment, he rarely allowed himself to become upset or annoyed. He never interfered but, in his detached way, was extremely kind. Because of this, and despite his dislike of the untidiness of family feelings, he all too often found himself in the middle of them.

"We would simply like to see more of you." He softened his tone and lifted a slightly ironical eyebrow. "And the country suits you. You relax when you're here. It would be nice," he paused to sip his coffee, "to see more of Sinéad too."

"You will, I hope. Things are going to change..."

"Mmm. She rang, by the way. She and her husband will be here by seven. She seemed surprised you'd already told me..."

"Did she indeed!" Bea snorted, then allowed herself a Jake-like growl of annoyance. "She really does behave as if I was the world's most indifferent mother!"

"Just a busy one." Charles's tact was oil on the waters of Bea's annoyance. She calmed down, pulled a wry face and changed the subject. Slightly.

"Talking about mothers," she said, "how's Jude?"

"As ever." Charles walked to the window with his coffee cup. When he was silhouetted there Bea thought that he'd definitely got thin. Maybe he was fit too.

"We'd better," he said, "empty the car before you go up to see her."

When they brought the fruit and vegetables in, the kitchen was filled with the sight and smells of food in preparation. The scrubbed pine table in the middle groaned with delights for the night's party. Charles's cranberry mincemeat pies, pecan snaps and cinnamon sugared nuts were annual treats. New, and delicious when Bea tasted them, were the chocolate truffles and bitter orange chocolates he'd added this year. A bowl of apricots waited with walnuts, breadcrumbs and celery to become a cordon bleu stuffing for the morrow's turkey. A similar stuffing had aroused unanimous family approval the year before.

"God, but you've been busy, Charles." Bea felt shamed.

"I enjoy it. And I do it because I want to. You know that." Bea nodded. She did know. Charles was truly a fine cook. He also enjoyed entertaining, so long as he didn't have to do it very often. Time alone was important to him.

Charles was homosexual. When he had told Bea, just before they bought Inverskena, she hadn't been at all surprised. As soon as he said it she realised she'd always known where his sexual preference lay. She'd simply never thought much about it.

Charles had always been self-sufficient, private. He'd never encouraged family involvement in his life. He was telling her about his homosexuality now, he'd said, so that she would understand why he would, most likely, be spending the rest of his life alone. Why there would be no children of his around Inverskena, no wife.

He hadn't said much more. He didn't have to. Bea had understood perfectly, felt his pain as he briefly explained that the one person he could have lived with was in Paris and would be staying there. He had not spoken of the person since, never discussed his yearly visits to the French capital. But over the years, Bea was sure that he had found a sort of peace in Inverskena.

During the Paris years Charles had become a skilled picture restorer. He now had a room at the back, lower end of the house in which he worked, with great passion and infinite care, on damaged and sometimes almost completely obscured pictures. Some of these he was commissioned to do, but the great majority were for his collection, what he called his "rescued treasures." He scoured the country, and France too when he visited, for pictures lost to view for years because of dirt, over-painting or over-varnishing. He could never fully explain what attracted him to a picture, what it was he saw in the murky canvases he carried away from antique shops and fairs, flea markets and house auctions.

Sometimes, it seemed to Bea, the more ravaged the paintings were the better he liked them. The only clue lay in his great dream. He'd told her once what it was.

"One of these days," he'd said, "I will rescue a real treasure. A masterpiece lost to the world. Sitting here in my room I will restore it, bring the artist to life again. It will be as if he had just finished painting, put his picture on view for the first time for the world to take pleasure in."

Despite his defensive grin Bea had seen that he

believed this, absolutely.

The results of Charles's passion hung on walls throughout the house. Some had proven genuinely old and interesting. Others were revealed as quite beautiful. A few were moderately valuable. Charles had not, as yet, restored a masterpiece lost to the world.

Bea, after standing the flowers in three large earthenware jars with water, studied a picture new to the kitchen. It hung over the heavy wooden mantel and was of a country fair.

"Very nice," she said before turning doubtfully back to the flowers. "You should have told me about the blue, Charles. I'd have chosen differently."

Charles eyed the massed white and red. "They can be made to fit in," he said and began to search through a drawer in the dresser Bea had bought while on holiday in Kerry.

At last, with a flourish, he produced a roll of indigo ribbon.

"You want me to tie that around the vases?" Bea hazarded.

"No point being half-hearted about a theme," Charles said. "Now, how about a glass of Black Bush before you visit the mother?"

Early as it was the idea seemed an excellent one to Bea. "Make mine a stiff one," she said.

Jake, in the drawing room, growled and gave the floor a heavy thump with his tail as they came in. Charles poured, generously, into two cut-glass tumblers. "You'll find Jude a lot feebler. In body anyway. She's still fiendishly alert most of the time." He handed Bea a glass and picked up his own. They raised them, wished each other luck and health.

"Is she behaving herself?" Bea, sipping some golden comfort, walked to the window.

"No, of course she's not! Nothing wrong with her tongue, you know..."

Charles sat in his favourite chair by the fire. His long, tweed-clad legs were stretched in front of him and he wore brogues. This rustic image was misleading. Charles disliked most country pursuits. He'd never in his life held a fishing rod, refused absolutely to ride, thought the hunt barbaric and would under no circumstances play darts in the local pub.

From the window Bea saw a round-faced woman arrive up the avenue on a bicycle.

"Alice Joyce is here," she said. "She's just going round the back on that old high Nellie of hers. How is her boy?"

"Not well." Charles contemplated the tip of a shining brogue. "He's to have another of those wretched operations in January. Alice continues to cope."

"She has to." Bea's tone held a harsh sympathy. She knew what it was like to be a mother alone. She felt a particular sympathy for Alice Joyce, rearing a handicapped child. There, she thought, but for the grace of God...Finding herself drifting back in time she shivered, briskly shaking herself back to today's reality.

"Does Alice still come every day?" she asked.

"Not every day, no. But I've asked her to come as often as she can while Jude's here." Charles was watching Bea closely. She sometimes wondered if he knew more about her past troubles than she'd told him. They had an empathy, she and Charles. Always had. To escape his gentle scrutiny she raised her glass again, smiling as she took a sip.

"Otherwise," Charles shrugged, acknowledging her

right to privacy, "she comes up twice a week. She makes good bread, keeps the place generally in order. I enjoy her company too. We are, you could say, mutually dependent. It's a good arrangement." He paused. "We've become friends."

This, for Charles, was quite an admission. He did not share friendship easily. Bea felt another stab of guilt.

"I really have been busy," she said. "And I've been tied up with someone. But I've sorted that out."

"Oh?" Charles raised an eyebrow but Bea shook her head.

"It's not something I want to talk about," she said, "but I would like to tell you about a new painter I'm going to show. See if you've heard anything at all about him. His name is..."

From somewhere in the rambling corridors above them there came the peal of a bell. Bea stopped. She and Charles exchanged silent looks. It had been like this when they were children, that same bell summoning them at all hours of the day and night. The peal came again, clamorous and insistent.

"She knows you're here, " Charles said gently. "You'd better go up."

"I'm on my way." Bea stood up. "She might even be glad to see me." This last was meant as a joke. Charles did not laugh.

Jude was still ringing her handbell when Bea pushed open the bedroom door. Charles, as usual, had put his mother into the smaller of the front bedrooms. It was stiflingly hot. The old woman sat in the brass bed, gaunt and rigid against several lace-trimmed pillows. She had arthritis in her spine and the pain showed in her strained face. The effects of a lifetime's drinking on her liver could only be guessed at. Bea stood at the foot of the bed, directly in the line of her gaze.

"Hello, Jude," she said.

Her mother did not reply. Nothing in her face indicated that she'd seen or heard her daughter. She lifted the bell again. It rang, deafening in the silent room.

"Hello, mother," Bea said and Jude dropped the bell.

"I have always told you never to call me that!" Her voice was cracked and rough-edged. "Ungrateful child, to take advantage of my feeble state. Why haven't you been to see me before this?"

"I've only just arrived." Bea was annoyed at herself for the small lie. But then the truth had never impressed her mother. "Anyway, I thought you might be asleep, until I heard the bell."

Old habits die hard, Bea thought. Here I am, protesting and defending myself as if I was twelve years old.

Her mother looked terrible. With her streeling hair and great, staring eyes—faded now but once the colour of Bea's own—she was a gothic horror. Always thin, she had become a wraith. The hand holding the bell was a claw whose bones seemed about to protrude through the fine, blue-veined skin. Shrivelled, lost in a winceyette nightdress with incongruous multi-coloured stripes, it was hard to believe she'd once been a fêted beauty. Only the tired skin sunk over high cheekbones held a clue. Her eyes sharpened suddenly as they turned on Bea.

"I heard you arrive," she was waspish, "a full forty minutes ago. Just as well I've learned never to expect anything but ingratitude and indifference from you. I suppose it's *something* that you're here at all!"

"Did you ring for something in particular, Jude?" Bea glanced toward the window, wondering if she dared open it an inch or two.

"I don't want you to open that window!" Jude almost screamed, giving a sharp ring on the handbell. Bea felt the beginnings of a headache. She had forgotten how extraordinarily perceptive her mother could be about things which affected herself and how very unaware she was of the needs of others, particularly her children.

"All right." Bea turned, assayed a breezy smile. "I won't touch it."

She saw that Jude had pulled back the bedclothes. Her long legs, skeletal and grey-blue, protruded from the bunched-up nightdress. On her feet she wore heavy purple bedsocks. Bea felt a wave of pity. The old woman in the bed was so terribly wasted. Wasted but cantankerous too, and full of poisonous carping.

"Do you want to get up?" Bea asked, without much hope that Jude would say no.

"Hand me my cane!" Jude snapped. "You don't expect me to stay here all day, do you? Charles would like that, of course. He'd like me out of the way. So would you all. But I won't stay here. I will join you downstairs." She gave a sour cackle and swung the stick-like legs out of the bed with surprising agility. Sitting on the side of the bed, she shook the bell impatiently at the slender walking cane leaning against a wing-backed armchair. Bea handed it to her and, to her immense relief, Jude at last put down the bell.

"You can help me to the bathroom!" Jude's tone was peremptory.

"It'll be chilly in the corridor," Bea warned as, ignoring her irritable shrug, she draped a shawl over Jude's shoulders. "Now slip your feet into these." Bea placed a pair of slippers on the floor in front of her and Jude, leaning heavily on the cane, shuffled them on over the bedsocks.

Bea knew better than to offer her mother her arm as they began to make their slow way to the bathroom. But she stayed close enough to be a prop if her mother should reach out. They were almost at the bathroom door when she did so, clutching her daughter's arm in a vice-like grip. Her hand was icy and she felt like a bunch of twigs. And about the same weight.

"In the nursing home I have a bathroom *en suite*. It's so stupid of you and your brother not to have modernised this house properly."

Jude made this point every Christmas. They reached the bathroom door and Bea was saved the need to reply, as she did every year, that yes, Jude had a point but that they had wanted to keep as much of the house's original character as possible. Jude would, as always, have snorted and refused to understand.

"There is no need for you to come any further," Jude snapped as she pushed the bathroom door open with the cane. "I'm only seventy-nine, you know, not a hundred. I insist on being left some dignity at least..."

Jude had been seventy-nine for three years now. Like Olivia, who had been thirty-eight for two years and was in fact forty, she abhorred age, adored youth.

"I'll wait here." Bea took up a position against the wall.

"You don't need to!"

Bea found the bathroom door slammed in her face. She could hear Jude on the other side trying to turn the key and, when she failed, pulling the small wicker chair into place against it.

"What nonsense," Bea thought and, for one of the

very few times in her life, smiled at an action of her
mother's. "I'm going to get some clothes ready for you,
Jude," she called through the door. "Give me a call when
you're ready to come out."

In the bedroom she went through her mother's
clothes, hung neatly in the large wardrobe by Alice Joyce.
She selected a high-necked blue wool dress. It buttoned
up the front so it would be easy to put on. Beside it she
found a blue plaid shawl. She had taken both out and
was closing the door when she saw the black fur coat.

CHAPTER FOUR

B ea reached into the wardrobe, pulled the coat to her and smelled its soft fur. As a child it had seemed to her to be the only coat her mother had ever worn, winter or summer. Its appearance had meant two things, aroused two emotions. It meant that Jude was going out and brought relief. But it also caused dread when it meant she was back, probably drunk.

After all these years, since she'd been a child living in fear of its black outline against the glass of the front door, it felt, and smelled, the same. Standing there, the coat in her hand, all of Bea's life since childhood seemed a dream. She was nine again. Waiting for her mother to come home. It was midnight. Olivia slept soundly in the next bed. Charles was behind the closed door of his own room. Their father, as so often, was not there. Jude had been drunk when she left the house and would be worse when she got back. The housekeeper had left at nine o'clock and Bea, as the eldest daughter, would be expected to help Jude to bed. Olivia, a thin eight-year-old, was excused such duties and Jude would not allow Charles to touch her. When he was ten Charles had been sent away to school by their father. This had allowed Jude to relinquish the last of her meagre interest in her son. Her aversion towards him was unrelenting.

By the time she was nine Bea had known all about the tragedy of her mother's life. About how she'd been a poet until marriage had destroyed her talent and given her children she didn't want. Bea knew this because Jude had told her, over and over again. None of Jude's children were left in any doubt about the fact that they had ruined their mother's life, rendered her unable to write, robbed her of her freedom. That she had no love in her heart for them was something they accepted when very young.

The one thing Jude did not talk about was her drinking. No one spoke of Jude's drinking. It was, supposedly, a secret. She drank, for the most part, in her room. Often she did not appear drunk at all. To those outside the family anyway.

Jude had been in her late twenties when she'd married Tom Hennessy. Spoilt, extravagant and self-centred she had published some poems in her early twenties and become something of a minor darling in Dublin's literary circles. When she married Tom Hennessy, large, awkward and rich, admiration had quickly turned to scorn.

"Beauty and the beast," the cognoscenti had tittered. "Won't last a week," they prophesied.

But Jude had known what she was doing. Tom Hennessy was a replacement for her doting, but ailing, father. She cared for him too, for a while and in her own way.

But Tom Hennessy didn't like poetry. He thought it a "waste of time" and resented being excluded while Jude wrote. So she stopped writing and concentrated, instead, on spending his money. Her own, left to her by her father when finally he died, she never touched.

Charles was born, after a difficult pregnancy and traumatic birth, when Jude was thirty-four years old. Swearing to have no more children she engaged a nanny and threw herself into the social whirl she'd abandoned during pregnancy.

But parenthood changed everything, for Tom as well as Jude. He adored his son and for a while was an attentive father. Jude, finding she had to share her husband's attention, retaliated by returning to the writing of poetry. But it was too late. The muse had departed and her earlier style was no longer fashionable. Her published efforts were greeted with scorn, her unpublished works littered every room of the house. Convinced that she would be great she carried on writing. To keep the reality of failure at bay she began drinking.

Jude was devastated when, at forty-one, she became pregnant again. Four months after Bea was born, her faith in breastfeeding as a contraceptive was shattered when she became pregnant with Olivia. By the time Jude was forty-three she was mother to a seven-year-old boy and two baby girls. She abandoned poetry writing completely, taking to gin as a more or less full-time companion. She fought endlessly with Tom. He could never find words to match hers and the fights left Jude glowing and triumphant. Tom took to spending less and less time at home.

For nine-year-old Bea, helping her mother to bed was never easy. Jude's drunken concept of time meant she took forever to climb the stairs. Stumbling, stopping, crying, Bea would coax and drag until she eventually got her mother to bed. Sometimes Jude would make her read to her until sleep came, obscure poetry which meant nothing to a child.

When Bea was eleven Jude tried to kill herself. This, ironically brought, a certain stability to the household for a while. Jude stopped her drinking and Tom Hennessy curtailed his. For a whole year the family took Sunday lunch together, each week in a different hotel. Jude seemed to enjoy this. Dressed in twin set and pearls she charmed waiters and smiled a distant, matriarchal smile on her family from the top of linen-covered tables. But she tired of the role.

When she began drinking again she retreated almost completely from family life. Tom Hennessy presented her with a handbell, to be rung in her room whenever she wanted anything. He then left her severely to her own devices and concentrated on the schooling of the daughters he'd so recently come to know.

Jude spent more and more time in her room. The handbell, which had come from a river boat, was very loud. It tolled, shrill and persistent, night and day, throughout Bea's teen years. No one ever considered taking it away from Jude and, in the end, it was the bell which drove her children away.

As soon as he took his degree Charles left home and, soon after, left the country. When she was eighteen, Olivia enchanted wealthy Albert D'Arcy with her cool, blonde beauty. She married him within six months. Bea, pregnant at nineteen, also married and left. Tom Hennessy stayed, until he died, in the house with its incessantly tolling bell.

Bea sighed for the years she had spent wishing her youth away, waiting to be old enough to leave home, wanting most of all to escape from her mother.

She dropped the coat, watched as it slowly swung into place between a long, shiny beaded dress and a maroon tweed suit. It was made of the skins of otters, an endangered species now. Like Jude in a way. Where her mother planned to wear the coat, or for that matter the beaded dress and suit, was anyone's guess.

Bea had turned to examine the few pieces of jewellery on the dressing table when she heard the crash from the bathroom. She whirled, fear lurching somewhere in the pit of her stomach.

"Oh, God, no!" she cried and instinctively touched the wood of the dressing table. Thoughts chased one another as she sped across the room.

"She's eighty-one. She's not invincible! Not really...We only think she is. Please God, not at Christmas time...Don't let it happen at Christmas time!"

Dry-mouthed she sped along the corridor to the closed bathroom door, heavy and solid like the others in the house. There was complete silence on the other side. She turned the handle and pushed. It didn't budge.

"Jude!" Bea called, urgently. "Jude, are you all right?"

There was no reply and she pushed again, harder. This time the door moved, but slowly and obviously hindered by the chair leaning against it. Bea leaned with all her weight and pushed. The door opened suddenly and there was a clattering noise as the chair toppled over. It was a large bathroom and, from where she stood, Bea could see no sign of her mother inside. Hear no sound either. She stepped through the door.

Jude was lying propped against the toilet bowl. She had taken her nightdress off and the shift she'd been wearing underneath, an incongruous garment in satin-coloured peach, hung like a bizarre shroud around the skin and bones of her cadaverous body. A few strands of hair dipped into the large glass of gin she held in an unsteady hand.

She didn't look up as Bea quietly crossed the bathroom and stood looking down at her. Ignoring her daughter she raised the glass to her lips, slowly removed the strands of hair and drained its contents. Just as deliberately she placed the empty glass on the floor and sat, hands in her lap, staring vacantly in front of her. Several feet away, by the bath, a gin bottle lay on its side. It was almost empty, a spreading patch of wet indicating where some, at least, of its contents had gone.

"Are you drinking it neat, Jude?" Bea asked. How her mother was drinking the gin didn't, she realised, really matter. But somehow she had to know. She couldn't see a mixer of any kind in the bathroom.

"Are you, Jude?" She could hear the harshness in her own voice but didn't care. Her mother turned her head from side to side, avoiding eye contact. Not for the first time in her life Bea wanted to shake her, scream at her to for God's sake stop ruining her life, the lives of everyone around her. But she knew her reaction was merely habit, an instinct from long ago. It didn't really matter what Jude did with what was left of her life. She had destroyed anything beautiful in it years before. Her heart, fossilised for so long, would soon cease to beat at all.

Bea picked up the gin bottle, stood the chair upright and sat down. Jude abruptly came to life.

"Give me a drink," she demanded. She retrieved the glass, holding it out imperiously.

"All gone." Bea tiredly turned the bottle upside down. A single drop fell on to the carpet. She watched it fall, sink without trace into the soft green pile. Like a useless, wasted tear, she thought. Like Jude's life. She blinked back a real tear of her own. She had thought herself past caring, incapable of being upset by her mother. She had been wrong.

"Bitch!" Jude, from the floor, spat out the word. She waved the glass as if it were the bell. "Cold-hearted, selfish bitch! You haven't changed..."

Bea's heart began to thump. I can't take it anymore. I'm out of practice. I've grown out of the habit of taking abuse, of being the object of her vicious hatred. I've grown soft with love and from being loved. To Jude she said, "Come on now, time to get back to bed. Any more bottles stashed away in here?"

Strange, a part of her mind was thinking as she searched, how the habit of secret drinking persists. There had been no need for Jude to hide the bottle of gin in the bathroom. She could have had it in her room, or downstairs, anywhere she wanted. No one expected her not to drink. Not now. Just another evasion of reality, she supposed. Like the way she'd fooled herself she could write poetry and pretended, a lot of the time, that she didn't have children.

"Get me a drink!" Jude made an effort to get up but slipped back into a sitting position. Bea leaned over her.

"Keep away from me, bitch! I don't want you near me! You want me dead! You all want me dead so as you can have my money! Well you won't get it! None of you! I'll see to that!"

The venom was unabated but Jude's strength was fading. Her drinking was controlled in the nursing home, Bea knew. This little spree was more than her relatively dry system could cope with.

"God knows where she got this," Bea felt a twinge of wry admiration as she carefully put the empty bottle into the bath out of harm's way. Stolen it from the drinks cabinet downstairs, most likely. Jude had always been devious, and successful, about getting drink. She went back to her mother.

"Get away from me! You've been a curse in my life since you were born! I didn't want to have you, I didn't want to have any of the three of you…"

Jude clutched at the side of the toilet bowl, trying to raise herself. When she failed she raised the glass and, with frail but effective fury, flung it at the side of the bath. It smashed and there was silence as the pieces tinkled into a pile on the carpet.

"That's it, Jude, that's enough!"

Bea, squaring her shoulders, pulled herself together.

She stepped behind her mother, deftly and firmly catching her under the arms. Ignoring her protests, she turned her round and half-carried, half-lifted her across the bathroom. She weighed very little, felt as though she might crumble into splintered bone at any second. By the door Bea stopped.

"You have a choice, Jude," she said coldly. "You can be dragged back to the bedroom like this, all the way, or you can stand on your own two feet and walk back. I'll lend you my arm to lean on. Which is it to be?"

Jude, by way of an answer, went absolutely limp.

"Right! You're not going to make an effort, is that it?" Bea tightened her grip under Jude's arms. "Remember, the choice was yours…"

She got Jude to the room and into the bed. She found another of the candy-striped nightdresses and slipped it over her head. Jude had stopped protesting, seeming to be dozing almost. Bea guessed she would sleep for a few hours. Just as well too. She tucked her into the big, old bed, left the handbell within reach. Jude was gently snoring, her mouth open, by the time she left the room.

In the bathroom she stood for a minute looking at the broken glass, the dull patch where the gin had soaked into the carpet. Then she opened the window, wide, letting the clean air fill the room. Growing up with Jude hadn't all been bad, she thought. Jude's particular brand of non-mothering had given her resilience, an ability to tackle life head on. For that much she was grateful.

She cleaned up the mess and went downstairs.

CHAPTER FIVE

A lice Joyce was working in the kitchen. Her sleeves were rolled high on her freckled arms and her strong, skilful hands were kneading enormous quantities of brown bread dough.

"That seems like an awful lot of work," Bea said, after they had exchanged greetings. "Charles is too fussy by half. We could have bought the bread..."

"We could not," Alice was firm. "There's nothing but water and flour in shop bread. It'd be a shame to spoil the ship for a ha'porth of tar, give people any old bread with that lovely smoked salmon your brother's got in. Anyway," she threw a hostile eye at Charles's carefully prepared delicacies, "my bread will give them a mouthful of decent food at least..."

Bea laughed. "Forget I said anything."

"Don't mind me," Alice grinned. "I'm too fond of my food—I could do with eating less..." She patted a capacious hip. "Will you be staying down for long?"

"I'm not sure," Bea hedged. She hadn't yet told Charles that she would be leaving on Stephen's Day. "It depends. Who is going to be home in your house for Christmas?"

"All of them! Even the lad that went to America last

year. It'll be the first time in four years we'll all be together. Joseph'll enjoy it..." So would Alice, to judge by the look on her face.

It was a round, pleasant face, surrounded by soft, curly brown hair which she kept very short. Bea had once tried to persuade her to grow it longer but Alice protested she had no time for tarting herself up. Nor had she.

Twelve years before, when the eldest of Alice's four children was ten and the youngest just a year, her husband Matt had taken a boat to England. He had not come back. He had not written either and money for his children had been infrequently sent to say the least. Alice, deeming the task almost impossible, had never tried to trace him for maintenance. It would, she said, be a waste of time. Once located he would simply move on, become lost again.

"If Matt Joyce doesn't want to pay there's no court in any land will make him," she'd explained to Bea. She didn't have to. Bea understood only too well the impossibilities of getting maintenance from an unwilling husband.

"If there were divorce here I'd at least be rid of him," Alice said. "As it is the bugger can come back any time the going gets rough over beyond. I'm still his wife, in law anyway. It makes me sick, it really does. But I've the children. They're the love of my life and he gave me them at least..."

It hadn't been easy but she'd done well by the love of her life. She'd worked, at anything and everything, any time and anywhere she'd been able to find jobs. In the process she'd picked up paramedical and housekeeping skills and could cook, clean, sew and iron with superhuman efficiency. Two of her children had left home, a third would soon finish school. But Sean, ill and suffering from multiple handicaps, would always be with her. Bea asked about him and they discussed his imminent operation.

"He's so happy in himself," Alice spoke reflectively as she divided the bread into loaves. She put them into the oven and Bea felt the blast from its heat redden her face. "He's that happy he spreads it around. He makes people feel good. You'll come and visit him before you go?"

"I will," Bea promised. She took a quick look into Alice's questioning brown eyes and turned away. Charles would have told her about Sinéad's marriage. She wouldn't, of course, approve. She would think Sinéad too young, which she was, and consider marrying in haste a bad thing. But Bea didn't want to hear Alice's forthright and sound views at the moment. So she said nothing and Alice kept her counsel. She could, sometimes.

"I'll make the mulled wine," Bea said. "It'll taste better if it gets a bit of time to mull..."

"The cauldron you used last year is in the small cupboard," Alice pointed. "Was your mother all right when you went up to her?"

"Fine," Bea spoke with her head in the cupboard. "She wanted to use the bathroom."

In the darkness, as she rooted for the cauldron, she allowed herself a smile. To use the bathroom! What a euphemism for secret drinking! There was no point in moaning to Alice about the scene upstairs though. She had enough problems of her own to think about. She found the cauldron, scoured it clean and made the syrup by mixing sugar, cloves, cinnamon, nutmegs, lemon and orange peel in some water.

"All the usual suspects rounded up for tonight's bash?" she asked Alice as the smell of the heating fruit and spices began to fill the kitchen.

"Apart from your own lot, you mean?" Alice grinned.

"Apart from my own lot," Bea agreed with a return grin.

"That fat-arsed, hairy-nosed Larry Dowling will be here of course. He wouldn't miss it, invited or not..."

Bea laughed outright. Alice's dislike of the village's leading publican was legendary. Nor did she make a secret of the reason why. Matt Joyce, before his departure, had spent almost every penny he earned or drew in dole in The Huntsman. The publican should have made it his duty, Alice felt, to send him home to his wife and children with at least some money in his pocket. He never had.

"Don't know why your brother asks him anyway..." Alice sniffed at Bea's loud laugh.

"Because it's easier to ask him than not," Bea said.

"It's not as if Charles even takes a drink in his pub," Alice pointed out. "He goes to Liam Murphy's place whenever he ventures out for a drink. Liam's a decent man, for a publican. But that other..."

"Well, Larry does give us glasses every year..."

But only, Bea knew, because Charles paid for them. She didn't care much for Dowling herself and felt she was defending the indefensible.

"Hummph!" Alice snorted. "He won't stay long, which is a small consolation. He'll want to serve the pre-midnight Mass customers himself..."

Talk of Dowling had put Alice off discussing the other guests and she began to make pastry. It was another of

Alice's beliefs that you couldn't have a proper party without traditional mince pies, straight from the oven. Fancy, complicated food was, she held, about as useful as a chocolate teapot and made people feel awkward. She argued the point every year with Charles and every year made her mince pies after he'd finished making his "fancy" food. Everyone devoured them, especially Charles.

Bea had lined up the bottles of red wine, was pouring the first lot into the syrup, when Charles came into the kitchen.

"Preparing the gruel?" he asked and Bea nodded.

"I want to show you something," he beckoned. There was a light in his eye that Bea knew well.

"Now?" she asked. She didn't in the least feel like viewing one of Charles's "finds." But Charles hovered impatiently while she filled the cauldron with wine and turned the heat low under it. Alice winked as she followed him out of the kitchen.

"I've found a real beauty this time," Charles led the way at a trot to the studio/workroom he'd created for himself at the back of the house. It was a long, low room which had once been three dark cubicles in which servants slept. A wide window on to the orchard kept the room in touch with the seasons. It also gave a fine view of the grotto housing a stone gargoyle in the middle of the apple trees. Definitely a Victorian folly, it gave Bea the shivers. Charles thought it amusing.

All the walls in the room were hung with Charles's latter-day follies in rows almost to the ceiling. A lot of the pictures had a Dutch or Flemish look about them, a style of which Charles was very fond. Apart from the pictures the room was furnished with a day-bed, a fine old escritoire, a high-backed leather chair and a long work table at which Charles now stood.

"There! What do you think?" He reverently touched the picture lying there.

Bea scrutinised it carefully. It seemed to be some sort of pastoral scene with flowers, bright and beginning to look cheerful, doing something in the corners. There was a lot of cleaning still to be done.

"It has possibilities," she said cautiously.

"I think so." Charles seemed pleased enough with this. "It'll be a while yet, of course, but this could be very special. I have a suspicion..." He stopped, looking mysterious.

"Yes?" Bea tried not to be too encouraging. She had been around Charles's suspicions and mysterious faces before.

"I'll confound you all yet!" Charles was quite perky as he ushered her out of the room. At the door she turned to stick her tongue out at the gargoyle. Then, with an anxious look at her watch, she hurried to retrieve the flowers.

In the conservatory she began to arrange them in vases.

"How was Jude?" Charles leaned against the door.

"Drinking," Bea said. "She had a bottle of gin stashed away in the bathroom."

"I thought she might have one somewhere," Charles shrugged. "One disappeared yesterday. I'll get Alice to bring her up some tea..."

"She's sleeping," Bea had hardly said the words before, faintly but quickly becoming louder, the bell began to peal.

"She *was*!" Charles said. "That's probably a demand

for tea. She's reasonably polite to Alice—knows she's immune to her slings and arrows I suppose. She still behaves as if I don't exist..."

He left and a minute later, with some relief, Bea heard Alice go upstairs. The bell stopped ringing.

In the silence Bea deftly arranged and distributed the flowers throughout the house. The sprays of Dutch ilex she carried into the hallway to display in a corner opposite the tree. On the limed oak table in the living room she placed vases of the daisy-like flowers. Going upstairs she put a great cluster of chrysanthemums beside a group of marble cherubs on the landing. She was on her way to Sinéad's room with a vase of carnations when she heard Jude querulously arguing with Alice, whose answering tones were briskly no-nonsense. Resisting the temptation to intervene she went back downstairs.

She distributed a few more vases and came at last to the painted African leaves. These she carried to the dining room and placed on the small William IV sideboard. Sitting there they reflected in the mirror on the wall behind it. She was turning away when something in her own face made her stop. She stood, still as stone, and stared.

"Oh God, no!" The exclamation, through stiff lips, had a stricken sound. It was as if she had seen a ghost. "When did this happen to me?"

The face staring back at her was Jude's. Not Jude as she was now but a younger Jude, with some beauty still in her face. "I used not to be so like her..."

Bea tried to push away the fear the image created in her, the feeling that she was contemplating her own mortality. There was a boniness about the face in the mirror she'd not noticed before. The skin was thinner and pulled tighter across the cheeks than it used to be. The eyes were darker. They were Jude's eyes.

"It's the lighting in here," Bea shook herself. "It's because the window is behind me..."

She closed her eyes, tight. When she opened them again the woman in the mirror was gone.

"Welcome back!" Bea sketched a shaky salute at the more familiar image of herself.

She was crossing the hallway when she heard Alice on the stairs with Jude.

"Stop that old nonsense!" Alice was saying. She had a firm hold on the older woman as they descended the stairs together. "You'll get a cup of tea and some toast. When you've that inside you we'll think about a glass of gin. Maybe..."

"You're hard, Alice Joyce. You're hard on an old woman..." Jude's voice was whining. Bea hadn't heard her like that before.

"Can you manage?" she called to Alice.

"We're doing fine," Alice made a dismissive gesture as Jude stopped to give Bea a double-barrelled glare. "I'll bring her into the living room. Maybe you could check the fire in there?"

As Bea moved away Jude raised her cane and pointed, tremblingly, after her.

"Jezebel!" she hissed. "Look how she turns her back on her own mother! The day will come when her own daughter will do the same to her. You mark my words!"

Jake, hearing the commotion, appeared with a growl in the hallway. When he saw Jude with the raised cane he barked vigorously. Jude quickly put it down.

"Come on now," Alice, smothering a grin, urged Jude down the remaining steps. Jake, with something like a yawn, disappeared again.

Bea added some logs to the fire, Jude's words echoing in her head like a curse.

"She is not going to spoil this Christmas!" She gave a last, stabbing poke to the fire and went into the kitchen. She had made toast and laid a tray by the time Alice joined her.

"Will you do it?" she nodded to the tray.

"She's gone all quiet," Alice said. "That's been happening to her for a few days now. She sort of drifts away. Maybe it's as well. She's not left herself much of a life, poor soul."

"No. She hasn't," Bea agreed as Alice took the tray. She felt tired, all of a sudden. And hungry. In the fridge she found some of Charles's excellent home-made pâté.

"Will you share this with me?" she asked when Alice came back.

"No, thanks. But it would do you no harm to eat a bit more than that." Alice picked up a pair of boots she'd left by the door. "I'm off home for a few hours. I'll be back around half-four. The bread's cooling. Your brother has some of his fancy bits and pieces to finish off. He could do with sharing that snack with you. He's been working like mad on that new picture for weeks now. I don't think he eats half enough."

With that she was gone, her sturdy figure disappearing round the side of the house with her bike. Bea laid a place for Charles, then called him. She wasn't surprised when he appeared from the direction of his workroom.

"Aha, *une bonne bouche*!" He rubbed his hands together.

"It's two o'clock," Bea said. "Time to eat something. By the way, have you ever heard of Miroslav Capek?"

She asked the question as Charles cut the bread.

"No. Sounds like a Russian warhead."

"Wrong. Not Russian. And not a warhead exactly." Bea took some of the bread. "He's a Romanian painter. I'm going to show him at the end of January. Maybe. Olivia discovered him."

"Olivia did?" Charles stopped eating. "Since when have you trusted Olivia's judgement? Since when," his voice was dry, "has Olivia *had* any artistic judgement?"

"She doesn't, I mean hasn't. She heard about him and went along to an Adams sale. A picture of his came up. It sold very well indeed."

Charles listened, non-committal, as Bea told him everything she knew about Miroslav Capek.

"He's had a rough time by all accounts. Seems he was a significant force in the Romanian art world and active politically until Ceausescu had him thrown into jail. He was beginning to be known abroad but the years in jail put an end to that. He escaped during the revolution and was helped to make his way to New York. He began painting again there, hard-edge abstractionist stuff. He was a hit in a couple of group shows, according to Olivia..."

"So, why does he want to show here? The real money's in New York. Are you telling me he paints for love?" Charles's tone was sceptical.

"Not exactly. Seems he wasn't able to cope with New York. The hype, speed, hysteria, all of that. So he found himself a rich Irish-American benefactor, or the American found him. It's not clear. Whichever, he was spirited away and is somewhere in Ireland now, painting away in secret and isolation..."

"I see. And the Adams picture—was it a new one?"

"Sort of. It was painted in New York and first sold there about a year ago. A New York picture was sold recently at auction in London too. No one, apart from the benefactor, has seen any of the new work. And he's wildly enthusiastic, according to Olivia..."

"Hmmm..."

"She says Capek's mine if I make a success of the January showing..."

"But why're you so keen? You've never been interested in hard-edge abstractionists?"

"That's true. But I've shown other work that wasn't to my taste. And I'm not committed yet to showing him—not until I meet him. But I run a business, Charles, and I want to expand. I've drifted into a safe, predictable niche in the market. I want a more international acceptance. Showing Capek can do that for me. He could become big and if he makes it then so do I. And now that Eastern Europe's opened up he could be my entrée there..."

"Don't bank on it," Charles's tone was dry. "A great many Eastern Europeans seem keen to shake the dust of their homelands off their feet. A mistake, in my opinion, but it'll take them a while to learn that dishwashers and a supply of videos don't mean freedom."

"Capek didn't come here to watch videos!" Bea was getting annoyed. She wanted Charles to be encouraging.

"Of course not. Your painter sounds as if he had good reason to leave Romania. I don't think you should invest your expansionist hopes in him, that's all."

"But do you think..."

"You'll make up your own mind after you meet him, Bea. Nothing I say now will make the slightest difference, you know that. He'll be interesting, at the least. And you've nothing to lose, have you?"

"No. He'll sell. That much seems certain."

"So why do you need my reassurance? You don't usually."

"I don't know. Because he's different, and I haven't met him. Still, all of that'll be remedied on Stephen's Day..." No time like the present, she thought, to tell him I have to leave.

"Oh?" Charles's eyebrows shot up. "You're meeting him on Stephen's Day? I didn't realise your visit was to be so very brief." He paused. "Sinéad will be pleased," he said and Bea groaned.

"There was no way round it, Charles. He's neurotically reclusive since New York. He agreed to a Stephen's Day meeting because there won't be any people around. I'll try to get back the next day..."

"Well, you know what you're doing, my dear. I can't see Sinéad understanding however. Especially since she's bringing her new husband to meet us. She's likely to think that if your painter wants the exhibition then he could stretch a point and allow you to have your Christmas holiday..."

"You mean that's what you think..."

"We all do what we have to do." Charles stood up. "Regardless of what others may think." He held up a hand as Bea made to protest. "Enough. I've got a special bottle which you and I are now going to share..."

Bea bit her lip as Charles left the kitchen. If he didn't understand then who would? Certainly not Sinéad...He was back in minutes, with a bottle of red wine and three glasses on a tray.

"A Pomerol '86," he poured. "About as decadent a wine as one could hope for!" He handed Bea a glass, then lifted the other two, a wicked grin on his face. "And it's just what we need, you, me and Jude, to toast Christmas and families! Come on..."

Bea followed to where Jude sat by the fire in the living room. The day outside had darkened dramatically and the flames from the burning logs flickered on her sleeping face as they stood looking at her. She seemed hardly to breathe and even in the warm firelight she was deathly pale. Sleep had not brought peace to her face.

"Is she all right?" Bea whispered.

"I don't see how she could be." Charles spoke gently. "But she's not about to die, if that's what you mean. She sleeps a lot. She'll sleep like this for most of the afternoon and be quite...lively...when she wakes."

He placed Jude's glass of wine on the small table beside her then raised his own to the sleeping woman.

"To those who give us life," he said and turned to Bea. "To mothers!"

"To mothers!" Bea echoed. The dark richness of the wine did her a world of good. "To Christmas and families," she added. They drank to that too, then had a little more before Charles left for the kitchen and Bea to unpack the clothes she'd brought with her.

There were two windows in Bea's bedroom, which was next door to the one occupied by Jude. The fire had been laid in the grate and, unable to resist the temptation, she lit it. As it crackled to life she pulled a small Slipper chair over to the window and sat looking out. It was quite dark now, the fields and trees secret and sombre. Bea hated the short, crowded days of December and, after a few minutes, closed the heavy curtains on the countryside's dismal mood.

She unpacked the velvet-trimmed jacket and trousers

she intended wearing that evening, then hung the green
wool dress she'd brought to wear for dinner tomorrow.
It was soft, simple and she felt good in it. She resisted an
impulse to open James's present and instead checked
that she hadn't forgotten any of her own presents for
the family. Reassured, she changed into a comfortable
sweater and jeans. The canopied bed was inviting and
she sat there, watching the flames' giddy dance, listening
in the silence to the occasional crackle of a log. Drowsily
she leaned back against the bank of lace-edged pillows
and contemplated the patterns made by the flames on
the lemon mousse walls.

She didn't realise she'd fallen asleep until she heard
Alice and Larry Dowling arrive together downstairs.
Accidentally, she was sure. Alice would never have
contrived to travel from the village with the publican.

Feeling treacherous, Bea stayed where she was,
knowing Alice would take in the glasses and give Dowling
short shrift. She was right. In less than five minutes she
heard his heavy Volvo crunch down the avenue. She
waited, like a thief, until the sound died completely away.
Alice sniffed loudly when she arrived down to the
kitchen.

"I fell asleep," Bea half-lied.

"I don't have much time to be sleeping myself," Alice
snapped.

Dealing with Dowling had not, obviously, been the
highlight of her day. She had changed into a grey linen
dress with a white collar. "There's a good bit of work to
be done here still," she added in a more conciliatory
tone.

For an hour Bea and Alice worked together, arranging
food on tables in both the kitchen and living room.

Guests would be expected to serve themselves, buffet
style. When Alice was satisfied things were as organised
as they could be, they sat and sampled the mulled wine.

"It's not bad." From Alice, whose only tipple was an
occasional glass of whiskey, this was praise indeed.

"Thank you." Bea sipped critically. "Do you think it's
sweet enough?" she asked.

"It's plenty sweet," Alice said. "Any sweeter and they'd
drink it like lemonade. You don't want drunken drivers
on your conscience. The guards are mad active on the
drink driving. No one's safe and a good thing too."

"Maybe you're right." Bea covered the wine. "You
didn't finish telling me who is expected tonight."

"Oh, just the usuals, like you said yourself. Agnes
Walsh, of course. She's running the village these days.
And the O'Malleys will be here. Nora's cancer has come
back, poor thing. But she's on the mend again, says she'll
beat it if it kills her!" Alice grinned. "She's a tough woman.
If anyone beats that disease it'll be Nora O'Malley. Brian
worries more about it than she does. For all his size and
rough way of going on he'd be lost without her."

Bea was saddened to hear that Nora O'Malley's breast
cancer had become active again. Nora was an exuberant
and colourful woman and what Alice said about her
husband was true. Brian O'Malley was the largest farmer
in the area and could be hard-headed, blustery and often
crude. He and Nora disagreed on most things but without
her he would be lost.

"Then there will be those antique-dealer friends of
Charles and the horse-trainer fellow and the family who
bought the old house the other side of the village."

Alice stopped, tilted her head in a listening position.

"Someone's early," she said. Bea listened and heard

it too, the sound of a car coming quickly up the avenue.

The D'Arcy family car, a red BMW, came to a halt with a squeal of brakes and great sprays of gravel. Bea, watching from the open door, wasn't at all surprised to see her sister get out of the driver's door. She slammed it shut and made for the house.

"Deal with your son, Albert," she called over her shoulder. "I've had enough of him for one day!"

She reached the doorway, where Charles had joined Bea, and made swift pecking noises in the air beside both their cheeks.

"The home fires are burning, I hope?" she asked archly. "I'm famished! That drive has undone all the good health I paid for at Forest Mere..."

With a shiver she pulled her musquash about her tall slim, frame and slipped past them into the hallway.

"*Plus ça change*," Charles murmured as he and Bea made their way to where Albert D'Arcy, awkwardly assisted by his son, was attempting to unload a variety of suitcases and bags from the boot of the car. Mark, wearing leather jacket and shades, seemed extremely disgruntled. Stephanie appeared sleepily from the back seat.

"Hi!" She sketched a wave at Bea, threw her arms around Charles. "Long time no see," she said.

Charles held her at arm's length, considered her for a moment. "You'll do," he smiled. "Made your mark on the modelling world yet?"

"Not exactly," Stephanie made a small moue and shrugged. "But I will."

She turned with a frown to where her father and brother were assembling cases on the gravel, her perfect profile seeming to justify her confidence. Her long, white-gold hair was brushed back and fell to her waist and she was almost as tall as Charles, who was 6' 2". She was as slim as a willow.

"Careful with my things, Mark!" she snapped.

"Look after them yourself!" Mark dropped the case he'd been holding.

"Children! Children! Not in front of the adults!" Bea, laughing, gave Mark a quick hug as his father straightened from a search of the boot.

"Bea!" Albert D'Arcy's round face split into a wide beam. "Give us a proper kiss!"

Bea did just that, laughing over her brother-in-law's head as he squeezed her tight. He was shorter than she by several inches and squarely built. When she got a chance to look at him his good-natured face seemed more than usually tired-looking. Living with Olivia had, she knew, its ups and downs. Turning her gaze on the array of luggage made her hope that last year's row, caused by Olivia and Stephanie expecting Alice to iron and hang every item, was not going to be repeated.

"Don't even think about it," Charles, reading her mind, picked up and started for the house with two large Louis Vuitton cases.

Jude was awake, but quiet. She gazed at her children and grandchildren, gathered in the living room about her, as if they were strangers.

"Hello, Jude." Olivia spoke loudly. Jude seemed not to hear. Olivia bent over, careful not to touch her mother. "Hey, Jude!" she said. Jude sighed and turned toward the fire.

"Best to leave her alone for a while," Charles suggested. "She seems to come and go. Alice is scrambling some eggs for her."

"Alice Joyce you mean?" Olivia snorted. "You've still

got that woman working for you? After the way she behaved last year? Really, Charles!"

"Care for a drink?" Charles, ignoring his sister, spoke to Albert, who nodded vigorously. Olivia had already helped herself to a gin and tonic. Stephanie was lounging in front of the TV and Mark, once he'd established that Sinéad hadn't arrived yet, had disappeared.

"You're early," Bea said. She threw a couple of logs onto the fire and they sparkled to immediate life. Jude moved irritably in the armchair but said nothing.

"Albert's idea. He thought you might need help..." Olivia threw herself into the armchair opposite Jude. "I hope you've got rid of that bloody dog, Charles. Or has it died? It's way past the age when dogs should be in heaven..."

Charles, at the window with Albert, didn't answer. But Jake, locked in the drawing room next door, began to howl. It was as if he sensed a threat to his existence.

"That is not the same animal, surely?" Olivia hissed. "He's dangerous! He almost savaged me last year! Albert, speak to..."

She stopped with a shriek as Jake torpedoed into the room followed by a jittery, defensive-looking Mark. With unerring instinct he made for Olivia.

"Get him off me! Get him away!" Olivia's shrieks merely fuelled Jake's gut feeling that this was an unfriendly human.

He bared his teeth and snarled, displaying all the characteristics of his war dog ancestors. He also shocked Jude out of her reverie.

"I didn't know he was in there," Mark protested. "I just..."

Jude began to laugh, rocking in her armchair to deep

cackling sounds. Jake barked, fiery eyes never leaving Olivia's face, pinning her where she sat.

"Good boy, that's enough now. Stoppit!" Charles caught the terrier by the collar and he became calm, biddable, as he led him from the room. Filled with the guilty feeling that she had willed the dog to attack her sister Bea became eagerly solicitous as the door closed behind Charles and Jake.

"Poor Olivia! He wouldn't have touched you. He's all snarl and no bite," she said. "I'll get you another drink..."

She tried a calming smile but it came out as a wide grin. She put her hand over her mouth.

"I'm not staying here with that animal roving the place! It's him or me! Charles will have to decide..."

"Better pack your bags so!" Jude had found her voice again. She was animated, quite joyful-looking. Her eyes shone with malice. "Your brother will make an unnatural choice, you know that. Out the door with you, my girl. Give your place to the dog!"

She cackled and held frozen-looking, blue-veined hands to the fire. Mark watched his grandmother with a dazed expression.

"Is she a witch?" His eyes looked slightly glazed as he asked Bea the question.

"I don't know," Bea grimaced. "Perhaps she is."

"Don't talk about me as if I weren't here!" Jude screamed suddenly and Stephanie, who'd been maintaining a detached cool, jumped.

"I'm not gone yet! And I've no intention of going for a long time to come. Where's my bell? Where is it? You!" She poked a bony digit in Stephanie's direction. "Bring me a drink. Gin, but a larger measure than your mother has..."

Stephanie looked helplessly at Bea, who nodded, holding her finger and thumb up to denote a small measure.

"Come on, Olivia, upstairs with you." Albert, who'd been quietly attentive by his wife's side, helped her to her feet. "A warm bath and you'll be your old self..."

"Christ, Albert, don't baby-talk me!"

Olivia, Bea could tell, was recovering. Even so, she was white-faced and shaky as she allowed herself to be led from the room by her husband. Stephanie followed. Mark sat opposite his grandmother, watching as she downed her drink in a gulp. She put the glass down and fixed him with a gimlet eye.

"Get me another!" she commanded. "A decent drink this time."

Catching his eye, Bea shook her head.

"Why not?" Mark spoke loudly and Jude turned.

"You still here?" she said nastily to Bea. "Don't you have something to do? I want to talk to this young man."

Mark stood up. "I'll get you a drink," he said.

"Don't, Mark," Bea spoke sharply. "She's had enough already today..."

"Enough? Who's to decide what enough is? If she feels she needs a drink then she should have it. Why not? Life's a shit anyway..."

He was, Bea decided, drunk. Must be.

"Please, Mark," she put her hand over his as he began to pour the drink. "She can't physically cope with any more right now. No matter what she says."

She spoke gently and, to her relief, Mark put the bottle down. He seemed to lose all interest and without a word left the room. Bea, only half-aware that her mother was shrieking at her, watched his unsteady progress to the door. He did not, she thought, look well. Curly-haired and on the short side, he had always had a lovable, choirboy look in the smoothness of his cheeks and the gentleness of his smile. All that seemed to have gone, to have been replaced by a strained and angry look.

"Bring him back!" Jude was strident. "Bring my grandson back He's the only one who understands me..."

Yes, Bea thought, and that's what's so worrying. To her mother she said, sharply, "Be quiet, Jude! You're going to eat some scrambled egg now. And I mean that: you are going to eat it. Otherwise you go up to bed and stay there, without the bell, until Stephen's Day when you go back to the home..."

"Take me back then." Jude was sulky, the fight gone out of her. Her strength was limited. It was amazing she had any at all.

Closing the brocade curtains Bea noticed that a wind had come up, saw the skeletal branches of the closer trees stiffly shaking.

Alice had the eggs ready when she got to the kitchen. "I kept well away from all that fuss," she said. "That poor old dog is just protecting what's his. He has the place to himself all year—wouldn't anyone behave the same if their place was suddenly invaded?"

This, Bea knew, was a statement. Alice did not want another opinion. "I suppose so," she said. "I only hope he's reconciled to company now."

"Oh, he's grand now," Alice assured. "Your brother had a chat with him. I heard her nibs coming to life too. I'll get her to eat this bite before anyone else comes. You go on up and get changed."

"If you're sure you can..."

"Go on," Alice was impatient. "You'll only be agitating

her if you stay."

Bea enjoyed a relaxing bath and slipped into her jacket and trousers. She was critically examining the result in the mirror when headlights on the bedroom window indicated a car arriving. She opened the curtain and looked down as it came to a halt. Sinéad didn't look up as she got out, linked her arm with that of the tall, fair-haired man who'd been driving, and came toward the front door.

CHAPTER SIX

B ea felt strangely shy and very, very nervous as she descended the wide staircase to greet her own daughter. Charles, resplendent in a dark green velvet jacket, had answered the clamouring doorbell. Sinéad was laughingly introducing him to her new husband as Bea approached.

They were a handsome pair: Sinéad, petite and with the vibrantly dark looks which were her inheritance from her father, and the tall, bespectacled and good-looking man by her side. He turned and smiled as Bea came close. She stopped and Sinéad turned in her direction too. Before either of them could do anything he took the initiative, and removed any awkwardness from the situation, by extending a hand to Bea.

"It's good to meet you at last, Ms Hennessy," he said. "And it's nice of you to let us have a share in the party..."

Bea gave him ten out of ten for diplomacy. In one stroke he had dealt with the fact that they hadn't met before and acknowledged her independent status. *And* he'd done it with a smile that was so reassuringly open it almost disarmed. Almost. Bea wasn't ready yet to relinquish her daughter to a man with a pleasant smile and easy manner.

"It's nice to meet *you*," Bea said and took the extended hand. He held hers firmly. Another small reassurance—though Bea sternly reminded herself that firm handshakes were the stock-in-trade of used-car salesmen and politicians.

Sinéad, who had been inscrutably watching their exchange moved closer. Smiling, Bea remove her hand and turned to her daughter.

"You look so well!"

She couldn't keep the relief out of her voice or stop herself from opening her arms in welcome. Sinéad, with some of the impulse of her younger years, fell into them and they embraced. Not the smothering hug of earlier years but not bad, Bea thought. Promising anyway, and more response than she'd got for a long time. When they parted, it was Charles who dealt with the small silence which threatened to stretch.

"Why," he asked, "are we standing here? There are fires lighting all over the place. Alice will take your coats..."

Alice, with impeccable timing, appeared brisk and smiling from the back of the house.

"So! You're a married woman, Sinéad! And what am I to call you? Mrs what?"

"Alice, meet Daniel Kirwan! And I'm still Sinéad Treacy—saw no reason to give up my own, perfectly good name!"

"Wish I'd had your sense!" Alice approved. "I hope you'll be very happy." But as she shook Daniel's hand she was, Bea noticed, carefully inspecting him.

The exchange gave Bea an opportunity to carry out some scrutiny of her own. Sinéad's husband was older than she'd expected. Six or seven years older than Sinéad, at least. His good looks weren't perfect, which was a relief. His face was a bit too square for that and his nose had definitely taken a punch at some time. But his eyes were a friendly grey and he had a self-assurance which she liked. The Louis Copeland coat he handed to Alice indicated that he wasn't exactly on the breadline.

As Alice left them Daniel turned abruptly and caught Bea's scrutiny. They looked at one another, carefully and questioningly. Daniel was the first to look away—but not without a small nod which recognised the bond they shared. We both care for Sinéad, the look said, we must try to be friends.

"How was the holiday?" Bea turned to Sinéad. She couldn't quite say honeymoon. Did sophisticated young people like Sinéad and Daniel HAVE honeymoons? Better to be safe, call it a holiday.

"Lovely!" Sinéad said and caught Daniel's hand. They smiled at one another, the conspiratorial smile of lovers remembering pleasure. Looks like it WAS a honeymoon, Bea thought. She felt absurdly pleased—but was surprised too by a small stab of envy.

"Well, well! So the bride has arrived!" Olivia's voice floated ahead of her as she came mincingly down the stairs. "We are to be allowed at last to meet the groom...!"

Sinéad stiffened as, wreathed in a dazzling smile and gilt-embroidered dress, Olivia swept across the hall. Stephanie, in a minuscule black creation, followed close behind.

Sinéad pulled her hand free of Daniel's as her aunt approached and Bea got a whiff of Poison, by Dior. How apt, she thought as she recognised the scent. Olivia has just succeeded in contaminating what was turning into a pleasant gathering.

"Daniel, I'd like you to meet my aunt, Olivia D'Arcy,"
Sinéad's voice was cool. "Aunt O, this is Daniel Kirwan..."

"Aunt! Aunt! Don't let's be so formal! You must call
me Olivia, please!" She paused, gave a tinkling laugh.
"Daniel! Such a...noble name! A Daniel came to judge
us..."

"Come to judgement," Daniel corrected, seemingly
unamused by the pun, as he gave a courteous nod.

"Seems like I'll have to introduce myself." Stephanie
tossed her hair and looked flirtatiously at Daniel. "I'm
Stephanie."

"We'd half-expected you to have a cloven hoof!"
Olivia said gaily before turning accusingly to Sinéad.
"Why have you kept this gorgeous young man away
from us?"

"Nothing deliberate, Aunt," Sinéad's tone was very
deliberate indeed. "Just a very crowded schedule. I didn't
get round to it."

"She kept him away because no one in their right
mind would marry into this family once they'd met us..."
Mark, giggling a little, stood by the Christmas tree.
Sinéad, looking relieved, flashed a sudden smile his way.

"Mark! Where've you been? I tried to get in touch
with you..."

"Oh, around. Here and there..." Mark spread his
hands vaguely. "And now I'm here. Nice to meet you,
Daniel." He made a small bow. "Do you fancy meeting
your granny-in-law? You'll enjoy her! She's a bundle of
laughs!"

As her family trooped into the living room Jude raised
her chin and, scrawny neck apart, managed something
of the old hauteur.

"Jude, this is Daniel Kirwan. My husband." Sinéad

smiled uncertainly at her grandmother as Daniel held out a hand. Jude ignored it.

"Nobody told me you were getting married," she snapped. "Why wasn't I at the wedding?" She turned a sudden, jabbing finger on Daniel. "Was *your* mother's mother invited?"

Daniel pulled up a chair and sat beside her.

"We didn't have any family there," he said gently. "Just ourselves. I'm sorry if you're offended..." Jude looked at him briefly before fixing her granddaughter with a penetrating stare.

"Marriage brought *me* no joy." She spoke slowly, her voice wheezy. "And I'm not offended because I expect no better from my granddaughter, given the way she was reared. Her mother is a trollop..." she gave a croaking laugh, eyes still on Sinéad. "But you may be safe enough, young man. I can see no trace of syphilis in your wife, in spite of her mother's morals."

Bea closed her eyes as Jude laughed again, a weaker croak this time. She's crazy, she thought. My mother is absolutely crazy. I mustn't pay any attention to what she says. Mark was right. She *is* a witch. A vindictive old witch...

When she opened her eyes Charles was handing a glass of wine to Daniel, another to Sinéad. Jude had shrunk back into her armchair and was again staring, impassively, into the flames. Maybe it had been a dream. Not even Jude could be so malevolent.

Alice, standing in the kitchen doorway, caught Bea's eye sympathetically. She made an upward movement of her head and Bea nodded. Firmly, without the least fuss, Alice came into the room, eased Jude out of the armchair and helped her unprotesting upstairs to bed.

"Togetherness! That's what Christmas is about!"

Olivia had draped herself gracefully along the *chaise-longue*. It would be another half-hour before the non-family party guests arrived. Sinéad and Daniel had gone to their room to freshen up and Bea had been shooed by Charles to join her sister and brother-in-law in the tranquillity of the drawing room. The fire glowed and from somewhere came the plaintive strains of a string quartet. The sudden peace was, Bea thought, like the calm before the storm. She hoped she was wrong.

"I've brought something to show you." Olivia reached a languid hand into a delicate, elaborately worked evening bag.

"Olivia, be a good girl and give your sister a break from work. She's on holiday. We all are. You can go over all of that next week, when we're back in town."

Albert's good-natured appeal merely annoyed Olivia.

"Don't interfere, Albert," she snapped. "You know nothing about it. This can't wait."

From the evening bag she produced some folded newspaper cuttings. Albert, with the air of a man who has said his piece and now wants to be left alone, began to pack tobacco into his pipe. Olivia, with a full glare in his direction, opened the cuttings.

"These," she waved them dramatically, "are what the New York critics had to say about Miroslav Capek."

She held them in the air but didn't get up. Bea, her reluctance to move overcome by curiosity, took the proffered cuttings from her sister. She sat by a reading lamp, spreading them on the small table underneath.

There were two of them and both spoke of an artist with a "committed vision." One detailed Capek's background but there was nothing in it that Bea didn't already know. The same review said that the paintings on show, eight of them, "explored extreme inner psychological states such as fear, madness, separation and love." They operated, it said, on "several levels, the artist speaking through seemingly empty spaces which were as articulate as those filled with figures."

Great, Bea thought grimly. So he's tormented, disturbed by all that's happened to him. But what are his pictures *like*?

The second review suggested he might have found a degree of peace. "These pictures," it said, "are about the nature of love. About how the desire is always there but can never be fully grasped." Good. So he'd found a girlfriend. Bea came at last to a description of the pictures. Capek's vivid colours were, the review said, "ambivalent and evocative of the instability of meaning in contemporary western culture."

And that was it. She would have liked fewer words like instability, torment, disturbed. But of his success with the critics in New York there was no doubt. His paintings said something to buyers too, judging by the numbers sold. The reviews were reassuring and she could use them in the catalogue. If she went ahead and showed him.

"Well?" Olivia was reading over her shoulder. "Those are prestigious galleries. That one in particular." She ran a vermilion nail over the review that had called the colours vivid. "You're lucky to be getting the opportunity to show someone like Capek. You *will* show him?"

"More than likely."

"For God's sake, Bea! What more do you want?"

"To meet him..."

The doorbell cut short any further argument on

Olivia's part. Bea slipped the cuttings into a drawer and joined Charles as he opened the door to Larry and Peg Dowling.

Peg was dressed in red. An unfortunate choice since it highlighted both the width of her hips and her pale as putty skin. She offered Bea a limp hand while at the same time giving Charles a thin smile.

"You've made a lovely job of the decoration," she said, a beady eye on the Christmas tree. Her husband, eyeing the garland along the staircase, nodded energetically by her side.

"Lovely job," he said.

This, Bea knew, could go on indefinitely, with the Dowlings lavishing compliments on things they would castigate in the pub later. She was tempted to make a caustic reply but the doorbell, once again, saved the moment.

"Go on in and meet everyone," she urged, "Alice will give you a drink..."

She opened the door to a huddle of shivering guests. First was Agnes Walsh and, on her heels, the O'Malleys. Within ten minutes the rest had arrived to spread themselves in groups through the rooms. Bea circulated, enjoying the good-humoured mood, glad the mulled wine seemed to be going so well.

Everything else seemed to be going well too. Sinéad and Daniel held hands and accepted congratulations from all sides. Olivia flirted with Brian O'Malley who, after a generous double whiskey, warmed to the flattery. What you'd call a meeting of minds, Bea grinned to herself. Both Olivia and Brian were hard-headed pragmatists who knew what they wanted and went after it.

Mark sat dreamily watching it all and Stephanie

chatted animatedly, about her career no doubt, to a
politely interested antique dealer.

Bea allowed an hour of this relaxed conviviality before
she went to the kitchen to get the Dom Perignon. A
bottle in each hand, she then went in search of the
newly weds. She found them by the Christmas tree,
Sinéad showing Daniel the paper bells and angel she'd
made as a child.

"This is your party too," Bea held up the bottles,
"and it's time to drink to you both."

"Oh, no!" Sinéad wailed, but laughingly, as Bea
popped a cork and the champagne flowed. To rousing
cheers Bea poured into long-stemmed glasses supplied
by Alice. When everyone had a glass she raised her own
in a toast.

"To Sinéad and Daniel," she said quietly, "may they
be very happy."

As everyone drank to the health of the young people
Bea caught her daughter's eye above the rim of her glass.
Sinéad winked, the conspiratorial wink of old. Bea winked
back, then enjoyed a deeply satisfying drink of champagne. Her heart settled down and the nervous stickiness
in her hands evaporated. Good God, she thought, I was
more uptight about this than I realised. But it was all
working out fine.

"I'd like to propose a toast too," Sinéad's clear voice
rose above the chat and laughter. "I'd like us all to drink
to my mother, the most..."

What Sinéad thought of Bea went unsaid as the
doorbell rang, piercingly shrill in the hushed hallway.

"Late arrival," Bea said, apologetic and with a puzzled
look around. Everyone seemed to be here already. Charles
frowned, slightly.

"Not anyone I've invited," he said. The bell rang again, loudly insistent.

"I'll get it," Bea said as she crossed the hall, glass in hand, and opened the door.

Walter Treacy, slightly dishevelled and widely beaming, stood on the step. "I'm home." He doffed an imaginary hat. "Home for Christmas."

CHAPTER SEVEN

Lightning didn't strike. Bea felt it should have, but found she was all of a piece, and outwardly quite cool, when she said, "Walter, this *is* a surprise. You weren't expected..." and stood aside to let him enter.

He had changed little over the years, even to the length of his hair. But then luck was always with Wally, in appearance as in everything else. Black-eyed handsome gypsy looks don't date and the fashion for the long hair he'd worn when Bea had first met him had come full circle. He didn't wear it quite as long now, she noticed, but there was just as much of it. Dapples of grey merely added to his rakish air and the lines in his face hinted at experience, not age. His long, stone-coloured raincoat hung open to reveal a dark red shirt and green bow-tie. On Wally the ensemble looked very good. In one hand he carried a Harrod's bag filled with brightly wrapped packages. His cavalier ways didn't seem to have changed either.

"I do not come empty-handed," he held up the bag and laughed—an infectious sound unless you'd laughed with him too many times before, as Bea had. "I bring gifts for my wife and gifts for the bride..."

Behind her Bea heard Sinéad's smothered cry. All of

her instincts urged her to run, protectively, to their daughter. But Wally had to be dealt with. She was not going to allow him to take over and ruin everything. She turned, calmly, to the curious guests.

"I don't think any of you have met my husband, Walter Treacy?" she said and smiled. She had no idea how bleak an expression it was. "Please get on with enjoying yourselves. There's all that food in there to be got through! Do help yourselves...I'll do the introductions in a little while..."

Charles, with a curt nod in Walter's direction, took Bea's cue and led the way back to the drawing room with Nora O'Malley.

"You'd better take your coat off," Bea turned coldly to Wally. "Then maybe we could have a private word in the library..." She was aware of a low murmuring, then a polite moving away of the curious crowd behind her.

"Walter! So you got here! Bea, you could be more welcoming to my guest..."

"Your guest?" Bea spun to face Olivia as she came, face wreathed in a smile, from the back of the house.

"Certainly!" Olivia planted double kisses on Walter's cheeks and faced her sister. "Someone in the family had to tell her father that Sinéad had got married. It seemed only decent to ask him to the celebrations..." She turned to Sinéad. "Don't you agree, my dear? It's my little surprise for you—what better wedding present than to have your absent father turn up to toast your health!"

Sinéad had become rigid. She stood with Daniel's arm around her, her face parched and frozen-looking as she stared at the father she hadn't seen for nineteen years and couldn't possibly remember.

Wally took a step toward her. "No!" The word was a

cry of deep distress. Wally stopped where he was, held up his hands and made a peace sign.

"I'm sorry," his voice was soft, low. It was as if all of the bravado had been knocked out of him by such unequivocal rejection.

"It was a bad idea to arrive like this. I should have prepared you. I should have written. Or telephoned. But I thought..." He paused, shot a hesitant, defensive look in Bea's direction. I thought your mother would forbid me to come, the look said. But when he spoke he said only, "I thought a surprise was the best thing..."

He sounded genuinely regretful. Sinéad, with a small sob, broke free of Daniel's arm and headed blindly up the stairs.

"Your talent for creating unhappiness remains undimmed," Bea's icy voice and demeanour betrayed nothing of the churning emotions she felt inside. Only from the darkening of her eyes to a steely grey-blue could something of her mounting fury be gauged. Looking at Wally, the picture of charming remorse, she felt her carefully built life slowly coming apart. She would *not* let it happen.

"This is all much ado about nothing!" Olivia shot an uneasy look at her sister's stony face. Wally, slowly and carefully, placed the parcels under the Christmas tree.

"I'll leave," he said. "I shouldn't have come. I'm sure to get a room in the village inn..." His tone was dry, his smile full of the irony of the situation.

"The innkeeper is here." Bea was curt. But she was caught, and she knew it. She would have to allow Wally to stay, give him a bed for tonight and tomorrow at least. She couldn't permit the Dowlings the pleasure of taking him in. Charles would be the one to suffer from the gossip and innuendo which would be the inevitable result. He would have to bear with the Dowlings, and others, as they enlivened village life for weeks to come with snide remarks and energetic speculation. And Wally, who was very good indeed at sizing up and turning situations to his advantage, would not disappoint them. He would amuse himself at The Huntsman by playing the wronged husband, the bereft father.

No, Bea thought, she couldn't do that to Charles. Not now he'd found a measure of peace. She was already guilty of neglecting him and Inverskena. She couldn't leave her marital problems on his doorstep as well.

She allowed Wally to walk as far as the door, a fluttering and agitated Olivia at his heels, before she spoke. "You can have a bed here, Walter," her voice had lost none of its ice, "Olivia will make one up for you."

Olivia whirled, eyes wide with astonishment.

"*Me?* Make up a bed?"

"Yes. Walter is your guest, after all. Alice will tell you where to get the bed linen. He can use one of the attic bedrooms."

Without another word Bea spun on her heel and made for the stairs. On the second step she stopped, turned and faced her husband.

"You are staying only because you've left me with no option, Walter," she said. "Not because I want you here. Or anywhere else in my life. After Christmas you will leave—sooner if you can arrange it. Do I make myself clear?"

"Absolutely." Walter's mocking tone followed her up the stairs.

Bea found Sinéad standing by the window in her bedroom. It was the same room she'd occupied for all of her teen years, the room where she'd dreamed lazy Sundays away, agonised over her changing body, held night-long giggling sessions with girlfriends. She'd even studied for her Leaving Cert in this room. But now she stood like a figure carved in granite.

"I'm so sorry this had to happen," Bea put a hand on her shoulder, tried to turn her away from the pitiless, wintry black outside. Sinéad, roughly, shrugged her hand away.

"Where's Daniel?" Bea asked.

"Bathroom," Sinéad said, shortly.

"Look, I know this is an awful thing to have happened. But Wally exists. He's your father. He was bound to reappear at some time in your life. It's just lousy timing, that's all. We can deal with it, Sinéad, you and I together. We can..."

"Is he gone?" Sinéad's voice was harsh, implacable. Bea took a deep breath.

"No," she said. "I had to ask him to stay..."

Sinéad lurched violently away. From across the room she turned to face her mother. "You've asked him to stay! *Asked* him! How could you! Couldn't you think of me? For once? About how I feel? He's never been a father to me and I don't want him here! I thought this was supposed to be *my* party? I bring my husband here to meet you and what do you do? You ask my father, who's been gone for nineteen years, to stay! It's always what *you* want, isn't it?"

"That's not true..."

"You've never been able to let him go, have you? You've hung on all these years. You could have divorced him, there *are* ways. Then he couldn't have reappeared. You could have got rid of him from both our lives. But you didn't. Anyway," Sinéad's voice became increasingly bitter, "if it wasn't him it would be the gallery somehow ballsing things up, wouldn't it? Demanding your time. Always one or the other. *Your* needs, *your* ego..."

Devastated, Bea listened to her daughter's tirade. How could two people who loved each other misunderstand each other so completely...She had not known Sinéad felt like this.

And how could Sinéad not have realised that Bea had never divorced Wally because of the upset and strain it would have caused? Sinéad had no idea how difficult it would have been, no understanding of how Bea's energies had been concentrated on surviving, making a go of the gallery. Nor, obviously, that it had been the gallery which had paid for her education, bought her the best of everything she'd ever needed. Bea had never complained to Sinéad, never talked to her about money or other difficulties. Now it looked as if she'd protected her too much from reality.

"Sinéad," Bea began slowly, "I know you're upset. And you've a right to be. But this," her voice quickened, "is out of court. Since the day you were born you have been the only priority in my life..."

Except, the thought came fleeting and painful, for one brief period. But Sinéad couldn't remember that. And if she did she would understand. Only Bea wasn't about to tell her. Not now anyway. Maybe never. She took a deep breath. Sinéad had turned away so she spoke to the mass of curly dark hair.

"You've said a lot of things here tonight which are both unfair and untrue. Obviously we need to sort them out. For now, it would help keep this a reasonably agreeable Christmas if you were to come downstairs.

Just be civil to your father, show him you've reached adulthood and don't need him. Do it for Charles's sake if not for mine, and for Daniel..."

"Your mother's right, Sinéad. It's the best way, given the circumstances..."

Daniel had come quietly into the room. He stood, almost as if keeping a safe distance, just inside the door. "No point in letting your father spoil everything for everyone. Seems to me as if he's done enough of that already."

"How the hell would you know? And where do you come on taking her side?" Sinéad swung furiously round to face him. Her eyes were almost black and her face sheet white. "You don't understand any of this, Daniel, so keep out of it!"

"I understand enough." Daniel sounded tired and Bea knew, suddenly, that this wasn't the first time Sinéad's personal demons had come between them. He walked to his wife, faced her squarely. "Cool it, Sinéad," he said. "You've taken this far enough for tonight."

"You're right," Sinéad swung her hair angrily. "I'm tired of it. And of you all. Get out of here, both of you. I'm going to bed."

Without another word she kicked off her shoes, began to unzip her dress. Behind her back Daniel made a curt nod in the direction of the door and Bea, sick at heart, left the room.

Downstairs, over the buzz of talk and laughter, Charles's wind ensemble delivered seasonal fanfares. Bea let the sound calm her as, for a few minutes, she observed the party. Walter was at his most charming and seemed to be enjoying himself. He had always had a way of insinuating himself into company, especially female company. Stephanie, her arm through his, was breezily introducing him to everyone as her "Uncle Walter." Glass in hand, bow-tie at an angle, Walter flattered, teased and enchanted most of those he met. Olivia, standing slightly apart, watched their progress with an arch smile. Bea wandered, dazedly, between conversations. Some she barely registered, some she joined in, briefly. It began to seem to her as if the party would never end.

"Don't you agree, Bea?" Nora O'Malley grabbed her as she passed. "Isn't it a nonsense to believe that the pre-TV Christmas of the thirties and forties was pure and wonderful?"

Nora, thin and pale but interesting-looking as ever, was, Bea could tell, quite tipsy. Well, more power to her. If she could drink and be merry while undergoing chemotherapy she deserved to be listened to.

"Believe it or not, Nora," Bea said with the brightest smile she could manage, "I don't remember the thirties and forties..."

"Of course you don't," Nora put an arm around Bea's shoulder and squeezed with surprising strength. "But you'll remember this Christmas, my poor dear."

So Nora at least wasn't fooled by the charade being enacted by Stephanie and Wally. Bea, afraid Nora's sympathy would weaken her and bring tears, moved quickly to where a drunkenly sentimental Brian O'Malley had pinned Olivia by the fireplace.

"The night Bobby Kennedy was shot," Brian's voice was loud, "I was driving along the Naas dual carriageway. I was in the Grand Central Cinema in Limerick when John Fitzgerald Kennedy was shot. I don't remember the film—" he gave a bellowing laugh—"but the news was on an *Evening Press* poster when I came out. Can you top that now? Where were you?"

"I was six months old," Olivia snapped. She tried to slip away. Liar, Bea thought. She was twelve at least. She couldn't understand why neither Olivia nor Jude could face the reality of their ages.

"You're sure you were that young?" Brian, to Olivia's consternation, peered closely at her face. Bea wondered if he was going to ask to see her teeth. He didn't. "I'd have taken you for older," he said instead. Olivia's fury made her look every one of her forty years.

Bea felt an arm on her shoulder.

"You all right?" Charles asked. She nodded.

"What about Sinéad?"

"Not so good."

"I was afraid of that. It's the season, you know. Bloody Christmas. It weakens people, makes them vulnerable. Too much false sentiment, dark melancholy." He dropped his arm. "She'll be fine in a few days. We'll be laughing about all of this by the New Year."

"I hope so..." Bea felt gripped by a dark melancholy herself. She wished Charles hadn't used the words; they described far too accurately the way she felt. From across the room Wally caught her eye. He had been laughing but stopped, solemnly raising his glass in salute. Caught, suddenly, in the bright reflection of Stephanie's glowing youth, he didn't seem as handsome as he used to be at all. Nor half so desirable. Bea turned away.

In the kitchen she found Albert with Agnes Walsh. Their judgement on Charles's "fancy" food was positive.

"Lovely food and lovely party," Agnes said.

"You're not going to be left with much of this!" Albert helped himself to a pecan snap as footsteps sounded in the kitchen behind Bea.

"Caught you at last! Where have you been all evening?" An arm she had never wanted to feel there again went round Bea's waist. "I was afraid you'd disappeared into the night."

Bea pulled sharply away. Holding tightly onto her glass, she stood looking at Wally. The candles on the table guttered and the flickering light played with the shadows on his face. His wide, wide smile seemed to shift, become crooked.

"Walter," she said stiffly, "have you met Agnes Walsh?"

"No, I've not had the pleasure. I would certainly remember..." Walter took Agnes's hand in his, raised it fleetingly to his lips. He was the Lothario he'd always been.

"How do you do?" Agnes's birdlike eyes were watchful. "We haven't seen you here before."

"No. But I hope you will see more of me in the future." Walter's smile became slightly wistful. "Though that of course depends on my wife."

"Oh?" Agnes, helping herself to the last of Charles's cinnamon sugared nuts, looked mildly sceptical. But anything she might have been about to say was interrupted by a distraught Olivia bursting into the kitchen.

"Bea," she cried, "do something! That wretched woman's got out of bed and is halfway down the stairs..."

Alice, who had her coat on and was preparing to leave, got to Jude before Bea did. Together they turned her round, then carried and coaxed her back up the stairs. On the landing she stood stock still, refusing to budge. A light gathered in her eye. "Count the spoons!" Jude spoke softly at first. Then very quickly, her voice rose to a shriek which carried clearly to the party crowd below. "Count the spoons! Check the silver!" she shrilled. "You never know what those people may have concealed on their persons! Count the spoons!"

Everyone left soon after that. Most would have left anyway, anxious to get to midnight Mass. They were all understanding about Jude, saying they knew how it was with old people.

"They're worse than children at that age," Agnes Walsh said as she wrapped her tiny frame into an enormous tweed coat. More than most, Agnes knew what she was talking about. Her own mother had been a querulous ninety-one when she died in the room behind the shop. She'd been buried five years before and Agnes was still slightly intoxicated by her freedom.

"But children grow out of it," Bea said, tired of excuses. "And the old die," Nora O'Malley was brisk. The wide, navy-blue cape she was pulling round her blew open as the frosty air from the open door caught it.

"Come on, woman," Brian O'Malley called impatiently from the doorway. But then, just as impatiently, he slammed the door shut.

"On second thoughts," he said, "stay where you are until I bring the car round. It'd freeze the balls out there..." This time, in a gust of frosty air, he went.

"He's started to fuss about me." Nora was indulgent. "I thought the day would never come. Time was when I could have done with a bit of fussing and didn't get it. But life's a contrary business, isn't it?" She became businesslike. "Too late to start cosseting me now!" She gathered the cloak around her, made Bea promise to come over for a drink the next day, "if you possibly can," and was gone herself into the cold night.

Bea surveyed the physical wreckage of the party. It wasn't too bad considering. Nothing that Alice and a few helpers couldn't clear in an hour or so in the morning. The emotional damage was another thing. But she wouldn't think about that now.

A voice called from the drawing room. Going in, she found Charles, Albert and Wally gathered with nightcaps around the dying embers of the fire. She sank into a chair with a drink of her own as far away from Wally as she could manage.

"Great party, Charles, terrific food!" Wally raised his glass. "I want to thank you for your hospitality. Bea too, of course. I realise it may have seemed a bit insensitive, arriving unannounced like that. But I thought it best to take the bull by the horns, so to speak. Take advantage of the season's goodwill." He paused, aware of a lack of response from his audience. "I may have been wrong but it was an honest mistake."

A silence, heavy and discouraging, grew as he finished speaking. Albert, embarrassed, hoped that by saying nothing he would avoid making things worse. Charles simply wanted Wally to go away. A log gave a long, dying splutter and Bea leaned back, closing her eyes. She was not going to make it easy for him either. Slowly, with a gracefully resigned shrug, Wally got to his feet. "I'll turn in then," he said. "See you in the morning." For a moment it seemed he would kiss Bea goodnight. Then he thought better of it and with a small nod in her direction left the room.

"Let there be no post-mortem." Charles's voice was dispassionate as Wally's footsteps faded across the hall. "Let us rather give in to the sentiment of the season and enjoy the peace of the moment."

The silence after that was companionable. Even so, a chill soon entered the room and, for Bea at least, the warm solitude of her bed beckoned invitingly. She said goodnight.

Crossing the hallway her eye was caught by a flash of scarlet in the kitchen doorway. Tiredly curious she turned to look. Olivia, wearing a red silk kimono, was pressed tightly against Wally as they kissed under the mistletoe. Their bodies moved easily together, Wally's hands urgently caressing Olivia's long back. Bea was aware only of a numb surprise. Olivia just wasn't Wally's type. Unless he'd changed dramatically.

In any event she certainly wasn't going to discuss it with him now. She reached for the banister but touched instead the holly garland and gasped as it pricked her. The couple under the mistletoe jumped hastily apart.

"Sorry to disturb you," Bea said coolly and began to climb the stairs. Wally was immediately on the step beside her.

"Annoyed, Bea? Jealous?" His eyes were wickedly black as he put a hand on her shoulder. "You don't need to be. A Christmas kiss, under the mistletoe. That's all it was."

"Let's get one thing clear, Walter Treacy." Bea shook his hand free, moved to stand on a step above him. "What you do, who you kiss, seduce or otherwise involve yourself with, ceased to be of interest to me nineteen years ago. All I want is for your visit to be over and my life to be free of you. This time for good.

"I don't believe you," Wally's voice was low, cajoling. "Let's make this a Christmas Eve to remember, Bea." He put both hands around her waist, pulled her down onto the step beside him. He held her tight, close. His body felt unfamiliar. "Let me come to bed with you and we can put the last nineteen years behind us. It'll be as if they never happened..."

Bea stared at him, rigid and disbelieving. Had he always, part of her wondered, been so profoundly arrogant, so brutally insensitive? Probably, that part of her answered. And you were nineteen and profoundly stupid when you met him. And in need of love.

The other part of her didn't think at all, merely acted. She tried to pull away. Wally tightened his grip, fingers digging into her waist. He was grinning as he bent his head, seeking her lips. That was when she brought her knee up, swift and hard into his groin. With a high-pitched squeal, a sound not unlike a pig, Wally jumped back.

When next she looked at him, from a distance of several steps up, he was frenziedly clutching himself with both hands. The expression on his face was a crazy mixture of disbelief and pain.

"Goodnight, Wally," Bea said sweetly. "Happy Christmas."

CHAPTER EIGHT

Marriage to Wally, when it was good, had been very, very good. But those times had been few. They had also been far between.

Bea, lying in her bed as the old house creaked around her in the night, felt wave after wave of memory sweep over her. The past was another country and she tried not to think about it too often. Nostalgia, regrets and sentimentality were, she strongly believed, a waste of time. She didn't understand self-pity. She was a doer and she kept moving.

But tonight, with Wally asleep in a room above her and their child distraught in another, she found it impossible to keep the past at bay. And once she started to remember she found she remembered too much.

It was the season too, of course. So much of everything that had happened to her had happened in this dark end-of-year month. The things Bea remembered with joy about Christmas time were astonishingly few.

She was nineteen when she met Walter Treacy at a summer party. She nearly hadn't gone to it and often, afterwards, wondered what the course of her life might have been had she stayed away. But the dark misery of the family house in Rathgar had contrasted so terrifyingly with the bright June days that she'd felt compelled to go.

It was the summer of 1970. She had just finished the first year of an Arts degree in UCD and had never felt so lonely in her life. Olivia had recently met Albert D'Arcy and was spending most of her time with him. Albert had money so Tom approved; Jude's silence in the matter was taken as approval too. Charles had disappeared into the freedom of a life of his own in Paris.

Bea didn't go to many parties. She hadn't yet learned to socialise and found smalltalk difficult. She hadn't the foggiest idea how to flirt and she didn't drink either, which was branding her almost a freak amongst her peers. She made only a slight effort for the party, putting on a long, muslin skirt and a purple, tie-dyed T-shirt she liked. She plaited her hair and tied it back with a purple scarf, then hitched up the skirt and cycled to Ballsbridge.

It was barely ten o'clock when she got there but already the top floor Waterloo Road flat thundered with Rolling Stones music, reeked with the pungent, musky smell of nicotine and marijuana. In the dim light there were bodies everywhere: upright and tightly together as they danced, inseparable and prone in bedrooms and dark corners, noisily lounging against walls, sweating in an impenetrable mass in the kitchen. Through the night they kept on coming, eagerly up the stairs, the thin, temporary link of student life bringing them together, giving substance and unity to their world.

But already, on that summer night, cracks were appearing in that world. Around midnight two guests arrived and announced that they were abandoning their studies, taking up gainful employment. One of them, a girl with violent red hair and pink leather trousers, said she was off to London to sell clothes.

The other was Wally.

"I've just sold a cartoon!" He waved a £5 note as he came up the stairs. "I'm on my way, folks!"

Bea couldn't take her eyes off him. He was laughter and fun, he was wanton charm. He was a vagabond who looked like a gypsy prince. He was everything she'd ever dreamed about.

He was also, she would discover later, sensual and exciting and able to give her the warm, warm love she'd never had in her life.

She stood, that night, wordlessly watching as people crowded around him, listened as he wisecracked and flirted. He was bone-thin in his jeans and crumpled shirt. His hair was too long and too wild. His grin was devilish and his black eyes reckless. Bea felt abandon stir inside, knew she could lose herself and didn't care.

She watched, knowing her jealousy to be unreasonable, as he stood talking to the girl in the pink trousers. He held a drink in one hand but the other stayed in his pocket, fingering the £5.

Unreasonable too was the violent hatred she suddenly felt for the muslin skirt, the tie-dyed T-shirt. On impulse she made her way to the bathroom. If he liked red hair *she* would give him red hair. Real red hair.

In a fever of anxiety she waited in the queue outside. She worried that he might leave, worried even more that he might disappear into one of the bedrooms with the girl. When she finally got inside the bathroom, the mirror was woefully inadequate. She just about managed to see herself as she loosened her heavy plait, fingered her hair into a tumbling mass which went halfway down her back. She bit her lips to give them colour. She had no make-up. There was nothing more she could do. It was the first time she'd ever done anything to her appearance for the sake of a man. And it worked.

Wally noticed her as soon as she emerged from the bathroom. She stood where she was and let him come to her. She felt strangely confident, indifferent to the irate glare of the girl in the pink trousers.

"And who might you be?" Wally reached out, lifted a lock of her hair. "Why haven't we met before?"

Bea smiled. For the first time in her life she felt glad not to be one of the crowd, happy for him to think her someone new.

"I'm a visiting alien," she said, "on a whistle-stop tour of the galaxy."

She was surprised how easy it was to flirt with him, how relaxed he made her feel.

"Want to dance?" he asked.

He held her tight. She leaned against him, afraid her legs would not hold her up. They were almost the same height and her cheek reached his exactly. For all his boniness his body felt hard against hers, and strong. The music was fast but they ignored it, swaying together in a slow, intense rhythm of their own; close, excited. She felt the urgency in him and went with the hot explosion of her own need when it came, moulding herself even more tightly against him. She didn't want the music ever to stop, the dance ever to end.

The crowd around them receded, dissolved.

"I like your hair," Wally's voice was hoarse. Bea moved her head and nodded, unable to speak.

"I like *you*," Wally said, and kissed her. The world exploded. Drunk with her need for him Bea allowed him to part her lips. As his tongue found hers she knew that all the emotions repressed during nineteen years of wanting to be loved, and to love, could be released by this man. And she knew she wanted them to be.

Hours later, it seemed, the music ended. They stopped kissing and Wally took his arms from around her. For an awful moment she thought he was going to leave her there. But he didn't. Instead he studied her face intently while she, aware that her expression must be adoring, returned his gaze.

He ran a finger across her cheek, went on down until he lightly touched a breast.

"You're lovely," he said softly. "What's your name?"

"Beatrice." Her voice was barely a whisper. "What's yours?"

"Walter."

They smiled at one another. There didn't seem any need to say any more, do anything else. The music started again and, wordlessly, they began to dance, close and tight as before. This time the girl in the pink trousers collided with them several times. The intrusions seemed brutal and Bea could feel Wally tensing each time she did it. The fourth time it happened he dropped his arms from around Bea.

"Come on," he said. "Let's get out of here..."

He held her hand, tight, as he pulled her through the crowd with him.

"Who is she?" Bea asked as they went down the front steps.

"Don't ask," Wally said, shortly. They had reached the street before she spoke again.

"Which way to your place?" he asked then. Bea waved in the general direction of Leeson Street.

"I live in Rathgar," she said. Wally shook his head,

took her hand again.

"Too far," he said, "for shank's mare. My place is closer, just around the corner in Baggot Street. Come on..."

But Bea pulled her hand free. It was cool in the street. The music was a dim throb in the background. Reality was all around.

"I have my bike," she said. "I must go home..."

Wally looked at her, disbelieving. "You can't," he said. "We've just found each other. I want to get to know you. You can't go..." he grabbed her arm.

"I'm going..." Bea, frightened by the intensity in his dark eyes, pulled her arm free and looked around desperately for the railing she'd locked her bike against.

"Please." Wally's voice was so gentle she had to strain to hear him. "Come back with me for ten minutes. I just want to talk to you."

Together they unlocked her bike and walked the short distance to his room, a first floor bed-sit with shared bathroom and toilet. They talked there, sitting curled on the bed, until four in the morning. By that time Bea knew that Wally had been studying Art but was intent now on learning from life. And on making money. She knew that he came from Galway, was the youngest of five children, never wanted to go back there. And she knew, most definitely, that she was in love with him.

And Wally knew something of Bea's story. He had coaxed from her details about Jude, what Tom was like, how they lived. He was quiet and said little while she talked about them. As light came into the sky and began to illuminate the tattiness of the room he stood up.

"Time for you to go, Cinderella," he said. "I'll call a taxi. Here." He pulled the five-pound note from his pocket. Bea was aghast.

"I can't take that..." she protested. "I'll cycle..."

"Don't be daft," he said. "Take it..." When she still shook her head he folded the note into her hand. "Look, woman," he said. "I want to live fast, die young and have a good-looking corpse. How is one, miserable fiver going to help me do that?"

She looked at the £5 in wonder as he went into the hallway to use the coinbox. It was all he had, and he had given it to her. Seconds later he was back.

"Got any change?" he asked. She laughed and gave him a shilling.

They huddled together under a blanket, aware now of the morning chill, until the taxi came. When Wally kissed her, Bea clung to him. She was filled with gratitude that he hadn't tried anything. He must have known that she would have been his had he wanted her. But, niggling at her happiness, came the awful fear that he might not see her, or even want to see her again.

The taxi driver, bad-tempered and tired, provided a solution to her problem. He refused to take Bea's bike. There was nothing for it but to leave it where it was, chained in the hallway.

"You can pick it up the next time." Wally was casual. Bea, lightheaded with relief, threw her arms around him, kissed him long and hard. From the taxi she waved until she could see him no more.

"My life has begun," she told herself as she sank into her bed. "I will remember this night for the rest of my life."

She'd remembered it for twenty-two years. It seemed unlikely she would forget it now.

Turning restlessly in her bed at Inverskena, Bea

wondered if Wally remembered too. If he remembered
any of the wonder and magic of when they first met. It
had been an enchanted time, the spell had bound them
for months. None of the things that had happened since
could take that away. And Wally *had* loved her then. As
much as Wally could love anyone. More maybe. He
simply hadn't been able to take the commitments and
responsibilities which grew with their love.

Wally didn't phone until three days after the party.
By then Bea was beside herself with anxiety, convinced
she would never hear from him again. She had decided
not to go back for the bike. She would leave it in his
hallway where it would serve as a daily reminder, a
constant stab at his conscience.

It was late evening when he telephoned. She almost
fell down the stairs in her attempt to get to the instrument
before anyone else. She needn't have bothered. Jude
didn't leave her room much by those days and neither
Tom nor Olivia was at home.

"Beatrice?"

She sat down when she heard his voice. She had to.
Her heart had begun to thump unevenly and her mouth
had gone dry. She leaned against the wall, cradling the
phone tight against her ear.

"Hello," she said. "Is my bike all right?"

"Seems all right to me. It's still there anyway!" He
laughed and Bea closed her eyes, savouring the sound.

"Good," she said. "That's good."

"Look, I may be cut off. I've no more change. Do you
want to come to a concert in Blackrock Park tomorrow?
You can collect your bike afterwards..." Did she want to.
It was all she could do to stop herself yelling yes. Yes and
yes. "That sounds...fun..." was what she actually said,

proud of her control.

They lay in the sun, two bodies among hundreds, and listened to rock bands belting it out across Blackrock Park. The highest temperature of the year, twenty-eight degrees centigrade, had just been recorded at Mullingar. Dublin Bay shimmered, the sky was a matchless blue. It seemed then, and in the weeks which followed, as if summer would never end, winter would never come and that they would never not be together.

They lived for each other. They shared ideas, dreams and, most of all, laughter. Life went on outside their cocoon and they took note, even talked about Bernadette Devlin's arrest and imprisonment in Armagh prison, felt shock when the Beatles broke up, when five people were shot in Northern Ireland. They cheered, joined in the mocking jokes, when the Catholic bishops announced in July that it was no longer obligatory to abstain from eating fish on Fridays. But none of it really impinged on the world they had wrapped themselves in.

For the first time in her life Bea understood joyous abandon. Wally, she couldn't help noticing, had that effect on people—especially women. He was an outrageous flirt, teasing and flattering wherever they went. She didn't mind. She was the one he had chosen, after all.

They made love, for the first time, in August. Ecstatic, rapturous love, all caution thrown to the winds. It happened in Wally's room, transformed by Bea over the months into a colourful oasis. It was a rainy afternoon, the first time in weeks that it had rained. They pulled the narrow divan bed over to the window and lay there, lazily watching the rain as it cascaded down the glass.

"Western wind, when wilt thou blow, / The small

rain down can rain? / Christ, if my love were in my arms / And I in my bed again…" Bea quoted dreamily, turning to smile at Wally.

"I'm here now." Wally's eyes burned, black as coals. Bea shivered. "I'm in your arms, Bea my love…"

They kissed, their bodies coming together. Feelings Bea had held back all summer began to rage out of control as Wally whispered loving words in her ear, began to kiss her more and more demandingly.

"I love you, Bea, love you, love you. Please let me."

"No," Bea said, once and feebly, before giving in to the same wild desire that had brought them together on the night of the party.

Somehow her T-shirt was on the floor, Wally's face buried against her breasts. It seemed right. It seemed wrong. He removed her jeans and it didn't matter any more. They lay, both of them naked, as Wally's lips and fingers explored every inch of her willing body.

"Wally, I think you'd better stop," Bea whispered, once. But she knew her voice didn't sound as if she meant it.

"Why? Don't you like it?" Wally's lips were to her ear. His breath felt hot.

"I like it…"

They didn't talk after that and Bea didn't protest any more either. When Wally parted her legs she was ready for him and when at last they came together it was as if she had been waiting a lifetime for the moment.

Afterwards they lay side by side, silent and at peace. The rain still beat against the window-panes but a watery sun was breaking through the clouds. Bea found it strange that the world seemed such as it had before. Suddenly self-conscious, she reached to pull a blanket over her nakedness but Wally stopped her. He raised himself on one elbow and looked, slowly, up and down the length of her body.

"Don't cover yourself, Bea," he said. "Don't you realise how beautiful you are?"

He pulled her close to him again and they lay quietly, bodies comfortably entwined, watching the rain ease off.

Very soon Bea realised that Wally was asleep. She thought about what he'd said. No, she hadn't realised she was beautiful. But she did know that she'd just crossed a threshold. She had left her girlish youth behind and entered the world of women. She was glad.

They made love frequently after that, always with joy and laughter and always in Wally's room. It became for them a love-nest. That autumn, Bea's course moved to the newly opened Arts block in Belfield and she began missing lectures. She blamed the distance but the reality was that she'd lost interest. Soon she didn't go at all. She got an allowance from her father and, after Olivia married in November, spent less and less time at home. Neither Jude nor Tom seemed to notice.

Sometimes, when she wasn't with Wally, Bea worried about her immortal soul. But deep in her heart she couldn't believe that what they did together was sinful and so she stopped going to confession. To go, she felt, would be a sin in itself since she could only make a false confession. She was not sorry and would not give up Wally. Both, she knew, would be necessary if she was to receive forgiveness. She worried more about becoming pregnant. Wally didn't like condoms and she couldn't bring herself to ask anyone about the Pill.

She didn't believe the family doctor would give them

to her anyway and was shy about going to a family planning clinic alone. As a vague precaution they worked out a method of contraception using "safe days."

Bea missed her first period around Christmas. Frantic, she took to washing her hair twice a day, running fast miles, taking long, hot baths, the things that she'd heard brought on a period. None of them worked and by mid-February she knew for certain that she was pregnant.

Wally was horrified when she told him. She watched, miserably, as he paced the room in front of her, his face dark and tensely brooding. When he suggested an abortion Bea mutely shook her head. She couldn't even think about it. He couldn't have paid for it anyway and nor could she. He was selling the odd cartoon still, painting some commissioned portraits. He earned just enough to pay the rent on his room and keep the wolf from the door. He didn't mention an abortion again.

For weeks Bea lived in a daze. She felt powerless, cut adrift, helpless and drowning all at once. Then, one Sunday morning in early April, she felt the baby kick. Everything changed.

"It's okay," she told the next kick. "I'm going to take care of you. Leave everything to me."

She was in the house in Rathgar and felt quite calm as she went downstairs to tell her father. She was prepared for any reaction except for his absolute desolation.

"I'm going to have a baby." She told him as she handed him a coffee. They communicated so little that she was unable to find a kinder way to tell him. Her father took the cup and put it down slowly. For a long minute he said nothing, just stared at the milky liquid. Then he began to turn the cup slowly in its saucer.

"I thought there was something wrong with you these

last months," he said and was silent again. He didn't look at her. Bea waited. She understood that he had to get used to the idea but was unable to make it easier for him. She just didn't know him well enough. But as the silence stretched, she began to panic. Maybe he was going to throw her out. She *had* to stay here, for a while anyway. Until Wally got on his feet, until they could afford to get married...

"This is a big house," she could hear the desperation in her own voice. "You'll hardly know there's a baby around..." Her father stood up, looked at her at last.

"Why, Bea?" he asked. "Why did you do it? Couldn't you at least have tried to rise above the hell of this family?" His eyes were those of a man who has lost all hope. He walked across the kitchen. By the door he turned. "I'll increase your allowance. But you can't rear your child in this house. It wouldn't be...suitable. Bring the father to meet me. We'll discuss some arrangement."

Tom Hennessy didn't like Wally, not one bit. But they worked out an "arrangement" which allowed Bea and Wally to marry in June, almost a year to the day from the time they'd met. It was a small affair, on a side altar. Jude refused to attend. She had come screaming into Bea's room one night, calling her a litany of names which began and ended with whore. She had not spoken a word to her daughter thereafter. Olivia and Albert had come but she could not get in touch with Charles. As per the "arrangement," Tom paid for the wedding, loaned them a small flat in a house he owned in Pembroke Street and told them to get on with it.

CHAPTER NINE

Sinéad was born in September. Bea was walking in Leeson Street when her waters broke. She stood, oblivious of the mid-morning crowds, holding her stomach as she looked the length of the street, at the traffic circling St Stephen's Green. She looked up, too, at the fast-moving clouds in the sky above.

"Everything is about to change...everything." She felt only wonder. "Will any of this look the same tomorrow?"

A girl about her own age passed on a bicycle, long hair trailing in the wind, long skirt flapping. Bea watched her, twisting the wedding ring on her finger. She became aware that people were looking at her oddly.

"Time to go," she told herself and turned calmly for the flat and her packed bag.

Bea had never had any doubt that she was carrying a girl but the reality when 8lbs, 3ozs of female humanity was placed in her arms, overwhelmed her. All she could do was lie there, holding her baby, repeating to herself, "I have a daughter, I have a daughter." Some time before Wally appeared, a few hours later, a more potent reality— that she herself was a mother—dawned on her.

Motherhood and Bea proved perfect companions. Wally, after an initial euphoria, found fatherhood less agreeable. In the beginning he marvelled at his daughter, even painted her at two weeks old. But as the months went by he became less interested, less in evidence about the flat. He couldn't, he said, work for the crying. He rented a share in a studio and Bea saw even less of him. His absence hurt, but she had Sinéad. Every day, even the coldest, she put her baby into a sling and took to her Stephen's Green. She got to know the other *habitués* of the park, built up a host of acquaintances. She was never lonely. She talked to Sinéad all the time, played music to her. Whatever she happened to be reading she read aloud.

She and Wally still made love. That part of their relationship remained a passionate joy to both of them. It was a bond which kept them close as the world outside tugged at Wally.

Bea's fragile security was shattered when she least expected it.

By January Wally's labours in the studio had produced enough pictures for him to show in a group exhibition. Bea, who hadn't seen the pictures, said she would like to attend the opening. She would bring Sinéad. Wally protested that it would be too crowded, that Bea wouldn't be able to see anything properly. He would, he promised, give her a private viewing, the day after. Bea laughed. She wouldn't miss the opening for gold, she said. And so she met the red-haired girl again.

Her first sight of her, as she pushed through the crowd toward Wally's pictures, was on her husband's arm. This time she was dressed in black and her hair was exotically curled. Wally was whispering in her ear and it would have been impossible not to know there was something between them. Bea was about to move away when they saw her.

"Bea!" Even in her anguish Bea could hear the anxiety in Wally's call. She turned, smiling coolly at the girl, who was slowly letting go of Wally's arm. On Wally she bestowed a dazzling beam.

"We won't stay long." She hugged Sinéad to her. "We're on our way out in fact..."

"Don't go..." Wally seemed to have forgotten the girl, who hovered nonetheless. "Come on, have a look."

He put an arm around Bea's shoulder and led her and Sinéad toward a large canvas awash with swirling colour. "There!" He pointed with a flourish at the title. It was called "Birth."

"See how you inspire me," he said softly, his arm still around her shoulder. Sinéad whimpered and Bea began to rock her back and forth.

"Yes." Her voice sounded flat, even to her own ears. She felt nothing for the picture though she knew that, technically, it was very good. "It's...great," she added, but knew she was making matters worse. Wally dropped his arm from around her shoulders.

"Jesus, Bea!" His voice was low but feverishly angry. "You could try a less bovine response! I need a bit of support! *Some encouragement*!"

"Seems to me you've got plenty of both!" Bea shot a razor-edged look in the direction of the girl in black. "You never *did* introduce me, that night at the party. Why don't we make amends now?"

Ignoring his furious protest she turned to where the girl stood, just feet away. She spoke coldly, and quite loudly.

"We've never met, formally, have we? I'm Beatrice Treacy, Wally's wife. This" she touched the top of Sinéad's head, "is his daughter, Sinéad." She held out her hand.

The girl ignored it. Instead she tossed her hair, tightened a pinkly-lipsticked mouth.

"My name is Liliana," she said. "Wally and I are old friends. Surely he's mentioned me." Her smile was nastily sarcastic.

"No. Wally's never once mentioned you. Out of sight out of mind, I suppose." Bea's smile was as bland as she could make it. She felt sick. Liliana scowled, pushed her hair back with a pink-nailed hand.

"That works both ways," she snapped. "Wally doesn't talk about you to me either."

"How very discreet of him." Bea smiled again. Sinéad stirred uneasily at the wild thumping of her mother's heart. "It seems a shame such old friends can't be more open with one another."

Liliana shrugged and Bea pointedly turned her back on her. As she did so she saw the girl crane for a view of Sinéad. For a quick moment she felt a vague sympathy. She, after all, had Wally's child. "And his love too," she told herself, fiercely. Liliana was an old friend, a flirtation. Wally couldn't resist flirting. That's all it was. She must believe that, in order to go on believing in their love.

Especially now that she suspected she was pregnant again.

Wally had disappeared into the crowd during her confrontation with Liliana. Bea knew that she and Sinéad weren't doing his image much good—a wife and child didn't fit with the reckless, witty and talented persona he liked to show his art world friends. She was, slowly, coming to know the real Wally, to realise that he wasn't at all the uncomplicated, life-loving boy she'd fallen in love with. She often thought now to herself how well his name suited him, given his Walter Mitty-like qualities.

She knew that he liked to think of himself as a man apart and that he was, behind his extravagant exterior, secretive and watchful.

None of it had bothered her before. But then she'd never before realised how completely Wally had cut her out of the major part of his life. Now, as she wandered through the people, listening to their bright chatter, she realised that nobody here knew her. Nobody at all. And she didn't know them.

The reality of her complete exclusion was like a slap in the face. She felt tired. Unaccountably she felt old too, and worn down. She clutched Sinéad to her and decided to leave. But then the speechmaking began, the official opening of the show. She was surprised to see a prominent politician doing the honours, a man she had thought in social as well as political disgrace. He praised the show, which was of course expected of him. But then he singled out Wally and another artist for special mention. The sudden burst of applause told her that this was unexpected praise and she felt a ridiculous surge of pride. She would have to stay and look at the rest of Wally's work. It didn't matter how badly she felt. He deserved her loyalty. It was ridiculous that she, his wife, didn't know his work.

As the speechmaking ended she pushed her way through the crowd again, to the wall where Wally's pictures hung. There were six of them, all very large. He had worked in oils, using strong, vivid colours. Apart from the picture called Birth, which had lots of yellow in it, the predominant colour was a shocking pink. The other five were all portraits of Liliana. They were good too, highly evocative of the sitter's sensuality, especially one in which she trailed a shawl between her legs. Bea could see why the politician had admired them.

She looked for a long time before she left.

Wally didn't come home at all that night. Bea waited until midnight before climbing into bed alone. At four o'clock she awoke to Sinéad's crying—and only then to realisation that her husband was spending the night elsewhere. It was the first time he'd stayed away a whole night.

It was another two days before she saw him. She was in the street, on the way back from a walk in the Green with Sinéad, when she met him on the front steps to the flat. They stood silently looking at one another, their breaths making clouds between them in the cold air.

"How did the show go?" Bea asked at last.

"I sold three," Wally said and put his key in the lock. It was then that Bea noticed he had a bag with him and realised he had been in the flat already. That he was in fact on his way out when she'd arrived. That he had merely come back for a change of clothing and hadn't intended waiting for her.

She said nothing as they entered the flat together, was silent as she went about preparing a meal, feeding Sinéad. Wally put the bag in the bedroom and threw himself, as if exhausted, into their one armchair. He closed his eyes and appeared to sleep. Bea waited until Sinéad too was asleep, and their meal on the table, before she spoke.

"Where've you been, Wally?" she asked. She tried to sound merely curious, careful not to appear hectoring. She had experienced flashes of Wally's temper before and she had no desire to see more of it.

"Don't ask," he said, shortly. "I'm here now, aren't I? Isn't that enough for you? Or do you want to own me, body and soul?"

No, it isn't enough that you're here now, Bea wanted to shout the words at him, explain that she wanted them to be friends again, the way they used to be. Lovers too. But she said nothing. Instinct told her he would go, maybe for ever, if she pushed him even a little. Instead she began to eat, forcing herself through the macaroni cheese she'd made because he liked it. She would sort things out some other time. Some better time.

"I liked the pictures," she said when she could trust herself to speak. Wally grunted not disagreeably. "The Nude with Shawl was very fine."

It had been haunting her evey since she'd seen it. She couldn't get the sitter's look of lazy sensuality, the arrogant invitation in her eyes, out of her head.

"It's sold." Wally sounded flat. "I got £150 for it…"

Bea gasped. It was a very good price.

"Who bought it?" she asked.

"Old boyfriend of Liliana's," Wally said. His tone told her nothing.

"Oh." Bea hesitated. "He must have been fond of her."

"You nosy bitch!" Wally turned on her suddenly. His face had darkened, become a tensely furious mask. Bea, frightened though she was, wondered if his real anger was at Liliana. "My friends are none of your business! Stop trying to smother me!" The words exploded from him.

"It's none of your business either who buys my pictures, who I paint, who I spend my time with! I won't be owned by you. Confine yourself to what you have to do here, to the child. I need to feel free or I can't work."

He came to a breathless halt and Bea, stunned, sat

looking at him. She'd never, ever, questioned him in the way he was implying. None of this was fair.

"You *are* free," she said quietly. "I've never put chains on you, Wally. You know that."

"Not obviously, oh no! You're much too cute for that! And far too clever, my little blue-eyed innocent! Your *need* is a chain. And it's choking me."

He stopped, putting his head in his hands. Despite all he'd said Bea longed to reach out and ruffle his hair, to comfort him. You fool, she reprimanded herself, and the moment passed. The Wally she had wanted to touch was not the man beside her. A few lines from Yeats came to her and with them a piercing realisation. She thought about them as she gazed at her husband's bowed head. "O body swayed to music, O brightening glance, / How can we know the dancer from the dance?"

She had mistaken the dancer for the dance, had thought Wally's charm and vitality were what he really was.

The realisation didn't stop her loving him. But her feelings underwent a subtle change in those silent minutes at the table. She felt older, more in charge, as she stood up.

"I got us some wine," she said. "To celebrate the exhibition. Might as well have it now. Better late than never and all that."

With determined cheerfulness she pulled out the cork and, filled with a terrible insecurity about their life together, took her first ever alcoholic drink. Wally raised his glass to hers, his dark eyes slightly mocking, and they toasted one another. Bea didn't mention her fears of a second pregnancy.

Three weeks later she had to. Morning sickness had

confirmed her fears and she was too ill to pretend. Drained from vomiting and feeling that any minute it might start again, she told him. He looked at her incredulously.

"Pregnant? For Christ's sake, Bea, how *could* you be pregnant? Didn't you *do* something? Aren't you on the pill? I thought, after the last time..."

"I didn't think it could happen, not while I was nursing Sinéad." Bea felt too miserable, too washed out, to suggest that *he* could have done something, that all the responsibility wasn't hers.

"You're sure?" Wally's voice held panic.

"Positive." She hadn't yet been to the doctor but she knew. The signs were unmistakable.

Wally stood up. His face had become very white. "You grabby bitch!" He spoke with controlled ferocity. "You did this deliberately. You're ruining my life. You're cutting off my air."

Sinéad began to cry as the door slammed behind him. This time he didn't come home for a week.

Bea's second pregnancy was hell. She felt sick all the time and even lost weight. When she told her father his face closed against her once again. He did not increase her allowance, which made her more dependent than ever on Wally. But by now he was selling more pictures and, always carelessly generous, gave Bea most of the money he made. She saved what she didn't actually need, some primitive instinct warning her she was going to need money and that she might not always have an income.

Of Wally himself she saw little. At first, when he didn't come home at night, she waited up for him. She stopped when the accumulated disappointments became a dull pain.

Olivia, by now pregnant herself, said she felt too wretched to visit. Albert was building his business while she kept immaculate house for him in Dun Laoghaire. Bea had, in fact, ceased to have any common ground with her sister.

Bea's second baby, a boy, was born in October. The birth was easy and she held him to her immediately, marvelling at his wealth of dark hair. Wally's delight at having a son surprised her.

"He looks like me too," he said, wonderingly. They decided to call him Oisín.

Oisín was an extraordinarily good and very beautiful baby. From the beginning he lay quietly in his cot, his huge eyes—the shape of Bea's, the colour of Wally's—taking in the world. Sinéad, thirteen months old now, stared back at him but seemed strangely afraid of touching her brother.

He was too good. When he was barely a month old Bea was persuaded by a visiting nurse to have tests run on her son. After three days in hospital she knew the worst. He had been born with a rare heart disease. They explained its causes in much detail, told her what treatment was possible. All she heard was the prognosis.

Oisín would not live more than a year, probably a lot less.

Bea did not cry. Not then and not for a long time. There didn't seem any point in spoiling any of Oisín's short, precious time with tears. She would give him the best year anybody had ever had. But Wally, disbelieving at first, wanted to have their son hospitalised.

"We can't look after him properly," he argued. "We can't give him what he needs. When he's in pain what will we do? How can we help him?"

"We can love him," Bea said. "We can let him know what life and love are like." And she refused even to consider hospital, finding in herself a strength of purpose she'd never known she possessed.

She *knew* that she could look after Oisín. She persuaded the doctors and they, with much advice and medication, allowed her to take him home. Without realising it she began to exclude Wally. She was absolutely convinced her loving care would give meaning to Oisín's life.

It was to be a shorter life than the doctors expected. Bea got the news of the deterioration of his condition two days before Christmas. The memory still brought an ache whenever she heard "Silent Night." She was on a regular hospital out-patients visit, sitting in a small, green room waiting for Oisín to be brought to her. Carol singers in the street outside sang the German carol and, for a moment caught in their bright mood, she hummed along with them. "Stille Nacht, Heilige Nacht..."

She stopped when she saw the doctor's face as he entered the room, without Oisín. She never since heard "Silent Night" without remembering his tired sadness, his resignation to a battle lost. He had been kind but to the point. Oisín had ceased to respond to treatment. There was little they could do but make him as comfortable as possible for the weeks which remained to him.

"But it's Christmas!" Bea's grief focused on one thing only. She could not imagine Christmas without her son. "You're not going to keep him here, are you?"

The doctor looked thoughtfully at her stricken face. "It will be his only Christmas. His one Christmas..." Bea pleaded brokenly.

"We'll have to take him in immediately afterwards," the doctor said eventually. "And if there are any developments..."

"Yes. Of course. I'll bring him in to you straight away if anything happens. Thank you, oh, thank you. It really will be the best thing for him. You'll see." Aware that she was babbling, Bea stopped short. The doctor patted her on the hand. "You can get him now," he said. "I'll arrange his medication."

Bea decided to wait until after the holiday to tell Wally. It was enough, she felt, for her to know that this would be the only Christmas the four of them would ever share together. No need for him to carry the burden as well.

But Wally left on Stephen's Day and she never did get to tell him. He went to get milk and didn't come back. This time Bea realised very quickly that he'd gone for good.

She spent most of the weeks which followed in the hospital. Her only company, apart from Sinéad, was that of the doctors and nurses. Albert was away, Olivia was caring for the new-born Mark and her father seemed unable to cope with the tragedy. Bea had never been very religious but she railed now against a God who would allow such a thing to happen, who could visit such suffering on an innocent.

Her rage, somehow, kept her going through the darkest hours, kept at bay the agony about what was to come. It also helped to make bearable her own feelings of inadequacy.

Oisín's smiles made things bearable too. In spite of his illness he managed a smile every day, his dark, luminous eyes lighting up when she came near. They followed her every movement as she talked to him, fixed mobiles above his cot, rocked him gently and sang—all the songs she'd ever heard. Even when blurred with pain, his eyes followed her. And only when he slept, and they were closed, did Bea leave him.

He began to sleep more. And Bea stayed all the time then, waiting. She held his hands, both of them together in her own. She kissed his face. His eyes flickered but did not open. She willed him to get better, knowing it was hopeless. She whispered to him about the life he could have.

"We'll feed the ducks when the days get longer. We'll watch the boats in Dun Laoghaire."

There was nothing more she could do. She felt sure he could hear her. She knew he understood.

She watched him die on a cold, dark day near the end of January. When he passed beyond medical help, the nurses gave him to her to hold and took Sinéad away. Almost as if she knew what was happening she went quietly, not once looking back at her mother as she sat on, still and dry-eyed, holding her dying son.

Nearly twenty years and she could still remember everything about that day. The aloneness. The quietness in the room apart from Oisín's small, laboured breaths. How soft and warm he felt in her arms, black lashes like half-moons on his cheeks. She kissed him and there was a terrible silence when he gave a last, wispy sigh and stopped breathing, dying as gently as he had lived. He wasn't yet three months old.

After a while she lay him in his cot again, fixing the clothes as if he were sleeping. She kissed him one last time and then she went to get Sinéad.

It snowed on the day of his funeral. The white silence

was unbroken as the small coffin was lowered into its grave in Dean's Grange. All efforts to contact Wally had failed. Jude came to the graveyard but didn't leave the car, Olivia stayed in another car with Sinéad. Tom was quietly drunk. Albert stood at Bea's side as she dropped a single, brave snowdrop onto the coffin. Her beautiful brown-eyed boy was gone. Forever. She cried then, tears which it seemed would never stop and which racked her body until she could feel no more.

But Oisín's life had not been in vain. Bea knew that even before the tears dried up. She would remember him with gratitude as well as with pain. He had taught her to be strong, to rely on herself. He had helped her to learn, during the months of caring for him, that she no longer needed Wally to give her life.

She had grown up, become someone who could take on life, with all its anguish and joy, and deal with it on her own.

A week later she folded up Oisín's clothes, gathered together his toys and packed the lot into sturdy wooden boxes. Sinéad watched all the while and, when it was finished, Bea took her, as a treat, to Grafton Street to buy her her own special soft toy. Sinéad chose a panda and named him Baba. She had him still. But she was only eighteen months when her brother died and she soon forgot him. Bea was happy to leave it that way. She had never since opened the wooden boxes.

In the weeks which followed Oisín's death Bea took a long, thoughtful look ahead at what life might reasonably hold for her. Her father would not pay her rent indefinitely, Sinéad would grow up and need companions. She herself needed to work—but what had she to offer the labour force? An unfinished Arts degree, some knowledge of the art world and pictures, some savings. Assets which no employer would appreciate. Self-employment seemed the only option and, in the end, opening the art gallery was a quite logical decision.

Despite Jude's objections, Tom advanced a loan to supplement her savings and Bea found a set of rooms not far from Merrion Square and the National Gallery. She reverted to her own name and the large, bright front room became The Hennessy Gallery.

The three to the back became both office and home to Bea and Sinéad.

By the following Christmas she was ready for her first exhibition. She had been surprised how easy setting up a business could be, now that she'd sorted out her life's priorities. She'd dealt confidently with decorators and workmen, shamelessly exploited her few connections in the art world. Feelings like embarrassment or shyness didn't come into it now she knew what she wanted. She was both surprised and delighted at how much she enjoyed dealing with artists; it was a plus she had not counted on.

Her first show was a success and The Hennessy Gallery was on its way. Bea was not yet twenty-three years old. By the time she was twenty-eight she'd moved to the Sandymount flat and paid Tom back in full. Two years later he died and she bought Inverskena with Charles.

Oisín had been dead two years before Wally got the news. He had dropped out, gone to India, deliberately cut links. When he heard, he wrote a long, moving letter telling of his distress. Bea read, slightly disbelieving. Wally, she knew, would be upset all right. But his overriding feeling would be one of relief that he had not been present for his son's death. That would have forced him to face reality, and real pain.

The letter helped Bea to put Wally, finally, out of her mind as well as her life.

She tried to do so again now, as the long night passed.

CHAPTER TEN

Christmas Day dawned frosty and chill. When she went downstairs at 7.30, Bea was met by Charles already at work in the kitchen. If he had seen, or heard, anything of her contretemps with Wally the night before he didn't mention it.

"I've made coffee." He indicated the pot on the range.

"Got a whiff upstairs," Bea smiled. "Why do you think I'm here at this hour?" She poured herself a mug of strong, black caffeine. "What time did *you* get up?" she asked.

"Early," Charles said. "Jake needed a walk. So did I and..." He paused and Bea waited for him to finish what he was saying. When it became apparent that he wasn't going to, she poured a second coffee and handed it to him.

"It's good," she said and waited again. Charles said nothing more.

It was still dark outside. The Christmas tree shone bright in the hallway as Bea took her coffee through to the drawing room. The fire was already lighting there and as she stood in the glowing darkness by the window Bea wished that the whole day could be so peaceful. A light came bobbing up the avenue, quickly followed by another. Within minutes she was able to make out Alice, then her daughter, as they came cycling unsteadily over the crunchy hoar-frost. They walked the last bit, laughing together as they rounded the side of the house. Bea felt a fleeting envy for their companionship.

In no time at all the house was cleared of the evidence of the party. Breakfast was to be a help-yourself affair of smoked salmon and Alice's bread, kippers for those who preferred, *pâté de foie gras* for those who dared. For real breakfast stalwarts there was a great pot of bubbling porridge with jugs of cream to help it down.

"Ye gods! Big fish with their heads sticking up at you early in the morning! Just what the doctor ordered!" Mark leaned in the kitchen doorway, blinking a little as he tried to focus on the kippers. He lurched across the room and took a seat at the table.

"How're you today, Aunt Bea?" He grinned widely at Bea.

"More to the point, Mark," Bea spoke more sharply than she'd intended. "How're *you* today? Are you all right?"

"Fine. Never better." Mark helped himself to some bread and Bea, thoughtfully, poured him a cup of coffee. There was something wrong here. She didn't want to think of the possibility that Mark had been drinking before breakfast. She smiled at him and he smiled back. The face might be thinner but there was a lot of the old, cherubic Mark in the smile. She relaxed. Alice touched her arm.

"I'll bring your mother down," she said. "And then I'll be off."

"Fine." Bea looked at her gratefully. "I'll put a chair in front of the fire for her."

It had turned into a bright, if stingingly cold, day by the time everyone finished breakfast and started on the present-opening ceremony.

Jude, alert as a sharpened razor, watched as Charles handed gifts around.

"I'm hardly an adequate Santa Claus," he said dryly, "but I'm all you've got."

It seemed a shame to rip apart the effects of Charles's decorative wrapping but Stephanie, the first to do so, gave a squeal of delight when she uncovered a pair of Japanese lacquer hairpins.

"Charles! You're so sickeningly original! How can anyone compete!" She pinned her hair back and immediately became exotically glamorous. Charles looked pleased.

"Wonderful!" Wally said. "But then you inspire such gifts, Stephanie!"

Stephanie patted the hairpins, tossed her head and smiled at him. Sinéad, looking pale but stunning in emerald green, pulled a grimace of distaste before turning her back on her father. She moved closer to Daniel. Her thin fingers played with her wedding ring, twisting it round and round. Daniel took her left hand in his, stilling the frantic movement. He smiled reassuringly and kissed the top of her head. Jude's eyes were fixed on Wally.

"That man," she said slowly, "has the eyes of a man who frequents prostitutes. And his wife," she turned her malevolent gaze on Bea, "has the eyes of a woman who knows it."

Albert, who'd been busy in the kitchen, chose that moment to enter with a tray of Irish coffees.

"My contribution to the festivities," he said loudly, neatly slicing through the *frisson* of tension.

Hands reached gratefully for glasses and Jude was ignored. For twenty minutes after that a spirit of childish excitement took over as wrappings were torn off, surprises spilled out. Even Jake caught the mood and wagged a lazy tail.

Charles, by far the easiest to buy for because his taste was so eclectic, was almost pinkly pleased with the eighteenth-century Wedgwood pâté dish Bea had found for him and the gold toothpick from Sinéad and Daniel. Olivia graciously threw her arms around her husband in gratitude for his gift of a silver pill-box.

"I'll take it everywhere with me!" she declared. "I need never again be without my Valium and Alka Seltzers!"

Sinéad, with a smiling thank-you, draped the coral silk net shawl that was Bea's present around her shoulders. There was general laughter as Mark opened the large Christmas cracker given him by his sister to reveal a black and gold designer condom. Jude, slowly opening her gifts, was silent until she came to the leather-bound diary Bea had bought her.

"This," she hissed, "is about as useful to a woman of seventy-nine as a bicycle. I do not expect to live more than another few months and I do not intend to spend the time filling this with the boring facts of my life." She held it out to Bea. "Take it back. You might benefit from committing your own thoughts to paper."

She dropped the diary on the floor. Bea, with a sigh, picked it up. No one who knew Jude doubted she'd live to be a hundred.

"Keep it, Jude. You might think of something to put in it." As her mother turned her face away, Wally thrust a small package into Bea's hand. He had dressed for the day in a rust-coloured, unstructured wool jacket.

"Open it," he urged. Bea looked at him coolly for a moment. His eyes, when they met hers, shifted under her gaze. For all his smiling *bonhomie* he was nervous, quite ill at ease. She took the package and opened it. The hexagonal Samson patchbox inside barely covered the palm of her hand. On the lid, circling a heart pierced by an arrow, there was an inscription. "Alas, love's dart gone to my heart" it said.

"Thank you, Wally," Bea's voice was detached.

"It's late nineteenth century," Wally said eagerly.

"I can see that," Bea said. "How very thoughtful of you."

Wally's gift to Sinéad lay wrapped on a table but, displaying a sensitivity born of his experiences the night before, he did not insist his daughter open it now.

"Well then," Charles briskly gathered up the glasses, "that would seem to conclude the greedier aspect of the day..." He hoisted the tray, gave an ironical smile. "Dinner will be the next big extravaganza. I shall be busy until then so you must amuse yourselves."

"Unnatural creature," Jude muttered and abruptly fell asleep.

"I'm off to Mass," said Albert as the door shut behind Charles. "Anyone feel like coming along?" He eyed his two children and Stephanie nodded.

"I'll come," she said. She glanced at Mark, asleep in a chair, and landed a swift kick on his thin, exposed ankle. Barely shifting himself he muttered, "Piss off, Steph," and fell back into a slumber.

"Lazy sod," Stephanie muttered.

"I couldn't *bear* that horrible, cold church." Olivia shivered and stretched lazily on a settee.

"We sinners have a special relationship with our maker," Wally laughed. "I'm sure he won't expect to see us there." He looked directly past Olivia at Bea.

"Don't be too sure about that," Bea snapped, and a look of triumph crossed her husband's face. Bea liked the local church, had intended going to a Christmas Mass anyway. It annoyed her that Wally should make it look as if she were doing so just to spite him. She was mollified however when Sinéad and Daniel, following her from the room, said they would drive with her.

The tiny, granite church smelled of evergreen leaves. The organist was thundering out the pedal notes of "Adeste Fideles" as they went through the doors and took their seats. The Mass was short, the sermon warmly charitable. The congregation—small since most parish members had already been to midnight Mass—squeezed cheerfully together and sang lustily. When it came to "Silent Night," Bea found she was able to join in with reasonable conviction.

Dinner, which began at four o'clock that afternoon, was everything it had promised to be. Five courses with all the trimmings, eaten over three hours in the elegant chandelier and candle-lit dining room. Not everyone stayed the course, but then not everyone was expected to.

The early brightness of the day had clouded over and darkness had fallen by the time they took their places around the rich mahogany table. It was laid, as always, with the nineteenth-century dinner service Charles had discovered while trawling through an old house for sale. Because it was monogrammed with the initial "H" he'd been unable to resist paying a small fortune for it. Each place setting had a white and gold cracker and the candlesticks at each end were of ivory. As soon as everyone was seated Bea lowered the adjustable Victorian chandelier so that it hung intimately a few feet above the table. Beyond its glow the dark green lacquered walls and cream curtains shimmered in shadow.

Jude, who had slept most of the day, woke to take her place at the top of the table. Sinéad, reluctantly, sat beside her. It was the furthest point from Wally she could manage.

"And the raven shall sit down with the lamb," Jude intoned with a malevolent look at her granddaughter.

"Why, Grandmama!" Sinéad smiled, "are you feeling lamblike today?" She shook out her white napkin as Jude glared at her.

"You, insolent child, are the lamb in question. I am the raven, the bird of death." She bestowed a cadaver-like grin on the table in general.

"Oh, but I've always thought the raven a noble bird!" Sinéad was wide-eyed. "Censure, after all, acquits the raven but pursues the dove."

Touché, thought Bea and hid a smile behind her hand. Jude froze into a sulky silence. At the other end of the table, the meal began with quail eggs in sherry jelly. Wally looked directly across at Stephanie. She had changed into a deep blue jersey slip dress. Her hair was still caught up with the Japanese hairpins.

"You look ravishing," he said silkily. "Good enough to eat."

Stephanie forked a quail's egg, looking at him a little tipsily. "What an *outré* sort of compliment," she said. "But thank you anyway, *Uncle* Wally." She stressed the title, giggling a little. "I'm famished, actually. Don't know when I've felt so hungry. Must be the stint in the church.

Or the country air." She popped the egg into her mouth and eyed Wally provocatively as she ate.

"Didn't sleep a wink last night for the country air myself," Wally said. "Silence too deafening. Took me until three o'clock to realise that there weren't going to be any sounds of life—no sirens, no ambulances. Looks like I've got out of the way of the peaceful existence."

He looked boyishly at Stephanie. Resist me if you can, his look said. I'm a devil but I'm charming, sexy and attractive and I live an exciting, big-city life. Stephanie looked back at him thoughtfully. She rested her hand on her chin, shaking her hair forward a little. She radiated youthful beauty and confidence.

Resist me if *you* can, her look said. Olivia, in burgundy velvet and long earrings, sat beside Wally and watched them both.

"Sounds like you've grown out of it all right," Stephanie said.

"You must come visit me in London." Wally took a finger of brown bread.

"Maybe I will."

"And maybe you won't," Olivia snapped. "Not while I'm paying hard cash for you to do a modelling course here!"

Wally shrugged. "I could help her in London," he said.

"I'll bet you could!" Olivia spoke through gritted teeth.

"I have my own contacts anyway," Stephanie whirled the wine in her glass and ignored her mother. "Even so, having an uncle there would be nice. And it's older people like you who're the ones with clout." She smiled delightfully at Wally who reached quickly for his glass of wine as she went on. "I mean, well, young people generally don't have much power, do they?" Stephanie seemed unaware of the body blow she'd dealt to Wally's ego.

"Not much," Wally agreed with a great lack of enthusiasm. Olivia, however, showed no signs of letting the subject drop.

"It's good to hear," she smiled encouragingly at Stephanie, "that the elderly *do* have their uses..."

"They definitely have!" Stephanie nodded vigorously. "And life is all about making the most of what others can do for you."

"Ask not what you can do for your country but what your country can do for you." Albert, sitting beside her, cocked an ironical eyebrow at his daughter. She looked puzzled.

"Yes, something like that," she agreed after a pause and attacked her starter again. Olivia watched her for a moment.

"Getting old frightens me." She sipped her wine and looked down the table at her mother. "I'm afraid of becoming ugly. I'm afraid of death." She sounded as if she meant it. Stephanie looked at her sharply.

"What nonsense!" she said stoutly. "You'll never be ugly! And you'll never be old either." She reached across the table and touched Olivia's hand. For a second Olivia looked as if she might cry. Instead she raised her glass to her daughter and husband and they smiled, drinking together.

Mark didn't eat. He sat opposite Bea and toyed with each course as it came. Not even the apricot stuffing, which he'd devoured the year before, tempted him.

"Off your food, Mark?" Bea pushed the carrot and

ginger soufflé his way.

"Does it look like I'm hungry?" he muttered and pushed the dish away from him. "I had breakfast, didn't I? All you people ever think about is food..."

"You may be right at that," Bea said brightly and nodded at the wine bottle. "Your glass is empty. Do you want me to pour you another?"

"Okay," Mark gripped the stem of his glass. Bea could see the white of his knuckles, the slight tremor in his hand.

"I've been thinking about pleasure." Jude spoke loudly.

"Jesus, no! She's off again!" Mark groaned and took a gulp of his wine.

Jude turned to Sinéad. "You, my dear, who are so clever with quotations, should learn from the wisdom of Lord Byron who said that hatred is by far the longest pleasure." She looked meaningfully in Bea's direction. "You should remember that men love in haste but they detest at leisure. Your mother knows that. Be sure you don't repeat her mistakes."

She never forgets anything, Bea thought, more in exasperation than annoyance. She's been planning how she would get back at Sinéad all through dinner.

"Don't worry, Jude," Sinéad spoke briskly. "I won't."

"Excuse me," Mark stood up suddenly. "Got to go to the bathroom." With telling control, he walked slowly from the room. Charles caught Bea's eye.

"Enjoy," he said, "and stop worrying. Every son rebels at some stage." He paused. "Every daughter too. How's the turkey?"

"Wonderful," Bea said. Daniel nodded.

"It's great," he said. "Your salad too. What sort of

cheese have you put into it?"

"It's an Irish goat's milk cheese. Called Croghan."

As Daniel and Charles talked food Bea realised, with surprise, that her daughter's husband was something of a gourmet. Accountants, she'd always believed, lacked the imagination to be epicures. Well, she thought, pleased, there's nothing like having your prejudices refuted.

Mark's seat remained empty. They had got to the pudding, already doused in whiskey and waiting to be lit, before he reappeared. He sat cheerfully in his place, seeming to have completely recovered his good humour, as Charles struck a match and the pudding blazed.

"I want to be cremated," Jude announced. "I have given it considerable thought and it makes sound economic sense. It is also hygienic."

The holly on top of the pudding cracked as it caught fire and, at the other end of the table, Stephanie began to giggle again. Jude dismissed her with a frigid look.

"I have developed an intense loathing for the prospect of having the physical remains of my body buried."

If she thought to put them off eating she was mistaken. Good wine had taken effect and she was ignored in favour of the pudding, with its foaming Cointreau sauce, as she went on, "...and I am sure my ashes will provide no greater problem than dust when it comes to the resurrection of the dead," before mumbling into silence and then sleep.

Sleep, for Bea came much later. She sat for a long time in her bedroom, holding James's present and listening as the day's final minutes ticked away on the French carriage clock given her by Olivia and Albert. She would open the wrapping after midnight. It had seemed

wrong, somehow, to expose his gift to the turbulence of
family life.

As the chimes struck the hour she unwrapped and
almost reverently lifted the string of Italian pearls from
their bed of black velvet. She studied them for several
minutes before going to the cheval-glass and putting
them on. They lay snug at the base of her throat, softly
luminous against the dark of her loosely hanging hair.

"Thank you, James," she whispered, a little sadly,
and took them off.

CHAPTER ELEVEN

Bea was surprised to find Olivia downstairs before her in the morning. She wore the red kimono and her face was freshly made up. "Going somewhere?" Bea asked.

"I thought I'd take a walk. Get some country air into my lungs," Olivia said. She looked out at the dark morning with its ghostly frost and shuddered. "But maybe not just yet."

"Aha! My favourite sisters! Good morning to you both!" Wally, dressed as he'd been on the night he arrived, breezed into the kitchen. He carried his case.

"You're leaving?" Bea didn't try to keep the relief out of her voice.

"Unfortunately, yes," Wally made no attempt to keep the sarcasm out of his voice. "A cup of the excellent-smelling coffee and I'll be on my way."

"Freshly made." Olivia poured him a cup, indicated a place beside her at the table. "We were *so* pleased to have you, Wally. *Must* you leave so soon?"

"Afraid so. I've a few things to see to in Dublin. I'll be there for a week or so." He looked quizzically over the rim of his cup at Bea. "Maybe we could have dinner?"

"I doubt it," she was curt. "I'll be busy. I've an

exhibition coming up."

"Oh? Anyone I know?"

"It's a group show. Some regulars, some new."

"You've decided to show him then?" Olivia interrupted eagerly.

"I'll decide tonight, Olivia, I told you!"

Wally looked quickly from one to the other woman and stood up. "Well, I'm off." He became businesslike. "I've an appointment in Dublin at ten." He gave Olivia a peck on the cheek and faced Bea.

"Goodbye, Wally," Bea said.

"You've changed," he said, sadly. "You're not at all the Bea I used to know."

"Thank God for that," Bea was brusque and Wally sighed.

"I'll be in touch," he said and blew her a kiss. "This is where I'll be staying." He produced a card with an address and, after a look at Bea, gave it to Olivia. "I expect to be around more often from now on. I find the auld sod has more appeal than it used to have. Maybe you can persuade my wife to think a little more kindly of me!" He smiled and was gone.

Neither sister moved, nor spoke, as the front door slammed and the faint sounds of a car on the gravel died away.

"He didn't say goodbye to Sinéad! How odd!" Olivia seemed genuinely surprised.

"Good God, Olivia, you can be so unreal at times! Of course he didn't say goodbye to Sinéad! He hasn't an interest in the world in Sinéad. What I would like to know," she looked thoughtfully at the lightening day and frowned, "is why he *really* came..." She shook her head as Olivia began to say something. "Oh, I know you invited him—and I'd prefer if we didn't talk about that. Not today anyway. But I know Wally, and he wouldn't have come unless he wanted something. Wally *never* used to do anything without a reason—and nothing in his behaviour during the last twenty-four hours convinced me he's changed. Not *even* the smallest bit..."

Ignoring a loud sniff from Olivia she began to get a breakfast tray ready for Sinéad and Daniel.

"You could give him the benefit of the doubt!" Olivia stood up and pulled the kimono around her. "He seemed to me to be *very* interested in the family. Some members of it anyway!" She yawned and stretched. "Think I'll forego the idea of a walk. A return to bed seems a much better idea..."

"What's Mark doing these days?" Bea asked the question casually as Olivia poured herself another coffee to take upstairs. Her sister shrugged.

"Apart from being moody and bloody difficult you mean? Not much. He'll be thrown out of Trinity if he's not careful. He hardly ever appears home and," she gave an exasperated sigh, "when he does, he won't talk to me."

"He doesn't look great," Bea said. "Maybe there's something wrong."

"Look," Olivia was snappy. "He's twenty years old, big enough to look after himself. I'm not a mind-reader. If there's something wrong he'll have to tell me." She swept from the kitchen.

"And a fat lot of good it would do him if he did," Bea muttered as she finished laying the tray and began up the stairs to Sinéad's room. Outside the door she hesitated, then knocked. When a sleepy-sounding Sinéad answered she simply announced the tray's presence and left it discreetly on the landing. Passing by ten minutes later she saw it had been taken in. She bit her lip. She still hadn't told Sinéad that she was leaving that afternoon.

Sinéad and Daniel did not appear until midday, walking right into a debate about whether or not the local hunt should be supported.

"Barbaric tradition." Charles was unequivocal.

"Spoken like a truly civilised city gent." Nora O'Malley laughed and shook her head. She'd called in the hope of encouraging the household along for a post-hunt port at The Huntsman. "You've not *once* attended the hunt in all your years here, Charles."

"Nor do I intend to." Charles produced a vintage port and began filling glasses. "All that business of blooding, digging out the unfortunate fox and throwing it to the hounds."

"Not the prettiest part of the hunt, I'll grant you," Nora agreed. "But it's greatly changed. These days people don't go in much for blooding and the fox doesn't get thrown alive to the hounds any more either."

"It's still a gory business," Charles said firmly, "and I'd prefer not to have anything to do with it."

"Well, I think the hunt *looks* lovely," Stephanie laughed. "All those prancing thoroughbreds and the riders in their red coats! I for one would love to go along and see them coming back."

"It's elitist," Sinéad said, "and underneath it all it's downright cruel. There must be a fairer way of keeping the fox numbers down."

"Well, as the only one here who has ever actually hunted," Nora, smiling, looked around the gathering, "I feel obliged to defend it as a part of country life. It's a proven way of culling foxes. The codes of conduct are transgressed by some hunts, of course, but, by and large, hunters behave as decently as people in any other walk of life..."

"Oh Nora! How *can* you defend it!" Sinéad sounded disgusted but Nora, quite unperturbed, sipped her port.

"Because, my dear child, I've seen the reality. Hunting is risky, thrilling and exhilarating. It's the supreme test of horsemanship. Nine times out of ten the fox escapes. If he's killed at all it's out in the open and it's all over very fast."

"You'll be telling us next that the fox-hunter is in touch with nature and has enormous respect for the countryside and its wildlife!" Bea smiled mockingly at her friend.

"Now that you mention it," Nora nodded.

"And that the fox is a crafty, wily devil anyway..."

"Yes, *and* he's a pest. He eats all the pheasants, not to mention the carnage done to chickens and to lambs in the lambing season."

"It's all too wearying and emotional for me." Olivia passed a languid hand over her brow. "But a trip to the pub sounds fun. Count me in. Albert too, of course."

Albert, reading contentedly by the fire, sighed.

"Sounds like a drinking session not to be missed," Daniel smiled. "What do you think, Sinéad?"

"When in Rome..." his wife gave a resigned shrug.

"Are any of the male riders under thirty?" Stephanie asked idly.

"Quite a few," Nora laughed.

"Then I'll come too," Stephanie said decisively.

Bea felt panic descend. At this rate she was never going to get a quiet opportunity to tell Sinéad that she would be leaving for Dublin in a few hours. It looked as if she would have to go along to The Huntsman and try to seize a suitable moment there.

"No point in taking all the cars," she said. "I'll drive you and Daniel."

"And Mark," Sinéad said. "I'll rattle him up. He looks as if he could do with the fresh air."

When Mark came downstairs with Sinéad a few minutes later he complained loudly that any venture into the fresh air might kill him. He was wearing shades again.

"Country air is lethal," he said. "There's too much of it…"

"Oh, shut up," said Sinéad and shoved him toward the door.

When they got there, The Huntsman was crowded, smoky and the atmosphere good-humoured. Albert managed to get seats in the inner sanctum for Olivia and Stephanie.

"Looks like we're stuck here."

Bea sank into the last available squashed chair in the main bar. Mark sat opposite, on a bench against the wall, and, in response to Sinéad's invitation, sullenly ordered a pint of shandy.

Left alone with him, Bea had to bite her tongue to stop from asking what the matter was. He hadn't removed the shades and was rubbing his face in an agitated fashion. As a distraction she studied the copy of Desiderata on the wall behind his head. "Exercise caution in your business affairs," she read, "for the world is full of trickery." Vowing to take Larry Dowling's advice to his customers to heart she looked around to where Sinéad was helping Daniel get the drinks at the bar. They were laughing together as they began to carry them back. Oh God, Bea thought, it's going to be pure hell telling her I have to go. And it's going to have to be done in the next hour.

"Hey, Mark, move along and make a bit of room there." Sinéad put the drinks down and nudged her cousin. Mark didn't respond. Looking at him, Bea wondered if he'd dozed off. It was hard to tell because of the shades. Sinéad shook him impatiently.

"Mark!"

"Fuck off! Leave me alone..." Mark reacted with a wild jerk. His voice was slurred.

"What's wrong with you?" Sinéad became concerned. "I've brought your shandy. Now move along a bit and make some room."

"No!" Mark grabbed the drink and drank greedily. As he put the empty glass back on the table he knocked over Daniel's pint of Guinness.

The black liquid spread quickly in Bea's direction, over the edge and onto her jeans and boots. Mark began to laugh, louder and then louder until the sound became a rasping whinny. Heads turned curiously in their direction. Mark stopped.

"I'll have another." He held his glass out to Daniel. Bea stood. "Come on, Mark," she said. "I think you'd better have the next one at home. I'll take you back." The spreading stain felt sticky, and cold. Peggy Dowling, her face openly disapproving, appeared with a cloth.

"Bit of an accident here, was there?"

She began a vigorous clean-up, studiously ignoring the stain on Bea's jeans. Mark, who was still holding the empty glass, suddenly dropped it onto the table where it smashed, scattering broken pieces everywhere. Peggy, with a frightened cry and hand to her mouth, leaped back. Mark began his strange laugh again as she took her hand away and, disbelieving, looked at the oozing blood.

"Stop it, Mark, stop it!" Sinéad looked from the injured woman to the contorted, laughing face of her cousin.

"Daniel," Bea's voice was commanding. "Would you get Mark out of here and into the car, please? I'll follow in a moment. Take it easy, Peggy. It looks worse than it is. Here, lean on me."

Ashen-faced, Peggy leaned against Bea as she helped her through the now silent crowd. In the kitchen they discovered that what Bea had offered as reassurance was in fact true. The wound was not deep and a plaster and some TCP were all that were needed.

When Bea got outside Mark was hunched over in the back seat, Sinéad a concerned huddle beside him. Daniel, sitting in the front, raised an enquiring eyebrow as she got into the driver's seat.

"Superficial," she said. No one spoke again until they got to Inverskena.

Mark lurched from the car as soon as it stopped, pushing past Charles where he stood in the front door. Sinéad and Daniel followed him.

"Bit of a fuss in the pub with Mark." Bea explained briefly.

"Thought there might be," Charles said, and she looked at him enquiringly.

"Something bothering him, I'd say," Charles went on casually. "I found him wandering about out here yesterday morning, early. He'd no shoes on."

"In the frost?"

"In the frost. I didn't like to say anything before but it looks to me as if he's..."

A loud whooping came from the back of the house. Bea and Charles were the first through the house, the first to find Mark astride the gargoyle. He had taken off the shades and was using them as a jockey would a whip. Tears were streaming down his face.

"Oh, sweet God," Bea whispered and stopped. Charles spoke briefly to Daniel and they moved together, one to each side of Mark. He didn't protest as they lifted him from the gargoyle but became quite limp and dazed as they carried him between them to his bedroom.

Sinéad followed. Bea, making tea in the kitchen, was joined shortly by Daniel and Charles.

"How is he?" she asked.

"Calmer," Charles said. "He'll probably sleep for a while. I'll call Albert."

"Give him a while with Sinéad first," Daniel suggested. "She thinks she can get through to him..."

"It's not just drink, is it?" Bea looked from one to the other of the two men. "Is he cracking up, do you think?"

Images of Mark, as a child and boy, hopcotched through her mind as she looked from one tensely concerned face to the other. How had the child who used to run to her with wild hugs, the curly-haired boy who'd put beetles in her breakfast cereal, become the deathly pale, self-absorbed young adult in the room upstairs? Daniel was shaking his head.

"I don't think it's a breakdown exactly," he said.

"He's on something." Bea suddenly realised the truth.

"He needs help," Charles said. His voice became cold. "And he needs a mother who will concentrate attention on him."

When Bea brought up the tea Mark was lying on the bed. Wan and red-eyed, he stared through the window with a vacant expression as Sinéad tried to talk to him.

"Tea," Bea announced brightly. "Hot and sweet." She put the tray down and began to pour.

"Come on, Mark, it'll warm you up at least." He didn't move. "Just leave it," Sinéad said. "I think he'll take it for me." Bea nodded. At the door she turned.

"I'll ring your parents now," she said. She was unprepared for Mark's reaction.

"Don't bother!" He almost shouted and his face, when he turned to her, was filled with loathing. "I don't want to see them. I don't want them near me. If you bring them here, I'm leaving! I'll just get the hell out."

"Leave it," Sinéad said softly to her mother and Bea nodded.

Outside the door she stood for a long time, head bowed as wave after wave of inexplicable sadness swept over her. Oisín would be Mark's age, almost, had he lived. She had watched her nephew grow and drawn parallels all the time with how her son might have been. In the oddest of ways, too, Mark had always seemed more of a brother to Sinéad than to Stephanie. But the stranger in the bed behind the door wasn't Mark. And there didn't seem to be much she could do to bring back the nephew she loved.

In her bedroom Bea hastily threw clothes into her bag. She was about to do the unforgivable again. She was leaving things to Charles. And, this time, to Sinéad and Daniel too. But only overnight. She would insist on wrapping up the business with Capek quickly and come back down in the morning.

Along the corridor she heard the sound of Mark's door open and light footsteps as Sinéad came along the landing.

She opened her own door and stood there quietly until Sinéad drew abreast of her.

"Sinéad!"

Her daughter stopped. She looked preoccupied and tired as she stood with the tray in her hands. Bea wanted desperately to take it from her, smother her in a hug that would say more than any words ever could.

"He's dozing," Sinéad said. "I'm going to get a book and sit with him."

"Fine. I'm sure that's the right thing." Bea took a deep breath. "Sinéad, I'm going back to Dublin, just for the night. I'm leaving now. I have to meet a painter. He's a solitary individual, to put it mildly, and tonight's the only time he'll see me. I'll be back in the morning."

"That's all right," Sinéad interrupted in a flat voice. "Your company for Christmas Day is as much as we should have expected."

She didn't look back and she continued along the landing and went on downstairs with the tray.

CHAPTER TWELVE

A mist descended as Bea came to the outskirts of Dublin. By the time she turned onto the Grand Canal it had become heavy enough to necessitate turning on the car's fog-lights. Falling like a grey shroud on the empty, darkened street, it added to the morgue-like feel of the city. She drove along the eerily quiet canal as far as Portobello before meeting another car and as far as Baggot Street Bridge before she met anything that could be called traffic. The closer she got to Sandymount the heavier the mist became.

"I hope Capek got here." The thought struck her as she headed down Sandymount Avenue. "Just my luck if he's caught in fog somewhere."

She pulled into the parking lot in front of her flat at seven o'clock. She would have nearly two hours to gather her thoughts, change her clothes and maybe even phone James before getting to the gallery for her nine o'clock rendezvous with Capek.

The house was in absolute darkness as she let herself through the main door. Knowing that the tenants of the other two flats were abroad for the holiday she'd have been worried if it were otherwise. A sudden need for peace overwhelmed her and she took the stairs two at a

time. It felt good to be enclosed by her own walls again.
She liked the silence, the semi-dark of the single up-
lighter she flicked as she came in.

For a while she sat in the peaceful familiarity, lazily
watching the city lights circling the bay out as far as
Howth. Her own company was restful, a pleasure after
the chaotic days *en famille*. Her eyes began to close as
she slipped deeper and deeper into the armchair.

"Enough!" She jolted herself upright. "Get your body
into the bath, woman, and yourself organised!"

The bathroom was somewhere Bea had put a lot of
thought into. She had a theory that bathroom decor
wasn't taken half seriously enough and had determined
to recreate for herself the sense of pleasure and style
she'd once encountered in a 1920s French hotel. French
doors led from the bedroom into its white and green
tranquillity. She'd chosen the green because it reminded
her of the Mediterranean on a sunny day, the white for
the sense of space it created. Her bath was large, curving
into a corner. A gloriously palmy plant flourished by its
side and a lily-white Lloyd Loom wicker chair sat under
its spreading leaves. Wall to ceiling shelves held books,
bright towels and some of the plates she collected
wherever she went.

The rest of the flat reflected her individual taste just
as strongly. The living room had large sofas covered in
grey and white ticking and sisal rugs scattered across
shining floorboards. A built-in window seat in the kitchen
meant she could breakfast, and often did, with a full
view of the sun coming up over Dublin Bay.

In the dining room she'd gone for strong colours,
burgundy with cream because she liked their warm
feeling. Everywhere she had worked clever things with

lighting so that a flick of a switch could change the mood of a room or corner. And everywhere, too, there were pictures. Followed from the hallway in they constituted a history of the gallery's progress and her own changing taste.

She decided to wear navy, a simple V-necked dress by Pat Crowley. Businesslike too, in its understated way. James's pearls added a touch of extravagance and reminded her that she should phone him. She began to dial, then stopped. Enough is enough, she told herself firmly. What I do *not* want tonight is more emotional hassle. I want to go quietly, and calmly, into the night and meet my prospective exhibitor.

Maybe it was the late hour, or the fact that the mist had lifted a bit, but there was a lot more energy in the streets as she drove to the gallery. Nothing like Dublin's usual bustle but enough to make her worry that Capek would make a rabbit-like bolt at the sight.

"Party crowds," she bit her lip. "I hope they don't scare him off."

A light drizzle began to fall again as she parked and ran for the gallery door. It was 8.45pm. She would have time to turn on the heating and make things welcoming before he arrived.

When she'd moved to Sandymount with Sinéad Bea had extended the gallery back into the rooms they'd lived in. This had given her space to show experimental work by her stable of regular artists or, when an exhibition was big enough, to take the overspill from the main gallery. The main exhibition room was large, square and white-painted. Grey columns broke up the floor space; two long windows broke up the expanse of wall. It was cool and uncluttered, an ideal environment in which to show pictures.

In her comfortably chaotic office Bea settled to wait, spreading the New York cuttings on the desk and browsing through them once more. Pretentious the remarks might be, but there was no denying that Capek's work had caused a stir in the Big Apple. There, at least, the critics believed in him and saw a developing market for his work.

He did not arrive at nine o'clock. A conscientious time-keeper herself, Bea was immediately impatient. When he had not come by 9.10 she moved to watch from the main gallery window, which faced the street. He might, she thought, have difficulty in finding the gallery—though the sign outside could hardly be missed. A drizzle still fell and knots of people drifted by under the refracted street lights. None of them seemed to be in a hurry and none of them looked anything like a Romanian painter. Bea had no fixed idea what Capek might be like, but she didn't somehow see him belonging in any of the laughing, festive groups on the pavements.

He would come alone, she was sure. And he would be carrying pictures, naturally. But beyond these facts she had to use her imagination. She did, and in her mind's eye saw him as gaunt, hollow-eyed, very tall. He would be dressed in black, have piercing grey eyes and a nervous tremor over which he had control only when he painted. Or maybe he would be diminutive, with fair hair and high, Slavic cheekbones under cold blue eyes. He might be neither of these images of course. He might be wizened, old before his time from prison sufferings.

No one remotely fitting any of her figments appeared in the street. The drizzle turned to rain and cars swished by. None of them stopped. By 9.30pm she had decided he was not coming.

"I'll give him another fifteen minutes," she thought. "If he's not here then, I'm leaving."

Anger grew with her impatience as she paced between the two windows. Had Capek any idea of the trouble he had already caused her? If this was how he behaved *before* any agreement was reached then he would be torment to work with and show. At 9.45pm she turned off the lights and grabbed her coat. She took one last look into the street, and saw the man.

He was wearing an old-fashioned trilby and long grey raincoat and stood on the pavement, looking straight at her through the window. He carried a large portfolio. Passers-by threw hurried glances his way before moving quickly past. He seemed to create a silent, watchful space around him.

"That's my man." Bea spoke aloud as if to defy the uneasiness she herself felt, watching him. "That hat! Does he *have* to look like the spy who came in from the cold?" She waved to him and, though it was so slight a movement that she couldn't be sure, thought she saw his head bow in response.

"I'm coming," she mouthed and was relieved to see him moving toward the steps of the gallery.

He fitted the tall, dark version of her imagination, though he wasn't at all gaunt. In fact he looked quite substantial as she smiled at him from the open door and indicated that he should enter.

"I hope you didn't get wet," she said, with determined courtesy. He didn't answer as he passed into the hall and went through the open doorway of the main gallery. Once inside he stood the portfolio against a wall and turned to face her. He reached out a long, slender hand.

It did not shake.

"I am Miroslav Capek," he said. "I hope that we may work together." His voice was deep and only slightly accented. Bea took the proffered hand. It did not feel calloused, as with some painters. He shook her hand briefly, but firmly.

"I hope so," she said and looked questioningly at the portfolio. The painter looked nervously at the street outside. "You have another room?" He gestured from the ceiling light to the uncurtained window. "I prefer not to be so exposed..."

"Of course," Bea said. "We can use my office. It's warmer there anyway."

Did he really think people were going to stop and peer through the window? And what if they did? Life before the revolution must have been fraught indeed to have made him so jittery.

Miroslav Capek laid the portfolio on her desk. It was of an old-fashioned kind and he immediately began to pull open its binding strings. Bea watched his hands, deft, sensitive, a few streaks of paint on one. He still wore his coat and hat.

"Please." She touched one of his hands lightly. "Take off your hat, at least. And perhaps you would like a drink while we discuss things?"

She took off her own coat again, then opened the fridge and studied the contents, frowning. She hadn't left much in the gallery over Christmas, a few bottles of Australian Chardonnay. When she turned, a bottle in her hand, she saw that the painter had removed the trilby and raincoat. He was wearing a heavy-knit black polo-necked sweater.

"I will take a drink, yes," he said. "Whatever you have."

His eyes were grey all right but she could never have imagined such a grey. Dark, like gun-metal, and with the same sheen. Penetrating, they seemed to see much more than they looked at, and to have seen much more in the past than they had wanted to. The rest of his face, undeniably handsome and creased in the barest of smiles, helped to soften their intensity a little. Bea opened the bottle and filled two glasses. She was glad to turn away, even briefly, from the scrutiny of those eyes.

"Your health." She handed him a glass.

His glass touched hers, with the utmost grace and a tiny clink, before he took a deep breath and swallowed the wine in one gulp. He handed her the glass and bent once more over the portfolio. Under the sweater she could see that his shoulders were quite broad, his arms muscular. She sipped her own wine, thoughtfully. He was an attractive man, but it was better for her not to think about that just now.

He lifted a picture from the portfolio. It was a startlingly effective work, its impact immediate and confusing. It was hard-edge, as his other work had been. The outlines were sharp, forceful, the colours strong and wildly contrasting. She took it from him and stood it against the wall, where the light was best. He'd worked in oils, using deepest red, celestial blue and lurid gold-green.

"What else have you got?" she asked. He produced three slides. "I have another, unfinished, in my studio," he said as Bea held the slides to the light. Even in tiny squares she could see the same forceful, startling quality apparent in the picture he'd brought. He had used similar bright colours, the same aggressively blunt outlines. She felt just as confused.

"I have aimed for clarity." The painter seemed to read her thoughts and she looked at him a little nervously. He was scrutinising the painting by the wall again. Clarity was not a word she'd have used to describe the pictures. With their hard lines and vibrant colours they seemed to her to hint at a divided personality. Probably at anger too, or a deep, controlled pain.

Or maybe they were simply clever and it was the restrained tension of the man standing beside her which suggested these things. She stepped away from him a little to study the picture by the wall. What was undeniable was that it managed, paradoxically, to be both striking and contained at the same time. Like the man. This tension was what gave the pictures life, she thought. And commercial potential. She wondered how it affected the man.

"You have decided?"

She looked at him and was surprised at how anxious he seemed. Being shown obviously meant a great deal more to him than his laconic behaviour suggested. She looked at the picture again. She had built up a stable of regular buyers over the years and this work would definitely not be to their taste. It wasn't to her taste either. But it was time to attract new buyers. She had gambled in the past. It had nearly always worked out.

"I can fit in two," she said, "I don't have space for any more."

"But you must take them all. I will finish the one in my studio as well." He picked up the picture by the wall, holding it in front of him. "You *must* show them all!"

"I *can't* show them all! I'm already committed to showing three other artists. I don't have the wall space."

"Your second room, you can use your second room."

His agitation was intense.

"Please try to understand," she said. "I have to get pictures framed, listed, catalogued. Even if I have the space I would need to have had your pictures before now to have them ready in time."

"I will have them here in a few days...I promise..."

"But two pictures in a group show is not such a bad beginning."

"Yes. It is good. I am thankful. But..."

She felt nailed to the ground by his eyes, the haunted expression there. They betrayed more than an artist's ordinary need to have his pictures shown.

"Please. You must listen to me." He sat down, spread his hands and then brought them together. The gesture was oddly theatrical in its supplication, but moving too.

"Of course."

Bea poured him a second glass of wine. She had barely touched her own. She shoved it across the desk and he drank it as he had the first one. She could see how desperately controlled his actions were, noting a muscle working convulsively in his jaw as he put down the glass. He seemed to her like a wild, trapped creature. Images of the hunt came to her, visions of a panic-stricken, terrified fox staying just ahead of the baying pack. He put his hands on the desk. They almost touched hers. Instinct made her tinglingly aware of something else—that the man in front of her was holding in check an explosive sexual energy.

"In prison," he began, "in Jilava in Bucharest, I had time to reflect. I considered what is important in life and I decided that nothing is important. All is transient, perishable. Man lives, and dies, and in between brutalises his fellow man." He smiled. "Art alone has some value,

for it can be civilising. And for me the act of painting
brings peace, for a while. In prison I swore never to paint
again for money. But now I find that the reality of
freedom has made me a prisoner once again. My mother
and sister are still in Romania. My mother is old and will
not leave the land where my father is buried. My sister
will not leave my mother. The money I send makes life
bearable for them both..." He paused, and drew a deep
breath. "It is a long time now since I had money to send
them. I need to sell all of the pictures I have ready."

His voice trailed away. The room whispered with
unspoken horrors of Jilava prison. He studied his hands
for a moment before reaching to touch Bea's lightly. She
didn't move. He came round the desk and stood behind
her. She was acutely aware of him, of the stifling intimacy
of the small office. She wanted him to touch her; she
was afraid he would touch her. And still she did not
move. It would be unprofessional to allow him see the
effect he was having on her. It would probably severely
embarrass him too. She sought refuge in speech.

"You could have made more money in New York
than you'll ever make here," she said.

She found she wanted to know why he had fled from
a beginning which seemed to promise so much. He didn't
answer at once but she waited, more aware of him with
every silent second which passed. He moved silently
and she could tell he was at the window. She turned and
studied his back as he spoke.

"But only if I had continued to paint," he said. "And
I had stopped painting. I was unable to make any more
pictures. In New York I found I had exchanged the hell
of life under Ceausescu for a hell of another kind. It is
a city fit only for the calculating heart, the beast who

will destroy his fellow for gain. Even to gain one dollar. It is a machine, that city. It grinds and devours and has ceased to be human. I could not paint there."

"I understand," Bea said, and she did. She loved New York herself, and was invigorated by its energy and excitement. But she could easily imagine how the other side of those qualities could affect a sensitive artist, especially one who'd spent years incarcerated in the dark horrors of a Romanian prison. New York's neurotic, grabby hedonism would not be reassuring, at all pleasurable, to such a person. It would be far more likely to prove destructive.

"I am glad," she said, "that you have found some peace in Ireland."

He turned at that. He seemed more relaxed and was smiling a wry smile. He spread his hands again and took a step closer to her. Too close. One step more and their bodies would touch. The idea excited her. But it unnerved her too and she took a step away from him. She had to get them out of this small room.

"I'll show you the main gallery," she said. "You didn't have more than a glance at it as we came in." He didn't move.

"I *have* found peace in Ireland," he said. "You cannot understand what peace. Here, the world has ceased to be a fractured, ugly place. In Ireland I am beginning to feel..." He stopped. This time his smile was quite beautiful, transforming his whole face. "Just to feel," he ended, softly. He ran a hand through his thick, almost black hair. He was close enough for Bea to note the series of tiny scars criss-crossing his left cheek. A shiver ran the length of her spine. She drank her wine, in one gulp as he had done.

"Come," she said firmly. "You must have a look at the gallery."

He followed her until he stood in the middle of the room where he stood looking around him. He gave an appreciative sigh.

"It is very fine," he said. "My pictures will hang well here." His unspoken query about how many she would show hovered in the air. Bea said nothing for a few minutes, calculating, hanging his pictures in her mind's eye, gauging the space.

"All right," she said eventually. "I'll take all five of them. I'll use the second room. It'll mean spreading the other pictures about a bit but that may not be a bad thing. And I'll need the lot here in a week. One week from today."

He smiled and Bea smiled back. She felt quite lightheaded. It's the wine, she told herself. But she knew better.

"Right." She became businesslike. "We'd better wrap up the business details."

"But naturally." He followed her back to the office.

Briskly, Bea opened her desk diary, faced him in determined fashion. A ghostly smile touched his face.

"I trust you," he said. "I know you will pay me for the works that sell." His eyes, slightly mocking now, smiled into hers. "Trust is necessary in all relationships."

"Even so."

Bea, determined to keep control of the situation, explained briefly how the gallery operated, explaining that forty per cent would be taken in commission.

"In New York it was seventy per cent," he said, agreeably.

"Will you come to the opening?" He did not, as Bea

had expected, recoil from the idea.

"Yes," he said and, after a slight hesitation, went on. "But not to have my picture in the newspaper or any such publicity. This would take away my privacy."

"Fine," Bea said. "Buyers like to meet the artist. If all goes well you may make enough to build a stockade around your hideaway."

"Maybe. Or maybe, in time, I will not want to."

"For now, can we arrange a way of making contact should I need you?" Bea did not want him disappearing into his fastness without establishing at least this link. Having Olivia as go-between gave too much power to her sister. But a shuttered look came over Capek's face and he began to tie the strings of the portfolio together again.

"Things are bound to come up," Bea said gently. "I must be able to get in touch with you."

He clutched the portfolio to him and spoke quickly.

"Forgive me. I am jealous of my privacy, especially now it has brought me such peace and made it possible for me to work again. Where I live it is impossible for you to contact me but, if you agree, I will ring you from a nearby telephone once every week."

"Okay," Bea agreed. "Once a week then."

They agreed on dates and she jotted them into the diary. They agreed too that he would get the four remaining pictures to her early in January.

"I am glad we have come to an agreement." He sighed a long, relieved sigh. "Do you feel that we could perhaps be friends as well as business associates?"

"I hope so." Bea spoke cautiously. She wondered what exactly he meant by friends.

"You are married?" He asked the question so abruptly

that Bea, without thinking, shook her head in denial.

"I thought not," he said. "You seem to me a woman used to being alone. Unusual in one so beautiful."

Bea was used to passes, oblique and otherwise. But for once she was not quite sure that a pass was actually being made. Capek was quite expressionless and gave the impression of merely checking on something about which he was mildly curious.

"Not quite alone," she smiled. "I've got a daughter."

"Ah! So you were married once?"

"Yes. I was married once. I still am, technically. But not in any real way, not for twenty years." She gave a small dry laugh. "Irish law has a way of imprisoning people in a marriage. Even after it's long dead."

He was looking at her strangely and she stopped. She'd said too much anyway. She didn't usually talk about her private affairs like this. And anyway, why should he be interested in her life? He seemed to find his own, with its nightmarish memories, difficult enough to deal with.

"I think it's time to go." She was aware that she sounded abrupt but he stood immediately.

"Of course," he said. "I have taken too much of your time already."

"How did you get here?" Bea asked, curiously, as she moved with him toward the door.

"By car. I am not so stoical as to do without transport in my mountain home!"

"I can't offer you a lift, so." Bea spoke lightly. She wanted to ask where he'd learned such almost classical English but was afraid he might feel patronised. She would ask him some other time. She knew instinctively that there would be other times, longer conversations.

Outside the rain had stopped and, apart from a few dark, scurrying figures, the street had become eerily empty.

"And rooks in families homeward go," Bea quoted, half to herself, and was surprised when a broad smile lit up Capek's face. "And so do I!" he ended the quotation and bowed deep. She clapped her hands in appreciation. There could not be too many Romanians so familiar with the poetry of Thomas Hardy.

He reached for and held one of her hands.

"Take care," he said, "until we meet again." He raised her hand to his lips and brushed it with the breath of a kiss before letting it go. "I lied to you," he said softly. "In prison I came to realise that love too can sometimes make life bearable."

He touched her face lightly and was gone, moving quickly along the street. He kept close to the railings of the houses and in a minute his tall figure had rounded the corner and was out of sight.

Bea drove slowly home. Her head buzzed with confused impressions of Miroslav Capek. He could paint, of that there was no doubt. As a man he was intelligent, sensitive, intense. And very private—though she didn't blame him for that. He was also, and she acknowledged ruefully her own susceptibility, sexually a very attractive man. As she slowed down to allow a lucky drunk to cross the road in Ballsbridge she acknowledged too that it was a long, long time since she'd been so drawn to a man. Especially an artist, a breed from which she usually fought shy. Wally had been the last.

Agreeing to show five of Miroslav Capek's pictures had created problems for Bea. Increasing the size of the exhibition meant she had some immediate work to get done. Picture-framers and printers would have to be

contacted, commitments got from them before they
began taking New Year orders.

All of this meant that it was going to be impossible
for Bea to get back to Inverskena the following morning.

She groaned as she considered her choices. If she
went back down the chances were she would never have
the exhibition ready in time. If she didn't, the cold war
between herself and Sinéad would sink to even lower
temperatures. On the other hand, even if she did return,
there was no guarantee that Sinéad would be at all
welcoming. All things considered, their relationship was
something which would have to be sorted out at another
time.

Maybe, indeed, time itself was the only thing which
would sort matters out. Time and a little help from Daniel.
Bea was finding that she had great faith in Daniel.

She shivered in the sharp breeze from the sea as she
climbed the steps to the flat. It was dark in the recess of
the front door and she didn't see the man until he stepped
out of the shadows. "You've taken a long time to get
here," he said and took the keys from her nerveless
fingers.

CHAPTER THIRTEEN

When Bea tried to speak, her mouth was quite dry. She had moved quickly enough from a sudden, paralysing fear to awareness that the man on her doorstep was Wally. But the knowledge didn't eliminate the effects of the shock, the terrible dread of attack she shared with almost every woman who lives alone. She stood, trembling a little and speechless, as Wally opened the door and slipped her keys into his pocket. He took her arm and ushered her inside.

"Where to now?" he asked. He closed the door with one hand, holding firmly onto her arm with the other. It was this, the proprietorial insistence of this action, that returned Bea to her senses, and goaded her into action. And words. She spoke with a cold, emphatic fury.

"*Now* you can get out of here, Wally Treacy!" With a violent jerk she broke his tight grip on her arm. "How dare you come to my home uninvited! And how dare you lie in wait, frightening me half to death!"

"Whoa there—calm down." Wally, laughing, held up a hand as if fending off attack. His trivialising of her fear added fuel to Bea's anger.

"I will *not* calm down! Let me make the situation between us absolutely clear, Wally. I am *not* prepared to accept your invasion of my privacy. You are not welcome here. This is *my* life and you have no part in it. No part at all. I don't want you here. In fact I want you to get out now and never come back! *And* I'd like my keys, please." She held out her hand but Wally moved back several steps until he was leaning against the wall. He crossed his legs and took the keys out of his pocket, dangling them just out of her reach. In the shadowy hallway his face had a fiendish look.

"Temper, temper," he laughed softly, seeming quite unperturbed. It was as if he had come prepared for her to be angry. "You really do look quite magnificent when you're angry, dear heart. Histrionics suit you—you should give way more often. All this self-control you've developed!" He made a tut-tutting noise and shook his head reprovingly. "Doesn't suit you at all. Unbridled passion was always much more your thing. Okay, okay I'm sorry! Just take it easy for a minute."

He stopped dangling the keys and held up a placatory hand as Bea, moving quickly, opened the front door. A blast of cold night air rushed in.

"Out!" she hissed. "Or I'll call the guards! I mean it..."

"Listen, Bea, please," Wally's demeanour changed. He was a small boy now, apologetic and crestfallen. "I'm sorry if I frightened you. Really I am. But I had to see you and this was the only way. You'd have hung up if I'd telephoned. And if I'd come buzzing at the intercom you wouldn't have listened or allowed me up to your flat—would you?" He sounded wistful.

"How astute of you, Wally," Bea knew sarcasm was cheap but couldn't resist. "No, I wouldn't have allowed you up and I'm not going to do so now, either."

"Listen, Bea, please!" Wally, moving away from the wall, came closer to where she stood. His teasing manner had gone. He looked worried. "There are things solicitors can't sort out. Sinéad, for instance."

"Sinéad is over twenty-one. *And* she's a married woman." Bea, aware that she sounded bitter, softened her tone. She had no desire to allow her own hurt about Sinéad complicate things. "She doesn't enter into this any more."

"But I need to talk about her. My daughter has become a woman and I don't know her! I *want* to know her. You *must* help me, Bea. Look, I don't expect you to forgive me—why should you? But I have no one else. No other children. I want to know the one I have."

"But she's not a child, Wally, as you so accurately pointed out. She's a woman. And there's nothing I can do." Bea spoke with lethal precision. "Sinéad didn't grow up overnight, you know. It took twenty years and you weren't here for any of that time. Not for a year, not for a month. Not even for a day. She's of an age to make her own decisions about the people she wants in her life. And she doesn't want to know you. You're a stranger. As far as she's concerned you've arrived twenty years too late."

"Don't you think I know all that, Bea? Don't you think I've suffered?"

"Frankly, no. I don't think you've suffered at all. I don't think you've any capacity for real feeling, Wally, beyond concern for yourself that is."

"You're wrong," Wally's voice was low. He lifted her hand, placed the keys in her palm, then closed her fingers over them. He looked at her. "I can't describe"—he faltered and stopped. He cleared his throat and went on more firmly. "If you could just be friends with me, Bea, then Sinéad might."

"No, she wouldn't. Us being friends wouldn't impress her one bit. Quite the opposite in fact. She's a very single-minded young woman. I can't imagine where she got it from." Bea allowed herself a small smile. But there was no humour in her voice as she went on. "You could, at any time over the years, have come to see her. It would have meant a lot to her, knowing her father cared about her. All of her friends had fathers. She often asked about you…You had so much time to make amends. But it's too late now."

"I wanted to visit. I really did. But I couldn't face *you*. Forgive me."

"It was too late the day you walked out the door. I can never forgive you. I don't want to. What you did, Wally, was heinous. Deserting your dying son placed you beyond contempt." She stopped and looked at the keys in her hand. When she looked up Wally was staring sightlessly through the open door behind her. His expression was desolate. But Bea did not stop, draw back from what she had to say. It had to be said, at last, if only to put some of her anger and hurt to rest. She had no pity in her heart for Wally. "All Oisín needed was love, the security of his small place in the world for a few weeks more. But you couldn't wait, Wally, not even that long. So he died without his father's hand, or face, anywhere near him."

She stopped again, this time to compose herself. She thought of her baby's brown eyes, his dazzling smile. She marshalled the strength his death had given her years before. "You killed any feeling I had for you by leaving then. You divorced yourself from decency when you left that day. And you divorced yourself from your daughter by not coming back."

There. She had said all, or most, of what needed to be said. She felt drained. Taking a breath she turned toward the stairway.

"Wait, Bea, please!" Wally's voice was hoarsely pleading. Bea stopped but didn't turn around as he went on. "You're right. Everything you say is right. I was worse than a bastard. I deserve your hatred, your disgust. In my defence let me say that I was young, and confused. I was terrified by the responsibilities I saw building up around me and wanted to be free. I knew your father would look after things. He always had. He loved you, Bea, even if you couldn't see it. That's why he hated me so much. But people change, you know. *I've* changed." Bea turned at that.

"No, you haven't. You haven't changed one bit, Wally. You're the same self-centred, vain little man you were then." She could feel her anger beginning to boil again and she stopped. She had said enough. She was not going to allow Wally Treacy to reduce her to a screaming virago in her own hallway.

This house, and the flat upstairs, were filled with good memories. She would not allow him to contaminate them. "I think we've said all that needs to be said." Her voice was gentler but none the less final.

"I want to visit his grave," Wally said and Bea felt as if she had, suddenly, been dealt a body blow. The breath seemed to leave her.

"No!" Her cry was involuntary and she repeated it twice more before she could stop herself. "No! No!" The word projected her horror and primitive need to protect her dead child.

"You can't deny me the right to see my son's grave, Bea! It would be inhuman."

Without a word Bea began to climb the stairs. She took the steps two at a time and had almost reached the top before she realised that Wally was following her. For the first, and only, time since moving into this old house she wished for a lift. It would destroy the house's character, ruin its architectural pedigree but at that moment she didn't give a damn. In a lift she could have escaped Wally. She walked briskly to her flat door, then stopped. "You might as well come in," she said.

Wally took off his coat and threw himself into a sofa. Bea, without offering him a choice, made black coffee. She was not going to offer him alcohol and risk having him here all night. Risk the other effects of alcohol either. She wanted coffee herself, so he could have coffee.

"Nice." Wally looked around appreciatively. "Very nice."

Bea said nothing. She was watching the lights of a ferry as it sailed slowly across the dark of the bay. The familiar sight calmed her, bringing her back to everyday realities. One of these was that she had never, ever, wanted Wally in this flat.

"Oisín is buried in Dean's Grange," she said. "I'll give you the grave number and draw you a map of how to find it. Then I want you to go." She stood up.

"I was hoping you'd come with me," Wally put his cup down carefully and jerkily pulled a packet of Gitanes from his pocket. He was right, Bea thought, to be nervous. She was feeling quite murderous.

"You were?" She was caustic but controlled as she sat opposite him and began to draw a map of the graveyard. For an instant her control gave way and tears filled her eyes, blurring the paper in front of her. It was such a private part of her life, that small bit of ground which held her baby son. She went there every month and had never wanted to share it with anyone. Certainly not with Wally. Bending over the paper she closed her eyes, tight. When she opened them she could see clearly again. She finished drawing the map.

"I've made it as simple as possible," she said. "It's to the back, near a large elm. His gravestone is easy to spot too. It just has his name and a short quotation." She looked up to find Wally standing, idly studying her pictures.

"Oh?" he turned. "What's the quotation?"

"I chose a line of Ben Jonson's. It's from something he wrote when his own son died." She kept her voice steady as she quoted. "Farewell, thou child of my right hand, and joy."

There was a silence as Wally stubbed out his cigarette.

"I'll go there tomorrow," he said. "I wish you'd come with me."

"No." She would not share Oisín's grave with him. Wally, acknowledging the finality in her tone, sat opposite on the sofa again.

"I'm tired, Wally, I'd like you to leave now," Bea said.

"Mind if I telephone for a taxi? Unless of course…"

"Be my guest," Bea cut him short and indicated the phone with a sweep of her hand. She was not going to offer him a bed, which was obviously what he was about to suggest. Nor did she intend driving him wherever he was staying. She knew only too well how Wally would behave in either situation. She began to gather up the cafetiere and mugs.

"What happened to the car you had at Inverskena?"

"Cursed thing wouldn't start for me tonight," Wally frowned as he dialled. Something else which hasn't changed, Bea thought as she washed the mugs in the kitchen. Wally had never had much luck with cars. He only needed to sit behind a wheel for mechanical problems to develop. He was a lousy driver too. She had finished clearing up when he appeared in the doorway.

"Taxi'll be here in ten minutes," he said. In the brighter, kitchen light she looked at him closely. He did not, she had to admit, look half-bad.

Remembering Stephanie she wondered idly how young the women he bedded were these days. He twitched a little under her gaze, then gave her a wide grin. "Leaving was the best thing I ever did for you, Bea. I'd have destroyed you. You'd never have become the woman you are today."

"And you might not be the man you are today." Bea brushed past and out of the kitchen. From the front window she watched for the taxi. Wally stood close beside her.

"The gallery is doing well, then?" he asked, conversationally.

"Yes, very well." Bea, glad of the safer, unemotional ground of business, answered brightly. "I'm quite established now." She gave a gentle, self-deprecatory laugh.

"So I hear. *Very* established in fact. Big name openings, stable of wealthy buyers, every show a success."

"Where did you hear all that?" Bea looked at him in surprise. Wally raised an eyebrow, made a mischievously vague face.

"Oh, I've a few contacts left still in Dublin. All of them are envious admirers of The Hennessy Gallery." He looked around the flat. "They're not exaggerating, I can see that. You've done well, Bea."

"I'm doing well but I'm hardly the social queen you seem to think."

Wally lit another cigarette. "Anyone interesting lined up for the group show Olivia was talking about?"

"Yes, as a matter of fact, there *are* a few interesting pictures coming in..."

"Oh? By anyone I know?"

"Maybe you do. He's a Romanian. Sold at auction in London a while ago. His name is Miroslav Capek."

"Can't say I've heard of him. You think he's interesting?" Wally stubbed out the half-smoked cigarette. Bea, watching the dying coil of smoke, wondered if it was talk of divorce, or of Oisín, which had made him so nervous.

"Yes. Definitely interesting," she said. A movement in the quiet road below caught her eye. "Your taxi."

"Maybe I'll pop over for the show. When did you say the opening was?" The taxi driver was coming up the steps but Wally seemed in no hurry to go.

"I didn't say. And it's invitation only." Bea picked up his coat and handed it to him. "Goodbye Wally," she said. "You'll be hearing from my solicitor."

For a second his eyes darkened and his mouth formed a tight, angry line. Then the moment passed, so quickly that Bea thought she must have imagined it. Wally's face, as he turned at the top of the stairs, wore only the most whimsical of smiles.

"I'll be around," he said. "I'm expecting an Irish goose to lay a golden egg one of these days. In the meantime, *au revoir!*"

With a cavalier wave he turned and plunged quickly

down the stairs. Bea locked the door, then watched from the window as he climbed into the waiting taxi. She didn't return his final wave.

Alone, she thought about phoning James and looked at her watch. Too late. Best to go to bed. She would do it tomorrow. As she bent to turn out the light a piece of paper on the floor caught her eye and she picked it up.

Looking at her map of Dean's Grange she wondered if Wally had ever intended going there. She looked at it for a long time before she decided that no, it had all been just another of his games. Oisín would not be getting a visit from his father.

She went to bed feeling tired, but curiously at peace. She hadn't telephoned James but she *had* taken the first step toward instituting divorce proceedings against Wally. As she lay there, drifting between wakefulness and sleep, a pair of penetrating, dark grey eyes invaded her consciousness.

"Goodnight to you too," Bea muttered, sleepily.

CHAPTER FOURTEEN

I t was still dark when Bea awoke next morning. She lay for a while, enjoying a few languorous minutes before attacking the day. She had dreamed in the night, a benign, happy dream which had left her with a sense of well-being. She could remember laughter, warm feelings. As the dark lightened against the curtains she closed her eyes and tried to recapture it. But it had gone, retreated into the limbo which holds on to happy dreams. She burrowed deeper into the bedclothes. Still it refused to return. With a sigh she got up.

Bea didn't usually waste time in the mornings. It was her way to work hard, almost obsessively, until she got each exhibition just right. This morning she quickly abandoned the idea of working at home—too comfortable—and headed instead for the gallery. The day had dawned clear and sharp and she drove slowly, enjoying the empty, unhurried feeling in the normally churning thoroughfares of Baggot Street and Merrion Row. The city had not really returned to work yet; that would take several more days, maybe even a week. It was not Dublin's way to rush to the end of a holiday period.

First she set to work on the catalogue. This took a couple of hours but by that time she had got together a draft which would shape the finished product. Next she went through the guest list she'd used for the last show. She knocked off some names, added others.

After that she studied Miroslav Capek's picture. It would have to go to the framer, that very day if possible. She telephoned Conor Molloy, who did all her framing, but got no answer. This did not mean he was not at home. Or even that he was busy. It usually and simply meant that he was not answering the phone. Bea wrapped the picture carefully. He would be annoyed when she turned up at his door. He would argue and protest overwork. But she would, in the end, persuade him to frame both this and the other additional pictures. It was a charade they always went through, even when Bea got pictures to him months in advance. And he, always, produced beautifully finished work at the very last minute. He had never once let her down. The idea of using anyone else never occurred to her. Conor Molloy was, for Bea, the best.

She was retrieving her keys from the desk when her gaze fell on the silent and accusing phone. It was wrong of her to put off calling James. *Very* wrong to put off phoning Sinéad. And foolish not to telephone her solicitor to initiate the divorce proceedings. She groaned and put the picture down while she juggled the relative conflicts of each conversation. A chat with James offered, she decided, by far the most pleasant prospect. She dialled his office. He would, she knew, be one of the minority back at work that day. She got through to him immediately.

"Bea!"

He sounded pleased and she gave thanks for his good nature, his capacity to put things behind him and carry on as if differences didn't exist. A part of this she knew had to do with his extremely good manners. She thanked him for the pearls and they talked, fully and warmly, of their respective Christmas experiences. Now that they were past Bea was able to give witty accounts of family dramas. It was part of her survival technique. Laughter, she found put everything in perspective. They were both laughing when James's secretary interrupted to remind him, frostily, that there were calls waiting.

"So, will I see you tonight?" James asked.

"I'd rather not," Bea said slowly. "Could we wait until after the weekend? I'd planned to bury myself in work for a few days, get some things sorted out."

"Fine," James said immediately. "Lunch on Monday then?"

They agreed a restaurant, and to meet at 12.30 in the Horseshoe Bar of the Shelbourne. James ended the conversation quite formally. He was most discreet when speaking from his office.

Bea then rang Inverskena. She did so immediately and without planning what she would say to Sinéad. The plain truth would have to do. She'd never quite got the knack of dealing in anything else anyway.

The call proved more difficult even than she'd imagined.

Sinéad, monosyllabic at first, shocked her by announcing that she and Daniel were returning to Dublin. With Mark. When, very carefully, Bea suggested they might stay a few days with Charles, her daughter cut her rudely short. Bea knew then there was something wrong. Sinéad was very fond of Charles, and he of her. Daniel had been getting on very well with him too. There had to be a reason they'd decided to leave so suddenly.

That reason had to be Mark. He was the bit which didn't fit. Bea, her mind a jangle of questions, knew she wouldn't get any information from Sinéad on the phone. She didn't, in fact, get anything else from Sinéad either. Not acceptance of her invitation for drinks on New Year's Eve, not even good wishes when they said goodbye.

She replaced the receiver slowly and thoughtfully. Sinéad's responses had been more than just rude. They had been evasive. She would call Charles when he was alone in the evening. He at least would tell her what was going on. She felt sure something was.

The call to the solicitor yielded only an answering machine that told her the office would be closed until Monday. She felt both impatient and reprieved.

"I'm hungry." She spoke aloud as her stomach rumbled. A sandwich, in company, seemed like a good idea. *En route* to Conor Molloy's, she stopped at Doheny and Nesbitt's pub.

Apart from a few journalists it was quiet. It was usually alive with commentators of every persuasion and this lonely condition did not suit it. Bea read a couple of the morning papers and found herself wishing the holiday would end. She felt a great need to see the streets teeming again, to hear the pubs noisy. She wanted things to be busy and normal. She had had enough of this peace.

Conor Molloy, as she'd expected, was irritable. But he agreed, as usual, to do the framing and called her, as usual, a bully. Then he offered her a drink, which was not at all in character. Bea had a large whiskey. She had another two hours later while she enjoyed a long soak in the bath, listening to Vivaldi's *Four Seasons* and trying not to think of any of her life's complications. She was feeling very relaxed when she phoned Inverskena but found Charles most reluctant to discuss Sinéad and Daniel.

"Please, Charles, just tell me why they left. It's to do with Mark, isn't it?"

Insisting on an answer Bea felt that she *was* a bully. She could almost hear Charles squaring his thin shoulders, could definitely hear him take a deep breath before coming abruptly to the point.

"Mark has a drug problem and Sinéad, I'm afraid, was the one who found him injecting himself." He ignored Bea's shocked gasp. "He is, however, keen to effect a cure and Sinéad is more than keen to help him. No, Bea, don't interrupt. You wanted to know. This is something you'll have to allow her do. Mark will not seek professional help and, because of that, it's my opinion that Sinéad can do more for him than anyone else. He trusts her. And she won't be alone. She has Daniel and she has promised to seek expert help as well. Take my advice, Bea, and keep out of it. It's between the two of them now. Let them get on with it."

Bea, her eyes fixed on a watercolour which hung over the phone, was fighting an instinct to yell at Charles. Instead she explained, very softly,

"Mark is like a son to me, Charles. Sinéad is my daughter. You are asking me not to help them in what could be, without exaggeration, a life or death situation. How *can* I stand aside?"

"Because you can't help. Not in this instance. You could, in fact, do a lot of harm. Trust has to be built between those two. If they feel they're doing it alone, it may just work. Believe me, I know what I'm talking about…"

He stopped. Bea, knuckles white as she gripped the

phone, struggled with the knowledge that he was probably right. If Charles said he knew what he was talking about then he did.

"Mark is staying with Sinéad?"

"Yes. And Bea, *please* don't discuss this with Olivia and Albert. Play dumb about Mark and where he's staying. He doesn't want his parents to know and I'm afraid we've no choice but to humour Sinéad and Mark in this"

"But they'll worry. At least Albert will."

"They've covered that. The plan, apparently, is for Mark to phone home once a week. Keep them off his back was how he put it..."

Dimly, over the line, there came the sound of a bell. Bea, with a quick stab of guilt, realised that she had forgotten to ask about Jude.

"Seems a bit down," Charles said when she asked him now. "She wants to go back to the nursing home and they agree I should bring her in. They're expecting me within the hour so I'd better go."

"Charles, wait! She's not well, is she?"

"She's been better. But you know Jude. The original phoenix."

"But can you manage her on your own? Is Olivia going with you?"

"Olivia and Albert have gone for a drive. Stephanie has offered to help. Don't fuss, Bea. We'll manage."

Long after she'd said goodbye Bea sat by the phone. This time she focused on another picture, a bright watercolour of young people on a beach. It was fairly amateurish and she'd bought it mainly for its sunny atmosphere. Now, looking at it, she could see an underlying tension as they squabbled over a ball.

Nothing, she thought, was ever as it seemed. Or as you wanted it to be.

CHAPTER FIFTEEN

Sinéad, lying drowsily in her bed at Inverskena, wished Daniel would come back. He'd gone downstairs for coffee and for something for them to eat. She was ravenous. Good sex always made her hungry.

And sex with Daniel was very good. Life with Daniel in general was a pleasing affair, as she had known it would be, almost the first time she'd met him. He was everything she'd never had, and always wanted, in her life. He was calm order, he was rock-like dependability. He was interesting too, and fun. But most of all he had a way of looking at her, of touching her and bringing her to glorious, blazing sexual life. She had never, ever put so much effort into anything as she had into capturing Daniel for herself.

He had happened at a time when she'd felt adrift, desperately in need of someone to love her. Someone she could love in return. All her instincts about Daniel had been positive. She had known that he was the type who would be faithful unto death, and she needed that. She could not share and she did not want to be betrayed, ever again. It had simply been a matter of convincing him that he was ready for marriage. She would not settle for anything less.

Losing Bea had devastated Sinéad. Her mother had been the one constancy in her life, an adored bulwark in an uncertain existence. They had been a unit, inseparable and sharing. Sinéad had defined herself by her mother. She had been Bea Hennessy's daughter and that was all she had been.

It had all ended when Bea met James Harte. In spite of the accusations Sinéad had levelled at her mother two days before, she had always admired Bea's determination and devotion to the gallery. There had been times, when she was a lot younger, that she had been peeved at Bea's not turning up at a school event. But she'd always understood, knew that without the gallery she wouldn't have been in such a school in the first place. No, the problem wasn't the gallery.

James Harte was the poison that had infected their lives. Within weeks of meeting him, Bea had rejected her daughter, transferred her loyalty and given her love to a man who was nothing more than a walking cheque book. Sinéad, struck dumb by the horror of what she saw happening, had been unable to say anything, to utter a single word of protest. She was convinced her mother was making a terrible mistake. James Harte was cold and self-seeking, anyone could see that. Anyone but Bea. He was a typical egotistical business type, concerned with his image and wanting it to be bolstered by having an elegant woman at his side.

Image was so important to James Harte. It was apparent in his designer label clothes, in the green, careful-not-to-be-too ostentatious Jaguar he drove.

Nor could Bea see either how he treated her, Sinéad. How he patronised her, asking about college as if enquiring whether or not she still played with dolls. A couple of times he'd invited her to accompany himself and Bea to concerts. Play gooseberry while he courted her mother! She'd given the idea a pretty swift chop and he'd dropped it as an approach.

She could perhaps have taken it all if Bea had ever once discussed the relationship with her. But she hadn't. She'd never even mentioned it. To go from sharing everything to sharing nothing; that, for Sinéad, had been the unkindest cut of all.

Bea had even ceased to pay attention to Sinéad's life in college. She had nattered on about letting her go, about not interfering. All very well if all had been very well. But life in Belfield had been hell. Bea, of course, had presumed she knew all about it. Just as she presumed to know about everything. Only she didn't know anything about UCD today or how completely it had changed from her time there. That had been in old God's time anyway, when Belfield was nothing more than a glorified creche.

Sinéad had been overawed by the sheer numbers on campus, utterly confused by the sprawl of the place, lonely because not a soul she knew was doing Arts. Once, when she'd tried to explain that lectures on crowd control might be more useful than hours spent on Aristotelian theories, James Harte had begun to laugh. Bea, who'd been paying attention until then, began to laugh too. After that there had been no point discussing with Bea her fears that Arts was not for her.

When she'd decided to share a house with three old schoolfriends Bea had been agreeable, giving her a generous allowance, probably because she wanted to be rid of her. Daniel, lovely Daniel, was the elder brother of one of the girls. Their parents had retired to the South of France and, keeping a protective eye on his sister, Daniel had called often.

A thud on the bedroom door brought her rudely back to the present. "Room service! Get out of that bed, woman, and let me in!" Daniel's call, cheerful and loud, was accompanied by another thud.

"Door's not locked." Sinéad stretched, then burrowed deeper into the bedclothes. There came a third, much louder, thud.

"I have to tell you, ma'am, that all services will be withdrawn if you don't get out of that bed and open the door. Now!"

"Just push."

"Furthermore, I will take this tray away and eat every morsel it contains myself. Alone. In the kitchen with Jake."

Grumbling and giggling Sinéad pulled herself out of the bed, wrapped the duvet around her and shuffled to the door.

"What've you got?" She peered at the laden tray.

"Porridge. Fruit. Yoghurt. Boiled eggs. Brown bread…"

When they'd finished eating they made love again. Desire and the mood were always present. All it took was for Daniel to reach over, touch her hair. And for her to turn, meet his warmly loving eyes.

"Such soft hair," he murmured. She caught his hand, laughing as she kissed his fingertips, one by one. She ran her tongue lightly across the palm, to his wrist. She felt his body's quick response and she pressed close to him, wanting his kiss.

"That breakfast has given me new energy," she whispered.

"Me too," Daniel said huskily. He lifted her hair from the nape of her neck and caressed the length of her body. She forgot everything, gave herself to the joyous pleasure of their desire for one another. Everything else went away, melted like snow. Nothing was important, not even the niggling fact that she'd forgotten to take her contraceptive pill again. Afterwards she lay with her ear on his chest, listening to his heartbeat.

"Slow, slow, quick, quick, slow," she murmured. "Like an old-fashioned dance rhythm. What can this mean, my love?"

"Maybe that I'm past my prime," Daniel said, and Sinéad looked up at him thoughtfully.

"When was your prime?" she asked, half-seriously.

"When I was about twenty," Daniel laughed, and wound a strand of her hair around his finger. "I really burned up the town that year."

"I'd have hated you then," Sinéad sat up, tracing his lips with a finger. He looked vulnerable without his glasses. "I much prefer older men." She lay down again and Daniel held her tight. She took a deep breath.

"Talking of burning," she said, "Mark's really on fire with something."

"Yes?" Daniel knew that, provided he didn't push her, Sinéad would tell him everything she'd learned in the time spent with her cousin the day before.

"He's been doing drugs." She spoke matter-of-factly. Daniel stiffened slightly and she rushed on before he could say anything. "But it's all over now, really it is. He's ended it. He's taking something called physeptone, a prescription drug to help with withdrawal symptoms. Yesterday, he doesn't know why, he had an adverse reaction to it and just freaked out."

"Mmm. What was he taking before?" Daniel spoke carefully.

"Experimenting with this and that, anything that came his way. You know."

"I think I do."

"He's not an addict or anything, Daniel. Nothing like that. He was just messing around. Curiosity, he said. All his crowd were doing it. It's just..." she stopped.

"Just what?" Daniel kissed the top of her head.

"Well, that he's changed so much. He's so miserable. I suppose that's understandable because he's not feeling great. But he's surly. And that's not like him. He used to be so happy-go-lucky. He's changed so much he's like a different person. He sounded downright depressive a lot of the time. And sort of angry too. He kept saying the world stank."

"What's he doing with himself, apart from messing about with drugs?"

"Don't be judgemental, Daniel," Sinéad pleaded. "He's supposed to be studying for some business thing in Trinity. He was really interested, I remember, when he started. He says now that it's deadly boring. Crap was the word he used. He's talking about packing it in."

"Great," Daniel said, shortly. "That'll give him all the time in the world to experiment."

"Look." Sinéad was becoming impatient, "I know he's finished with the drug thing. He needs support, not condemnation. Problem is, he's been living away from home, more or less. He's not keen to go back to living with Olivia and Albert. He doesn't seem to know what he wants to do with himself."

"Do you want me to talk to him? Man-to-man sort of thing?"

Without turning, Sinéad could feel him smile. Daniel was the least macho man she'd ever met. Man-to-man was not his style.

"No," she said. "I'll have another go myself. In fact I'll get dressed and trot along to see him right away."

Half an hour later she was knocking on the door of Mark's attic bedroom. Now that Wally had gone he was all alone on this floor, which was not ideal, in Sinéad's view. She'd have preferred him closer to everyone. But he'd always liked the attic, even as a child.

There was no reply to her first, fairly timid, knock. She tried again, louder this time. There was still no reply but now she could hear distinct sounds from within the room.

"Mark!" she called, "Are you in there?"

There came a crashing sound, followed by a low moan. Then a whimper. She quickly pushed open the door and entered the bedroom.

Mark was on his knees on the floor. It was obvious that he'd fallen out of the bed and was trying to get back in. The sounds he was making were now more like a cat mewing. On the floor beside him there was a needle and hypodermic syringe.

"Oh my God, Mark, no!"

In seconds she was beside him. Clumsily, she tried to lift him onto the bed but he resisted her help.

"Leave me alone! Get away from me!"

He tried to shake her off but his strength wasn't up to it, his fluttering hands unequal to the task of pushing her away. He had taken his pyjama top off and his torso seemed to her terrifyingly emaciated and fragile-looking. She continued to lift and pull him and, when she at last got him against the pillows, saw for the first time the hideous reality of his scored arms.

If she needed further evidence of his addiction it lay

with the matches, burnt spoon and cottonwool on the bedside table.

"Oh my God, Mark!" she said again. It seemed to be all she could say.

He had been filling her with lies. Hypodermic needles and burnt spoons were not the stuff of doctors' prescriptions. She gazed bleakly at his thin, wasted arms, at the ugly purple tracks caused by injecting drugs, at the hideous spreading discolouration which made the skin seem like a diseased thing. An abscess oozed on one arm.

She picked up his pyjama top and draped it around his shoulders. He didn't try to stop her but when she looked at his face she saw that he was smiling at her. A cold smile.

"Surely you didn't believe me, little cousin?" His tone was sneering. But Mark wasn't the sneering type. Not the Mark who'd believed in magic and wanted to be a magician. Not the Mark who'd taken her to her Debs only three years before.

"What were you injecting, Mark?" She tried hard to keep her voice from trembling. He looked away from her.

"Just a little snow. Brightens up the day. Makes for the good life."

"Really? From where I am, your life doesn't look so great!"

"Don't be so fucking sanctimonious! You've never tried it. I'd let you have some if I had any left." The cocky sneer died on his face and for a moment fear showed on blanched features.

It passed and he was jauntily mocking as he went on.

"But that was it! My last shoot up of the festive season!"

He closed his eyes, took a few deep breaths and smiled to himself.

"Snow is heroin, isn't it, Mark?"

"Snow is heroin," Mark mimicked. "And snow is heaven. It's also junk, horse, scagg—whatever you're having yourself."

"Why did you lie to me? Why did you tell me you'd come off it?"

"Because that's what you wanted to hear. And I wouldn't want to disappoint my sweet, innocent little cousin, would I?"

"Oh shut up! Just shut up, Mark! You've become such an almighty pain!" Now that she was sure he wasn't going to die, Sinéad felt angry at her cousin and was able to say what she thought. "You think this is all so bloody clever, and cool. If you could see yourself! You're pathetic! You look like shit."

She stopped. She couldn't bring herself to use the word death, the only one she felt adequately described his appearance. Mark opened his eyes. They were unnaturally bright, his pupils unnaturally small.

"But I feel great," he grinned. "Nothing else matters. Appearance is all show, a middle-class obsession like consumerism. No need to get yourself into a sweat, old hen. Think of me as a bit of variety to the family."

"We've got more than enough variety in this family already! We could give half of it away and not even miss it!" Sinéad spoke with unconscious bitterness.

"Ah, but we've never had a dope fiend until now…"

"We didn't need one," Sinéad snapped. "Why, Mark? Why are you doing drugs?"

Mark shifted in the bed before answering her. He put his arms into the pyjama top.

"Why not?" His cavalier manner became truculent as he asked again, "Why the hell not? I like it. I like how it feels. It blocks out reality, puts things on hold." He reached out and caught her arm in a surprisingly strong grip. "Look, you don't understand. When you have a turn-on it's like putting a video on pause. Everything stops. Every shitty thing in the world. It's better than sex. Better than anything." His glittering eyes dropped from hers and he let her arm go. He groaned.

"Then you come down," the fear was back in his face "and you're off, running around looking for a score so that you can push the pause button again."

They looked at one another for an endless minute. Mark was the first to look away.

"What is it you're trying to escape, Mark? What can't you face?"

"Jesus, Sinéad, how can you ask me that? You of all people! You know my folks, you know what sort of mother I've got! Selfish bitch, she's never given a damn about me. Not even when I was a kid, certainly not since I've grown up. I'm not tall and handsome, not at all the sort of son she wanted. She wanted someone she could show off, a socially desirable son. And what did she get?" Mark paused, gave a sort of twisted grin. "She got me, didn't she? Little Markie. Not big enough to be noticed, not even small enough to be a dwarf. Mr In-Between." He gave a laugh which ended in a cough. "Then there's my father. He's so concerned with making money and keeping her happy he wouldn't notice if I grew an extra head. I'm nothing to either of them."

"I've never heard such whining self-pity in my entire life!"

Sinéad exploded, but just as quickly calmed down.

She knew that what she said next, how she handled Mark over the following minutes, could be crucial.

"Look, I know they're not perfect. But they're what you've got, so you might as well get on with things. You're a big boy, Mark. Time you stopped laying the blame on Albert and Olivia. Albert's okay, anyway. Olivia, I grant you, is a major pain in the ass. But you're you and this," she affected a jokey New York accent, "ain't no dress rehearsal, man. This is life and the only one you've got."

He'd closed his eyes again and it was impossible to tell whether or not he was listening.

"What I'm saying, Mark, is that it's time to enter the adult world, make the most of what you've got. It's not so bad, really. It can be pretty good, in fact."

"All right for you to talk," Mark was sullen. "You've got your Mr Perfectly Clean to see you through. I suppose you consider marrying that boring jerk an adult move?"

"Yes, it was," Sinéad said, quietly.

"Well, whatever turns you on," Mark shrugged and then looked at her slyly. "And of course you've been lucky enough to have Bea for a mother."

Sinéad froze. Her voice dropped by several degrees to a cool below zero.

"I've made a life without Bea. In spite of her, in fact. I could have done drugs. I'd just as many excuses as you, if I wanted to look at things that way. Just as many opportunities too."

"Three cheers for the righteous Mrs Kirwan! Wouldn't the world be a better place if we could all be a bit more like her!"

Bea stood up.

"You're right," she said, in a small defeated voice.

"You always did have a way of making me face myself. And I *am* being self-righteous. It's just that I don't know how to handle this, Mark." Her voice broke. She was close to tears. "You're more than just my cousin, you know that. You're my friend, you're sort of my brother. I can't stand to see what's happening to you. It's as if you're destroying yourself in front of my eyes, and I can't do a thing about it. The Mark I knew is gone away. I'm so frightened he won't come back, that this other Mark will…"

She stopped. Mark had turned away from her, there seemed no point in saying any more. "Okay. If that's the way you want it. I'm going. But if there's anything I can do, well, you know where I am. Any time." She was halfway to the door when he called her.

"Sinéad! Don't go!"

His voice had lost all belligerence. He had pulled the duvet around him and curled into a ball. His head was still turned away and when he spoke his voice sounded like that of a small boy. "Please understand what's happened to me. I'm more afraid of living than dying. I'd rather run the risk of dying when I turn on than go on living without a hit."

He stopped and the silence filled every corner of the bedroom. Sinéad, through a blur of tears, looked from his hunched, bundled shape to the familiar blue wallpaper, up to the skylight window where clouds chased each other across the sky above. She tried to say something but could only manage a choked sob.

"Help me, Sinéad, for God's sake help me!"

Mark's utterly desolate cry unlocked her paralysis and she went to him. Sitting on the bed she pulled him to her. Holding him tight she began to rock back and forth as she whispered reassurance, told him she was with him, that together they would sort it out. She felt his tears on her arm and knew that the Mark she had grown up with and loved like a brother was not lost.

She wouldn't let him down, not now he needed her. She knew what she had to do. She let him go and stood up.

"Right." Her voice was firm. "We'd better work out a strategy, Mark. Plan how we're going to get you off this stuff. To begin with you'd better look at me!"

She shook the lump in the bed. Even through the duvet she could feel the thinness of his contours. Slowly, he shuffled into a sitting position. He managed a shaky grin, one with more than a ghost of the old Mark about it.

"You look so damn healthy," he said ruefully. He began to scratch at the side of his nose, already red and quite raw from previous scratching. He sniffed. His eyes, quite red-rimmed, had become watery. Sinéad understood now why he had been wearing the shades.

"That fix doesn't seem to have done you much good." She sat on the bed and studied him closely.

"I had to cut it. My tolerance has built up and I need more than I can get these days. I popped some jolly beans yesterday to pep me up a bit. I haven't got any left."

"What's a jolly bean?"

"Amphetamine," Mark said shortly. He moved restlessly in the bed. "Look, if you really want to help why don't you go downstairs and get me something to drink? Cola or lemonade—anything so long as it's sweet. I don't suppose Charles has anything as ordinary as a Mars bar in his gourmet kitchen?"

His tone had become belligerent again. Sinéad wanted

to remind him that he had asked her to help, to yell at him to stop being such a boor. But she didn't. She was learning, fast, about the effects of the drug on his personality.

There would be months of selfishness and self-pity to put up with if she was to pull Mark back into the land of the living.

"Cola or lemonade, right. A Mars bar? I'll see." She reached up, pushed the skylight open with its rod. "Don't go anywhere until I get back," she smiled.

There were no Mars bars. No cola or lemonade either. She made up a tray with orange juice, cereal, a pot of tea and large bowl of sugar. She was crossing the hallway when the phone rang. As she stood, uncertain what to do with the tray, the front door opened to admit Charles, a grumbling Jake at his heels.

"I'll get it," he said.

Charles picked up the phone and Jake fixed Sinéad with a gimlet eye. Don't, he seemed to say, move another inch while he's busy and I'm looking after things.

"Nice Jake! Good old Jakesie..." Sinéad cooed softly. Jake bared his teeth. Impossible to tell whether this was a yawn or a threat but, on balance, it was far more likely to be the latter. Sinéad lost patience.

"Oh, come on, you stupid dog! I'm just going about my business. Why don't you go about yours and leave people alone? What did I ever do to you?"

Jake began to wag his tail. He came to her and, like an overgrown geriatric cat, began to rub himself against her. Sinéad all but dropped the tray.

"Why, you contrary old bugger," she said, careful to use the same tone as before. Jake sat and held up a limp paw.

"Don't worry. Don't say another word, please."
Charles, on the phone, indicated that the caller wanted
to speak to Sinéad. With Jake slavishly following, she
put the tray on the table by the tree, fingering a
decoration while Charles finished what she could now
tell was a conversation with her mother. It was apparent
that Bea was not coming back to Inverskena.

Sinéad felt as if someone had delivered a soft, but
telling, punch to the lower part of her stomach. The
sensation grew from disappointment to anger as she
realised that she'd very much wanted Bea to be here,
that she had been subconsciously planning to discuss
with her what she might do for Mark. A blue snowman
came away in her hand from the tree. She held it tightly,
took a deep breath and willed her feelings to go away. Be
realistic, she told herself. Bea's not coming back was to
be expected. It really made no difference to anything.

"Fine. Take care. No, everything's great. Mark's in
bed and Jude's been more or less sleeping since you left.
Yes."

There was a pause while Bea spoke at the other end.
Charles interrupted what was obviously a busy flow of
words.

"She's here now. I'll put her on."

As Sinéad picked up the phone, Jake, with a lingering
glance at her, followed Charles to the back of the house.

"Sinéad, I'm so sorry. Things have snowballed here."
Bea was always sorry. It never stopped her doing what
she wanted to do. "The end of January exhibition is
going to be bigger than I'd intended and I need to—"
Sinéad cut her short.

"It doesn't matter," she said, "Daniel and I are leaving
today anyway."

Daniel didn't know this yet. Nor did Mark, who would be coming with them. Sinéad's plans were taking shape as she spoke.

"Oh? I thought you might stay around for a few days. Daniel and Charles seemed to get on so well and Mark—"

"We've decided to leave today," Sinéad was curt. She heard her mother take a deep breath.

"I wonder," she hesitated briefly then went on, "if you're not busy for New Year's Eve would you and Daniel like to come for drinks that night?"

"Sorry. We're busy." Sinéad's rejection of the invitation was instinctive. She had no intention of easing Bea's conscience by allowing her pour a few sentimental drinks into them while the boats hooted in the harbour and James Harte flashed his gold cuff-links. "See you next year," she said and hung up before her mother could say anything else.

Mark drank the entire carton of orange juice and half-heartedly spooned some of the cereal. As he did so Sinéad told him what she planned to do. He made no objections so she left him to get dressed and pack.

Daniel had left the bedroom and gone downstairs. Unfortunate, Sinéad thought, since she'd have liked to have explained things to him in private. Still, she could save time this way. She would pack their things now, then explain what was happening to Daniel and Charles. It might in fact be better to present the plan as a *fait accompli*.

But neither man saw it quite as she did. Charles was unexpectedly unsupportive and Daniel was less than enthusiastic.

"Move Mark in with us while you nurse him off

drugs?" His habitual cool was severely tested, she could see that. "That is what you're suggesting?"

"Yes, Daniel. That's right. It'll only be for a few months, until he gets on his feet again. He agrees. He has no one else."

"I'm quite sure he agrees, but you are seriously misguided, Sinéad my dear, and may do more damage than good." Charles sounded quite annoyed. "The boy needs professional help, and residential treatment in a therapeutic centre. You won't be able to do it. You may, as I said, make matters worse." Sinéad bristled.

"I'm not the idiot you seem to think I am, Charles! I have thought about it. I know I can help him."

"You don't know enough about it," Charles was adamant. "Whatever you propose doing, Mark is going to need more help than you can give him."

Sinéad made small, tight fists of her hands. To Charles she seemed like nothing so much as a small, black-eyed terrier.

"But I know him better than anyone! And I care about him more than anyone!"

Charles, in his heart, acknowledged the truth of this. Daniel was looking thoughtfully at his wife. Sinéad looked from one to the other.

"I intend getting him physeptone on prescription. I'll see him through the withdrawal symptoms. Then I'll work on getting him back to being the old Mark."

"The old Mark became an addict. He needed the drug," Charles's voice was uncharacteristically hard and Sinéad listened, attentively, as he went on. "A cure is a lot more complicated than you realise. Coming off drugs is not the real problem. That's just physical and can be dealt with relatively easily." Looking at him, at his tense fingers as they sought the comfort of Jake's wiry curls, Sinéad knew that Charles was talking about something he was very familiar with.

"It's the psychological problems afterwards that are the real difficulty. That and staying clean."

"I take your point, Charles." She spoke gently when he finished. "And I know you're right. But I just know that Mark won't go into residential care. It has to be done this way."

"Right." Daniel sounded decisive. "Then we'd better sort out a few things. You'll have to take advice, Sinéad, from someone in the field. A drug counsellor, perhaps. And you'll have to be prepared to take all the shit which goes with the drug lifestyle. He won't be cured overnight. I'll be there for you, but not all the time. And what about when you're at college? Who keeps an eye on him then?"

"I'm not going back. I'm taking time out to see this thing through."

"I see." Daniel said nothing else. Charles said nothing at all.

"I'll go to check that he's packed his things." Jake began to follow Sinéad from the room but she shooed him back.

"Promise me one thing before you go," Charles said, calling the dog to him. "Promise me you'll take the advice of whatever drug expert you consult. Promise me, Sinéad, that you will listen, very carefully, and that you will do everything he or she says. Will you do that?"

"I'll do that, I promise," Sinéad spoke lightly. This strangely intense Charles made her uncomfortable. "Scout's honour," she held up three fingers.

Charles smiled, his usual vague smile, and things

seemed much more normal again.

"Good luck then," he said.

Charles stood in the doorway for a long time after their car had disappeared down the avenue. He fingered the hastily written note Sinéad had left for Olivia and Albert. It briefly explained that Mark had returned to town with herself and Daniel.

She was taking on so much, marriage and Mark's cure, all at once. But she was her mother's daughter, in more ways than either she or Bea realised. She needed to take charge, just as Bea did. She was under the impression she'd taken charge of her own life when she in fact still... Well, that would probably sort itself out, in time.

Taking charge of Mark's life was a different proposition. She really had no idea, no idea at all, of what that was going to entail. He, Charles, had known, the day Mark arrived at Inverskena, that he was well and truly addicted. He'd seen it all before. Ahead of Sinéad there would be lies and broken promises, depression and maybe even suicide attempts. Mark would manipulate her and probably steal from her. He would almost certainly try to bring his addict and pusher friends home.

But there was a chance, an outside chance, that she might bring it off, help him to a cure. Charles hoped she would. He himself had failed, years before, when he'd been called on to save the life of someone he'd held very dear.

Jude's bell echoed, dim and lonely. Jake followed Charles up the stairs to her room.

CHAPTER SIXTEEN

For Bea the weekend passed in a necessary blur of work. Several times she had forcibly to keep herself from dialling Sinéad's number and once, a mood of utter desperation descending, she grabbed her coat and got as far as the car. Only Charles's warning, and the conviction that he was right, stopped her putting the key in the ignition and heading for Blackrock.

On Sunday the nursing home told Bea that Jude was herself again and she took this as a good omen. She would have to accept that her own grown daughter knew what she was doing.

She walked from the gallery to the Shelbourne to meet James on Monday. He was waiting for her when she got there. It was a cold day and she was glad to be enclosed in the dark comfort of the bar.

"Must we go and eat?" she asked with a shivery laugh as James kissed her. "It feels so cosy in here."

"I've booked a table. But if you'd prefer I'll ask if they can fit us into the Saddle Room."

"No. Once I've thawed out I'll be raring to go again. A port might speed the process."

Sipping her drink Bea watched James's face as he chatted lightly about his daughter and grandchild. He was wearing a navy double-breasted suit and grey wool crew-neck sweater. He really was, she reflected, a most civilised man. On impulse, she leaned across and kissed him fully and lingeringly on the lips. He looked surprised, but pleased too. And only faintly embarrassed. "What was that all about?" he asked. Bea laughed and, feeling a lot warmer now, slipped off her coat.

"That," she said, "was a proper thank you for my Italian pearls." She fingered them where they lay, a creamy contrast to her aubergine silk shirt. "They really are lovely, James."

They stayed another half-hour, enjoying one another's company, acknowledging the greetings of acquaintances, before leaving for the short walk to the restaurant. It was James's choice and too fashionable by far for Bea's taste. But, with its sage-green and blue decor, mirrored walls duplicating the glow from table lamps and vast arrangements of mimosa and fronds, it had undeniable style. Background music from a string quartet helped to soothe fevered brows. A *maître d'* moved smoothly between tables, remembering people and flattering egos.

It seemed to Bea that the faces at the tables were exactly the same as when she'd last lunched here. The plates in front of most held salads, but then the food, while good, was not what attracted customers. Discreet but vigorous people-watching was the main attraction. Eyes everywhere busily assessed newcomers, noted knowledgeably who was dining with whom. It was a restaurant to be seen in and Bea knew, without a doubt, that she and James were being closely observed. She nodded as people she knew caught her wandering eye and found herself in turn observing, unconsciously at first, who was dining with whom. It's contagious, she thought ruefully. A waitress, young, pretty and almost intimidatingly self-possessed, hovered with note-pad.

"I'll try the slivers of smoked salmon with citrus fruits to begin with," Bea said. The girl, with deeply disapproving expression, took her order. Bea, risking even more severe disapproval, ordered breast of chicken and leeks to follow.

A salad lunch was not an option she ever considered.

"I'll try the salmon too," James said and this time the girl nodded with vague agreeableness. "With a char grilled fillet of beef to follow…" The waitress left, with a loud sniff, and was replaced by a wine waiter. James chose a Chablis he knew Bea liked. Waiting for it to arrive they debated possible reasons for the waitress's irritability.

"Maybe she's on a diet?" Bea suggested, "Or maybe she's really an out-of-work…"

"Beatrice! James! How lovely to see you both! And together! What luck!"

Bea, heart sinking, recognised the voice and its owner's Bruno Magli pumps as they stopped beside her. She fixed a smile on her face and looked up at Lorraine Johnson, over-dressed and over-anxious charity fund-raiser. Lorraine was ubiquitous. In pursuit of funds she organised endless parties, dinners, balls and galas. She was a close friend of Olivia's and uniquely well informed about the private life of anyone with a useful bank balance.

"How are you, Lorraine?" Bea tried to be enthusiastic. James made as if to stand up and Lorraine fluttered long, burgundy-coloured nails at him.

"Please! Don't let me interrupt! I just had to say hello…" her eyes were fixed on the Italian pearls and

Bea, self-consciously, began to finger them. Lorraine, with a slight smile, turned to James. "You look so relaxed, James. Christmas must have gone well."

"Very well, thank you."

"I'm told, Beatrice, that you've got a most exciting exhibition coming up soon. Someone mysterious and new along with the usuals I hear."

Bea felt a flash of annoyance. Lorraine's information could only have come from Olivia and she hadn't spoken to her sister since meeting with Capek. Olivia was being really presumptuous, passing on the word that he was in the show without checking with her. It was almost as if she was intent on making it impossible for Bea not to show the Romanian. Still, now that she'd decided, word of mouth was about the best publicity you could get in Dublin. And Lorraine had one of the biggest mouths around.

"He's not exactly new, Lorraine. He just hasn't been shown in Dublin before."

Lorraine's voice dropped to a dramatic whisper. "Rumour has it that he's someone who suffered dreadful persecution in one of the collapsed Communist countries—and that Martin Scorsese wants to make a film of his life! I heard too that he's fabulously good-looking. Is it all true? You have met him?"

Across the table Bea caught James's quizzical, half-amused expression. She had not yet told him about her meeting with Capek.

"Some of it's true, Lorraine. And yes, I've met him…"

"Aha!" Lorraine's eyes were sharp with curiosity. "Well? Is he interesting?"

"Yes. Definitely interesting. I'll be showing five of his pictures. I'll send you an invitation."

"I suppose I must wait until then to know more." Lorraine sounded wistful. Bea merely smiled as the waitress, quite pleasant now, placed their entrées on the table. James, pointedly, picked up his cutlery. Lorraine, social animal that she was, knew better than to push things any further and made her goodbyes. With a sigh of relief James began on his food.

"So he's surfaced at last, your Romanian painter?"

"Yes." Bea, spearing a sliver of smoked salmon, hoped James would not ask when she'd met Capek. To admit she'd been back in town the day before calling him would be hurtful. "There's quite an interest developing in him, though the film thing is nonsense."

"So. He's interesting. He's fabulously good-looking," James was smiling widely. "But will he sell?"

"Yes. He'll sell. He's sold well already, in New York and at auction."

"Mmm." James helped himself to a glass of water. "Will I like his stuff?"

"No. It's not your kind of thing." James bought now and again but only pictures he liked, never for investment purposes. His taste was for figurative work, pictures with lots of movement and life. "Mmm. Why are you showing someone you're not keen on yourself?"

Bea looked at him in surprise. She sometimes forgot how astute James could be.

"Because I'm in the business of selling pictures—and there's a demand for his work. Anyway, I do like it."

Their main course arrived and they ate in silence until James said, "I missed you."

"I missed you too, James," Bea smiled.

"I've been thinking things over. Why don't we live together? We don't need to get married. We don't intend having children…"An expression of sudden alarm crossed his face. "Do we?"

"No, we don't." Bea gave a reassuring laugh, then fell silent. For James to suggest cohabitation without marriage was a huge compromise with his principles. He had obviously thought long and hard during their days apart. Bea was moved. But still she couldn't say yes. The timing was all wrong. She wasn't ready. She had an appointment to see her solicitor about her divorce that very afternoon. Maybe she would feel differently afterwards.

"Oh, James, I do appreciate the offer."

"That's not an affirmative, I take it?"

"Not for the moment, no." It was the moment, Bea supposed, to tell James about her divorce plans. But she just couldn't face the ensuing conversation, with explanations about Wally's visit and Sinéad's upset. In a week or two, when things were more sorted out, she would tell him everything.

"You could keep your flat." James filled her glass as he spoke. "Stay there whenever you wanted. You wouldn't need to work so hard. No more rushing about, no grabbing sandwiches. You could have leisurely lunches, champagne breakfasts. I want to give you those things, Bea. You deserve them."

Bea said nothing. It always came back to this, to James wanting to provide a life for her. But she had a life. She would not even think about living with him, or marrying him, until he fully understood that. It was the root cause of her inability to say yes and she wondered, sadly, if he would ever understand. She looked slowly around the other tables. At most of them, it seemed to her, the women who lunched had discontented faces. Married, wealthy, they were killing time, living

vicariously off other people's lives. She never wanted to
do that.

"No, James," she said firmly. "I do not deserve that
kind of life." They parted amicably an hour later.

Olivia called to the gallery the next day. Bea was
dealing with a customer and waved her through to the
office. When she joined her sister minutes later, she had
opened a bottle and poured two glasses of the
Chardonnay.

"To celebrate," she handed one to Bea. "Lorraine
telephoned. I must say, Bea, I was disappointed not to
have heard from you yourself that you'd decided to show
Capek."

"I've been busy. I thought you were staying in
Inverskena until the end of the week?"

"Albert had to come back. Work. Look, Bea, if you
need any help with this thing, any help at all, don't
hesitate to call me."

Bea looked at her sister in surprise. Olivia never offered
to help anyone with anything. Bea could only suppose
the social cachet which seemed to be growing around
Capek made her want to be involved.

"No thanks," she said. "Everything's under control."

"Good. Well, remember, I did offer. Must rush now.
I'm lunching."

She finished her wine quickly and left. Bea watched
her as she strode to her car, three-inch heels hitting the
pavement like bullets.

"Must be some point to those lunches I don't quite
get," she thought and went back to work.

Miroslav Capek's four pictures arrived, via a railway
courier, two days later. They'd originated, Bea noted, in
Tralee, so his hideaway was somewhere in Kerry. That

made it very much easier to understand his devotion to his secret place. Kerry, as far as Bea was concerned, came pretty close to satisfying the heart's every desire. With its westerly light and wild Atlantic views it was a painter's paradise too. Not that the picture in front of her looked to be greatly influenced by such obvious sources. The colours were subtler than before but the style was the same: hard-edged and unrelenting. She searched for a note. There was none.

Miroslav Capek telephoned later that evening, however. He was checking, he said, that the pictures had arrived. Bea reassured him and he ended the conversation with a polite wish for her good health. He promised to phone in a week.

On New Year's Eve Bea visited Jude, telephoned Charles and, finally, Sinéad. There was a limit, she told herself, to discretion; good wishes and normal courtesy had to be maintained. Daniel answered. He was friendly but distracted, loud music making it difficult to hear what he was saying. Sinéad, when she came on the phone, sounded breathless. "Few people here," she said, "Difficult to hear you..."

"How are you?" Bea raised her voice.

"Fine. Fine. I'm sorry. It's hard to talk. Hang on." She put the phone down and the music stopped. Her voice came on the line again. "How's work for the exhibition going?"

"Very well, thanks." Bea felt pleased. It was a very long time since Sinéad had taken an interest in the gallery.

"You'll come to the opening, I hope?"

"Sure. We'll see you then. Happy New Year!" A loud blast of music drowned her final words and the line went dead.

Bea, getting ready to meet James, considered the call. If Sinéad and Daniel were giving a party things must be going quite well with Mark. The thought cheered her and she was lighthearted as she slipped into a short, coolly sophisticated, black dress, hung a pair of long silver earrings from her ears. She was looking forward to the evening ahead but even more so to the dawn of a new year and new beginnings.

CHAPTER SEVENTEEN

S inéad sat and waited for Mark to wake up. She had
been waiting an hour already, since she herself
had woken at seven o'clock. Mark had been lying to her,
using her. She was determined to know what he was up
to and was going to get the truth, even if it meant sitting
by his bed all day. She had listened, credulously, for
three weeks, but that phase was over now. She was not
going to be taken for a gullible fool any longer. There
would be no more lies, no more manipulation. She would
see to that.

Working on Mark's cure had had its ups and downs.
Some of the downs had hit the bottom but, even so, it
had been looking good. He had begun to eat. He'd started
to sleep again too—real sleep and not just a dope-induced
zonking out like now.

Then, three days ago, he had left for a walk at midday
and not come back until late evening. He had been
dismissive of her fretting. Things were cool, he said. He
was clean, his head was together. He had needed to get
out of the house, that was all, needed some sort of normal
existence or he'd go mad.

Next morning he was gone before she got up. When
he didn't come back at all that night she'd gone

frantically to his room and searched it. The drugs, a collection of different types of pills in a plastic bag, weren't even well hidden. Furious, she realised how sure he'd been of her trust, how confident he'd been of his ability to fool her. Everyone had told her what it would be like: Charles, Daniel, the doctor, the drug counsellor. She had listened and thought herself on top of things. She hadn't even been close.

From what she now knew about drug abuse she guessed Mark's collection contained LSD, probably barbiturates and Diconal—or some of the other opiates he'd told her he was finished with. The size of the cache worried her. There looked to be far too many pills for just his own use. He must be trading, or selling.

Staring at the collection Sinéad knew Mark had been lying to her for at least two weeks. Not the first week, when he'd been really shattered. He had even helped throw out some friends of his who'd arrived on New Year's Eve. No. The lies had begun a few days after that, when he'd started taking the daily walks to Dun Laoghaire.

She looked at him. God, he looked dreadful. As a joke she'd bought a child's Mickey Mouse duvet cover for his bed. Under it now he looked like a very sick joke. His skin was the colour of dirty laundry and his hair, which for a while had begun to look normal, was again matted and limp. He made gurgling, distressed sounds as he slept. He showed no signs of waking and, for a couple of minutes, Sinéad contemplated leaving him, waiting downstairs. But she knew that wouldn't work. She had to trap him here in the bed, where he was vulnerable and couldn't escape her.

She had made sure of this by hiding all his clothes.

Apart from the T-shirt and underpants he was wearing when he'd fallen into bed she hadn't left him a stitch of clothing. Not even shoes. It was now mid-January and freezing hard outside. He wouldn't get far, if he did make a run for it, without being picked up.

Yawning, she sipped some tea and opened the book she'd brought to help keep her awake. He wasn't going to escape her this time.

But reading proved impossible. Not with her thoughts chasing one another. She was discovering so much. Not only about Mark and drugs but about herself too. It seemed to her now that she had known nothing, either about drugs or life, when they'd got back from Inverskena.

Mark, very subdued, had begun to shake in the car. Within minutes of arriving home Sinéad had been on the phone, making contact with a doctor friend, checking out a drug counselling centre. Both had agreed to help once they realised that Mark was refusing absolutely to go on a residential detox programme. That night, Sinéad had got physeptone on prescription and taken careful note of how she should use it to wean Mark off heroin. Next day she had spent several hours with a drug counsellor. Afterwards, she'd felt equipped to deal with almost anything.

Mark's mood had been one of the bleakest depression those first few days. He had paced continuously and refused to eat. Sinéad had spent long hours talking to him and, in three days, came to understand something of the hell that was his life. Something too of the monstrous reality of Dublin's drug culture.

"You don't want to know this stuff," Mark had protested, irritably, at the beginning.

Sinéad had been adamant. "Yes, I do. I want to know everything. When you began taking stuff, what you've been taking, how you get it. Everything. I need to know, Mark, so that I can understand what's going on with you. So that I can help..."

They were in the small living room. Mark, lying back in the black Le Corbusier sofa which was Daniel's pride and joy, looked at her with empty, disbelieving eyes. But he began telling her anyway.

"I was sixteen when I began to..."

"Sixteen! But we were together a lot of the time then! How come I didn't know? Sixteen...!"

"It was nothing heavy then. Smoking cannabis, doing magic mushrooms, that sort of thing..."

Sinéad stared at him. The trusted confidant of her teen years, the chubby-faced younger cousin she'd felt so protective of, had been taking drugs. She started to say something but Mark silenced her roughly and rudely.

"Shut up, Sinéad. Just shut up! If you're going to ooh and aah and make eyes at me like a bloody sheep I'm not going to tell you anything. You wanted to hear it—so just listen. Okay?"

"Okay." Sinéad was cowed by his ferocity, hurt by his hostility.

She reminded herself that this was a drug-induced personality. She reminded herself of it many times as he talked.

"I got the mushrooms early in the mornings at my father's golf club. It was a fun thing. They helped me get in with the crowd at school who were doing cannabis. But the spring I was studying for my Leaving Cert I began to get ambitious. Hash just wasn't enough any more. The really cool dudes in school were doing coke and acid. Remember me then? Fat, slobby little Mark. No one at home gave a fuck about me. No one anywhere else gave a shit either. I was a joke, a pimply blob to be patted on the head now and again. Like a dog. But the dudes in school reckoned me when I began to come up with money..."

He began to pick at his broken nails. He *had* been fat, Sinéad remembered. She'd never known it worried him. When he had started to lose weight she had thought it just a growing-up thing, the natural shedding of puppy fat. Puppy fat. What a cruel irony, given Mark's image of himself! At the time she'd been too wrapped up in her own problems to think any more about it. That was the year her mother had met James Harte.

Still picking his nails Mark went on.

"I got into coke and acid." He tried a crookedly evil grin. "Cocaine and LSD to you, little innocent. It got me through the Leaving Cert. I wasn't addicted or anything. Everything was cool. Then school finished and I was on my own. The dudes all split to the four winds. So that summer I started going into town. Pretty soon I got into the dope circuit there. It's not hard, once you've got the bread."

"Where did you get the money?" Sinéad couldn't resist the question. At first she thought Mark wasn't going to answer but then, abruptly, he began speaking again, fast and furiously.

"At home. My father's careless. He doesn't ask about things like missing cheque books because he assumes my mother's used them and doesn't want a row. The same with cash. And credit cards. I even worked a way of getting money from the bank, but that's riskier. Everything's possible when you're desperate. You find ways of doing things. Anyway…"

He shook a cigarette out of a pack and twitchily lit it. Sinéad shoved an ashtray his way, resisting an urge to open the window and blast the room with cold air. He drew hungrily on the nicotine, then blew a smoke circle. Sinéad knew he was gathering his thoughts and didn't push him. He wanted to talk now, she could see that.

She was unprepared for what came next.

"I met a girl." He watched the circle of smoke get bigger, then disappear. "Her name was Cleo. She was… terrific. I'd never met anyone like her before. She had long black hair and she was wild. She was three years older than me and she knew everything. She was brilliant, And she liked me. That was the strange thing because otherwise she didn't give a fuck about anyone or anything but her music. She played the flute and she was sort of a composer, when she wasn't doing heroin. Which of course was the other thing she cared about.

"She was into a heavy drug scene. It was really strange that she fancied me. She was beautiful, she could have had anyone. She said I reminded her of someone but she wouldn't say who. Her dead father, maybe. I dunno. Anyway, she laughed at me, called me a kid for doing coke. Heroin was the top, she said. She told me I'd never really be part of the scene until I started doing heroin."

He shrugged, pulled nervously on the cigarette. "I wanted to do it anyway, it wasn't just because of Cleo. She was the push, that's all. She got me some red-hot stuff and everything was cool. She had a place in town and I started to stay there a lot. I wasn't the only one. There were other dudes too but I was her *numero uno*. That's what she said anyway. I didn't care as long as I got to be with her. I felt good when I was with her. She could handle dope, she taught me things. She used to detox every so often and stay clean for maybe a couple of weeks. Then things would come at her, problems she had, and she'd start shooting up again. She always had money."

Mark coughed and put out the cigarette. He stared sightlessly at the grey skies outside. Sinéad wondered what he was really looking at.

"Then she went away for a while. Her mother died, I think. She didn't like to talk about her family. While she was gone I got the place in Trinity and I decided to cool it. I got myself detoxed and off the heroin. I wasn't really addicted, not physically anyway. I needed it when I was around it, that's all. I was really interested in the Trinity course and chuffed that I'd got the place. So I kind of drifted away from the drug scene.

"I was still doing coke now and again, but that was alright. I could handle that. Then Cleo came back."

He was looking at his shoes now, just as sightlessly as he'd looked at the sky a while before.

"She was really low. I think there was some pretty bad stuff going down in her family. She came into Trinity and found me and that night I started shooting up heroin again. I started spending time at her place again too and things started to get out of control pretty fast. Cleo couldn't seem to get enough of the stuff. She was like a zombie most of the time, zonking out and sleeping for hours and hours. But still she wanted me with her. In case she OD'd or in case someone got her stuff while she was asleep. In case she didn't wake up. She didn't trust anyone else and you couldn't blame her. She was in with all sorts of heavies, weirdos some of them. I was still interested in the Trinity thing and that kept me together, some of the time. But I was shooting a lot of dope too. I used to get pretty down, because of Cleo mostly. Which was strange because dope usually kills your feeling for everyone but yourself. But then dope brought us together so that made it different. Cleo started talking about killing herself but I didn't pay much attention. She talked about a lot of wild things. In May we went to the Trinity Ball. She cleaned herself up and did her hair. She wore a purply black dress thing and she was the most..." he searched for a word, "exotic woman there. We had sex before we went, for the first time in months.

"She brought her flute along, to entertain the masses she said. She brought some dope too. That was to entertain ourselves, she said. Things got a bit blurry after a while because I was drinking and shooting up but I remember her sitting in a tree in New Square at one point, playing her flute. After that I lost her but I was stoned so I didn't look much for her anyway. Just before dawn there was a big commotion and an ambulance came screaming in through the Pearse Street gates. Most people were gone by then and I was sitting under the tree, waiting for her to come back."

He stopped and it was a long while before he went on. When he did his voice was flat, unemotional.

"The ambulance guys went into a building and came out with a body covered in a blanket. I knew then Cleo wouldn't be coming back. I knew it even before some crazy kid rushed over and pulled the blanket away and I saw her. She still had the needle in her arm. She'd been dead a couple of hours."

He put his head in his hands and began to cry. He did it silently, his body heaving and shuddering but no sounds coming. Sinéad, close to tears herself, sat rigid and undecided. If she went to him he might stop talking and the talk seemed to be acting as a purge. But to sit and watch such grief seemed an unpardonable cruelty. A light tap on her shoulder resolved the crisis.

"I've brought some tea," Daniel said and she looked up at him gratefully. She had no idea when he had slipped into the room but he was, as always, there when needed.

He left and she poured Mark a cup of tea, liberally sugaring it.

"Tea," she announced and placed it on the small table beside him. She put a handkerchief into his hands. After a few minutes he blew his nose and picked up the cup. He began to talk again.

"Things got seriously bad after that. I started having nightmares about Cleo and how I'd let her down. But after a while I put things together and knew that she'd planned it. She'd meant it when she said she wanted to kill herself and she'd wanted to do it in a big way, on the night of the ball. She was like that. She liked scenes and to be the centre of attention. She'd have been really pissed off to know that there was only me and that stupid kid who pulled the blanket around for her final exit. Christ, what a crock."

He shook out another cigarette but didn't light it. He rolled it between his fingers and went on talking.

"The guards talked to me about her and everyone in college knew she'd been my girl. It kind of put me beyond the pale with a lot of people. Not that I gave a shit. But it did mean that the only time I felt really comfortable was when I was in the bars around town where they scored dope. That's where home was."

He grinned widely, seeming to think this a good joke.

He finished the tea and indicated that he'd like another cup. Sinéad poured.

"I used to go into a place off Grafton Street where I was considered a real heavy. I'd feel ten feet tall. I could see the kids there watching me, knowing who I was and thinking I was great. But I was in the pits about Cleo and doing more and more dope.

"With her gone, nothing seemed to matter. My allowance was never enough so I used go home for money and clothes when I thought there would be nobody there. Sometimes I misjudged and ran into my mother. I think she knew what was going on but she never said anything. Maybe she couldn't face it. I sold everything I could take from home. Then I got into trading drugs, coke and acid mostly. I was mixing with criminals. I knew the guards were watching me but I didn't care. I didn't care about anything. I saw Stephanie a couple of times in bars in town and I ignored her. She came over one night and called me a little shit and I laughed at her. It was about what I expected from her, with her poncy friends and rubbish about modelling. This was in the summer and I slept anywhere and everywhere. Outdoors sometimes.

About September I drifted into a squat in Castleknock. I reckoned that was about as far as I could get from home without leaving town. Somehow, some of the time, I functioned. I still went to lectures now and again. Just before Christmas I went and got myself detoxed. But when I came out I heard that one of the heavies who used to hang around with Cleo had got AIDS. I've seen someone die of AIDS and that really scared the shit out of me. I was so nervous I started shooting dope straight away. I got myself a nice little score for the holidays and went down to Inverskena with my mummy and daddy.

The rest you know."

He leaned back and closed his eyes. Looking at him Sinéad felt both sick and angry. She longed to put the clock back four years.

Instead she poured herself some tea. It was cold and she couldn't drink it.

Using physeptone they got through the next few days relatively easily.

On New Year's Eve everything changed. They had decided to spend the evening quietly, watching TV. At about seven o'clock Daniel answered an insistent ringing on the doorbell.

"We're visiting Mark."

The man who spoke was taller and older than his two companions. He had closely shaven hair and a skull earring. He stepped languidly into the hallway and the others, a fair-haired youth and thin, mousy girl, followed. All three wore leather.

"Tell Mark it's party time," the man with the earring said. The girl giggled as he hoisted a ghetto blaster on to his shoulder and turned it on full blast. The youth stayed close to the door and looked around disparagingly.

"He's otherwise engaged." Daniel took off his glasses, carefully placed them beside the phone. Sinéad's heart did a sickening somersault before lodging uncomfortably somewhere in her throat.

"I'd like you to leave." She forced herself to confront the man with the ghetto blaster. "If you don't I'm going to call the Guards!"

He didn't even look at her. He kept his eyes on Daniel, coldly calculating.

"Mark phoned us." He spoke softly. "He said to come and get him."

The telephone rang and Daniel, standing beside it, picked it up. Calmly he wished Bea a Happy New Year and signalled to Sinéad. Taking her cue from Daniel she spoke to her mother in as normal and friendly a fashion as she could. The heavy metal roar seemed to get louder as Bea asked how she was and Sinéad, suddenly furious, covered the phone.

"Do you mind?" she snapped. "I'd like to speak to my mother!"

The man grinned and turned off the music. Sinéad asked about the exhibition and, as Bea chatted, she had a desperate urge to tell her what was going on. As if reading her mind, the tall man grinned, and turned the music on full blast again. Daniel moved to face him and Sinéad, feeling quite sick, hurriedly finished the conversation. The girl began to giggle uncontrollably and the youth moved in from the door.

"I've changed my mind, Steve. I don't want to go to the party," Mark spoke from the top of the stairs. "So just cool it, man, and leave."

"Hey, Markie! Good to see you!" Steve, with a wide grin, displayed a set of silver-capped teeth which matched the earring. "We're offering fun times, my man. Get your gear and come on."

"I don't have any gear. I'm clean. Go on, Steve, split."

Mark came down the stairs, stopping three steps from the end. He looked at the girl.

"Get him out of here, Susie," he said. The girl grinned.

"Whatever you say, Mark. Nice pad you got here." She giggled, rubbed herself against Steve. "Come on, lover. We're wasting party time." She took him by the arm and Steve, with a scowl in Daniel's direction, left the house with her.

Afterwards, Mark refused to talk about the incident. Sinéad didn't pursue things but Daniel had a few harsh words with him about inviting trouble like Steve to the house. Mark, to Sinéad's surprise, agreed without argument. Afterwards, he was subdued and didn't talk much for a couple of days. Then he began to unburden himself again, recounting over and over the awful details of his four, drug-ridden years. Some of it Sinéad would have preferred not to hear. She didn't really want to know about the chances he'd taken to get heroin, about how and where he'd stolen money, about the criminal gang he'd been involved with. She found his naked hatred of his parents hard to take too and longed to shake him when he blamed them for all the mistakes in his life. She didn't, however. She went on listening and learning, and slowly she began to put the pieces of her own life into perspective.

Through it all she administered physeptone, once a day and in exactly the proportions prescribed. Toward the end of the first week in January Mark began eating again. Proper meals, four courses. He began to sleep normally too. He fidgeted less and glanced at the newspaper when it arrived in the mornings, watched TV with some interest.

Sinéad began cutting down on the amount of the substitute drug as she'd been told to. Soon Mark was on a minimal amount. He was sometimes depressed and moody and she knew it was time to begin the second phase of his cure. His psychological dependence would have to be broken. He would have to be motivated back to a normal, active life.

He seemed quite cheerful the day he announced his intention to take daily walks to Dun Laoghaire. He needed the exercise, he said, and Sinéad agreed. He began to leave each day at the same time and the walks did indeed seem to do him good, both cheering him up and tiring him out.

But the sea air and exercise had had very little to do with his improvement. Sinéad knew that now. Drugs, fresh supplies and new highs, had been responsible.

Mark groaned and turned on his side so that he was facing her. Behind closed lids, his eyes moved rapidly. Sinéad watched carefully and waited. After a few more minutes of troubled half-sleep he opened his eyes. When he saw her he closed them again and made a small, whimpering sound. Sinéad stood and leaned over, shaking him.

"Come on, Mark, wake up!"

He groaned again and struggled into a sitting position. He held up both hands as if to fend off blows.

"Stop! Don't say a word!" He kept his eyes closed and his voice had a cringing tone which set Sinéad's teeth on edge. She said nothing as he went on.

"Everything you want to say about me is true. I let you down. I'm a complete shit. I'm useless and..."

"Self-indulgent." Sinéad, her voice scissors-sharp, cut short his litany. "And now you can just shut up and listen."

Mark scowled, balefully watching her through partially opened, bloodshot eyes.

"You're all of the things you say you are, and more. You're being kind to yourself, in fact. But talking isn't enough any more, Mark. I know what's been going on. I know you've been meeting contacts in Dun Laoghaire. I know you've been lying to me and I know you've been supplementing what I've been giving you with your own supply of uppers and downers."

She nodded toward the drawer in which she'd found the pills and Mark's eyes rounded in sudden, fearful comprehension.

"All gone," Sinéad went on briskly. "Every one of them. Flushed down the loo."

Her cousin looked at her in appalled disbelief. Sinéad said nothing, waiting until his expression changed to sick despair. When it did she knew he had at last taken in everything she'd said.

"The whole lot?" His voice was barely audible. He licked dry lips and collapsed in a crumpled heap against the pillows.

"The whole lot."

Sinéad watched him carefully. His lips were white-flecked. She could see that his mouth was parched. She hardened her heart against an impulse to offer him a drink. He would go through a lot worse than thirst during the next four or five days if he agreed to what she was about to propose. He straightened a little, trying to speak. Sinéad silenced him with a look of icy intent.

"I'm only prepared to go on helping you if you do cold turkey. Either that or you leave. I don't care where you go. I'm not going on with this indefinitely. I'll be here for you while you come off—but you have to do at least fifty per cent of the work yourself. So," she took a deep breath, "there it is. I'll leave you to make up your mind."

Mark shivered, looked at her with loathing, and turned away.

Downstairs, Daniel was reading the paper as he breakfasted on yoghurt and toast. Sinéad wrinkled her nose when he offered her some of the yoghurt.

"Any coffee left?" she asked. He poured her a cup. "How is he?"

"Deciding his future." She briefly explained her ultimatum.

"Sounds fair enough," Daniel turned to the paper's financial page. "As long as you feel you can do it."

"I can do it," Sinéad said shortly.

She gave Mark a full hour to make up his mind. Standing over him again she saw that he'd become sweaty and feverish. Withdrawal had started already.

"This is your answer," he rubbed his brow. "I want to get off this gear. Only you had better be prepared for what cold turkey is like, too."

CHAPTER EIGHTEEN

B ea was becoming anxious. It always happened to her before an opening. It didn't seem to matter that 95 per cent of her shows were a success, that people *always* came to her openings, that reviews over the years had been uniformly good. She always became anxious.

There was less reason than usual to worry about the current show. The three other painters she was showing with Capek were all well known and popular. The show had been prominently highlighted in an *Irish Times* article with broad hints given that it could be a show worth keeping an eye on. A prestigious art magazine had said much the same thing in an article about "exciting things to come in a popular gallery."

Arrangements had gone well too, more smoothly than usual in fact. With just a day to go, the pictures, miraculously, were all back from the framer, the catalogue had arrived from the printers without a mistake, the caterers had already delivered the glasses and wine and the actress who was to open the show had confirmed that all was well. Feedback from around town indicated too that most of those she'd invited would be turning up for the opening. This last was not something to be counted on in Dublin, a city where invitations were accepted casually and often forgotten.

Miroslav Capek would be coming. He had assured her of this in his last telephone call, two days ago.

He'd been meticulous about phoning once a week but his conversation had been limited to monosyllabic replies to Bea's questions.

All of these reassuring points meant nothing as she walked critically around the gallery, adjusting pictures here and there, frowning as sudden doubts about positioning assailed her.

"Leave it and go home," she told herself, aloud and firmly. "If you allow yourself to change once you'll have to change the whole lot."

"Is this a private conversation or can anyone join in?" Olivia, enveloped in palest musquash, stood in the doorway.

"You seem to have joined in already," Bea said dryly, then shivered. "Close the door, will you? We're not all dressed for arctic conditions."

Olivia sauntered into the middle of the room and surveyed the picture-hung walls. From the faint whiff of brandy underlying her expensive perfume Bea guessed that she'd been having an extended lunch.

"Looks well," Olivia said. "Those," she pointed, "are the Romanian's pictures, I take it?"

"Yes. What do you think?" Bea was not simply being polite. Olivia's judgement could not be called a litmus test exactly but she did have an unerring instinct for the commercial.

"They're wonderful." Her sister's voice was breathily enthusiastic. "They're so...so...brave!"

Bea supposed this meant Olivia liked the pictures. She began turning off the lights.

"I'm having an early night," she said. "Otherwise I'd offer you a glass of something." Not, she thought as she looked at Olivia's unsteady progress around the room, that she needed another drink. "Can I drive you home, Olivia?"

"Certainly not! Why on earth would I want to go home at seven o'clock? What would I *do* there all evening, for God's sake?" She stood, waiting for an answer. Bea, a little wearily, realised the question wasn't mere rhetoric. "You could talk to Mark, discover what he's doing with himself."

The words were out before Bea could stop them. But once they were said she decided to go for broke. For weeks she herself had resisted asking questions or interfering. She had phoned Sinéad several times, holding herself in check and discussing pleasantries. She had not once mentioned Mark and Sinéad had not once hinted at what was going on. Bea felt the constraint dreadfully and she was damned if Olivia was going to escape all responsibility for her son.

"How is he, Olivia? He didn't seem very well to me at Christmas."

"Oh, Mark is looking after himself these days," Olivia was offhand. "He's left home, to all intents and purposes anyway. He telephones. Other than that I have no contact with him. Ungrateful brat."

Bea snapped off the last of the spotlights. "Do you know where he's staying?" she asked as Olivia followed her to the office.

"No, and frankly I don't care. He's been difficult as hell these last couple of years. Living elsewhere, having to fend for himself, may make him realise just how much I've done for him all his life." Olivia produced a compact, began to lipstick her already red lips. "Albert worries, though. He's constantly nagging about him. His son, his son, his duty to his son, that sort of nonsense. Just as well he's in Hong Kong this week. Gives me a rest from his harping about the boy. He seems to think Mark is not attending Trinity any more. Where he gets the idea, I don't know..."

"When did you last see Mark?" Bea asked the question with her back to her sister. To face her would have meant betraying her anger.

"Oh, God knows. Christmas, I suppose. His allowance is paid into the bank, and cashed, every month. He must be all right if he's spending money. Don't be so boring about him, Bea. He's twenty years of age. Old enough to look after himself. Sinéad's only a year older and she's married. Do you worry about her?"

Yes, Bea wanted to shout. Yes, I worry about her. I worry about them both. About your son because he's a drug addict and about my daughter because she is trying to cure him. I worry because I don't know if she can cope and I don't know if he's getting better. Instead she said, "I'm going home now, Olivia," and led the way through the gallery to the front door. Her sister, grumbling a little, followed her. While Bea locked up she looked at the black, starless sky and pulled the fur tightly around her.

"Hope bad weather doesn't keep your guests away tomorrow," she said. "What about the guest of honour? Is he coming?"

Bea decided to be deliberately obtuse. "Who exactly do you mean?"

"Capek, of course." Olivia was quite snappy. "He *is* the most important painter in the show, isn't he?"

"Not necessarily. The others have respectable reputations, a strong following. And I expect all my exhibitors to make an appearance."

"God Bea, you can be tiresome. People are interested *only* in Capek. I know that even if you don't."

"Exactly *who* is running this business, Olivia, you or me? I'm mounting a group exhibition. *All* my painters are important."

"Of course they are," Olivia stifled a yawn, looking vaguely along the street as she tried to locate her car. "But you've met him. You know how attractive he is. The man himself will be as big a hit as his paintings at tomorrow's opening, you'll see." She lifted a hand gloved in pigskin. "*Au revoir* 'till then. And do get some beauty sleep. You look as if you could do with it." She was gone then, coat swinging as she carelessly swept down the street to the SAAB parked near the corner. Bea, heading into the bitter night without the anaesthetising effect of alcohol, fumed at Olivia's overbearing presumption. Wondered about it too.

She hadn't discussed meeting Capek with her sister. Hadn't said anything about his being attractive or otherwise. Olivia's imagination was in overdrive. If she couldn't handle drinking lunches better she should abandon drink, or lunches. Or both.

Next day was cold, with heavy skies threatening rain which refused to fall. Bea had put from 6 to 8pm on the invitations but at four o'clock, finding the anxiety unbearable, she left the gallery and went for a walk. She wandered down Grafton Street, allowing herself become absorbed in the lively street life. She listened a while to a couple of very young violinists, wondering at their enthusiasm in the face of icy temperatures, then had a coffee in Bewleys'. When she could delay no longer, and gauged it time for the caterers to have things set up, she began a brisk walk back. She arrived in the gallery, flushed and breathless, to find the caterers at work and the phone ringing. It was 5.30pm.

"Hello?" She pulled off her coat as she picked it up.

"Are you all right? Why weren't you there? I've been ringing for a half-hour or more. Is anything wrong?" Sinéad's voice, high-pitched and anxious, came down the line. Bea laughed, then made calming noises.

"Of course I'm all right. I went for a walk, that's all. You *are* coming, I hope?"

"Yes, I'll be there. That's why I'm ringing. Daniel and Mark are coming with me. We're leaving now. See you in a little while."

Bea smiled as she put down the phone. Sinéad had been worried about her! Genuinely concerned! She chatted with the caterers, gave a few critical tugs to her olive-coloured silk pants and tunic and poured herself a glass of wine.

The first guests, a couple of academics who had bought loyally over the years, arrived just before six. By five minutes past the gallery was thronged, very early indeed to have a full crowd. Bea, busy greeting guests and ensuring that everyone had a drink, found herself all but swallowed up, completely unable to measure initial reaction to the pictures. She would have to stand back, absorb what people were saying, when the rush died down.

But the rush didn't die down. People kept on arriving, far more of them than she remembered inviting Sinéad, Daniel and Mark arrived with a cluster of other invitees. Bea barely had time to register how tired Sinéad looked, how much more alert Mark seemed, before the actress who was to open the show made a breathless entrance.

"I'm not late, am I?" She looked around the milling crowd, ran a hand through her tousled locks and appeared frantic.

"Relax," Bea smiled. "You're in plenty of time."

The actress was not, Bea knew, half so frantic as she seemed. It was simply that her role for the night was that of conscientious, concerned art-lover.

Olivia had met her at the Adams auction of Capek's picture and she had expressed an interest in his work. When she'd dropped into the gallery in early January it had seemed a good idea to ask her to open the show. Famously pretty, she had tonight opted for the severe chic of a simple grey flannel suit with velvet collar and buttons. Its minuscule skirt showed off her Fogal fine wool tights and her very good legs. Bea handed her a glass of wine.

"None for me, thanks." She shook her head, eyes busily picking the crowd for faces she knew, or should know, or who should know her. "I've gone all healthy. Given it up forever. I'll have a Ballygowan."

Bea spoke to a passing waiter and he reappeared in seconds with the mineral water.

"Impressive crowd," the actress said as she sipped. "Has the painter himself arrived yet?"

"None of the painters has arrived," Bea said.

"The Romanian is the one I want to meet. I've met the others before. Everyone wants to meet him." She made an expressive gesture towards the crowd. "But then you know that. When do you expect him?"

"Oh, any time now," Bea crossed her fingers. She hoped the actress wasn't going to concentrate solely on

Capek in her opening remarks. Through the crowd she saw her favourite art critic arrive. At almost the same time she caught Sinéad's eye and beckoned slightly. Sinéad, always quick on the uptake, began to make her way through the throng.

"I'm going to leave you with my daughter for a few minutes," Bea said, introducing them. As she moved away she heard Sinéad discuss a recent role played by the actress on TV and thought, not for the first time, how good her daughter was at handling people.

She greeted the art critic, glad to see he was in good form. Dauntingly honest, he could be acerbic when he felt he had to be. Usually he arrived for a viewing before the opening but tonight, like everyone else, he wanted to meet Capek.

The other painters, two men and a woman, arrived together. "Good crowd," said one, with a wry smile. "Good for all of us," Bea said and he grinned, agreeably.

"Relax, it's going well." James placed a light kiss on her cheek. She had not seen him come in and smiled a relieved smile as she returned his kiss. He was an oasis of calm and she was very glad to have him around.

Olivia and Stephanie, arriving just then, made a spectacular entrance. Olivia wore a sequinned tuxedo with black leggings, Stephanie stunned in thigh-high leather armoury boots.

"Mark is here," Bea said, as she handed her sister a drink. "He is?" Olivia looked vaguely around but Stephanie, spotting her brother, refused a drink and made directly for him.

Two of Bea's other artists sold pictures. Placing red stickers, she dawdled, picking up the tail end of conversations.

"...pretty bold stuff..." "...hear he's selling for mega-dollars in the States..." "...but *where* in God's name would I hang it?" "...is he here?"

This last she heard on all sides as she made her way to where the actress stood, looking genuinely frantic now as an elderly politician tried his charm on her. Sinéad made an apologetic face as Bea, firmly and politely, extricated her speechmaker from his attentions.

"Excuse us," she said. "Time to open things officially." She clinked a couple of glasses together and, in the expectant hush, announced the opening speech. To her relief the actress was gracious, light and generous to all the painters in the show.

Just, however, as everyone was about to clap and resume the serious business of gossip and drinking, the actress seized the hour and went for the drama of a passionately concerned ending.

"One painter this evening deserves a warmer than usual welcome." She tossed her hair, allowed her eyes to flash. "I am sure the others in this group show will not begrudge the extra attention to Miroslav Capek. He has come, literally, through hell to be with us..."

She stopped, allowing a well-timed pause to take effect. The crowd shuffled its feet, looked self-consciously around, wondering if the painter was amongst them. He would hate this, Bea thought, glad he hadn't arrived yet. *If* he ever did. She tried to concentrate on the speech.

"A few short years ago we watched, convulsed with shock, as our television screens showed us the execution which brought to a grotesque end the Ceausescu regime in Romania. We absorbed the shock in comfort, confident that such things would not touch us. But of course they will, they do so now, as the world order continues to change. Miroslav Capek, who suffered hideously under the regime, is a manifestation both of what was and what can be in the future. It is through artists like him that Eastern Europe, separated and beyond our ken for too long, will at last be able to share with us the wealth of its culture. Miroslav Capek has already shared his unique vision with the West through a number of successful shows in New York. We are privileged that he has chosen to live and work among us here in Ireland. I hope we know how to make him feel appreciated and very, very welcome."

The speech was well delivered and the applause was robust. Bea, clapping along with everyone else, wondered a little cynically what the actress hoped to gain. Publicity, she supposed.

"Thank you," she said as the chat level rose again and the party got seriously under way. "That was quite a...delivery!"

"You liked it?"

Bea was saved further discussion by the sale of another picture. As she stepped back from placing the sticker she collided with a body standing very close behind her. "Sor..."

The apology died on her lips as she looked into the penetrating grey of Miroslav Capek's eyes. A nervous smile touched his face.

"A very fine speech," his tone was dry. Bea was acutely aware of his closeness, of the smoky smell from his heavy, grey tweed jacket. Not a cigarette smell, more like that from a turf fire. Someone pushed against her and she fell against him. She moved back, quickly, shocked at the ripple of excitement the contact had aroused.

"Have you been here long?" Even to her own ears she

sounded nervous. She must sound like a fool to him.

"Two minutes, maybe three." He looked around, uneasily. "You have a big crowd of people."

"Yes. And you're the main attraction." Bea tried to keep her tone light. She did not want him to take fright and leave. She was aware of a hush developing as people began to notice Capek. The painter too became aware of it. His face grew tense and for brief seconds it looked as if he was going to made a run for it. But, with an expression which make it seem as if he was grinding his teeth, he silently stood his ground.

"Would you like to meet my daughter?" Bea asked. Sinéad at least could be relied on to be sensitive to his reserve. He didn't seem to hear her, so Bea touched him lightly on the arm. It was rigid. His whole body was rigid.

"Do they like my pictures?" He didn't look at her as he asked the question. His voice was hoarse. "Have they bought any?"

"Not yet. But they will. At your prices they sell more slowly."

"Of course, I understand."

"Bea!" Olivia, arms outstretched and beaming hugely, burst through the crowd. "How can you be so mean as to keep the man of the moment to yourself!"

Capek took a step backwards as Olivia stopped in front of him. This time Bea was quite convinced he was going to flee. She took his hand firmly in hers.

"I don't believe you've met my sister," she said, "though she acted as go-between with your benefactor for some time..."

Olivia, with kittenish coquetry, held up her hand. Bea, about to finish the introduction, felt a tap on her shoulder.

"Excuse me Ma'am, I don't mean to be rude. But I have a car waiting outside and time, as they say, is money. I would like to discuss the purchase of two of these pictures..."

Leaving Capek to Olivia's tender mercies, Bea turned to study the man to whom time was money. He was American; that was obvious from his accent. He was about forty-five, several inches shorter than she was, overweight with reddish hair and no eyelashes. None that were discernible anyway behind his oversized spectacles. Pinky-white eyebrows bristled in tufts above the frames.

"By all means," Bea smiled. "Perhaps you would show me which two you are interested in."

She followed him as he led a bustling way through the crowds towards the front of the gallery, noticing that he carried a carefully marked catalogue. He stopped in front of the picture Miroslav Capek had brought with him the evening he had first come to the gallery.

"We'll have this one," he said, "and this one." He pointed a stubby finger at a second Capek picture. "And I'd be obliged, Ma'am, if you could conduct our business quickly. My man is double-parked out there and I don't want a parking fine added to the bill."

He rubbed his hands together and Bea, glancing through the window, saw a silver-grey Rolls-Royce just in front of the gallery. It was, as the man had said, double-parked. Fleetingly, she wondered why the owner of such a car would balk at a parking fine, preferring to conduct his business in a frenzied fashion. Time, as he'd said, must indeed be money.

"Come with me," she smiled again, hoping to calm him down. "My office is this way. Do you want to pay a deposit, or the entire sum?"

"I'd be glad if you would put stickers on those before we move, Ma'am. Don't want any mistakes. My client wants those two particularly."

"Please don't worry." Bea affixed a red spot to the corner of each.

In her office the man sat squarely into a chair and placed a cheque book on the desk. Bea had never seen such freckled hands.

"We'll pay you a deposit of one-third of the price of each picture now." He began to write. "And the rest when I collect them. That all right with you?"

Bea, reading across the desk, saw that he had worked out the sum exactly. She saw too that the cheque was drawn on a Japanese bank.

"That's fine." She pulled a ledger toward her. "May I know who you're representing? You are not, I take it, buying the pictures for yourself?"

"Damn right I'm not. Don't care much for pictures. No, Ma'am. Good food and a day on the golf course are more my style. My name's Sam Winegold and I'm a corporate lawyer." He slipped a card across the desk. "I represent a company of Japanese bankers who're due to set up business in your Financial Services Centre here in Dublin. Seems your painter is something of an investment and they want a couple of his pictures on their walls when they move in a month from now. Well, time is money! If everything's all right I'll be going."

"Yes." Feeling slightly dazed by the speed of Winegold's delivery, Bea took the cheque, looking at his card as she stood up. "I don't know too many corporate lawyers."

Winegold, already halfway to the office door,

chuckled. "We're not such a rare breed, but we're an expensive one. Only the *very* successful can afford to pay me. Roughly exchanging the rate, dollar against punt, I'm worth £300 per hour." He moved through the gallery, talking loudly and at speed, oblivious of curious glances. Bea saw Miroslav Capek watching them and wondered what he would think of the home his pictures had found. "I couldn't take that kind of money from little old widows, now could I?" Winegold chuckled again but Bea, in the face of his sublime insensitivity, felt obliged to defend the widows.

"They'd hardly come to you anyway, would they?" she asked.

Winegold stopped, wagged a hairy, reproving finger at her. "You'd be surprised, Ma'am, you'd be surprised. There's a certain kind of American widow needs legal help and comes to me. Usually their husbands were businessmen who looked after things financial for them. They leave pretty helpless ladies behind..." He bustled ahead once more. "My mother is my best customer. If I were to charge her! Boy, does she waste my time." They were on the steps now. Bea, still slightly dazed, felt her hand gripped in his, firmly pumped up and down. "Goodbye Mr Winegold." He didn't seem to hear her. Still holding her hand he went on talking.

"The widows don't know how to use the time. They spend the first hour just getting their thoughts together. More time, more money wasted. I feel bad about it. A company would never do that. They realise time is money. I feel much better working for a company." He let Bea's hand go at last. "Great party you have here, sorry I can't stay. Good parties are as rare as forty-year-old dodos these days."

With a last, low chuckle he headed down the steps.

Before he'd even got to the pavement the uniformed chauffeur had opened the car door. Once inside, Winegold waved briefly before the car shot at speed into the night. Feeling slightly exhausted Bea turned to go back inside.

"He bought two pictures?" Miroslav Capek stepped through the door, a sudden wind lifting the dark hair off his forehead and giving him a boyish look. He was wearing the coat he had worn on his first visit.

"Yes. They're to hang in the offices of a Japanese bank. A lot of people will see them."

"I suppose so." His eyes held hers. "I am leaving now. I cannot stay. But I must tell you; I am working very well. My pictures are changing…I would like you to show a full exhibition of my work before the end of this year. Can you do that?"

"I don't know…I'd need to…"

"Please, do not say anything now. If the other three pictures sell, then we will talk. That is fair?"

"That's fair," Bea said. He reached for her hand, took it in his.

"I am thinking of you while I work," he said and raised her fingers to his lips. "Only of you." His kiss was a bare, whispering contact. He let her hand go, slowly, and touched her cheek. "I will telephone."

She watched him walk away until the cold drove her back inside. There she found Sinéad and Mark preparing to leave.

"So soon?" she asked. "And where's Daniel?"

"Bringing the car round," Sinéad said. "He has an early start in the morning so we're leaving now." Bea thought again how tired she looked.

"Good party, Aunt Bea," Mark said. "Nice pictures. Pity about some of the guests."

"Oh come on, Mark, you're always carping about something." Sinéad pulled at his hand impatiently and Mark grinned, obligingly allowing himself to be dragged away.

Bea went with them to the door where they waited for Daniel. Hoping he wouldn't notice she took a closer look at Mark. He was still too thin, still pale. But he was definitely more relaxed. a lot less intense. He'd abandoned the black leather too, for denim.

"Glad to see your new man sold a few," Sinéad said. "He's a bit of a hunk, isn't he? James had better watch out." She waved to Daniel as the car drew in to the kerb. "Good luck with the rest of the evening. I'll be in touch."

Bea felt strangely sobered and rather flat as she drifted among the remaining guests, exchanging greetings, dealing with another Capek sale (red stickers on two seemed to have helped a regular buyer make up his mind) and, at last, bidding the final guests goodnight. She didn't feel at all hungry and regretted the arrangement for a small dinner party later. She should, she knew, have invited Miroslav Capek. But he wouldn't have been interested and, anyway, she felt sure that he and James would not get along. They were too different.

That, at least, was what she was telling herself tonight. She was too tired, and too confused, to face the possibility that there might be another reason she hadn't invited Capek. And that it had a lot to do with her own feelings for the painter.

CHAPTER NINETEEN

B ea awoke early, and with a blinding headache. This, she knew, was the result of too much to drink the night before, and too little to eat. Refusing to allow James spend the night, pleading exhaustion, hadn't helped either. Acutely aware of his hurt, and feeling guilty, she had slept badly.

An almost cold shower, followed by fresh orange juice and a walk in the sharp, easterly wind on the beach, improved her physical condition dramatically. It was a help too that this was the last day of January; the morning was encouragingly bright, with winter definitely on the run.

When she could put it off no longer she walked to the village for the morning papers. She told herself there was no need to rush, that art reviews weren't necessarily used immediately, that they were often held over for days, that it didn't mean anything if the show wasn't mentioned. Unable to convince herself of any of this she covered the last fifty yards to the tiny newsagent at a trot. She bought all three dailies and, with enormous restraint, kept them folded under her arm until she was sitting with a coffee in the nearby delicatessen.

Two of the papers had reviews of the show. Both

were kind. Once she'd established this Bea sat back and read them properly. The first, written by a critic she was not familiar with, concluded that the show contained something to please most tastes.

All of the artists were mentioned, Miroslav Capek singled out. His pictures, the critic said, were strong, unequivocal. An exciting contrast to everything else in the show. They were works to be reckoned with and, in the critic's opinion, displayed evidence that the artist might become great.

The second review, written by the critic Bea particularly admired, was less fulsome in its praise. As a group show it worked well, he said. Three of the painters, whose work he was familiar with, showed of their best. The fourth, the Romanian Miroslav Capek—whose reputation was growing—had shown some pictures which were technically clever, startlingly effective. They would, the critic had no doubt, prove both popular and profitable. It was his view, however, that they inclined a bit toward the internationally anonymous.

Bea walked home thoughtfully. Overall, the reviews were good. It was the nature of critics to let their prejudices hang out. None of them was going to change the decision she had made before falling asleep the night before.

She had decided to show Miroslav Capek again. She would mount the full, solo exhibition of his work he wanted. She would organise it for October and let everyone see what he was really capable of—for better, for worse.

Bea was in the gallery later that morning when the call came from Charles. She knew immediately that something was wrong.

"What is it, Charles? Has something happened to the house? To you? You're not sick, are you?" Her heart lurched slightly at the thought that Charles, so often her bulwark, might be ill.

"No, Bea, there's nothing wrong with me. It's Jude. She's dying."

Jude had been moved to a smaller room. It was away from the main part of the nursing home and was very quiet. Bea was the first to arrive—Charles's 2CV was not made for speed and he refused to drive anything else. Bea, unable to get Olivia, had left a message on her answering machine. She had not phoned anyone else. It seemed to her that Jude's death was something her children alone should share. She had had neither affection nor concern for her grandchildren and so, Bea reasoned, it was not fair to expect them to bear witness to the distress of her death. As Jude's children, on the other hand, she, Olivia and Charles owed their mother life at least.

Jude was unconscious, breathing with difficulty. Bea sat by her bed, waiting. Death hovered several times over the next hour but Jude resisted it, struggling painfully on. The only sound in the room was of her rasping breaths, the occasional and terrifying silence when she stopped. Bea silently willed her mother to hold on until Charles arrived. She wasn't sure exactly why.

Maybe it was, simply and selfishly, that she did not want to be alone with Jude when she drew her last breath. But no: it was more than that. Because she also wanted her mother, quite desperately, to open her eyes and know, before she went, that she had been cared for. In spite of everything. To know, before she faced death, that life held forgiveness, generosity—even that terrible pity at the heart of love. Then maybe, just maybe, Jude would find it in her heart to express a caring sentiment of her own. To reassure her children, however vaguely, that bearing them had not been the ruinous curse she always said it was.

Jude stirred and it was Bea now who caught her breath. The woman in the bed was a wraith, her body barely disturbing the flat spread of the counterpane. A hand plucked at the white cloth, bony fingers seeking something to hold. Bea placed her own hand over her mother's but the agitated plucking did not stop.

"Jude," Bea called her softly. "Can you hear me, Jude?"

Silently, the hand went on plucking the threads of the counterpane. Bea lifted her mother's other hand, held it. It felt dry, light, withered. Like a leaf. She heard voices outside the door and then Charles, thank God, was in the room.

"She's still alive?" Bea nodded. He sat on the other side of the bed, indicating to the nurse who had followed him in that she should go.

"Has she said anything?"

Bea shook her head. Did Charles too, she wondered, hope for a word from Jude before she died? She looked at him, thin and bony and so very like his mother in appearance, and knew that he did.

They sat together, in silence, and watched as Jude died. Once, it seemed to Bea that she tried to say something. Her lips moved and her breathing came in several quick, painful gasps. But no words came. The nurse came back, bringing tea on a tray.

"She asked for you last night, Miss Hennessy," she said, handing Bea a cup. "It was very late so I didn't call you. I didn't think she would go so quickly. I'm sorry."

"Did she say anything in particular?"

"What she said didn't make sense. She was rambling a bit. Something about helping her upstairs. She didn't want to go alone."

"I see. Thank you." Bea bent her head. Jude had known last night, then, that she was about to die. And she hadn't wanted to be alone.

The nurse tucked Jude's hands under the bedclothes and left the room. As the door closed, the dying woman pulled her hands from beneath the clothes and, with infinite weariness, opened her eyes.

"Hello, Jude," Bea said. Her mother looked at her and then, slowly and painfully, turned her head toward her son.

"Just you two then." The words were the barest whisper. "Just you two..."

"Don't try to talk," Charles said gently. "There's no need."

"There was never any need." What might have been a smile touched Jude's lips. "Never."

There was silence for a few minutes until Bea asked, "Can I get you anything, Jude?"

"She...won't...come...now..." The words came in jerky breaths. Jude laid her hands, palms up, along each side of her body. Her wish was quite plain and Bea and Charles took a hand each. Jude, very slowly, closed her fingers over theirs. She looked straight ahead. Her lips moved again and the words came quite clearly.

"The strife is over," she said, "the battle done." She closed her eyes then and her hands, as life left them, slowly released theirs.

For a long time Bea and Charles sat by the bed.

Nothing in their mother's life had prepared them for her dying. She had never allowed them to love her and had never given them love herself. All her energy had been spent in hating. So there had been no place in her life for warmth or care. She had seemed impregnable. She had seemed immortal.

But she hadn't been immortal. Maybe she had never even been impregnable.

Tears, silent and hopeless, streamed down Bea's face. She should have been able to get through to her mother. There must have been a way. She hadn't tried hard enough. She hadn't tried at all. No one should be allowed live such a cold, dreadful life.

An arm went around her shoulder, lifted her from beside the bed.

"Come on, time to leave her now. The nurses will have things to do."

Bea leaned against Charles and for a long moment, together, they looked for a last time on the dead woman. Then they turned away and walked from the ward.

As she'd wished, Jude was cremated in Glasnevin Cemetery. It was a small funeral. There were no friends to mourn her since she had, years before, alienated anyone who presumed to that status. Not even all of her immediate relatives attended. Stephanie was away, on a modelling shoot which had come out of the blue and which was, she said, "the most important thing that's ever happened to me." Albert was away too, on a business trip. James attended and helped to bring the number of mourners to seven.

It was a bright day, but bitterly cold and with a sharp wind howling around the little chapel.

The ceremony was short, no one wanting to prolong a situation in which grief was so ambivalent. Proceedings ended with Sinéad, as Jude's first grandchild, reading from Louis MacNeice. Bea had chosen lines which her mother had often, in those darker midnight hours so long in the past, demanded be read to her. Sinéad's clear young voice gave them meaning as never before.

"There will be time to audit the accounts later, there will be sunlight later and the equation will come out at last." Jude, Bea felt sure, would have approved for once. The curtains opened and the coffin, with dreadful and speedy finality, slipped away.

Afterwards they gathered in the nearest pub. It seemed indecent to break ranks and disperse without at least a drink in Jude's memory.

"It's still hard to believe." Olivia was pale and seemed slightly shaky. She was dressed in black, relieved only by large silver earrings. She had not been home the day Jude died, had not learned of her death until late that night. As a result she seemed not to have come to terms with its reality. She fiddled with her beer mat. Shook the ice in her gin and tonic. Called for an extra slice of lemon. Mark, sitting opposite with Sinéad and Daniel, watched her closely.

"She seemed so..." Olivia searched for a word.

"Indestructible," Bea suggested gently.

"Yes. Almost immortal. But of course she wasn't..."

"No," Charles said. "She was only human, after all." This produced smiles and everyone relaxed. For an hour then they celebrated Jude, remembering examples of her verbal excesses, her bitchiness. It seemed by far the most fitting way to mourn her passing.

In the later afternoon Bea, Charles and Olivia went

to see Jude's solicitor. Bernard Ward was a pernickety
man, almost as old as Jude had been. He had offices on
the quays, opposite the Four Courts, and had insisted
they come to see him immediately, if not sooner. Since
Charles had no desire to hang around town, he had
asked to have it over and done with that day. Olivia had
grumbled, complaining that such formalities were a waste
of her time when the contents of the will were already
known. But she had come along anyway, driven, Bea
was sure, by a masochistic curiosity about how much
Jude had actually been worth.

"This will simply torture me," she admitted as they
sat waiting for the slow-moving Ward to appear with
the papers. "All her money going to fund the poetic
outpourings of idle brats."

"It might encourage a new Eavan Boland or a Brendan
Kennelly," said Bea.

"More likely to produce graffiti!"

Olivia tapped her fingers irritably on the side of her
seat as Bernard Ward appeared in the door. Sitting at his
desk he coughed, blew his nose and looked carefully at
each of them.

"I won't keep you long. Her will is brief." He adjusted
his bifocals and read: "I leave all that I possess to my
daughter Bea, on condition that at least half of the total
be spent on setting up a poetry foundation in my name
in TCD. She may do what she likes with the rest."
Ignoring Olivia's shocked cry, and the stunned silence
which followed it, the solicitor put the will down and
turned to Bea. "Your mother was worth almost a million
pounds. £902,003.00 to be exact. Her will was drawn up
almost twenty years ago. It is quite in order."

Bea, her head reeling, asked him to read the two

sentences again. Rather testily, he did so as Olivia, her
face white, got up and left the room. The second time
round Bea was able to absorb the will. She had been left
almost half a million pounds.

"But why?" Bea looked pleadingly at the solicitor.
"Doesn't she explain, say any more? Did she say anything
to you when she was drawing it up?"

"Nothing." Ward's prim voice was decisive. He closed
his mousetrap mouth and began to gather up the papers.

"The will is, and I hope it is unnecessary to remind
you of this, completely legal. I have seen to that. There
is no point in anyone in the family contesting its terms.
Now, if you'll excuse me, I will start on the arrangements
right away." His tone was dismissive.

"But how did she come to have so much money?"
Bea desperately needed to know more.

"Much of it was inherited from her father, I believe,"
the solicitor frowned at his watch. "And a few early
investments, made on your own father's advice, seem to
have paid off. Now, I really must ask you to leave."

Olivia was sitting in her car, still white-faced but in
an almost frenzied anger, when Bea and Charles got to
the street. She got out as they came towards her.

"The bitch! She couldn't even leave peace behind
her! But she won't get away with this. I'll contest. I'll
fight you, Bea. It's not fair that you should have all that
money. There's not a court in the land will uphold a will
like that."

Bea counted to five and took a deep steadying breath
before she exploded. "You're a fool, Olivia! You're doing
exactly what Jude wanted you to do! God, but she'd
really enjoy this! Here you are on the day of her funeral,
threatening court action...You're right on cue, Olivia!"

"Don't mouth self-righteous bullshit at me, Bea! You're half a million richer than you were an hour ago so don't lecture me on how I should behave! How do you think I feel…"

"Not so good," Bea conceded. "But court action isn't going to make you feel any better. We need to discuss the whole thing. Sort something out. It doesn't have to be done Jude's way. She's gone…"

They stood, silent and indecisive, in the chilling cold. Clouds had darkened the earlier sun and litter, caught by the wind, whipped around their legs. Seagulls, escaping worse weather on sea, swooped and shrieked bleakly down the river. Bea was filled with a feeling of desolation. We three have never, she thought, been so apart. Jude has done this.

"I'll sort something out," she said. "As soon as I get the money and have the bequest thing organised."

"There's no need," Charles frowned. "Frankly, Bea, I'd prefer if you didn't."

"And frankly, Bea, I'd prefer if you did." Olivia's nose was quite blue with cold, her eyes streaming. It was hard to tell if the latter was caused by grief, anger or simply the wind. "I think sharing the money is the least you can do. That is what you're proposing, I take it?"

"That's what I'm proposing. There will be no need, Olivia, for you to take me to court. Will we go now, Charles? It's damn awful cold here."

Charles nodded, took her arm. Olivia snap-closed a button on one of her black, fur-lined gloves and got back into her car. Bea and Charles walked slowly to where Bea had parked, a couple of hundred yards further down the quays. Charles had left his 2CV outside her flat in Sandymount.

"Why do you think Jude did it?" Bea asked as she put the key in the ignition.

"Because she wanted you to have the money," Charles said simply. "She made that will twenty years ago. She's had plenty of time to change it, to work out even more devious ways of creating dissension. But she didn't. She left it as it was—ergo she wanted you to have it. Take it, Bea. Use it. Olivia will recover."

"No, she won't. You know she won't. And I can't believe Jude wanted me to have it either." Bea bit her lip. "*Why* would she want me to have it? She did nothing but abuse me her life long." She got as far as Christchurch before a set of traffic lights stopped her. Studying the cathedral's façade she was aware of nothing but an awesome grey hulk. The lights changed. In Dame Street they got stuck in traffic. Charles made a disgruntled face.

"This is why I never come to town," he said. "Life is too short." Realising what he'd said he flashed a wry grin Bea's way. They laughed, briefly but together.

After Charles had taken his car and gone, Bea sat in the darkness of her flat and watched the city lights circling the bay. A ferry moved out from the port, passed slowly by the Baily lighthouse and onto the horizon. She was aware of a need to cry but tears refused to come. She could not, in truth, say she would miss her mother. But it was impossible not to mourn a life so unhappily and bitterly spent.

"She was eighty-one," she told herself, aloud. "A long life by any standards. But not a good life."

Drink, scorn for her children, malice: they had all kept her going. Maybe they were all she wanted. She'd never really wanted to be involved. Maybe the poetry too was only an excuse to opt out.

Outside it had started to rain. The sea, under the heavy sky, tossed in annoyance. Bea thought of the ferry passengers and hoped they would not have too rough a crossing. Tiredness made her turn at last, and reluctantly, from the world outside. The sea, the ferry, the city lights— they were all a distraction. The hours alone, in bed with her thoughts, had to be faced.

As she lay there in the dark, death's awful finality came home to her. Jude was gone, for ever and ever. And the answers to all the questions she'd never been asked were gone with her. No one would ever know now why Jude had lived as she did. There was no way now of knowing whether she'd ever felt any love for her children.

It had not been like this when Oisín died. Her mother's death, faced now, at last and alone, filled Bea with a sense of her own mortality. The woman who had given her existence was dead. Life's unremitting cycle was making its rounds, making her think, for the first time, of her own death. It had seemed too distant a thing ever to contemplate, until now. Almost something which happened to other people but would never come to her. She would never again feel so comfortably impervious to death's cold touch.

Much later, as the darkness began to lift toward dawn, Bea's habit of taking charge of her life reasserted itself. There was too much to be done to allow melancholy take over. Jude's money would pay for the divorce. And a holiday in the Cayman Islands. She would use some of it, too, to fund a magnificent catalogue for Miroslav Capek's October exhibition. The rest she would put into accounts for Sinéad, Charles and Olivia. Jude would not be pleased.

CHAPTER TWENTY

Sinéad was doing something she had often seen her mother do. She was watching the sea while she thought, letting the wide vistas of the bay put things in perspective.

Her grandmother was dead a week now and she hadn't been in touch with Bea since the funeral. There were messages from her on the answering machine; she hadn't replied to any of them. Not because she didn't want to. She did, desperately. But this was a time when she felt she should be offering support to Bea but she knew that she couldn't. She was afraid that as soon as they began to talk she would weaken, smother her mother with her own needs and problems. She was terrified of howling like a child for the sympathy of her mother's understanding.

All of her resentful bitterness toward Bea had gone. With it had gone confidence in her own judgement about a lot of things. Events of the past weeks had forced her seriously to assess her own life and how she had handled it. She had learned a lot about herself. The trouble was, she didn't yet know quite what to do with the knowledge.

Mark was getting stronger every day. But getting this far had caused pain and hurt to both of them. Mark,

from the depths of his anguish, his fury at needing her
and at her power over him, had lashed Sinéad with home
truths. Unable to deny their accuracy, she had faced
them. She was still facing them.

God knows how Daniel was feeling. He was quiet,
supportive as ever but strangely uncommunicative.

The five days of Mark's cold turkey experience had
been sheer hell for all three occupants of the house.
Mark had tried, at first, to go it alone. He had closed the
door of his room and told them to keep away. It was his
life, his problem. He would cope with the few rough
days ahead on his own. He would prefer it that way.

By the evening of the first day Sinéad and Daniel
were aware of him relentlessly pacing his room. For the
first time Sinéad wished she hadn't had the floorboards
bared and varnished. A carpet would at least have muffled
the unremitting reminder of his torment. It was worse
when they went to bed. His room was next to theirs and
so it was impossible not to hear his low moans, sudden
sharp cries and rushes to the bathroom.

"There must be something I can do," Sinéad
whispered. Daniel tightened his arm around her.

"Leave him alone," he said. "Let him try to make it
on his own. It'll be better for him in the end if he does."

A cry in the next room was followed by a thumping
sound.

"He's banging on the wall," Sinéad said. "Maybe he
wants someone to go in to him."

"No, he doesn't." Daniel was firm. "Try to rest. You
might even fall asleep."

He kissed the top of her head and turned away. Within
minutes Sinéad heard his breathing become regular. How
could he sleep? She lay closer to his large, warm body,

envying him, slightly resentful. Gradually, the agitated sounds in the next room grew fewer. After a while they stopped altogether. At about two o'clock Sinéad too fell asleep.

She awoke at four and knew immediately that Daniel was awake too. The moaning had started again, but this time it was punctuated with gabbling sounds. It was as if Mark was trying to say something.

"Oh God, I can't stand this." Sinéad got out of bed. Daniel said nothing. "I'm going in there."

She knocked loudly on the bedroom door. The sounds continued remorselessly and she knocked again. When there was no answer she opened the door. The light was on. Mark was huddled in a foetal ball in a corner. His arms were clamped around his knees, his eyes tightly shut as he rocked himself to and fro. As she watched he began to gabble again, unintelligible sounds but obviously an attempt to comfort himself. Perhaps it was intended to give him courage too. His face was pasty, white and sweaty. Even so he was shivering. She went to him.

"Mark." She touched his arm. He didn't seem to feel or hear her. She got the duvet from the bed and put it gently around him.

"No point," Mark opened eyes that were almost blind with pain. "Cramps. Diarrhoea too. Can't stay here long." His body gave an uncontrollable shudder. Sinéad left and came back with a heavy sweater and some hot, sweet tea. Not at all gently she persuaded him to don the first and down the second. Afterwards, and for a little while, he seemed better Sinéad went back to bed. But things had changed. The tea and sweater had re-established that they were in this thing together. For now anyway.

The next day was worse. Mark became feverishly hot mid-morning, and by the afternoon had what appeared to be a raging flu. His temperature shot up, his eyes took on a wild look. His body ached, he complained that his throat was on fire. The diarrhoea had passed but he was still suffering from spasmodic cramps. Sinéad, worried that he was going to die, panicked and would have gone for a doctor. But Mark, fixing her with hot eyes, stopped her.

"I don't want a doctor!" It was a command, weakly given, but absolute. Sinéad hesitated. Mark closed his eyes, as if blotting her, or something else, from sight. "I've seen this before," he said. "It'll pass. Nothing a doctor can do. Just get me a drink and leave me alone for a while."

It did pass. By the next day the fever had become less of a raging inferno, the cramps less agonising. But Mark's mood swings were wild and Sinéad stayed away for a lot of the time.

Long silences developed. She had got used to his pacing and now the silences unnerved her even more. Through them she waited for the furious sounds of anger when it gripped him. He was full of sudden rages. On the fourth day he turned one of these on Sinéad. She had brought him some tea and toast.

"I suppose you think you've done this for me? Held poor little Markie's hand while he kicked the dope habit? Well, my super-smug cousin, let's get something straight before you start polishing your halo! I did it myself. I'm not there yet but what's been done so far I did. Not you. I'm the one who went through it. I could have walked out of here any time—but I didn't. I stayed."

"I know that." Sinéad spoke quietly. "And you can

go the rest of the way too." It was not an issue. Of course he'd done it. But he was angry again and she didn't understand why.

"Bloody right I can. And without leaning on anybody too. Not on you, not on anyone. I don't need a prop. That's something you could learn from me, cousin dear."

"What do you mean by that?"

"I mean you could learn to stand on your own two feet." In spite of herself Sinéad was angered, goaded into defending herself. "Stand on my own two feet? What do you think I'm doing now? If there's one person in this family able to stand on their own feet it's me. I've always been my own person!"

"Come bloody off it, Sinéad. You've always been Bea's daughter. You made a lot of noise about being yourself, doing your own thing. But what did you actually *do*? You did Arts because Bea did Arts, not because you'd any interest yourself. And then, when Bea stopped holding your hand, found someone to hold *her* hand for a while, what did you do? Why you bit her and found yourself another hand to hold. Good old Daniel's this time. I might have fucked up my life with drugs, Sinéad, but you're no shining example of the life well used yourself, you know."

"None of that's true. It's not true at all!" Sinéad heard her voice rising and tried to calm herself. "How can you say such things? And what do you know about my life anyway? You've been doped out of it for years, you said so yourself!"

"Doped but not totally blind and stupid." Mark was shivering again. Automatically, Sinéad put the sweater she was holding around him. His eyes filled with tears and he turned away.

"Look, Sinéad." His voice was thick. "I could see what was happening to you because, through it all, I cared about you. You're the only one in the family I gave a toss about. I could see what happened to you when Bea got involved with that boyfriend of hers. You behaved like a stupid, jealous cow. Why couldn't you share her? Then getting married like that! Jesus, Sinéad!" He turned to face her. He was still shivering and his eyes were bright with unshed tears. "Why did you do it? To spite Bea? Or because having lost Bea, you wanted another prop?"

"Stop it, Mark, stop it!" Sinéad covered her ears. She didn't want to hear this. She didn't want to think about it.

"Okay." Mark's voice was quietly serious. "But I think it's time you had a powwow with yourself. Or with me if you want to. Maybe, while you're sorting me out, I could sort you out too? *Quid pro quo* sort of thing? Because I know you, Sinéad. You're going to get tired of this." He waved an arm around the room. "The housekeeping novelty hasn't worn off yet, and I'm a diversion for the moment. But in the long term you have to find something to do with yourself."

"I'm going back to UCD..."

Mark shrugged. "Why? What'll you do with an Arts degree? Come on, Sinéad, *talk*. It's good for me to listen! Keeps my mind off this."

His body went into spasm and he hunched into the sweater. Drinking the by now cooled tea, he spilled some. Sinéad began to talk.

They talked every day for a week. They talked late into the nights, going back, in the quiet of the midnight hours, to the source of so much of what they'd become.

They talked about the family and about growing up, about childhood dreams and fantasies. They shared memories of the events and moments which had caused real pain and of the highlights which had brought liberating laughter. And, with abandon and illumination, they discussed their parents, comparing notes on the kind of people they perceived them to be. Toward the end of the week they began to talk about themselves, about the kind of lives they wanted. By then Mark had started to eat and sleep and Sinéad had begun to face a lot of things about herself and about her relationship with her mother. She had also persuaded Mark to attend a daily counselling session.

She felt good about things by the end of the week, but extraordinarily tired. She knew she had been neglecting Daniel and promised herself she would make it up to him. The tiredness she put down to weeks of broken sleep so she treated herself to a few early nights. They made no difference to the way she felt. If anything she felt worse.

Then, one morning after Daniel had left for work, she dragged herself from the bed to be nauseously sick in the bathroom. When it happened for a second, then a third morning, she was forced to face what she'd been trying to avoid even imagining.

At the end of January her doctor confirmed that she was two months pregnant. She left the surgery and drove to the pier in Dun Laoghaire and, in pouring rain, she walked its length. Her head reeled as her emotions lurched from joyful acceptance of the life within her to hysterical rejection.

She was twenty-one and she was going to be a mother. She was just getting her life together, sorting herself out, deciding on her future. A baby had no place in her reckonings. And then there was Daniel. She loved Daniel, more and more as time went on. But he didn't want children yet. He had said so before they married.

She had offered to take the Pill and he had agreed, happy with the surest form of contraception so long as she was happy taking the responsibility. Only she hadn't taken responsibility. Not really. She'd been casual about taking the Pill, missing days and sometimes weeks. How, she wondered now, could she have been so careless?

Her face and ears were tingling when she got back into the car. Her waxed jacket had protected her somewhat from the rain but her hair and feet were soaking. It was almost four o'clock when she got home, leaving her just enough time to bath, organise Mark, pick up Daniel and get to Bea's exhibition opening by six.

Jude died the next day. Sinéad was upset, though mostly for Bea's sake. A mother was a mother and, good or bad, she was a part of you. Bea was bound to be distressed. But at the funeral she seemed to have things, and herself, in hand. So much so that Sinéad felt any offer to help would be superfluous.

In the week which followed she experienced a tiredness unlike anything she'd ever imagined. Daniel and Mark, noticing this, put it down to the effects of Jude's death and were solicitous. They had become quite friendly and the household, after six harrowing weeks, had assumed a more relaxed mood.

Now, watching the sea and thinking, things began to fit into place for Sinéad. She was feeling better too, not quite so tired. She would tell Daniel tonight. Now that Mark seemed positively on the road to recovery. Now that it seemed likely she and Daniel would have the house to themselves again in a few weeks. Now that the winter was passing. Now that she would soon be beginning to show.

She got into the car and drove home. As she came through the door the phone rang.

"Hello?"

"Hi, Sinéad. It's Stephanie. Look, I won't waste time. A little bird tells me *mon petit frere* is *chez vous*—true or false?"

"He does spend some time here, yes."

"My, but you sound cautious! You needn't worry, I'm not about to rush round with mummy dearest by the hand. I just wondered if we could meet for a drink tonight? You, me, Daniel and Mark?"

She paused and Sinéad waited for her to go on. She had never felt close to Stephanie and drinks with her, especially tonight, didn't appeal. On the other hand, it might be a good idea for Mark to begin building bridges with his sister. It might also be a good idea to get Mark into a milieu removed from the drug culture. Stephanie's idea of a place to meet was bound to be carefully civilised, tasteful in decor and clientele. Still, she wasn't going to make things easy for Stephanie. She was going to have to explain herself further.

"This is fairly out of the blue, isn't it, Stephanie?"

Her cousin cleared her throat before replying. "I suppose so. It's just that I see so little of Mark these days. He told me himself he was staying with you, actually. I'd just like to meet him. That's all. And I know he won't come along on his own. He will if you come too." She sounded flat, and sad too. As if the truth hurt. She sounded in fact like the Stephanie Mark had talked about during the long nights of their shared confidences. Like the sister he insisted was "one big front" and not nearly as sophisticated as she pretended. Nor half as confident. Sinéad heard herself agreeing to the pub Stephanie named and a time to meet.

Daniel, who had work to do, agreed to go only reluctantly. Mark was frigid about the idea at first but came round after some coaxing. Stephanie had chosen the modern bar of a city-centre hotel which was, when they got there, almost empty. Sinéad was relieved. She couldn't have faced the posturings of Stephanie's circle. Even the bar was a bit too self-conscious for Sinéad's taste. But Stephanie, who was sitting on a stool when they got there, obviously thought it the place to be. "Here I am!"

She waved gaily and, jumping down from the stool, rushed noisily to greet them. She was wearing a very large pale blue sweater and matching leggings. Her hair was caught back with a blue ribbon and she wore no make-up. She looked about fifteen.

"Thought you'd never get here! The barman's muttering about giving me a glass of white wine, for God's sake! Actually asked me if I was eighteen! It's not as if I haven't been here before."

"Big brother's here," Mark grinned. "What's everyone else having?"

Stephanie, linking Mark's arm, went to the bar with him while he ordered. Daniel and Sinéad found seats for them all.

"He's getting there." Daniel watched Mark thoughtfully. Brother and sister were laughing together, Stephanie with an arm around Mark's shoulder. He was still painfully thin but that very fact accentuated the family resemblance.

"Yes." Sinéad reached for Daniel's hand and held it.
"The trick now is to keep him motivated. His counsellor
is good and that's a bonus. He's sorting through a lot of
stuff about Olivia and Albert too. He's got months of
work, maybe years, ahead of him still. But once he gets
back on top of things in TCD the going should be easier.
Providing he keeps away from the drug scene, that is.
He's on his own now, more or less."

"Yes. You've done a good job. You handled the
situation well." Sinéad felt herself go slightly pink. Daniel
wasn't lavish with compliments.

"I learned a lot."

"It would have been difficult not to."

"About myself I mean. About how wrong I've been
about...a whole lot of things."

Daniel was watching her closely. His expression was
polite, nothing more. But Sinéad knew him well enough
to know that he was acutely interested in what she had
to say. Even anxious.

"I think it's time I stood on my own two feet." She
looked at him directly as she spoke. "I think it's time I
stopped hiding behind you and did something with my
life."

Daniel tightened his hold on her hand. He began to
say something. Sinéad put a finger to his lips.

"Don't speak. Let me finish. I've decided to do my
exams—but only as a challenge to myself. I'm dropping
the subjects I was doing and in October I'm going to
take up Psychology. I'm not an Arts student, there's
nothing for me in that area. If I'm going to be any good
at anything I feel it'll be to do with counselling and
psychology. I just know I could be good at it. And it
means letting go of Bea too. I've finally stopped expecting

her to live her every breathing moment for me." She came to a breathless and hurried halt. Her jaw was set and she was quite flushed.

Daniel let her hand go. He studied a point somewhere in the middle of the room.

"I wish I had a drink," he said. "Then I could drink to you, to your future. To your very good luck." He closed his eyes and gave a deep, and what sounded like a very relieved, sigh.

Sinéad looked at him curiously. "Is that all you're going to say! I've put myself through the wringer, faced demons, shaken them off and finally decided to grow up and all you have to say is good luck!"

"Yes. That's all you need now. You've done the rest yourself." He pulled her close, kissed her with such serious intent that she pulled away in giggling protest.

"Not here, Daniel!"

"All right, it'll hold. Now that I know." He paused, looked at her seriously. "I've had a few demons on my back this last week too. I thought I was losing you. I watched all the work and commitment you put into helping Mark and was sure you must think me dull and predictable. I felt you were growing out of me, regretting rushing into marriage."

Sinéad looked at him open-mouthed. "God, Daniel, how could you think that? I love you. That will never go away. And I could never have helped Mark without your support."

"Not true. You'd have done it anyway. Still, it'll be good to have the place to ourselves again, now that we know where you're going."

"Yes. But not for long, I'm afraid."

"You're not moving someone else in?"

"I am. But not until August. I'm pregnant, Daniel."

CHAPTER
TWENTY-ONE

B ea, at a concert with James in the Royal Hospital at Kilmainham, was feeling at peace with the world. In the month since her mother's death she had adjusted to life without her and got used to the idea that Jude was never again going to cause pain.

Bernard Ward, though greatly disapproving, had done as he was told and made Jude's money payable to various accounts. Bea had arranged for the half-million pounds for the poetry foundation to be administered by a poet in TCD. A man of enormous humanity and warmth, he was the antithesis of everything Jude had been. Bea could think of no one more suited to act in her name.

The rest she had divided equally. Charles and Olivia already knew they were richer by some £125,000 but Bea had yet to tell Sinéad. She was finding it almost impossible to pin her daughter down to a meeting and was resigning herself to a peripheral role in her life.

Losing herself in the music, a Beethoven string quartet played by a visiting quartet, she banished thought and began simply to enjoy. She liked coming to the RHK. Its size and stony grandeur made an occasion of any event. Beside her James seemed, to be almost asleep. He was just back from a two-week trip to the west coast of the

US and the golden glow he'd picked up there suited him.

"You should have come along. You'd have enjoyed Oakland," he'd said, briefly and pointedly, when Bea had expressed envy.

At the interval they headed downstairs for a drink. A cold night and threatening storm had not kept people away and a robust crowd pushed and shoved its way to the bar. Standing back, Bea willingly relinquished the battle for service to James. She was idly studying the *mêlée* when she saw Wally.

He had his back to her and was leaning against the curve of a stone arch. Even so, there was no mistaking him. Holding a drink he was concentrating all of his attention on the animated chatter of his blonde, and quite lovely, companion. Bea's first thought was to wonder how he had got hold of a drink so quickly. She decided he had left the auditorium before the interval. Then, as the shock of seeing him wore off, the real questions asserted themselves.

Wally never did anything without a reason, so what was he doing in Dublin? And how long had he been around? He had cut his ties with friends over the years and she had made it clear that *she* didn't want to see him. Was he in touch with Sinéad? Or was his companion the attraction?

Bea studied the blonde as closely as she could without drawing attention to herself. About twenty-four, she reckoned, and probably a model. Pretty enough, certainly, and slim enough. Her eyes shone adoringly as she looked at Wally.

"No ice, I'm afraid," James handed her a dry sherry. She almost grabbed it, effusively thankful in an effort to disguise a sudden panic as Wally turned their way. She did *not* want James and Wally to meet. Wally would not behave well and James, well, she just did not know how James would react. With dignity she supposed. She cursed the fact that she had not told him about initiating divorce proceedings. It would be hurtful and insulting if he were to find out here from Wally. She *had* to keep them from meeting.

"I don't really want a drink at all." She took James's arm. "Not without the ice. Could we go back upstairs now? It's quite chilly down here."

It was too late. Wally, with his now sulky-looking companion, was by her side. "Bea, my darling Bea! What a surprise!"

He put a hand on both her shoulders and grinned widely before kissing her lightly on the lips. Bea stiffened and stepped back. He was tipsy and, Bea saw, playing his "broth of a lad" role. A bright silk scarf gave a rakish look to his black wool dinner suit.

"You look wonderful, as ever!"

His eyes, openly and with a hint of possessiveness, slowly appraised her. Bea, uncomfortably aware of a silent James, turned reluctantly to make the introductions. His face had become a polite mask.

"James, this is Walter Treacy. Walter, I'd like you to meet James Harte."

The two men looked at one another, then James held out his hand. For a split second it seemed to Bea that Wally would ignore him. Then he nodded, briefly touched James's hand.

"Hope you're taking good care of my wife." He turned to Bea. "She deserves the best. She's a very special lady."

"You're quite right," James was very, very cool. "Bea *does* deserve the best. And I intend to see that she gets it."

"Oh?" Wally's eyebrows shot up. He ignored the smouldering fury of the girl by his side and continued to look at Bea. "And you're quite sure you can give it to her? That you know what she wants? She's mighty independent, my lady wife." James whitened a little and Bea felt a surge of anger. Wally had a gutter instinct for an opponent's Achilles' heel. And there was no doubt that he saw James as an opponent.

"I'm aware of *all* Bea's fine qualities." James's tone was light.

"Then you'll know all about her loyalty. Phenomenally loyal, our Bea." Wally's meaning could not have been clearer if he had waved their marriage certificate. Bea turned quickly to the blonde girl.

"Are you enjoying the concert?" she asked and the girl shrugged.

"Not really," she spoke with an English accent.

"Could *you*, perchance, be the reason my wife is divorcing me after twenty years?" Wally looked at Bea as he asked the question of James. Without turning she could sense how betrayed and humiliated James must feel.

His innate decency would prevent him telling Wally, in front of her anyway, what he thought of his crude behaviour. A strangled gasp from the girl told Bea that Wally's impending divorce was news to her too. She seized the moment. Two could play at Wally's game. "He'll be a free man quite soon, my dear. Didn't you know?"

But her anger dissolved as she looked at the girl. Her earlier confidence had completely disappeared and she looked hurt and very unsure of herself as she twirled her glass. She was obviously in love with Wally, or thought she was. She probably harboured dreams of marriage.

Wally would have used Bea as the tragic reason that this
was not possible. Well, he'd have to think up another
excuse after tonight. Knowing something of the pain
she must be feeling, Bea felt nothing but compassion for
the girl.

"We haven't been introduced," she said gently. "I'm
Bea Hennessy."

The interval bell rang as she held out her hand.
Without a word the girl turned abruptly on her heel and
headed for the cloakroom. Bea looked at Wally.

"See you in court," she said.

James drove, directly and in silence, to Bea's place
after the concert. Earlier, in the good beginnings of the
evening, he had suggested they end the night with a
meal. Neither of them mentioned this as they came out
into the cold night, got into the car and headed for
Sandymount. Dinner *a deux*, in the strained atmosphere
left by the meeting with Wally, was not an appetising
proposition.

Once in the flat, and without asking, Bea poured
James a large Black Bush. Straight, no ice, the way he
liked it. She poured a second glass for herself, also straight.
She had a feeling she was going to need it. James, after
a savour of the whiskey, came straight to the point.
"Why didn't you tell me you'd started divorce
proceedings, Bea?"

"I was going to."

"That's not an answer."

Bea took a long drink before beginning, slowly, to
explain. "Because it's something I'm doing for myself.
Not for us, not for you. I should have done it years ago.
You were right about that, James. But Wally never
bothered me all those years, never once came to Dublin

in all the time Sinéad was growing up. I dreaded the fuss, the acrimony, meeting him, the upset to Sinéad, the cost. But all that's changed now. He's come back and I don't want any part of him in my life. That's why I'm divorcing him, to be free of him. Completely free of him forever."

"I see." James looked into the dull gold depths of his Bushmills. He took a long drink. "And when you've got your divorce, what then?"

"Then I'll be in a position to make decisions...or at least *a* decision."

"I see," James said again.

Bea knew that he did. Knew that he saw very clearly that she was avoiding the issue of giving him a yes or no to his proposal of marriage.

"If you'd been more honest with me you would have spared me a lot of tonight's embarrassment," James spoke stiffly. "As it was, both myself and that young woman were made to look very foolish."

"I'm really very, very sorry, James." Bea flushed.

Of course she should have told him. It had been cowardly not to. She'd simply been avoiding another confrontation about marriage. But to James it must look as if she had behaved no better than Wally, playing her cards close to her chest, keeping her options open.

"It never occurred to me that you and Wally would meet. I never *wished* for you to meet."

"Obviously," James's tone was dry. He finished his drink and stood up. "I think we'd better call it a day, Bea. While we're still friends. If you decide, when your divorce comes through, that you're able to cope with the idea of marrying me, well, just give me a call. I'll be around." He picked up his coat. "But not indefinitely."

Bea walked silently to the door with him. She couldn't trust herself to speak. She did *not* want him to go. Not like this, not at all. She wanted very much for him to stay, to be her warm, loving James until morning. She could not even bear to think about not seeing him again.

But she could not promise marriage either. So she said nothing, even when they got to the door onto the street. Silently she returned his brief kiss, looked at him wordlessly as he ran a finger down her cheek.

Long after he had gone she stood there, aware of the cold but hardly feeling it. When at last she closed the door she had the feeling she was closing it on something precious, something she might live to regret for the rest of her life.

The flat seemed unbearably empty, lonely in a way she'd never noticed before. To divert her thoughts a little she listened to the telephone answering machine. There were two messages. One was from the artist she was showing next, the other was from Sinéad. "Just saying hello!" Her voice was cheery. "Hope you're well. We're fine. I'll be in touch soon and we'll have lunch. Byeee!" Bea snapped off the machine.

"That's it." She spoke aloud to the empty room, then began to pace. "I may have buggered up one relationship but at least I can take my relationship with my daughter in hand! Tomorrow, whether she likes it or not, I'm going to pay her a visit. And we're going to have a talk. I'm putting my life in order and she's going to hear about it. I want her to know I'm divorcing her father— before he tells her. And I want her to know about Jude's money."

The resolve, and a plan for the morrow, helped a little. But it was still a long, lonely night.

CHAPTER
TWENTY-TWO

Drawing up outside Sinéad's house early next morning, a Saturday, Bea felt angry. She had decided to allow herself feel that way; anger kept at bay the misery she knew would swamp her if she began to think instead of James.

The day, filled with snappy showers of hail, was typical of early March. It matched her mood perfectly. Sitting in the car she looked at Sinéad's home for several minutes. It was a new house, smallish, red-brick and part of a curving, cul-de-sac development. Its newness did not appeal to Bea but there was a certain efficiency about the design which could not be faulted. All the houses were neat. Grass-free, cobblocked gardens ensured that the imminent spring growth would not upset their order. Most of the houses boasted a burglar alarm. They were, Bea thought, the predictable, respectable, first-time houses of middle-class aspirants. She felt a lurch of disappointment that Sinéad should have chosen to live so cautiously.

Stifling her prejudices she got out of the car, and stood on the pavement looking at the house in front of her. It had no burglar alarm. The windows were uniformly curtained. It could have been the house of a stranger.

Her daughter had been living here for more than three months and she had never once been invited to visit. An invitation would, at the very least, have been a courtesy. Bea's anger gave a lively twitch.

Whatever her faults as a mother she deserved better treatment. Anger saw her through the gate and helped her keep her finger on the bell until a mildly irritated-looking Daniel opened the door. His expression changed quickly to astonishment and then, as he opened the door wide, became welcoming. It occurred to Bea that Daniel did not often allow himself to be caught off guard. "Bea! Great to see you! Come on in."

The warmth in his tone was gratifying. Sincere or not he was making an effort. She stepped into the bright hallway and found herself having to swallow, in one great gulp, her prejudices about the taste and style of those who lived in suburban Dublin.

Sinéad and Daniel had made this small house intrinsically and uniquely theirs. The hallway and stairs were, quite simply, a statement about their individuality, their uncluttered style of living. A large, black-framed mirror hung on the palest of lime-green walls. Underneath, on a pale green glass shelf, a wide black vase held an arrangement of white flowers. Opposite, a black telephone rested on a discreet black table. The colour on the walls was echoed in the carpeting. The overall effect was of dramatic simplicity.

"Nice." Bea smiled appreciatively as Daniel closed the door behind her. "Very, very nice." Ahead, through an open door, she could see part of the kitchen. High chrome stools stood beside a granite worktop.

"Sinéad's shopping." Daniel sounded apologetic. "She'll be back soon."

He took her coat and led the way into the living room. Bea looked around with naked curiosity as he left to hang her coat. The colours here were palest blue and black. Glass doors divided the living space from the kitchen so that light from a small conservatory at the back of the house flooded the entire area. A Turkish kilim picked up the honey colour from the varnished floorboards. Two black futon chairs had blue cushions and, by the window, Bea instantly recognised a black leather-and-chrome sofa as a Le Corbusier.

She laid the flowers she had brought on a low black lacquered table.

"Coffee?" Daniel appeared through the door from the kitchen, the smell of freshly ground coffee following him. He wore a faintly embarrassed look and Bea nodded, smiling with what she hoped was friendly reassurance.

"Look, Bea," Daniel began immediately she sat on one of the chrome stools in the kitchen. The coffee was Bewley's dark roast and Bea sipped appreciatively. "I'm sorry we haven't had you here before now."

"You wouldn't have me here now either if I hadn't invited myself," Bea pointed out, but mildly. She in no way blamed Daniel for the resounding lack of invitations.

"We've, ah, been a bit tied up since Christmas," Daniel said. "We still are, in a way. But we'd planned to remedy things in the next few weeks."

"It's all right, Daniel, I understand. Really I do. Let's say no more about it. Point is, I'm here now." She looked around the kitchen, bright and with an outdoorsy feel because of the conservatory, before putting down her coffee and slipping from the stool.

"Do you mind if I have a look around the rest of the house? Just to satisfy my disgusting curiosity."

Daniel laughed. "Why not!" He waved an expansive arm. "Here you have the kitchen. To the back you'll find a conservatory and upstairs you'll find three bedrooms..." He began to lead the way to the hallway but Bea, catching his arm, stopped him.

"Hold on, just a minute! I'd like to take it in." She played lightly with her fingertips on the black lacquered table in the dining corner of the kitchen. The chairs around it had pale oak frames and black fabric upholstery. "Which of you is so keen on black?"

"We both like it. It began with the Le Corbusier and went from there."

She followed him up the stairs and from room to room in wonder at a style which was so completely the antithesis of her own but which, nevertheless, she found she liked. The floorboards had been polished and the paintwork everywhere was pale. Splashes of colour in rugs and on walls gave startling life to the smooth simplicity of it all. Even the bathroom, small and windowless, managed to be interesting.

Its walls were lined with creamy tongue-and-groove panelling. The bath had been boxed in with polished timber to match the floorboards. Towels were folded in baskets and a calico Roman blind impersonated a window.

Only one room was at odds with the cool tones and ordered mood of the house. The smallest bedroom looked and smelled like unruly abandon. It was a turbulent mess of clothing, books, magazines, music tapes, and the air was sour with stale cigarette smoke. The bed was unmade and the curtains still closed against the light of the day. Even if Bea had not already decided she was tired of discretion it would have been impossible not to comment.

"You have a house guest." Her tone was dry.

"Ah, yes."

The expression on Daniel's face wished the room, and its chaos, into oblivion. He adjusted his perfectly straight spectacles, cleared his throat. "That's, ah, the reason we haven't felt free to invite you over. We've been a bit, ah, preoccupied. Well, Sinéad has been preoccupied, to be precise." He closed the bedroom door. "Why don't we have another coffee? Maybe you'd like yours with a dash of cognac this time?"

Following him down the stairs Bea felt a rush of sympathy for this straightforward, decent young man who had married her daughter. None of the existing situation was of his making, after all. Given the circumstances, he was being remarkably generous. Then too, there was the fact that she was his mother-in-law, a breed surrounded by social jaundice. God knows how he really felt about this visit. She heard herself give a small, involuntary click of exasperation at the situation she found herself in.

Daniel, pouring a dash of cognac into her coffee, looked at her sharply and tilted the bottle so that it became a liberal flow. Bea grinned, relaxed again. It was time to stop pretending, put their relationship on a more equal basis. Lifting the mug to her lips she caught his eye over its rim and held his gaze.

"Daniel, I know about Mark." She spoke slowly. "I've known all along only Charles made me swear not to interfere." She put the mug down. "But to hell with all of that. I've gone along with this silence and cunning long enough. *Now* I want to know how Mark is, how it's working out. Is he anywhere near a cure?"

Daniel had seemed impassive as she spoke. When

she finished he smiled widely, however, the open, relieved smile of someone glad to have things said at last. Bea guessed that dissimulation did not come easy to him.

"I thought from the beginning that you must have known what was going on. I didn't really see how Charles could have kept it from you."

"And how right you were! So—how is Mark?"

"He's fine. Really." Daniel grinned and looked at her, frankly friendly now. "He's got the drugs out of his system and is working hard on breaking the psychological dependence. Your calling today is a bit of a coincidence because he's in the process of moving out, going home. He's gone to meet Stephanie somewhere. They should be back soon."

Bea was silent. All this has happened, she thought, without me. Mark is on the way to recovery, thanks to Sinéad. She felt quite lightheaded with relief and, as quick tears pricked her eyes, bent her head over the mug again.

"I'm so glad," she murmured when she could trust her voice. "So very glad. Was it very difficult?"

"Oh, there were a few sticky patches." Daniel was laconic. "I don't imagine Sinéad would fancy repeating the exercise next week or anything. Certainly not now she's..." He stopped as a key sounded in the front door. "Talk of the devil," he grinned. "Do you want to surprise her—or will I tell her you're here?"

Bea felt suddenly unsure, the heart for a confrontation leaving her. She looked at Daniel, undecided, and saw his surprise as he grasped her confusion.

"I'll tell her," he said gently. "Wait here."

It seemed to Bea that he took an interminable time

telling Sinéad that her mother had come to visit. She was about to sally forth and hang the consequences, when Sinéad burst into the kitchen. Her cheeks were flushed and eyes suspiciously bright as she threw her arms around Bea.

"Oh, God, mother, it's good to see you. I'm so sorry I've been such a total slob about inviting you."

"Well," Bea extricated herself and took a look at her daughter. "I'm here now."

But Sinéad would not stand still. She buzzed around the kitchen, storing groceries, chattering gaily. She wore a loose white shirt over navy-blue leggings and seemed to have put on a little weight. It suited her. Bea had never seen her look so well.

"Mark and Stephanie will be here for lunch." Sinéad spoke from the depths of the fridge. "Will you stay and eat with us too?"

"Of course she will," Daniel was looking critically at Sinéad's purchases. "Did you remember garlic? And the mangoes?"

Sinéad, pulling a face at him, plonked two bags on the table. "I haven't become bovine quite yet," she said, then turned hurriedly to Bea. "We're having spaghetti—but Daniel makes a great sauce."

Bea, pondering Sinéad's remark about being bovine, watched idly as she and Daniel worked together on the lunch. They seemed genuinely happy, exchanging glances, once even touching hands. She offered to help but they both, adamantly, pooh-poohed the idea. She chatted to them in desultory fashion about the gallery, about a recent conversation with Charles. And she watched Sinéad closely. Becoming bovine. Putting on weight. Could Sinéad possibly? Bea tried to put the suspicion out of her mind.

The arrival of Mark and Stephanie put an end to any chance of more intimate conversation.

Mark, almost maniacally cheerful, made no effort to hide the fact that he was moving his things out, or that he had been staying in the upstairs room. As they sat to eat he positioned himself beside Bea and poured her a glass of Chianti.

"I'm not a tragedy any longer, Bea." he grinned hugely. "I'm all recovered and on the way to my first million. Once I get through with Trinity..." He stopped as Sinéad's frantic grimaces got through to him.

"Oh dear moi!" Stephanie giggled. "I do believe, *mon petit frere*, that you've let another family skeleton out of the cupboard."

"It's all right." Bea spoke directly to Sinéad. Her tone was dry. "I've known for some time. I bullied Charles into telling me." She turned to Mark, put a hand over his. "I'm very glad for you, Mark. It's really great to see you in good shape again." Impulsively, she reached an arm around his shoulders and hugged him.

"It was nothing. A cinch." Mark tried for a nonchalance which didn't quite come off and stopped abruptly. There was a small silence which Stephanie, sounding surprisingly tough, ended.

"Mark needs better friends. No more wanky people who can't cope. He needs people like Sinéad, and Daniel, and me."

Mark stood up, interrupting her.

"I'd like to propose a toast." He raised his glass. "To Sinéad. Without her I wouldn't be here today. And I mean that. Mightn't be anywhere visible, in fact. To Sinéad."

Sinéad blushed while they stood, glasses raised, and drank to her health. As they began to sit down Mark, face serious, proposed a second toast.

"To Daniel," he said. "Who also played a blinder—and without whose brilliant support things wouldn't have been possible."

The lunch was a less emotional affair after that, everyone drinking too much wine and relaxing into the intimacy of people who have little to hide from one another. Daniel's Bolognese sauce was as good as Sinéad had promised and the salad she herself had prepared won general acclaim. Afterwards they ate mangoes, Mark's request as a dessert. Unable to cook, he had offered instead to demonstrate his one, foolproof way of eating the fruit. Knife in the air he demanded attention.

"The mango is eaten thus."

Bea, watching with affection as he began his party piece, marvelled at how far he had come since the painful episode at Inverskena on Stephen's Day. He looked well, lean now rather than thin. His eyes were bright and hair once again full of crisp curls. Assessing him critically she realised he had the makings of a very attractive man.

"Bea, you're not listening!" Mark's tone was severe and Bea jumped guiltily.

"Sorry," she said and Mark, with a frown, continued his demonstration.

"Place the fruit on a plate. Thus. Take a sharp knife and cut through to the tip of the stone, thus. Cut right around, carefully. Then, even more carefully, insert a spoon inside the skin and over the stone. Work it all the way round, separate with a knife and...*Voilà!* It turns inside out."

Only it didn't. The fruit adhered stubbornly to the

skin. Mark, amidst gales of derisive laughter, tried and failed with a second mango.

An hour later the last of Mark's belongings had been packed into Stephanie's Golf.

"See you soon." Mark hugged Sinéad briefly as his sister impatiently blew the horn. He punched Daniel playfully on the shoulder, kissed Bea and then they were gone, Stephanie executing a sharp and noisy turn in the small cul-de-sac. Sinéad looked at the sky, still bright and with only a few mildly threatening clouds.

"Fancy a walk along the Ho Chi Minh Trail?" she asked.

Bea, hiding her surprise, immediately nodded agreement. In the past, when Sinéad was younger and had had something to confide, they had always walked and talked along the Trail, a causeway which ran from Sandymount Strand to the South Wall. It was dubbed the Ho Chi Minh Trail after the local politician responsible for putting it there; residents liked to say he looked like the Vietnamese revolutionary.

She couldn't think of a better place to unburden herself to Sinéad. But she wasn't at all sure that she was ready to hear what she felt increasingly sure Sinéad wanted to tell her.

After the drive from Blackrock they had the causeway almost to themselves and started along it at a brisk pace. Winter was dying on the high banks to the land side, new buds and greener grass appearing everywhere. On the sea side the tide was in, cold green-grey waters tossing against the rocks. The air invigorated and refreshed them, clearing their heads of the effects of wine and lunch.

Bea, bracing herself against a sudden squally wind, came straight to the point. She had a feeling that Sinéad's news would make conversation about divorce and money unseemly somehow.

"There are a few things I want to tell you." Sinéad, turning to look at her, linked an arm through hers in much the way she had always done. "Thought you might have," she grinned.

"Thought it the minute I heard you'd come visiting. You *never* impose, mother. There had to be a reason for you to come calling out of the blue."

"There was," Bea paused, took another deep breath and plunged in, head first. "I'm divorcing your father. I've started the proceedings already. I don't expect Wally to be helpful exactly and the whole business will take several months yet. But I'm determined to go through with it."

"Why?" Sinéad sounded merely mildly curious. "I mean, why are you doing it now? And how? I suppose you're talking about a divorce in the Dominican Republic or somewhere like that?"

"Yes. The Cayman Islands actually. As to why, I'm doing it for myself, just to be free at last. To be a single, divorced woman, have that status at least. It's what I've been, in fact, for twenty years."

"You're not going to marry James then?"

"I'm not going to marry James. James and I are no longer an item. We split up last night."

"Oh mother! I *am* sorry! What happened? Are you very upset?" Sinéad, impulsively, put an arm around Bea's shoulder. She had to reach up to do it and the position was so awkwardly incongruous that they both laughed. Compromising, Sinéad again linked her arm through Bea's and gave it a squeeze. Bea went on talking.

"Yes. I'm upset. So is James. It's partly my fault because

I haven't been able to make up my mind to marry him. But Wally was the direct cause of last night's break-up."

Sinéad listened with gratifying attention, and without interruption, while Bea related the events of the evening before. It felt good to tell someone. It was especially good to be telling Sinéad. Coming to the end of the story Bea realised that she was sorting out events as she talked, putting things into perspective. She was also, and the realisation was a shock, treating Sinéad as an equal, and an adult, for the first time ever.

"James was right. We couldn't go on as we were. The strain was becoming huge and we seemed unable to meet without the issue of marriage coming up. Wally's carry-on was simply the straw which broke the camel's back, so to speak."

"I can see that." They stopped and Sinéad looked thoughtfully at a sea which was becoming more grey than green as clouds filled the sky. "But I'm sorry it happened. I know I've behaved badly, like a proper cow in fact, over the last few years. Mostly it was because I was madly jealous of James. Jealous of how happy you were with him. I didn't admit it to myself, of course. I didn't even realise it for a long time."

It was Sinéad's turn to talk, and she did, telling her mother about her voyage of personal discovery in the months since Christmas. She didn't mention her pregnancy. Not at all sure how Bea would take it, she had decided to save that news until other things had been thrashed out. In every other way she was unsparing of herself, giving Mark full credit too for helping her see herself as she had been.

"Anyway," she gave a small rueful laugh as she rushed to the end of what she had to say. "Now that I've cleared a lot of stuff out of my head I can see James more clearly. I can see what an ideal companion he was for you. But that's all. I don't see him as your life's partner. I'm sure he loves you, in his way, and he's gorgeous and all that. But love is not enough. He doesn't really *appreciate* you. You deserve someone more imaginative, someone more, well, *exciting*. Someone who will let you be yourself, love you for being just that but encourage and stand by you when you need them. You've never had that from anyone, not even from me."

"Hold on, hold on just a minute!" Bea, laughing, tugged at Sinéad's arm, then stopped and faced her. "I can see that you've been sorting things out all right—but let's not go overboard! I doubt very much if the man you describe exists! Anyway, I think that what I need now is time on my own."

"But you've *been* on your own! All these years! Don't you *want* someone by your side?"

"But I haven't been on my own, darling. I had you. And I've still got Charles, friends, the gallery. Life has been full, and it's been good. It still is."

"Don't put me in the past tense," Sinéad spoke quietly. "You'll always have me. And I'll always have you. We've just gone through a bad patch. Maybe it was necessary, a way of helping us separate and lead our own lives."

"I think perhaps you're right."

They walked in silence for several minutes. Bea was surprised, even chastened, by Sinéad's clear vision of things, a little awed by her confident way of putting it into words. An unfamiliar feeling, which she slowly recognised as security, stole up on her. She had regained a daughter and more. She had, in Sinéad, a friend who would, from now on, stand by her. It was more, much more, than she'd hoped for when she'd set out for her daughter's house that morning. She said nothing of this when next she spoke.

"But I don't want a man in my life unless it's someone who will be separate too, allow me lead my own life in my own way."

"Exactly what I was saying!" Sinéad's laugh was triumphant, turning to a chortle as she went on. "What you need is a New Man! You know, someone who has got his head around the idea of women being equal and who'll treat you accordingly."

"Yes." Bea's tone was dry. "A rare and treasured breed, my dear, even twenty years after the contraception train." Sinéad looked blank and Bea laughed. "Never mind," she said. "All of them are spoken for anyway."

"Not all. What about your new painter? He looked okay to me. A bit intense but *very* attractive. And a man who's been to prison is hardly going to want a confined relationship." Bea, in spite of herself, felt a flush creep from her neck on to her cheeks. The memory of Miroslav Capek's eyes, his lips brushing against her hand, the feel of his tall body as she fell against him. She shook herself, pulled her collar around her face. Her voice was steady when she spoke.

"I don't think Miroslav Capek wants any kind of relationship just now. What he wants is peace. He's happy and very glad to be on his own."

"Wouldn't be too sure about that." Bea could feel Sinéad looking at her closely but refused resolutely to meet her gaze. With a small, meaningful, cough her daughter changed the subject.

"I got the impression there were other things you wanted to say to me."

"Yes."

They had rounded the head and Bea took a couple of deep breaths as the quickening, heavier winds rushed at them. They strengthened her resolve. If she and Sinéad were to be adult, trusting friends then there was something else her daughter should know. It was time she knew that she'd had a brother.

"When you were very small, a little more than a year old, I had a baby boy."

Beside her she heard Sinéad gasp, then stop. But she kept on walking, quite briskly, until Sinéad ran to catch up. She started to talk again, but looking straight ahead, as soon as her daughter drew abreast.

"His name was Oisín and he was beautiful, with huge brown eyes. But he had an incurable heart disease and he died when he was three months ond. You were a kind and good sister to him while he lived. But you forgot him, after he died, in the way that children forget the things which made them unhappy. And because you forgot about him, and never asked about him, I didn't talk about him to you as you got older. You had enough to cope with. Wally had gone, even before Oisín died, and you were missing a father. Asking you to accept your brother's death, remind you of him, seemed an unnecessary cruelty. As the years went on there seemed less and less reason to burden you with it. Even so, I always intended to tell you, someday. Today."

Bea was proud of the steadiness of her voice. When she had finished she looked at last at her daughter. Sinéad looked shaken and distressed and, trying to decipher what else she read in that strained face, Bea realised that her daughter was appalled. Walking slowly now, Bea waited, saying nothing. Sinéad needed time to come to terms with the revelation. Bea could only hope for her understanding.

It was fully five minutes before Sinéad spoke.

"It would be easy for me to say you should have told me. That was my initial reaction and if you'd told me this months ago I wouldn't have understood at all why you kept it quiet. But I think I understand now. At least I'm trying to." Her voice cracked, just for a moment, before she went on. "I think I can see how things were for you. My father, *his* father, had left. You didn't have the kind of parents who gave you much support—not emotional support anyway. It must have been terrible…Oh mother…"

Her voice broke and she stopped, turned and threw herself into Bea's arms. Bea held her as she went on, words muffled in the tangle of her wind-blown hair. "I don't think I've ever appreciated you as much as I do this minute."

"That's good." Bea, embarrassed, was brisk. "Now let's get moving again. It's cold and I haven't finished."

Sinéad stood back, tossed her hair out of her eyes and looked at her mother with a level gaze. At that moment she seemed, to Bea, very grown-up indeed.

She said, "I want to know all about my brother. About how he died and why exactly my father wasn't with you. But we have a lifetime to catch up on those things. I have something I want to tell you first."

Bea, recognising the inevitability of what was coming, controlled an urge to tell Sinéad to be quiet, not to tell her just yet.

"I'm going to have a baby." Sinéad's face was transformed as she said the words, happiness giving it colour and radiance again.

Bea swallowed, took both her daughter's hands in her own. "I thought you might be. I'm so very glad for you."

Now that it was out, now that she was faced with the fact of becoming a grandmother, she found she didn't mind. Not too much anyway.

"There's rain in that wind," she said. "Let's get back."

In the flat, Bea made tea while Sinéad talked about the expected late August date of her baby's birth and her plans to study Psychology in October. Listening, Bea became aware of just how much her daughter had changed in the time they had been estranged. Her interests were not what they used to be. She was much more analytical about life, about people.

With a mixture of regret and relief Bea acknowledged to herself that Sinéad had *needed* to be free of her, and her influence, in order to find herself.

The walk had given them appetites and Bea got together a snack of pâté and cheese with the tea. Sinéad, who had declared earlier that pregnancy had given her a constant ravenous hunger, began immediately to slice the cheese.

"There's one last thing I have to tell you," Bea said as she poured the tea.

"I don't know if I can take any more." Sinéad looked slightly wary.

"You'll manage this," Bea smiled. "It's simply that Jude left me some money."

Sinéad, her mouth full and unable to say anything, rounded her eyes in astonishment.

"Yes, I was shocked too," Bea admitted. "Everyone was, especially poor old Olivia. Anyway, the point of all this is that I've divided the money. I've put £125,000 into a bank account in your name. Maybe you could use it to buy a bigger house, now the baby's coming."

Sinéad found her voice. "I like that house." She sounded defensive. "But £125,000! You're not joking, are you?"

"I'm not joking. Now drink your tea before it goes cold."

In the days which followed Bea tried to get used to the idea of becoming a grandmother. Being delighted for Sinéad's sake, pleased about her obvious happiness, was one thing. Accepting her own, imminent role of grandmother was quite another. If Jude's death had led to an awareness of mortality, then becoming a grandmother seemed to hasten old age. She tried to envisage the baby, the joy she knew she would willingly share in when it arrived. But she couldn't—and in the end she stopped trying. Time, she hoped, and the reality of the baby when it came, would make her more enthusiastic about the role. Help her accept too that having a grandchild at forty-one did not automatically consign her to a rocking chair and shawl.

"Be positive, Bea!" she admonished herself, trying to put the image out of her head. "Ridiculous vanity!" she told herself too, and to more effect.

Easter was early that year and Bea, declining an invitation to visit old friends in Tuscany, opted instead to spend the holiday at Inverskena. Despite her resolution she'd managed only one weekend there since Christmas. She would take Charles out to eat, maybe the O'Malleys too. On the phone to Sinéad she told of the plan.

"Sounds great," Sinéad said. "Look, is this a private party for you and Charles or can anyone join in? It's just that Daniel has three days free at Easter and it *would* be nice to spend them at Inverskena. We had to leave in such a hurry after Christmas."

"Of course it's not a private party. It'll be good having you there."

Charles was in excellent form when Bea arrived on Good Friday. Jake was less appreciative but she ignored him.

"I've something to show you." Charles's impatience was palpable.

"Can't it wait?" Bea felt like nothing so much as a glass of wine and a chat with Alice, who had already called a greeting from the kitchen.

"No it can't." Charles was firm. "It won't take long anyway. Come on."

He led the way, almost at a canter, to the back of the house and into his studio. In the centre of the table, lit by the late afternoon sun through the window, there was a picture.

"There! What do you think?"

Bea didn't know what she thought. Even in the light the murky colours made it difficult to see what exactly had attracted Charles to such an obscure canvas. She could just make out a river, lots of fern, some figures on the bank.

"Looks...nice." She looked at her brother. "Is there something special. I can't see...?"

"There certainly is."

Charles didn't seem at all put out. "None of the dealers at the auction saw it either. I didn't myself. But I had a feeling about it, a hunch. It's grown stronger since I've brought it home. I haven't begun to work on it yet but I *know* I'm right this time. This is a very, very special picture." He touched it lightly and Bea looked again at the dull browns and greens, trying to see what Charles saw, feel what he felt. A brighter spot near the top caught her attention.

She pointed. "What's that?"

"That's the reason I bought it. A sunflower, I think." Charles looked at her, pleased.

"I'd like a drink now," Bea said.

Alice, in the kitchen, was sympathetic but not sentimental about Jude.

"She had a good innings," she said, "for a woman who abused her body the way she did. But it's a lonely enough thing when your mother dies. Changes you a bit too. I suppose you've found that out?"

"Yes. I've found that out."

Alice stopped what she was doing and sat a while. She looked tired. Bea had been in touch and knew her son had come through the operation. Alice confessed that he now needed a lot of nursing.

"But you know, because I know now that he has a future, and that he'll live a normal life, I don't mind at all. I can see him getting better every day."

"I've brought him something," Bea said. Followed by Alice's tut-tuts about extravagance, she left the kitchen to get the box from her car.

"It's very big-looking," Alice sounded doubtful as, puffing, Bea returned and put it on the kitchen table.

"Normal sized," Bea assured her and lifted the lid to reveal the computer inside. Alice gazed at it in silence for a long while.

"He'll love it, Bea," she said quietly at last. "God bless you. It'll make a world of difference. He'll really come on now, with this to occupy and educate him. Thank you." The simplicity and sincerity of her appreciation told Bea she'd done the right thing. She closed up the box again.

"Daniel will set it up for him tomorrow and Charles can give him lessons in using it. In a couple of months he'll probably be giving lessons himself."

Sinéad and Daniel, brought immediately on arrival to see Charles's latest picture, tried and failed to see what was special. After that Charles stopped talking about it. It was as if, having given each of them an opportunity to spot gold, he had abandoned all hope for them.

Before night fell Bea took a short walk across the fields around Inverskena. She picked some wild violet and cowslip, added kingcup. They made a sunny, springlike arrangement on the living room table. Fiddling and rearranging them she heard a bell ringing, faintly, from upstairs. She stopped to listen but heard nothing more. Jude had gone from Inverskena too.

They ate next evening in a restaurant where the low beams were reflected in the polished crystal of the glasses. Brian and Nora O'Malley came along, Nora looking much better than she had done at Christmas and with her hair grown back. It was one of those nights when the mood, good-humoured, was matched by the food, excellent, and seasoned by the ambience, which was mellow.

Much later, in bed, Bea lay for a long time listening, as she had so often done before, to the old house creaking around her. But she had never before felt lonely in the way she did tonight.

"What is wrong with me?" she wondered. "Everything is working out well. Things are so much better than they were at Christmas. I miss James, of course. But I can manage without him. And I don't want his kind of marriage. I've got a full life. Is it that I'm afraid my passion is all spent? That abandon has left my life, and sex?" She gave herself a mental shake. "Come on, Bea. Get a grip. You're a loner. Accept it. You're not a team player. You've learned not to be. But..." The small, inner voice nagged, would not be still. "All right," she sighed, accepting what it said. "I know how to be alone—but not yet. What exactly I'm going to do about it is another thing."

She fell asleep wondering, and dreamt of a place where cowslips and primroses grew on a cliff-top and large, bright canvases floated on the sea below.

CHAPTER TWENTY-THREE

The months between Easter and the high summertime of July passed quickly but un-eventfully for Bea. She hosted two exhibitions in that time, one a newish painter showing a clever set of portraits, the other a regular with her biennial show. The latter produced some lively pictures and Bea enjoyed showing them.

Canvases continued to arrive at irregular intervals from Miroslav Capek, always delivered by Iarnród Éireann courier. His colours grew stronger, more vibrant, but his stark, hard-edge style did not vary. Looking at them as they arrived, critically assessing each one for a frame, Bea found herself wondering what it would take to make him change, try for a more realistic style, or even more movement. It would be interesting to see how he developed after this show, which would certainly sell.

Her confidence in his commercial power was greatly boosted in May when the last of the pictures she'd sold in the January exhibition turned up at auction in London. It was sold, to an anonymous buyer, for twice the price she'd got for it. Her only regret was that Capek would not get the extra money.

On the other hand it meant that, without her lifting

a finger to promote him, Capek's reputation was growing. Even so she was nagged by the idea that he could be something else, be another kind of painter. His style was too deliberate, too calculated. He worked, she felt sure, under self-imposed constraints, though he hinted at changes happening when he telephoned. If only she could meet with him, talk to him. She felt sure she could make a difference. If only...

She tried to stop thinking about him. It wasn't easy. When he telephoned at intervals, the calls were brief. But they were reassuring. He was working well. He was pleased with what he was doing. He hoped she was too. He felt things were happening with his work. The mountain, the sea, the peace, they were all, he said, new influences on him. Maybe, after this show, he would be ready to try something different.

Fearful of breaking his concentration, of losing the productive mood, he would not come to town before October. When Bea said she would like to come to Kerry, pay a visit to his studio, he was gently off-putting.

"I am not yet ready," he said. "When we meet I want to be able to give you all of my attention. I am alone here and it is good for now. I see no one except the people in the village who sell me my food. And those at the petrol station, the railway station. It is enough for now. It is better this way. It is good for my work and it is good for me. I will telephone again in seven days."

He ended all of his calls in the same abrupt fashion. It was almost, Bea thought, as if he was afraid of saying too much, of becoming involved in a conversation.

During those months, too, Olivia took to calling into the gallery more than she used to. It seemed to Bea that her sister was quite often at a loose end. She could think of no other reason to account for the visits. Stephanie was getting more and more work, featuring in magazines and newspapers as both working model and gossip item. Mark was immersed in his business studies and was, according to his mother on a mid-morning visit, developing a new relationship with his father.

"I must say," Olivia was petulant, "he seems to pay *me* very little attention. He has plenty to say to Albert, huddling with him and talking business whenever they're together in the house. He's becoming quite passable-looking too—" her voice took on a wistful note—"but whenever I suggest lunch he seems to be busy."

She looked irritably through the latest of the Capek canvases to arrive. Bea, secure now in her own friendship with Sinéad, felt a stirring of sympathy for her sister. But only some. Olivia herself was responsible for Mark's alienation and it would take more than a few invitations to lunch, now that she found him socially acceptable, to gain his trust. Bea thought of Jude, of how she had made a lifetime's achievement out of uncaring selfishness, and hoped that Olivia would not repeat the pattern. There was still time to win her son back, but luncheon invitations were not the way. She tried, tentatively, to say as much to her sister.

"Maybe you should talk to him. Get to know him a bit better."

"Don't be ridiculous!" Olivia, pacing restlessly in the small office, made an exasperated sound. "He's twenty years old. What on earth would I talk to him about? They're all so boringly predictable at that age. Anyway, he's turning into a clone of Albert so that gives us even less to talk about."

"He might surprise you. Why not try?" Bea, watching

Olivia's nervous itinerary around the office, strongly suspected that her sister knew about Mark's drug addiction. Her reluctance to talk to him seemed to Bea an avoidance tactic.

"You *are* aware that one of Capek's pictures sold in London, I suppose?" said Olivia, who often changed the subject of conversation like this when things became even vaguely personal. Bea, aware that to pursue things would be fruitless, abandoned Mark as a subject. Time, she reckoned, would either distance mother and son further or bring them together. It all depended on what, if anything, Olivia decided to do about mending bridges. On present evidence she didn't intend doing much.

"Yes," Bea said now, looking thoughtfully at the growing pile of canvases. "I know he sold in London. It should put his prices up considerably for the October show. Help bring over some UK buyers too, perhaps." Olivia looked abstractedly at the canvases.

"I'd try to persuade Albert to buy one if he weren't such a damn philistine." She looked at her watch. "God, I need a holiday."

She's killing time, Bea thought. Killing time. She hated the phrase but it suited Olivia's dissatisfied spirit better than any she could think of.

"Olivia, why don't you get a job of some sort?"

"Me? Get a job?" Olivia snorted. "With 300,000 unemployed, who'd employ *me*? What can *I* do? And it's not as if I needed to work." She took a compact from her bag, studied her flawless face with a critical frown.

Her reply surprised Bea. It seemed to imply that Olivia had at least considered the possibility of a job. Encouraged, she went on. "You could set yourself up in some business. Open a boutique perhaps."

"I'm working on something," Olivia became vague, appeared to lose interest. She pointed a finger at her lip. "Look, I've got a cold sore." She sounded peevish.

"I don't see anything," Bea groaned. Olivia's mercurial conversations could be exhausting.

"Well, it's there. I can feel it." Olivia poked gingerly at her lip and the lines of dissatisfaction deepened along her smooth, pale cream skin. She snapped the compact shut. "I have to go now anyway." She gathered together the fashion magazines she'd brought with her and, with a brief wave, swept away in a dazzle of scarlet and white. Bea heaved a sigh of relief.

By the end of July most of the Capek pictures were with Conor Molloy and Bea was feeling very much like a holiday. It was looking too as if her divorce papers would not come through before the end of the year and she did not want to wait that long before getting away. She needed time to think and she needed to do it away from everything familiar. Away from everyone familiar too.

She had bumped into James a couple of times at social gatherings. It was the nature of the city, given its size and gregarious temperament, and she would probably go on meeting him. She wanted, for a few weeks at least, to be somewhere she could not possibly meet James, never in a million years bump into Wally. Sinéad was due at the end of August. A two-week holiday now would get her back in plenty of time for the birth. On impulse she rang her old friends in Tuscany, asked if they had a bed and was rapturously encouraged to travel immediately. Two days later she was on a plane to Milan.

Dublin slouched on through a hot and sticky August.

Daniel, waiting in the bar of the Abbey Theatre for Sinéad at the interval, didn't begin to worry until the last person had left and gone back into the auditorium. As the door closed and the noise inside died to an expectant shuffle he eyed the ladies', toilet doubtfully. It was unlikely that Sinéad had come out and gone back to her seat without him. On the other hand, she had been in there a very long time.

A burst of applause told him the curtain had gone up on the second act. Maybe she'd met someone she knew in there. Or maybe she was...No. She couldn't be. It was fully two weeks yet to her due date. On the other hand, she'd been enjoying the play. So what was keeping her?

He knocked twice, loudly, on the door of the ladies'. There was no response. He called Sinéad's name, cursing the upbringing and inhibitions which prevented him from simply bursting in. Still there was no response. "Would you like me to go in to see if your friend is okay?" The voice, calm and female, was balm to his ears.

"Would you? It's my wife actually, she's pregnant." The woman, whom Daniel remembered serving them earlier from behind the bar, smiled reassuringly.

"Take it easy," she said and disappeared through the door. In less than a minute she was back.

"Your wife's in labour," she said. "Go to her. I'll call an ambulance."

Daniel always remembered the next hour as a frenetic blur of set pieces. First there was Sinéad on the floor, a crazy mix of pain, fear and apology on her face as he tumbled through the door. He heard her say something about "rotten timing" before she closed her eyes and clenched her hands convulsively. He got down beside her holding her in the way he'd been instructed at the few pre-natal classes he'd managed to attend. Talking to her soothingly, in a voice that belied the sick fear inside him, he cursed himself for not having made the effort to get to more of the classes. Even more he cursed the lack of courage which had prevented his coming through the door to find her. If anything happened to her he would blame himself for the rest of his life. If anything happened...

Then the ambulance people, competent and reassuring, were taking her from him. He held her hand on the journey to Holles Street paced the corridor after she was taken from him again by hospital staff. He sat briefly in the fathers' waiting room until he was defeated by the cigarette smoke and controlled hysteria of a trio of first-time fathers, the cavalier machismo of a father of six. He was standing by a window, trying not to think about the evening Sinéad had told him she was pregnant, when a doctor tapped him on the shoulder.

"You can see your wife now," she said. "But we should talk first. We can do it more privately along here."

He followed her to a small room, helpfully festooned with mother and child advice. He tried not to see this as he sat on a hard plastic chair. The doctor, who looked to be about Sinéad's age but must have been older, perched on the side of a desk, the only other piece of furniture in the room. She was kind, courteous and to the point. The baby was premature. Labour had slowed down. There was a risk of complications.

"Please believe me, we're fully in control. Her own doctor is away but we're doing everything he would have done anyway. We're monitoring the situation carefully but it will be some time yet before she gives birth. The baby's heartbeat is very strong."

"Will it be all right for me to be present at the birth?"

"I can't promise that at this stage, I'm afraid. It's not a completely normal situation. But please don't worry. Two weeks premature is not a great deal and it may even be that your wife's dates were slightly out. You can go to her now. The very severe contractions of earlier on seem to have eased off."

Sinéad was sitting on the side of the bed. She was wearing a white smock and had caught her hair back. She looked very, very young. Daniel kissed her and she smiled.

"It's just the family taste for drama," she said. "I couldn't resist it. I'm sorry about the fuss at the theatre but to save my life I couldn't have got off that floor! I thought I was going to give birth there and then."

"I'd no idea it could happen so suddenly."

"Well," Sinéad pulled a face. "It wasn't all that sudden. I *did* have a bit of a warning. I had twinges this morning and again during the first part of the play. But I convinced myself it couldn't be labour. I didn't want to panic, raise a false alarm or anything. I kept hoping it would go away." She clutched at his hand. "Oh God, Daniel, two weeks premature! I hope she'll be all right. What did the doctor say to you?" Sinéad was convinced the baby would be a girl. They both were.

"Only that everything was going to be fine. Look—shouldn't we do something about getting your things here? Is Mark around? He's still got his key to the house."

"Yes, he's around and that's a good idea. Tell him my bag is—Oh, God!"

She ground her teeth together and gasped in pain. The hand holding Daniel's tightened to a clamp as beads of perspiration began to trickle down her forehead. She tried to breathe slowly and rhythmically, tried to concentrate on all she'd learned at the pre-natal classes. She had determined, from the very beginning, to have her baby naturally, had been adamant that she did not want an epidural or any kind of what she called "medical interference." She had wanted too to have her baby here in Holles Street, the hospital where she herself had been born. That part of her plan, at least, was working out.

Daniel, wiping her forehead, hoped the rest of it would work out too. Sinéad smiled at him, biting her lip in a way he'd seen her mother do. Her eyes, as the contraction passed, were worried.

"It's not right, Daniel. There's something wrong."

Daniel squeezed her hand, telling her not to worry He had never felt so inadequate in his entire life. Another contraction gripped her, a long one this time. As it passed Sinéad sank back on to the pillow. A nurse appeared, a jolly fair-haired girl with freckled skin and determined manner.

"You might feel better walking around," she suggested. "Some women say it helps to be on their feet. Want to give it a try?" She was helping Sinéad off the bed as she spoke. "You won't be ready to deliver for a while yet anyway."

"If it helps." Sinéad stood uncertainly on the floor. "Why not?"

The nurse draped a dressing gown around her shoulders as, with her arm through Daniel's, Sinéad began to walk slowly down the corridor. She covered the distance once before another contraction doubled her over in excruciating pain. By the time they got her back to the ward it had become obvious that hers was not going to be a normal delivery.

The decision to deliver Sinéad's baby by Caesarean section was arrived at reluctantly. Sinéad herself fought it. She wanted her child to arrive in the world naturally, was prepared to put up with the pain, did not want a surgical delivery. The medical staff were firm, the young doctor sympathetic; there was no alternative to a Caesarean section. Her baby had not completely turned in the womb and was in danger. A natural birth would take time and time was running out.

Sinéad, bitterly disappointed and weakly crying, heard only the last phrase. She acceded to the inevitable and was taken away for the operation.

Daniel waited. He felt numbed, powerless, cripplingly unable to do anything to help Sinéad, the medical people, even himself. His wife and his child might be in mortal danger and all he could do was sit. He had an urge to thump his fists on something, yell aloud his frustration. Instead he telephoned Mark.

"I'll be there in fifteen minutes. Less. Don't go away." Mark was businesslike. Daniel waited again.

He hadn't smoked for eight years but he needed a cigarette now. Anything to pass the time, to keep him from stopping every nurse and doctor who passed, pouncing on them for news of a patient most of them knew nothing about. He desperately wanted to go out for a drink but was afraid to leave the hospital. He wished Bea was there and cursed irrationally her need for a holiday. She was needed here. She was a mother, Sinéad's mother. She knew about these things.

And Sinéad needed her, though she hadn't admitted it. Only once, and then half-apologetically, had she wondered aloud about contacting Bea. Almost immediately she had decided against it. Daniel had no such qualms. Bea's presence would have been an anchor, a tangible and reassuring link with Sinéad.

He drank machine coffee and again tried to obliterate memories of the evening Sinéad had told him she was pregnant. They would not go away.

Totally unprepared for the news, he had felt shock at first, then a feeling of absolute panic. He'd had no idea, none at all, that Sinéad was pregnant. Afterwards he wondered at his own stupidity. All the signs had been there, but he'd explained them away. Sinéad's uncharacteristic tiredness he'd put down to sleepless nights and those endless talks with Mark. Her weight gain, which had surprised him because she was normally so weight conscious, he'd blamed on the endless amount of coffee and biscuits she shared with Mark. She'd been taking the Pill. She'd never said anything about wanting a child.

He'd retreated a little, into himself, as he'd absorbed the news. Sinéad had taken his silence to mean he didn't want the baby and had immediately set about convincing him that the pregnancy was perfectly timed, that it would be the best thing ever to happen to them.

"We'll have a wonderful child. She'll be tall like you and sensible like me."

He had stopped her with a finger to her lips, then pulled her close and whispered into her hair, "Be quiet, woman, let me think."

And because she knew him she'd been quiet, for a very brief while, while he came to terms with parenthood.

He found himself focusing on a pint of Guinness, full-headed and waiting on the bar counter. Fatherhood. A child which would be his, Sinéad a mother, things never the same again.

"Well?" The query had ended thirty seconds of silence.

"Well, well." He'd grinned, letting her wait a while longer. "How long have you known and not told me?"

He'd been angry then to discover she'd known for weeks, aghast that she should have imagined he would not welcome the baby. They had been lousy company for Stephanie and Mark when that pair had eventually joined them. Quite early in the night they had left them to their own devices and gone home.

To make love. That was the part of the evening he was trying hardest to forget now. All that life, all that love. Sinéad with her black hair tumbling on to her bared shoulders. Her small face laughing up at him, teasing, as he cradled her in his arms. Other images too, of other times. Of her black eyes when she was angry, her black eyes when she was sad. Thinking of her he could almost feel the creamy softness of her skin, smell the flowery perfume she always wore. He remembered her abandon when they'd made love that evening, the peace and loving confidences they'd shared afterwards. He tried to remember his life before he'd met her, a short sixteen months ago. He could remember nothing.

The waiting, not knowing, was becoming almost unendurable. He got another coffee from the vending machine. It was vile and reminded him only of the very good coffee Sinéad usually made. He finished it anyway and got another. It was something to do.

"I've brought you something with a bit more kick in it than that," Mark's voice, and his hand on Daniel's shoulder, were a blessed relief and distraction. Daniel turned and grinned weakly at him.

"What've you got?" he asked, and Mark held up a

brown paper bag. He patted a pocket and the sound of glasses clinked.

"The only thing for an occasion like this. Some strong Irish. Come on, let's find a quiet corner." It was after midnight now and the corridor a lot quieter. They found chairs a decent distance from the vending machine and Mark, with practised stealth, poured two large whiskeys. "Drink!" he commanded. "Talk later." Daniel drank.

Then he told Mark what the medical situation was. Then they both had another whiskey, slowly.

"I feel so bloody useless." Daniel ground the words out furiously. A combination of having the whiskey and saying out loud how he felt helped. Company helped too.

"My mother wasn't home," Mark said. "She might have come if she was. But Bea knows."

"Bea? You were talking to Bea?"

"Take it easy, man. Yes, I talked to Bea. She phoned when I was in the house collecting Sinéad's things. She'd been phoning all evening, she said. Seems she had some sort of premonition. She got into a bit of a flap when I told her things were happening and that Sinéad was in here. Maybe I wasn't, ah, delicate enough. Then when she wanted details I didn't have any. You were pretty brief on the phone, man, didn't tell me a lot. Anyway, I got the distinct impression she was rushing off to an airport to get a plane home."

"Sinéad will be glad to see her." Daniel didn't add how glad he would be himself to see her. "Pity she has to cut short her holiday. What sort of premonition did she have?"

"Just that things weren't good with Sinéad. Said she hadn't been able to shake the feeling since she woke this morning."

"Sinéad said she had pains this morning."

Mark, abruptly, and with a warning hiss, took the glass out of Daniel's hand.

"Be upright, man," he whispered. "There's a doctor heading your way."

Daniel stood, straightening his glasses, as the doctor, an elderly man this time, stopped in front of them. He pretended not to notice the whiskey.

"Mr Kirwan?"

"Yes."

"You have a baby son."

He had the impassive face of a newsreader, the staccato delivery of a man given to few words. Daniel sat down again. He tried to speak but the doctor held up his hand.

"Your wife is fine, considering. She's had a rough time and she is weak, naturally. She will need plenty of rest. But she should make a full recovery. No reason why she shouldn't enjoy another four or five confinements." Daniel's feeling of relief almost gave way to outrage. Was the man serious or was it his idea of a bad joke?

"When can I see her? See him?" He tried to keep the edge out of his voice.

"You can look in at the baby now. He's in an incubator but he's a strong child and we expect to be able to take him out tomorrow. You can see your wife for a few minutes after that. But *only* for a few minutes. And alone, naturally." He didn't exactly glare at Mark but the impression given was that males who weren't fathers, and who supplied whiskey on hospital corridors to those who were, were not what this doctor ordered.

"Wait for me!" Daniel commanded and charged down the corridor.

His son cried lustily all the while he stared at him, speechless and barely comprehending the reality of this person who would from now on be forever part of his life. He realised he was holding his breath and let it out, slowly and carefully. The tension in his body was replaced by a feeling of pure joy.

He thought at first that Sinéad was sleeping when he got to the small private ward. She lay very still and a nurse checking her chart was the only movement in the room. The nurse left immediately, warning him not to stay too long.

Sinéad's arms were pinned under the tightly arranged counterpane so that only head and neck were visible. He stood, studying her face. Strands of damp hair lay across her forehead. She looked tired, washed out in fact, but otherwise he could see no change. He wasn't sure what sort of change he'd expected, exactly. Some outward sign of what she'd gone through maybe. Some visible indication that motherhood had touched her. He looked along the bed. The bump had gone. That, at least, was a change.

"Have you seen him?" Her voice, clear and so very familiar, made him jump. Her eyes, in her white face, were darker than he'd ever seen them. But luminous too. He kissed her, gently and long, on the lips. She gave a great sigh of satisfaction as he drew away.

"That was nice. Do it again before you go..."

"Be glad to oblige. And yes, I saw him. He's beautiful. And noisy."

"Impatient. He's going to be an impatient person. I can tell. Look how he couldn't wait even to be born." She laughed, then, as the movement caught at her stomach, winced.

"Are you very sore?"

"Not exactly up to a night in Lillie's Bordello. But how're you? You look dreadful."

"Well, the father does his own bit of suffering, you know. Mark brought your things in. He was good to have around."

"From the smell, I'd say he brought in more than my clothes."

Sinéad grinned and pulled her hands from under the bedclothes.

"Hold my hand, Dad." Daniel held her hands, tightly. "We have no names for a boy," Sinéad said.

"No. Are you disappointed it's not a girl?"

"Of course I'm not. But so much for my feminine intuition!" She looked up at him, serious now. "There is one boy's name. If you agree, I'd like us to call him Oisín."

"Great name. Oisín it is." They were silent for a moment. Sinéad had told him about her brother and he had gone with her to visit his grave in Dean's Grange. "Bea knows you're here, by the way. She's coming home."

"I've ruined her holiday."

The protest was weak, unconvincing. Her hands in his grew limp and the elation with which she'd greeted him seemed to evaporate. The features in her pale face had become more sharply etched and under her eyes there were hollows he hadn't noticed before.

"You need some sleep," he said gently. "I'll be back in the morning."

"It *is* the morning." She gave a tired smile. Her eyes were closing. "I'll have Oisín with me when you come back, I hope." Another minute, he knew, and she would be asleep. He leaned down and kissed her. She smiled, her eyes already closed.

"That was nice," she said. Her breathing was regular as he left the room.

Mark was asleep too, lying on a bench downstairs when Daniel got there. Daniel shook him awake, steered him through the front door and waited in the street while he stamped his feet and woke himself up fully. Yawning, he got his bearings and tried to remember where he'd parked. Walking around Merrion Square to his BMW, they heard church bells begin to ring.

"Six o'clock," Daniel said. "What a night."

Sinéad had her son beside her when Bea arrived in the ward next day. She stood inside the door, eyes filled with tears and unable to speak. Exhaustion, emotional and physical, fought with relief as she looked at mother and son. Sinéad, wordlessly, held out a hand and Bea went to her.

"I thought I'd never get here." Bea put her arms around both of them, her voice husky. "I've been travelling for twelve hours. Everything went wrong— and I was so worried. Not knowing. How *are* you? How is he?"

"*I* thought you'd never get here either. And you can see for yourself how he is." As Bea lifted the baby Sinéad went on, carefully, "If it's all right with you we're going to call him Oisín."

But her mother, engaged in a mesmerised study of her grandson, didn't hear her. "He's like Daniel." She sounded accusing. "He's not at all like you when you were born."

"Mother, he's like himself. He's even got a name."

"Oh? What're you calling him?"

"Oisín. If you agree."

Bea agreed. Without hesitation and joyfully. When, reluctantly, she put the baby back beside his mother, she made a halting admission.

"You know something." She was blushing. Sinéad looked at her mother in astonishment. She had never before seen her mother blush. "I worried about becoming a grandmother. I don't feel grandmotherly and I worried about how I'd respond when the baby came. But all of that seems so ridiculous now. He's just adorable and wonderful. And that's grandmotherly enough for me!"

Bea's visit developed almost into a party when Daniel arrived with a bottle of champagne, Leonidas chocolates, and more flowers for a room already overflowing with blooms. Charles, equally laden, arrived on his heels. Oisín cried as the cork popped, stopped when his grandmother picked him up, fell asleep as they drank a first, then a second, glass to his health.

CHAPTER
TWENTY-FOUR

The weeks until the opening of the Capek exhibition passed with indecent haste. In spite of a relatively smooth glide through the arrangements Bea found herself in her usual state of pre-opening anxiety on the eve of exhibition morning.

She was also angry. The catalogue, into which she had poured money and devoted a great deal of thought, had just arrived on her desk. It was a sumptuous affair. Capek's pictures had reproduced to great effect on the strong, glossy paper, his life and career details were fascinating and impressive by turn. The designer had done Bea proud and it was, positively, one of the best catalogues The Hennessy Gallery had ever produced.

It would have been *the* best were it not for the blank space where there should have been a picture of Miroslav Capek.

The blank space made Bea angry. Capek had promised her a photograph. In a phone call shortly after Oisín's birth he had agreed to send her a couple of his New York publicity shots.

"My final canvases will arrive in one week. I will send the photographs with them," he had assured her. He had even made a joke, of sorts. "I am disagreeable-looking

in them—but then the camera never lies, they say." Bea
had laughed, glad to hear him sounding so relaxed. The
canvases *had* arrived, on time as ever. But search as she
might, she had been unable to find photographs in the
carefully wrapped package.

She had waited, impatiently, for his next weekly
phone call. It had not come. Nor had she heard from
him since. She was not even sure that he was coming to
the opening and she wanted to know.

A week before she had reluctantly phoned Olivia,
intending to ask her sister to act once again as a conduit.
She'd had some vague idea about asking Olivia to get
publicity shots from Capek's benefactor—who must by
now be anxious to get back the money he'd invested in
the painter. It could even be that her sister had a
photograph. Bea clearly remembered Olivia mentioning
that she had seen one. "Looks like a man to be taken
seriously," was what Olivia had said.

But Olivia was away on one of her thrice-yearly health
farm sojourns and would not be back until today, which
was much too late. So it had been that the printer, unable
to guarantee production of the catalogue if he was forced
to wait any longer, had gone ahead and printed. With a
blank space.

Bea's anger grew as she flicked through the catalogue.
For sheer style and discriminating professionalism it took
some beating, which made the blank space particularly
incongruous and brought the entire production
dangerously close to looking ridiculous.

She would, Bea realised, have to do something about
it. *What* to do was the problem.

It was unfair, inconsiderate, downright reprehensible
of Capek to treat her like this. Perhaps, now his work

had sold well in London, now that he was in demand, he no longer felt a need to humour her about the photographs, or even to bother coming to the opening.

"It's my gallery, my walls and my money funding all this. He could at least let me know."

It was *not* enough to tell her she was beautiful and cause her insides to churn. She was running a business. She could not afford to be sentimental. She should have insisted on the photograph long before now. She should have gone to Kerry too, to see for herself how his work was developing. Standing by the office window she glared, ran fingers through her hair and told herself to be rational. It was time to make a plan and to act on it.

"And be honest with yourself, Bea. What's the *real* reason you're angry? Hasn't it a lot to do with imagining you were more to him than simply the owner of an exhibition space? Isn't that what a lot of this is about, really? You *wanted* to mean more to him and your pride has taken a bit of a battering. You're also afraid that you've fallen for a subtle line in flattery. Oh, vanity of vanities, Bea, all is vanity. As Jude might have said." She took a deep breath and turned away from the window. "*Now* you're beginning to see things more clearly, my girl. So, if it was any other painter, someone you didn't fancy—" she winced as she faced the fact "—what would you be doing right now?"

Had she not been attracted to him she would not have been half as sensitive about his privacy. She would have gone through hell and high water to discover his Kerry retreat and then have sent someone, or gone herself, to get the photograph. But she hadn't done either of these things and right now the catalogue had to be salvaged.

As she saw it she had two options. The first was to go

with the catalogue as it was, attempt to laugh away the space or even turn it on its head and make it a talking point. She could hope that it added to Capek's mystique and, with a bit of luck, his prestige.

But it was a dodgy option and she ran the risk of ridicule if it didn't work. The art world was competitive; there were too many people willing and anxious to turn the laugh on her.

No. She would have to go for the second option—which was to get hold of a photograph, somehow. If she got one today she could have several hundred copies run off overnight and insert them by hand early tomorrow morning. It *could* be done. Sinéad would help.

Which made Olivia her only hope.

She picked up the phone and dialled her sister's number. It was answered immediately by a breathless Stephanie. No, she said, her mother wasn't home yet. She was expected around noon.

"Look Steph," Bea spoke urgently, "you don't by any chance know if Olivia has any photographs of Miroslav Capek, do you? I need one badly for the catalogue."

"Sorry, Aunt Bea, haven't a clue. She may have dozens for all I know but she certainly doesn't leave them lying around. Anything like that would be in her study—strictly out of bounds to the rest of the household, I'm afraid."

"I don't suppose you'd break a house rule for me?"

"Would if I'd the time but I'm late as it is. Really I am."

Bea sighed, believing her. She tried another tack. "I *absolutely* must have a picture of Capek. I'll come out there myself, around midday, to meet Olivia. But in case she's delayed, could you leave a key with a neighbour for me?"

"No need. Teresa will be here, cleaning, until three o'clock. She'll let you in. I'll tell her to expect you. Have to run now."

Bea, driving along the Stillorgan Road, tried to remember when last she'd visited her sister's home in Foxrock. Three years ago? Four years? And even then it had been by invitation, for a celebration of some kind. She seemed to remember that Olivia and Albert had, unaccountably, been fêting their wedding anniversary.

It was after eleven o'clock when she turned into the broad avenue they had moved to in the mid-eighties, when Albert's fortunes had begun to spiral upwards. The houses, though relatively new, were large and stately with well-tended gardens and swagged curtains on every window. It was deeply hushed, conspicuously free of children, dogs or any kind of street life. Bea rang the bell of The Laurels, standing back a little as its peal echoed through the house. Before it had faded she heard heavy footsteps coming toward the door.

"Come on, oh come on…" She was almost dancing with impatience as locks were slowly released and the door pulled deliberately open.

The woman whose malevolent gaze met hers was more a force than a personality. Large and square, she seemed, like a wall, to fill the entire doorway. Her hair could have been any colour but for the moment was a yellowy orange, wildly at odds with her washed-out complexion and pale, angry eyes. Belligerent was the word which immediately came to Bea's mind and the impression was confirmed when the woman spoke. She had a muscular voice.

"You're the sister, I suppose? I was just sitting down to my cup of tea. Well deserved, I might add."

"You must be Teresa! I'm sorry to have timed things so badly," Bea slipped nimbly past the woman and into the freshly waxed hallway. "Thank you for letting me in. There's no need to disturb yourself further on my behalf."

She smiled brightly, firmly too she hoped, before beginning across the hallway towards the stairs and Olivia's study. Teresa moved surprisingly fast. She had made another wall of herself, this time blocking the stairway, before Bea even got there.

"Mrs D'Arcy doesn't like anyone interfering with my work in the house," her tone was glacial. "She'll be here in an hour or so. You'll have to wait in the drawing room until then." She loomed, implacable, over Bea.

"I'd prefer to wait in my sister's study, if you don't mind." Bea, intent on meeting force with force, was adamant. Her force was as nothing compared to Teresa's however.

"Well, I do mind," Teresa's pale eyes held the glint of battle. "Mrs D'Arcy doesn't like *anyone* going into that study. I'm about to give it a bit of a clean out anyway and Mrs D'Arcy doesn't like interference with —"

"I know, I know."

Bea tried not to sound too frantic. She could hardly take the woman on physically; she wouldn't have a hope of success anyway. The stand-off seemed to go on for an endless time, Bea wondering all the while what Teresa would do if she *were* to make a sudden dash for the study. Trouble was, she couldn't actually remember which room it was. And, even supposing she got the right room, the chances of Teresa allowing her an undisturbed search were pretty remote.

With as much grace as she could muster Bea stepped back and went through the drawing room door.

"I see my sister's made some changes," she said brightly. "It'll be a pleasure to wait here. Don't bother to make me tea, Teresa."

Leaving the door open, to keep an eye on her, Bea supposed, the woman stomped off toward the kitchen. Sinking into one of four white-upholstered armchairs Bea looked at her watch. Eleven-thirty. At least half an hour before Olivia got here, probably longer since she was unlikely to arrive exactly on time. It was a nonsense making her wait like this. Ten minutes in the study was all she needed. She was being cowardly. The woman had no right to confine her to this room.

And what a room. Bea, studying the decor, fully appreciated Charles's profound aversion to Olivia's taste. It had been radically, and expensively, changed since last she'd been here.

Her sister had opted for white everywhere. The floor was covered in thick white pile and the windows draped in white muslin. A pair of ivory candlesticks stood in front of the marbled fireplace over which hung a portrait of a woman in white veils who could only be Olivia. Lavish white ornaments were strategically placed about the room, with pride of place given to a white elephant that had lilies growing out of its back. A cornucopia of white china grapes stood on a small central table and on each side of the glossily white folding doors to the next room there were alabaster Greek figures, one male and one female. The room showed no evidence of use.

"Dear God, Olivia, how *could* you," Bea groaned as she looked at the Greek figures.

A loud rap on the door made her turn.

"I'm going up now to do Mrs D'Arcy's study," Teresa's voice was slightly less disagreeable than before. Bea said nothing and Teresa, worried perhaps by her lack of response, went on. "There's some tea left in the pot. You can help yourself if you want." My reward for being a good girl, sitting as I was told, Bea thought.

Teresa stomped up the stairs, savaging the banister with a duster as she went. Bea ground her teeth, fuming. That bloody woman knows I want to get into the study, and she knows too that I can't do it while she's in there, she thought. A door opened at the top of the stairs, reminding Bea which room served as the study. Teresa had been of some assistance after all. If only she could be persuaded to leave the study for a few minutes.

As a vacuum cleaner began to hum upstairs Bea went along to the kitchen. She had poured herself a cup of lukewarm tea when the telephone on the wall beside her began to ring. She picked it up.

"Teresa?" The voice was Olivia's.

"It's Bea, actually." Olivia, on the other end of the phone, made a strangled sound. "Well, I know I don't visit very often." Bea was wry. "But there's no need to be so terribly shocked, Olivia. As it happens, I've got something of an emergency on my hands."

"An emergency?" Olivia was shrill.

"Yes. I badly need a photograph of Capek for the catalogue. I was hoping you might have one."

"Of Capek? Of course I haven't. What made you think I had a photograph of him?"

"Because you told me you'd seen one..."

"Oh, well...Yes, you're right. But that was ages ago. I don't even remember what I did with it. I'm sure I don't have it any more. Where are you, by the way?"

"In the kitchen. Please Olivia, this is important to me. Does Capek's benefactor have any photos? Could you..."

"Is Teresa there? Where's Teresa?"

"She's upstairs, cleaning your study…"

"My study! I want to speak to her. Tell her I want to speak to her *now*!"

"Is everything all right, Olivia? You sound…"

"Of course everything's all right. I simply want to speak to my cleaning lady."

"I'll get her for you when you tell me if you know of any photographs."

"Christ Bea, you're so bloody persistent. Look, I'll meet you at the gallery in a half-hour and we'll talk about it then. Now get Teresa."

"But why can't we talk now?"

"Because I want to drop by the gallery anyway and I need time to think about it. And I really think you should leave there right away, Bea. It's cold and I don't want to hang around outside the gallery waiting for you."

Bea put the phone down thoughtfully and called to Teresa from the hallway. It didn't take genius to figure out that Olivia wanted her out of the house, and quickly. The reason why was more difficult to fathom. Maybe she was expecting a lover to call any minute. In any case, it seemed a likely bet that, in her anxiety to get Bea out, she had lied about there being no photograph in the house.

Bea had to call twice to be heard above the vacuum. Teresa appeared on the landing.

"I'll take it down there," she said. "I forgot one of my polishes anyway. All this coming and going, disturbing me at work, no wonder I'm forgetting things." Muttering and grumbling she passed Bea and went on into the kitchen, closing the door behind her and leaving the way free to Olivia's study.

The temptation was more than Bea could resist.
Quickly, taking the steps two at a time, she headed up
the stairs. It would be stupid to leave without a quick
look at least. The study door had been left open and she
stepped quickly inside.

It was a plain room but then Olivia wasn't trying to
impress people here. It was adequately furnished with a
desk, swivel chair, filing cabinet and some shelving. It
was also untidy; it seemed unlikely that even the
redoubtable Teresa was allowed in very often. Or that
Olivia herself spent very much time here. The desk, an
Edwardian copy of an escritoire, was the only attractive
thing in the entire room.

Teresa had been attempting to stack and pile
magazines. Titles like *Ideal Home* and *Interiers d'aujourd'hui*
caught Bea's eye. She was more surprised to note copies
of a prestigious fine arts magazine and supposed that
Olivia must be reading up for investment purposes. A
couple of paintings leaned, faces inward, against a wall.
Vividly remembering the picture over the mantelpiece
Bea easily resisted a temptation to turn them around
and have a look. Instead, before guilt about invading
Olivia's privacy assailed her, she opened the nearest desk
drawer.

Inside there was a jumble of letters, receipts and
Olivia's passport—a burgundy EC one. Bea hurriedly
closed the drawer. She was already beginning to regret
having come into her sister's sanctum. She bit her lip
and opened a second drawer.

Staring up at her, from a dramatically lit black-and-
white photograph, was the face of Miroslav Capek.

It was a studio shot, very posed and theatrical. The
painter seemed to be in Shakespearian costume, or at

least Elizabethan garb of some kind. His expression was intensely brooding and the camera and lighting had been used to exploit the dark, penetrative quality of his eyes to great effect.

"He didn't mention he'd been an actor," Bea whispered aloud, "but then there are a lot of things about himself he didn't tell me."

The photo wasn't really suitable for a catalogue but if she eliminated the costumed shoulders and torso it would just about do. At least it looked quite recent. She turned it over, hoping to find a date on the back. She found one, and a lot more besides.

The picture had been taken less than a year ago, in London. The photographer's stamp was quite clear. There was a message too, in chillingly familiar handwriting. "Dear Friend," Miroslav Capek had written, "Portrait of the actor at rest—and ready to begin his Irish season. Hope scene is set."

She looked again into the drawer and saw another photo, a snapshot this time. Capek was grinning in this one, wearing his black sweater and posed against a green/grey landscape with the Skelligs rocks in the background.

More than a thousand words could have done, it told Bea where the painter had found his seclusion. In the years before Inverskena she and Sinéad had found their own peace in secluded holidays on the very same Kerry peninsula. She turned it over and read another message in the familiar writing. "Clean out of decent claret. Roll on the big bucks!"

Bea's blood ran cold. A suspicion, dark and dreadful, jabbed like the exploratory movements of a surgeon's knife. The more she tried to push it away the more it insisted, the deeper it plunged. Her feet, with a will of their own, moved quickly towards the paintings stacked against the wall. Her hands, unbidden, turned them round.

She was looking at them, and only half-believing what she saw, when Teresa's voice began to rage from the doorway.

"What're you doing with Mrs D'Arcy's things? Them's valuable pictures! She warned me you might try to get in here. I'm to..."

Bea's lifeless hands let the pictures go. Blindly, wordless, she pushed past the shouting woman and stumbled down the stairs. She was only half-aware of her in the doorway, shouting still, as she started the car.

CHAPTER
TWENTY-FIVE

B ea was scarcely aware of what she was doing when she turned off the road leading to the city centre and headed instead for Tallaght. It was the shortest way she knew to get to the main road south. The answers and the truth were to be found in Kerry, on a headland facing the Skellig rock. She knew it well.

Her mind would not be still, would not give her peace to decide rationally what she must do. Heading for Kerry was irrational but, instinct told her, the right thing to do. Out of the chaos of incidents and events of the last year, all of them now screaming at her that she should have known, or suspected, what was going on, one thing at least was clear. The proof of her stupidity, her gullibility, had stared at her from the two Capek pictures which had been facing the wall in Olivia's study. Pictures which were supposed to be in a Japanese bank.

She took the snapshot from her pocket, putting it on the dashboard in front of her. Thank God she'd had the presence of mind to take it; she was going to need it in her search for Capek. Or whoever he was. It was hard to think of him by any other name—she would call him that until she knew better.

No point in asking Olivia his real name, or anything

else either. Olivia, at best, would lie. At worst, knowing
she was cornered, she would try to maximise the damage
by shifting all blame onto Bea. The truth, every painful
bit of it, would be Bea's only defence.

Not that it would be much of a defence. The harsh
reality in the art world was that, as far as a dealer was
concerned, there was no defence possible against the
charges of misjudgement and credulity. It would be as
damaging to the gallery as corrupt dealing. Her reputation
and well-earned respect would be ruined. She knew the
score. She had seen it happen to others.

Or maybe she was wrong. Maybe there was some
crazy, but somehow logical, reason behind the scribbled
messages on the photographs. That's what it would have
to be—crazy logic. But she knew it would not be as simple
as that. Her hands were sticky on the wheel and
somewhere in the pit of her stomach a knot of cold
dread settled. She would dearly have liked to stop, sit in
the warm comfort of an anonymous cheerful pub with
a hot whiskey. Maybe there she could pretend this was
not happening, or that it was happening to someone
else.

She realised she had reached the old Tallaght village
only when a traffic jam held her up. She had no idea
how she'd got there, no memory of the route she'd driven
or the other traffic she must have encountered. She found
a handkerchief and rubbed the palms of her hands. As
the traffic began to move again she splashed cologne on
her palms and forehead. She turned when she came to
the signs for the motorway south.

For a while, anger replaced dread. Furiously, without
sparing herself, she cursed her unprofessional infatuation
with Capek. It was only when she realised that she had

covered at least five miles of motorway on what again amounted to automatic pilot that she began, at last, to take deep, calming breaths. The only place driving like this would get her would be to a cemetery, fast.

Kerry was six hours' drive away, the part of it she wanted to get to anyway. It would be almost seven, and very dark, by the time she got there. She knew the peninsula she was headed for and she hated driving there by night. There would be no lights anywhere, only the moon if she was lucky.

Traffic was light and the roads quite clear for the first part of the journey. She drove steadily, succeeding for long stretches in concentrating solely on her driving. She had not bothered with breakfast, had had nothing but Teresa's overbrewed and lukewarm tea all day. But by the time she got through Limerick and had reached Adare she knew she would have to stop for something to eat. She *had* to stay alert at the wheel.

Going through the city of Limerick, instead of using the ring road, had been a mistake. She had been badly delayed by traffic. As she sat in the chintzy comfort of The Dunraven Arms Hotel she tried to avoid the eye of the clock over the bar.

Darkness had been falling slowly over the countryside as she was driving along, the road ahead becoming dimmer all the time. Night would fall soon.

She finished her sandwich, had a second coffee and finally checked her watch with the clock over the bar. It was 5.15. She paid and forced herself to take a brisk, ten-minute walk through the village before getting into the Audi and hitting the road again.

She was thinking more clearly now and realising how the fraud had been carried out.

There was nothing new about the sort of scam Olivia and Capek had set up; she'd heard of similar schemes before. She'd just never expected to be the victim of one. She suspected too that Olivia and Capek were not alone, that neither of them was the mastermind. All that seemed certain was that together they had hyped Capek's pictures—if indeed he was the painter. He was more likely to be an out-of-work actor playing a bit part as a mysterious, reclusive artist. An easy enough role. All he had to do was brush up on his Eastern European accent, learn a tragic background story, retire to the country and make occasional, fleeting public appearances. A few phone calls and trips to the railway station when the pictures were ready and *voilà*! the scam was set up. There had been supporting players too, of course. And then there was the real painter...

"Bastard! Lousy, rotten bastard!"

Bea allowed herself the luxury and relief of a loud swearing session as she drove too fast along the lonely road between Abbeyfeale and Castleisland. The wide main street of that town was cheerfully busy and she was held up once again. A pedestrian ambled in front of her and she blasted her horn in alarm. Faces, mildly indignant, turned on her from other cars and the man stopped, shaking a finger. Bea gritted her teeth and willed him to move on. Unaffected by her frenzy he looked pointedly at her Dublin registration and wagged his finger again. "There's no need for that class of thing here," he shouted loudly enough for her, and half the street, to hear. "No need at all. We get by here without agitating people with the noise of car horns. We get by very well..."

Shaking his head and his finger by turns he ambled to the footpath and Bea was able to drive on. At Farranfore she took the road for Killorglin. She was almost at Glenbeigh when it began to rain, light sprinkling drops at first but quickly getting heavier.

"Hell and damnation!"

Bea wasn't at all sure if she was cursing the rain, her conspiring sister, or her own blindness in the whole affair. Certainly there had been signs aplenty that something was afoot. She would have seen them had she not been so wrapped up in other things—in James, Sinéad, Inverskena, Jude, Wally. If there hadn't been so much going on, if she hadn't been so attracted to Capek, if...

She could have been alert at the very beginning, when Olivia had come to her about the Adams auction. Olivia knew nothing about pictures, and cared less. Her interest in the Capek picture should have been a warning.

The picture had been put into the auction so that inflated bids could be made and an inflated price paid. Capek himself, in another role, might even have done the bidding. All he would have had to do was pay the Adams' commission. It was an old and well-tried trick. Then there had been the New York reviews. She had not even checked those, had taken them at face value. It was consoling that nobody else seemed to have checked them either—though given the thousands of galleries in that city the task wouldn't be an easy one. The further sale of a Capek picture in London, the same trick as at Adams, had merely copper-fastened a growing "reputation."

God, how they had used her! Arranging for her to meet Capek the night after Christmas had been a clever strategy, a nice piece of scene-setting. Alone, caught up in the mood of the season, it would be hard for her to resist the "tragedy" of the painter's life-story, impossible to resist his charisma. And he *had* charisma, and sex appeal too, damn him! He had been well chosen for the role.

Remembering his eyes, his way of looking at her, of standing close, she shivered involuntarily. It had been a superb performance, projecting mystery and vague suffering, seasoned with just the right amount of subtle flirtation and flattery. Could it *all* have been play acting?

And she hadn't even liked the pictures. Her instinct had been not to show them. But she had ignored her instinct, thus breaking one of her own golden rules.

The Japanese bank was never coming to Dublin, of course. Not the one represented by the preposterous Sam Winegold anyway. She had been taken in by him too— but why not? There had been no reason to suspect him. The two pictures he'd "bought" were no doubt destined to face Olivia's wall until Capek's reputation had become solid enough for them to be sold quietly to a genuine collector. The commission she herself had taken from the payment cheque would simply have been written off as an investment in the future of the scam.

But the other three pictures sold at the exhibition were a different story. They had all been bought, in good faith, by buyers she knew, all of them taken in by reports of Capek's growing reputation and promising future. They had been encouraged too by the Japanese bank's "purchase."

Tomorrow was to be the real killing, the chance to make some real money. After that there would be further pictures, another, bigger gallery perhaps. A painter's reputation, once established, was hard to destroy. Buyers didn't like to be made to appear fools, didn't care to have investment pictures brought down in value by talk of a fraudelent reputation either.

She had the option, of course, of saying nothing, doing nothing. She hadn't been the only one to be taken in. The critics hadn't suspected, the auction rooms had sold in good faith too. But she knew she couldn't do it. She was not going to be used any longer and she was not going to allow them get away with it. That way she would be able to go on living with herself.

The rain was really pouring down now, but the roads were reasonably good still and house lights, like will-o'-the-wisps, winked encouragingly from across the mountains. Soon she would have to leave the main road and head out onto the peninsula. There would be precious few house lights there. Those houses that were left, holiday homes most of them, were discreetly out of view. She would have to stop, make enquiries in the village nearest the headland. Otherwise she could drive around, searching, all night. Someone was bound to have noticed Capek coming and going and have some idea where he was staying. No one went unnoticed in a place like this. Especially someone who looked like he did.

She switched the windscreen wipers to top speed and slowed down a little as she saw the lights of the village ahead. Tightening her hands on the wheel she drove into the main street.

CHAPTER
TWENTY-SIX

A watchful silence fell as Bea walked into the pub.
She had expected as much. She knew this part of
the world, knew that as a stranger and woman alone she
presented a curious spectacle. The village was off the
general tourist trail but even so got its quota of summer
visitors. These were taken for granted, not much
commented upon. Ignored even, for the most part, in
the hope that they would move on quickly. It was a lot
more difficult to disregard someone who turned up on
a wet October night. It would be downright foolish,
indeed, not to pay heed to such an event.

There were five customers in the bar, all of them
male.

"Bad night," one of them said and Bea nodded.

"I'll have a small Paddy, please," she said to the
barman. Her voice sounded loud, intrusive, in the silence.

"It's no joke driving in the rain." The barman spoke
over his shoulder as he measured her drink, watching
her in the mirror, not spilling a drop. He was a man of
about fifty, heavy and florid-faced. The gleaming baldness
of his dome was patchily covered with long strands of
carefully grown and positioned side hair.

"It is," Bea agreed as he slid the glass across the

counter, followed it with a jug of water, "and it seems to be getting worse."

"What's the weather like above in Dublin?"

Bea didn't ask how he knew where she'd come from; she knew her accent would have been placed immediately. She only hoped he would prove as observant when she came to ask him if he'd seen a man answering Capek's description.

"Mild enough," she said and took a gulp of the whiskey.

"You'd be on your way to Kenmare maybe, or Cork?" Bea knew the barman didn't think she was on her way to either place; she was on altogether the wrong road. It was simply the tortured, Kerry way of asking her where she was going. She could tell him the truth, which was not at all what he wanted to hear. Not immediately anyway. But she had no time to play the game, not tonight.

"No. I'm on my way out to the headland." She nodded in a general, westerly direction, aware that the entire bar was listening. "I'm hoping to find a friend there. I've urgent news for him and there's no telephone where he's staying. Trouble is, I don't know where the house is, exactly. I was wondering if you could help."

"I don't know." The barman, in anticipation, was lining up a couple of pints. "Lots of people come and go out there. Most of them don't have much to do with us here in the village."

She had been wrong, Bea thought, to rush him. She took another gulp of her drink. But damn him, she needed to know.

"Look." She produced the snapshot. "He sent me this a few months ago. Does he look at all familiar to you?"

She tried to smile. The barman's expression became almost pitying. He thinks I'm a fool, Bea thought. And maybe I am. She put the snapshot on the counter and waited, trying not to watch his face too closely.

He lifted it, held it at arm's length and squinted. "I'll be damned if I know him—but it's hard to tell from such a small picture. There's a lot of people like him comes to stay around here, painting and writing like. I'll tell you what…" He slipped the snapshot into his shirt pocket and leaned over the bar counter conspiratorially. "If you were to have yourself another drink and wait in that corner there," he pointed to a bench seat by the window, "there's a man comes in about eight o'clock who'll know for sure who's living back on the headland."

Eight o'clock. Half an hour away. The wait would be worth it if the man really knew anything. The alternative was to drive on blindly, hoping somehow to find the house. It wasn't really an alternative.

"Fine." She put some money on the counter. "Maybe the rain will have stopped by then. I'll have the same again—and have a drink yourself."

The barman took her glass and poured her a second drink. He measured a double for himself. Bea, hoping he was telling the truth, retreated with her whiskey to the corner by the window. Only when she was safely tucked away did sporadic conversation break out again at the bar.

The first whiskey had both warmed her up and calmed her down. She sipped the second very slowly. She wanted to be absolutely in control when she confronted Capek. Or anyone else who might be with him.

Scraps of conversation drifted her way and she listened hard, hoping to pick up something, anything, which might be useful. Sounds of an argument rose above the general drone. "That's gospel truth," an old man banged a fist on the counter, "God damn me if I tell you a lie!"

"But the animal had the look of Tom Fitz's cow, I tell you." His younger companion was red in the face. He stood down from the stool he'd been sitting on. The old man banged the counter again.

"Maybe so—but that was a month after he bought her. I'm telling you the God's honest truth!"

"Come here to me, I want you." The younger man leaned over and spoke with quiet ferocity as he jabbed a finger at the other. Bea found herself craning to hear and pulled herself back. This was none of her business; it was unlikely that Capek would have involved himself with the cattle trade.

She tried instead to concentrate on her surroundings, attempting to imagine Capek in these murky environs. The ceiling was low, almost oppressively so, and had been turned nearly black by smoke and grease. The walls, almost the same colour, were covered with photographs, liberally autographed, of victorious Kerry football teams. Vacant spaces between had been filled with framed posters of pithy sayings. Bea read the one nearest which maintained that the perfect man was one "who never does a thing which is not right," and whose wife could tell just where he was, "morning, noon and night." A local wit had scratched, "He's dead, of course," under this wisdom.

Bea looked at her watch. It was ten to eight. The barman seemed to have forgotten her and the row about the cow had ended. The older man had, at any rate, accepted a drink from his companion. "Good luck to ye, anyhow." He lifted the pint and downed most of it in a long slug.

"Sláinte." His younger companion, calmer now, nodded.

The door opened and a gust of rain-sodden wind blew across the room. It was followed by a tall, stooped man, dripping cap pulled low over his brow, long coat wrapped tightly around him.

"Mike."

The barman greeted him loudly and beckoned to him. The man seemed not to have heard him as, slowly and methodically, he took off his cap, then his coat. He hung them on a hook inside the door before bending down to remove a pair of bicycle-clips. Straightening his jacket he walked to the bar and lifted the pint the barman had placed there in readiness for him. This act too was deliberate. Leaning across the counter the barman took the snapshot out of his shirt pocket. He handed it over with a few brief words and a nod in Bea's direction, then moved away as the man began to study it over a long, slow draught of his pint. He didn't once glance Bea's way. He had almost finished his drink before he got up and walked over to where she sat.

"You're looking for someone."

It was a statement, delivered in a flat, grey voice. In one movement he handed her the snapshot and pulled over a stained, plastic chair. He sat opposite her. "Could be I can help you."

He took a last draught of his Guinness and turned the empty glass meaningfully in large, bony hands. Bea called for another. The barman, she saw, had already drawn it. She asked for a cup of tea for herself.

"I'd be very grateful if you could." She pointed to the snapshot. "Have you noticed this man staying anywhere on the headland?"

"Could be that I have."

He put his empty glass on the table and both hands on his knees. Silently, while the barman delivered the new pint and Bea's tea, he studied her. There was nothing rude about his stare. It was simply curious. Bea, curious in her turn, returned his look. His face, with its high cliffs of cheekbones and square promontory of a chin, was handsome in a forbidding way. He seemed to her a lump of rock, a craggy mountain, like a part of the headland itself. Impossible to imagine him ever young; impossible to imagine him ever getting any older. If Capek was living on the headland this man would have seen him all right. She was sure of that.

She was worried about what he thought of her, whether what he concluded would convince him to impart information. Instinct told her he would form his own judgement, in his own time, and that there was little she could do to convince him. She waited as patiently as she could.

But it wasn't long before he said, "It's a reckless night to be driving out there," and jerked his head towards the west.

"I know." Bea tried to put images of the cliff road and the wild, howling Atlantic out of her head.

"Do you know the road?" the man asked.

"I know it in daylight. If you could tell me where he's staying," she pointed to the snapshot, "I'm sure I'll be able to find the house."

"You might, and then again you might not. You'll have to do a bit of walking maybe. You'd need a strong pair of boots going out there."

He looked pointedly at her feet and Bea had an urge

to hide her Jourdan pumps under the bench. Instead, defiantly, she stretched them in front of her. The man spoke again. "Look at my own boots now."

Bea, obediently casting her eyes down, was confronted by a pair of maroon Doc Marten bubble-toed boots.

"I bought them inside in Puck Fair. And I made a bargain with them. They're a size twelve. Eleven is what I usually take but these were the last pair and I got them cheap. I put insoles and a heavy sock inside and they made a fine fit. Fourteen pounds I paid for them and Christ but they're a great shoe for water." While he'd been talking, Bea had finished her tea. Damn him, she thought, he's not going to tell me anything. Patience stretched beyond endurance and she stood up.

"You're an impatient woman." The man's tone of voice did not change. "But I'll tell you now where to find your man. What did you say his name was?"

Bea did not sit down, "Capek. Miroslav Capek."

The man frowned. "Queer sort of name for an Englishman. But sure the English are a bastard race anyhow."

"You're sure it's the same man we're talking about?"

"I'm sure. He's been here since early in the year. Keeps himself to himself but I've seen him. I know every inch of that headland. There's nothing goes on there but that I don't know about." Bea ignored titters from the bar which told her they were being listened to. "Did you say he was expecting you?"

"No, I didn't."

"Only I think your man might already have company. But sure the more the merrier on a wintry night." This brought further titters from the bar. "Now then, here's how you'll get to him."

The road ahead streamed wet and muddy in the headlights. Rain, great torrents of it, beat on the roof of the car. She hadn't seen another moving thing since leaving the main road outside the village. Nor a glimmer of light. Nothing but blackness, wet and inky, everywhere beyond the car. She might have been swallowed into it.

There was a wind blowing up now as well. Not gale force but bad enough to shake the car. October weather was unpredictable. She was driving faster than any rational person should on a narrow, windy road like this. But it cut cross-country and would take miles off her journey along the cliff road. Time too, maybe as much as half an hour. She prayed, the first time she had really prayed in years, that he wouldn't have gone by the time she got there. She had to see proof for herself, the evidence of her gullibility. It wasn't enough that she knew, already, how she'd been used. She *had* to see.

She slowed down hardly at all as she met a flooded patch of road. The water, a lot deeper than she'd anticipated, hit the car with a wallop. She caught her breath, putting her foot down hard on the accelerator. The car cut through and away.

Then she was on a straight stretch of road again. The headlights picked up a set of cat's eyes along its centre. Another pair, yellowly misleading, appeared by the side of the road. They stared, unblinking, as she passed. Country cats travelled far in search of whatever it was they hunted. Sex and companionship she supposed. Primal instincts were the same, whatever the species.

Another two miles, according to the man in the pub, and there would be a sign for the cliff road. She rounded a corner and didn't see the cow until its huge head turned, staring at her in the headlights. A shuddering awareness of what could have happened made her slow down so that she didn't miss the small, obscure road sign when she came to it five hundred yards further on. From now on she knew there was nothing but stony mountain land on her right, an almost sheer drop into the Atlantic on her left.

She drove for another ten minutes before she saw a light, another five before she got to the cottage. Heeding her instinct, bitterly regretting that she'd ignored it for months past, she drove on until she found a widening in the road and turned the car. Hands clenched hard on the wheel, she drove back to the gate leading to the cottage and parked the car on the road. This way she would at least be ready for a quick getaway. If the need arose.

The wind almost knocked her off her feet as she got out of the car but once she entered the yard it was more sheltered. The man was right: her shoes were sodden before she got to the door.

It was quite a big cottage, with lights on in two of its rooms. A black Volvo, with English registration, stood parked in front. Voices came from inside. He was here then, and not alone. But then she hadn't expected he would be.

She took a deep breath and knocked on the door, hard.

CHAPTER TWENTY-SEVEN

B ea's knocking produced utter silence inside the cottage. She stood, keyed for the slightest response, as the night howled around her and the rain and wind went on building to a storm. Lights still shone in two of the cottage windows but the curtains were heavy and there were no chinks anywhere that she could see. She waited, half-poised for flight, forcing herself to look carefully around the shadowy yard, to take in the deep pools of black in its corners. She had come to the shiny, menacing bulk of the Volvo when her eye caught a sudden small movement along the wall nearest her. She stifled a scream.

"It's probably only a mouse. Or a bird. Maybe it's a small cat." She didn't want to think it was a rat. Rats terrified her. They carried poison, they jumped at your throat. Giving herself a strong shake she turned again to the silent, unopened door.

"I'll count to thirty and then I'll knock again." But by the count of ten she had lost patience and lifted the heavy knocker. She let it fall with a couple of resounding thumps and was poised for a third attempt when the door swung suddenly open.

The light was behind the man who stood there and

she couldn't see his face. He was tall, thin and, even in outline, dishevelled. She knew that, with the light falling full on her own face, he could see her clearly. But, still and staring, he said nothing. It didn't matter. She knew who he was, had known immediately he opened the door.

The wind, coming from the north-west, rushed through the open door and into the cottage. A woman's voice, petulant and high, demanded that the door be closed. The man who had called himself Miroslav Capek turned his handsome profile irritably in the direction of the speaker.

"Oh shut it, can't you!"

The low, dark voice was the same but the accent now was unmistakably English. He turned back to Bea, shoulders rising in a barely perceptible, nonchalant shrug. "This is *most* unexpected, very surprising indeed." His tone had a sardonic quality it hadn't had before. The wind rattled the door. "What a night to come calling! Do come in." He stood aside, gesturing elegantly that she should enter. Stiffly, without looking at him, Bea passed into the cottage.

She stepped immediately into a low, kitchen-cum-living room. A restoration job had preserved the traditional features of the cottage but added comforts the original inhabitants couldn't have dreamed of, nor afforded if by chance they had. The walls had been stripped back to stone, heating came from under the polished stone flags of the floor, dark ceiling-beams were hung with fishing rods and walking sticks.

It seemed unlikely that Capek or any of the other three people in the room had ever used any of them. None of them, Bea thought, were the kind of people to whom country pursuits appealed. As if to prove her point, the large, open fireplace was in use as a rubbish bin, the shelves of the old dresser covered in rows of empty bottles. A scrubbed deal table in the centre of the room was also littered with wine bottles, as well as the remains of a meal.

Her awareness sharpened both by anger and apprehension, Bea took everything in at a glance before focusing on the man who had risen to his feet as she came into the room. His expression, when she looked into his face, was so utterly shocked as to be almost comical.

"Good evening, Wally." Her greeting cut like lead pellets through the wine- and smoke-filled air of the room. "I *thought* I might find you here."

"Clever, clever Bea!" Wally sounded hoarse. He managed a rather sick grin. "And how right you were— as usual! Well, since you're here now you might as well *tar insteach agus lig do scith*, as they say in these parts."

He raised his glass in salute and kicked a wooden chair into the centre of the room. With a sweep of his hand he indicated that Bea should sit. The shock had not quite worn off and his grin had become a grotesque grimace. Bea ignored the chair.

"Don't waste my time, Wally. I'm here to find out exactly what's going on. For a start you can introduce me to your colleagues."

A low laugh made her uncomfortably aware of Capek, leaning against the wall just behind her. He leaned towards her and she felt his winey breath on her check. She took a step away from him—and came closer to her husband. The proverb about being between the devil and the deep blue sea came to her and for a moment she

felt dizzy, frightened. Wally, she knew, sensed her fear.
His face, now bearing a fully recovered smug smile,
brought a return of anger so savage it swept any such
timid emotions before it. Wally reached as if to touch
her and she stepped sharply aside.

"Calm down, dear heart. Everything can be
explained..."

"Don't—you—dear—heart—me!" Bea ground the
words out with a slow, ferocious intensity. "I want to
know who *he*," she jerked her head violently in Capek's
direction, "is." I want to know the full extent of
this...fraud. I want to know who else is involved, apart
from Olivia and," she threw a contemptuous glance at
the other two women in the room, "your friends here."

"All in good time, all in good time." Wally was
indulgent, conciliatory. "You're far too excited at the
moment to take in that amount of information. Have a
glass with us first. You've come a long way." He turned
to the blonde girl thrown in a chair by the fireplace.
"Get a clean glass, sweetheart, will you?"

Ignoring Bea, the girl tossed her mane of tangled hair
and reached for a bottle of scarlet nail varnish. "Fuck
off," she said. "You want to entertain your wife—you do
it yourself!"

His companion from the RHK concert was only just
recognisable. Her face was whey-coloured and her eyes
bruised with tiredness. She looked as if she had slept in
her jeans ånd T-shirt. For several nights. She also looked
quite drunk. She began an attempt to paint her toenails.

"I've had it with this whole thing. I should never
have come to this barbaric arse-hole of a place. Now
she's here, the money isn't even going to work out."
Tears streamed down her face as she stabbed at her toes

and fingernails with the varnish. Wally shrugged.

"What a silly little bitch you've turned out to be." He looked at the girl in disgust, then poured the last of the wine into his own glass. He sighed, contemplating the empty bottle. "We cannot continue without libations." His voice was saw-edged. Violently, he tossed the bottle into the fireplace where it crashed and broke against the old crane. In the brief shocked silence which followed, Wally left the room. As he did so the other woman, also looking quite different from the last time Bea had seen her, got out of the chair she'd been sitting in to strike a pose in front of the fireplace.

Bea, now feeling quite detached and strangely in control of things, wondered what role the actress who had opened her January show was playing tonight.

Without make-up and dressed in a loose black tunic over black leggings she looked dramatically beautiful. And stricken.

"This could ruin me." She spoke in a tormented whisper. "What are you going to do?"

"That depends." Bea was curt. "But I really don't see how you can be kept out of it."

"Depends! What do you mean depends?" The actress's voice had become shrill, out of control. The performance had ended.

"On the full story, when I hear it. When I know how many buyers have been conned and how much my reputation and gallery have been used to sell hyped pictures." Bea eyed the actress coldly, speculatively. "It seems to me you were involved from the beginning, certainly since the Adams auction. And you *did* deliver that very convincing speech at the opening. You were very moving indeed."

The actress whirled, titian locks writhing in distress, eyes flashing tempestuously. The theatrical effect was negated somewhat by the very real draining of colour from her face, the involuntary shake in her hands as she reached out to clutch at Miroslav Capek.

"Do something, Nigel! Tell her it was all a joke! You were going to come clean. It was only a joke! She made money out of it anyway! Tell her."

"Well, Nigel, tell me. Why don't you let me in on the joke?" Bea, with a tight smile, turned to the man leaning against the wall. "And maybe you could introduce yourself while you're at it? Nigel Capek doesn't quite ring true. I suppose you're a Smith or a Brown?"

"A Spenser, actually." The dark grey eyes were mocking. "Though I've grown fond of Capek, and of Miroslav. I rather got the impression you liked him too? He certainly liked you. Ah well, all good parts must come to an end. It was a good run while it lasted. And I did particularly enjoy those exclusive private performances for you, dear Bea."

Bea flinched. "I must commend you," she kept her voice cool. "You were most convincing. But, as you so rightly say, the show is over. You, I take it, were not the director too?"

"No. Simply the lead." Spenser dropped the cigarette he had been smoking carelessly grinding it into the flagstoned floor. "Your husband must take credit for the idea and planning." His voice tightened. "Seems he didn't plan quite well enough, however, or you wouldn't be here, would you? Not that it isn't delightful to see you."

"You can't stop, can you, Nigel?" The actress banged an explosive fist on the table. A glass toppled over and the dark wine spread quickly and ran onto the floor.

"Exactly how good a role *did* you play with *dear* Bea? Just how exclusive were those *tête-a-têtes*?

Spenser laughed, a throaty, genuinely amused sound. "*Very* exclusive," he laughed again. "Wouldn't you say, Bea?"

"I..." Bea sensed rather than saw the glass as it careered past her ear and crashed on the wall an inch from Spenser's head.

"You bastard! I put myself on the line for you! You promised this would change everything! But it didn't did it? You're the same lousy, self-indulgent egomaniac you always were! Nothing's changed! Nothing!"

Spenser's eyes darkened dangerously and he moved away from the wall. The actress, pacing up and down, didn't seem to notice.

"You couldn't keep your hands off, could you? Not even this once, not even with what was at stake. You had to satisfy your fucking ego, had to prove no woman can resist your almighty sex appeal. *You're the one who blew it!* It's your fault she's here! That everything's ruined."

She stopped as Spenser caught hold of her wrist, pulling her on to her toes so that her face almost touched his.

"Shut it, you stupid cow!" The scars Bea had noticed on his face months before had turned white, his mouth become a tight line. "It is none of your fucking business how I played my part. I played it well, I convinced." His voice became softer but no less menacing. "What I want now is for you to be a good girl and calm down while we work out a little damage-limitation here..." He loosened his hold but did not let go of her wrist. Flat on her feet again the actress looked at him, her eyes brimming with tears. For a moment their eyes locked and then Spenser bent down, whispering in her ear. She made a sound somewhere between a giggle and a groan and nodded. He freed her wrist and she turned, looking once, triumphantly, at Bea, before sashaying out of the room.

"I really do wish you'd sit down, Bea." Spenser's tone was conversational. "We'd all be more comfortable."

"I'm not at all interested in making you comfortable. And I'm leaving here in five minutes unless I get an explanation. I've seen all I need to see, anyway. The Guards can sort out the rest."

"Oh, I don't think they'll bother..." Wally's voice, almost in her ear, made Bea jump. He had come from a side room, a bottle of wine in one hand, glass in the other. He had a blithe smile. He said, "There's been no criminal offence. If people are foolish and greedy enough to buy pictures for investment purposes, or because they hope to make a nice, fat profit, well then..." with an eloquently dismissive shrug he put bottle and glass on the table, "they must take the consequences. The choice is theirs. And it was a choice. No one forced them to buy." He squinted at the label on the bottle and sighed. "Have to do for now. Better times ahead." He applied a corkscrew. "The pictures are original, and good. Their provenance may be debatable but I think you'll find it impossible, dear heart, to prove a case of criminal intent. What buyers want to admit they've been duped?" He raised his eyebrows questioningly as he deftly pulled the cork free.

"They don't need to," Bea said.

"I haven't finished, dear heart." Wally shook his head reprovingly and began pouring the wine.

"Much, much touchier than buyers are gallery owners,

as you well know. What gallery owner can afford to admit she has been duped? It would be business suicide." Humming gently to himself he filled a second glass of wine. "A bit of a breather would have improved this." He sounded regretful. "But needs must—and we all need a drink." He lifted his own glass, and took a long draught. "Mmm, not too bad. Now, take this, dear heart. I insist!" He handed Bea a glass which she took, carefully placing it on the table before pulling over a chair and sitting down.

"Good. Now we can talk business," Wally said. "Discuss what's to be done."

He sat opposite her. Nigel Spenser had meanwhile poured himself some wine and taken a seat at the top of the table. The girl by the fire seemed to have fallen asleep, the actress had not returned to the room.

Bea had been aware, with the part of her mind alert for the moment she must go, that the storm was worsening outside. The cottage was solid, its thick stone walls almost sound-proof. Even so the howl of a rising wind came through. Windows rattled as wind and rain beat against them and occasional gusts thundered down the wide chimney, sending eddies of chill air into the room. Bea, thinking of the drive home, felt a knot grow in her stomach. She looked at her watch. It was almost nine-thirty.

"Everything ready for tomorrow, then?" Wally's tone was cool.

"It was. I've cancelled."

The lie produced the desired effect. Now they would take her seriously, stop treating her like the fool they'd supposed her to be for the past nine months. Wally's expression, determinedly casual until now, froze and became grey. His mouth narrowed to a thin line as he fought to control a nervous tick in his jaw. Nigel Spenser swore hoarsely under his breath and reached for the bottle of wine.

"So Walter, you had everything tied up, had you?" he said.

"You stupid bitch!" Wally's voice was a low, restrained shout. "Why did you have to do that? You know you'll have to go ahead with it; why not tomorrow? You can't admit you've been had—not by one of the oldest tricks in the book."

"Oh, but I can. And I will. I'm not going to run my gallery on a lie and I'm not going to defraud buyers."

"For Christ's sake, Bea, grow up! This is not some sort of Utopia we're living in, where the good are rewarded and evil punished. This is the real world. Nobody'll thank you. You'll be ruined. No one will believe you weren't involved, that you didn't know what was going on."

"That's not altogether true," Bea spoke quietly. "Some people will know, enough people will believe me."

"But your judgement will never be trusted again. You can't win! Look, Bea, be sensible. We can salvage this thing." Wally's eyes, watching her face closely, became very still. He thinks he knows me so well, Bea thought. He thinks he has me all sewn up, still believes he can manipulate me. The realisation, as those dark eyes coldly assessed her, came in a flash of intuition. With it came strength, and not a little pity. Wally was a mess. Nothing had changed; he was still the self-centred adolescent she'd married, still avoiding reality and responsibility and still without anything of real value or joy in his life. The fact that this adolescent was a forty-three-year-old man made it all rather pathetic.

Pathetic too was the fact that he couldn't see, or accept, that she had changed. She had grown up. A long time ago. But how *could* he know? He hadn't been around for any of the things which had shaped her; not for Oisín's death, not for Sinéad's childhood and adolescence.

"What do you mean, salvage things?" Bea asked the question slowly.

"Easy. The cancellation can be turned round to become a plus. Mysterious artist insists on cancelling show. Refuses to exhibit. They'll go mad for his pictures when they think they can't get any more. Then, in a month's time, you announce that he's changed his mind, that you've got a bigger and better show together. I'll do a couple of extra pictures."

"*You'll* do a couple."

"Don't play the innocent, Bea, it doesn't suit you. You *must* have guessed by now that I was painting them."

"I suspected. I wasn't sure."

"Face it Bea. It's not going to stop here. It's growing, the whole scenario's changed. Tell her, Nigel."

The actor leaned back in his chair, hands behind his head. "Your husband wants me to explain to you that he's become excited by his own work. He sees possibilities. He thinks Capek could change and develop. Become a good painter in time."

"He's a *good* painter now," Wally's voice was clipped. "He's on the way to becoming a *great* painter..."

"But why," Bea, knowing the answer, still had to ask the question, "can't this happen to Walter Treacy? Why does it all have to be fraudulent, a con?"

Wally treated her to a look of dismissive impatience. "Because, my dear, simple-minded Bea, the work's done.

Capek is established. Painting as him, I can go on to make real money—selling *real* pictures. No one's going to buy Walter Treacy, not for years. I haven't the time to build a reputation."

"Of course you have. What you mean is you don't fancy the hard work, the lean times until you get there."

"Spot on. And why should I? Come with me, I want to show you something." Wally, his eyes alight with an energy and fire Bea remembered from twenty years before, jumped up from the table. He crossed quickly to the door leading to the back of the cottage, stopped and beckoned her to follow before passing through.

"Better do as the man says," Nigel Spenser was laconic. Bea looked at him as she stood up. His hair needed to be cut and he could have done with a shave but he was still one of the most attractive men she'd seen in a long time.

"I *did* wonder about your excellent knowledge of English poetry," she said.

"Ah, yes. I worried that that was pushing things too far. All in all," his eyes looked her over, lazily, "it was fun. Maybe we could run part of the act again some time?"

"I hardly think so." Bea's tone was dry. "You could, however, satisfy my curiosity about something. Those scars on your face—how did you get them?" Spenser put a hand to his face, one of the long, expressive hands Bea had thought so painterly.

"Ah, scars so bravely borne! A public school brawl, nothing more, I'm afraid. Now that *was* a prison, if you like."

"Have you even been to Eastern Europe?"

"My sweet innocent! Of course not! Nor to New York, for that matter. I'm quite a home-boy, really. This exotic place," he threw a sardonic look around the room, "is as far as I care to travel. But hark, yonder—your husband calls."

"Bea!" Wally's voice, then Wally himself, came from the back of the cottage. He stood waiting as Bea slowly crossed the room, then turned and led the way impatiently down a short corridor to the back. The windows to the back were larger and had no curtains. Remembering the cottage's orientation Bea guessed the room faced west, out to sea and the Skellig rocks. It had been used as a studio and smelled vividly of oil and paint, turpentine and stale cigarette smoke. There was an easel in the middle. Canvases and drawings, some finished but most incomplete and seeming to be experiments, were stacked in piles everywhere. Wally had been busy—but then he always had been a fast worker.

"Now, see for yourself." Wally crossed excitedly to a large canvas on an easel. "When I moved away from the hard-edge stuff things began to happen. Look."

The almost-finished picture on the easel was an explosion of movement and colour. A dramatic landscape, with swelling seas dominated by the massed grey and green of the headland, it was a vibrant statement about the lonely grandeur of the place, and it was very good. Exciting too in a way that the "Capek" pictures had never been. It was Wally painting for painting's sake.

"Well?" Wally was almost dancing with impatience.

"It's good." Bea stood back, looked at it for a long minute, then looked slowly around at the other, stacked pictures. A few were recognisable "Capek" specimens but most were alive with the heady vitality of the landscape on the easel. There was a portrait too, a rather lonely-looking nude of the young blonde girl now asleep in the chair by the fire. Bea was overcome by a terrible sense of loss. Wally could still paint. There had been no need for him to engineer an art scam to get pictures into a gallery. If he worked at it he could become a very, very good painter. Maybe even a great painter.

If he worked at it. But Wally would never work at it. Because for Wally getting his pictures shown was only a small part of what painting, and life, were all about. He wanted money, and he wanted lots of it—fast and easy. Not for him, he had made clear, the hard slog of building a reputation, developing his talent. He had taken the easy option, as he had taken it all those years ago when his daughter and baby son had needed him. When she, their mother, had needed him. Then, he had destroyed her love for him, lost forever the chance of knowing and loving his daughter. Now, he had destroyed his hope of recognition and lost forever his chance of making it as a legitimate and talented painter. No reputable gallery would show him once the story of the Capek scam got out.

And it *would* get out. Bea would not, could not keep quiet about it and his part in it. If she did, it would go on and he would to do it again and again. She could not allow him do that.

"For God's sake, Bea, you can't destroy me now! I've thought it through and here's what I'll do." Wally began to pace the room. He picked up a paintbrush and stroked it as he talked.

"I'll kill off Capek. He can be a suicide. If you just go ahead and show the pictures you have, then I promise— no more Capek. The buyers will have what they wanted—

pictures by a mysterious, powerful painter who died before achieving his full potential. They won't lose. The pictures will have a cachet and they'll increase in value. It's perfect, you know it is. No one will ever know."

"Of course they will. And it's fraud. The New York reviews will be discovered to be frauds..."

"But they won't, because they weren't." Wally was triumphant. His eyes blazed. "That was where it all began. I was spending a summer in New York and experimenting with that hard-edge stuff in a friend's studio. She put a few into a group show in a small Greenwich Village gallery. It was just after the December '89 revolution in Romania so we concocted the Capek story for a bit of a laugh. You know New York; it loves a good selling story, and angle to everything. Truth doesn't matter. When I got back to London from New York things were pretty tight." He spread his hands in a gesture of helplessness. "Miroslav Capek and his pictures were just begging to be revived."

"I'll bet."

Bea, examining a small picture of rock and grass, spoke bitterly. She could see how it had been. And how convenient a gallery-owning wife and a sister-in-law only too willing to help set her up must have been. She wondered what sort of cut Wally had promised Olivia and his various players, but didn't ask.

He would never tell her the truth. She shivered a little when she thought of how close the whole elaborate plot had come to succeeding. It would have done, if she hadn't gone to Olivia's house this morning.

Wally, as if reading her mind, asked, "How did you find out? We were nearly there..."

"It was all to do with your friend Nigel's tardiness in

sending me a photo for the catalogue. He promised me one but then it didn't arrive..."

"Christ Almighty!" The nerve in Wally's jaw twitched uncontrollably and the paintbrush he'd been holding snapped in two in his clenched hand. "So it's that bloody peacock who ruined everything. I told him there were to be no pictures. I told him that from the very beginning. I told him someone would be bound to see and recognise him. But he couldn't resist the chance to see his mug all over the place and so he told you you could have one. I found out and stopped him sending it."

"Well, you should have had him invent an excuse. Because I needed that photo and went out to Olivia's this morning to see if she could help. She wasn't there. But I found two photographs anyway. And I found the pictures bought by the Japanese bank."

"Just lying around?" Wally looked sick and incredulous.

"Oh no, in Olivia's study. Tucked away actually. But I was desperate and searching. I found the photos first. This one was most helpful." Bea took the snapshot from her pocket and held it up. Wally groaned, closed his eyes momentarily.

"You gave it to her?" Bea guessed. "The other, studio one as well?"

Bleakly, Wally nodded. "She was nagging on that she didn't know what he looked like."

He turned, irritably, and began rummaging through the chaos of paint tubes, brushes and rags on a table. When he found the cigarettes he was looking for he lit one with nervously jerking fingers and inhaled, long and deep. Bea knew it was time for her to go. There was no more to be said, no more to be discovered here. But a strange reluctance, an intimation of some kind that was linked with an inexplicable sadness, kept her rooted where she stood.

Wally stood by the window, looking moodily at the storm and blackness outside. As the silence grew between them, Bea joined him and together they watched the rain as it beat against the glass. It was impossible not to think of that other, rain-streaked window in Baggot Street, twenty years before. Bea had believed then, mostly in Wally. And Wally...She would never know what, if anything, Wally had believed in.

It was he who broke the silence.

"Look Bea," his voice was expressionless, almost as if he knew what her answer would be. "People like the pictures. Does it matter who paints them? Can't you just let it go?"

"You know I can't. It's unfair in so many ways. Unfair to real talent. Unfair to those who buy because they believe they're buying the work of an established and highly regarded painter."

"But we could make a lot of money, all of us. You too." He grinned with something of the old Wally devilment. "And that money would support real talent. Mine." He moved back to the easel, stood looking at his picture. Bea looked at it too, one last time.

"Keep painting, Wally," she said. "Try to sell a few." Her voice hardened. "Because I'm going to see that you reimburse at least some of the buyers."

Wally gave a short, derisive laugh. "You can try," he shrugged and then, before Bea could stop him, ground the cigarette viciously into the picture in front of him.

"Goodbye, Wally," Bea said. As she left, he was looking blankly at the damaged canvas.

In the main room, Nigel Spenser was pouring himself yet another glass of wine.

"Ah, the beautiful Bea!" He waved the glass in her direction, considerably drunker than before. "I hope your erstwhile husband has convinced you of the benefits of going along with our little scheme."

"'Fraid not, Nigel. It's back to treading the boards for you, to earn an honest shilling if you can."

She reached the front door and began to open it. Spenser's arm encircled her waist from behind and a surprisingly strong arm forced hers away from the latch.

"Don't go." He spoke into her hair, his voice low and pleading. "We had something. You know we had..." Before she could move he had turned her around, was holding her tightly against him, his eyes mocking but insistent. "Don't resist, Bea, go with it."

Bea, rigid with fury, tried to pull herself away. "Let me go!" She almost spat at him. "You vain, idiotic..."

"He likes it when they protest." The actress's voice was a rapier. "Don't you, Nigel? Don't you?"

With a sigh and a shrug Spenser released his hold on Bea. The actress, dressed now in a black négligé but effectively *déshabillée* glared at him in unhappy anger.

"Just trying to help in my own little way," Spenser said. "Once she leaves here, we might as well pack our bags and get out of the country."

"The things you do for the cause." The actress moved to his side. "You promised to come to bed." She bent forward, managing to reveal perfectly shaped breasts. Spenser grinned and reached for her.

"I did too," he said and then, more softly, "and now it's bedtime." Slowly and quite deliberately, he took one of her nipples between two fingers. Bea wordlessly lifted

the latch and slipped out of the cottage. She had pulled
the door behind her and was facing into the night when
she heard his voice, loudly laughing, calling after her.
"We'll meet again, Bea Hennessy, we'll meet again."

CHAPTER
TWENTY-EIGHT

On the way back Bea drove slowly. She didn't have any option. A gale-force wind buffeted the car, rain beating mercilessly against the windscreen, and the road, narrow and twisting though it was, ran ahead of her like a river. The pitch-black night offered no light or comfort.

Keeping as close as she could to the mountain, she tried not to think of the sheer drop on the other side of the road. Earth and stone, loosened by the force of the rain, formed slippery, muddy patches on the road, slowing her to a nightmarish snail's pace. Every so often a blast of rogue wind caught the car, shaking it almost out of her control, stretching her nerves to screaming point. Several times she imagined losing control and saw herself, trapped in the car, tumbling down, down, into the rapacious jaws of the Atlantic.

It seemed an eternity before the car coasted down to a reasonably safe level and the force of the gale abated. When she at last rounded a bend and saw the lights of the village in the distance she was aware of a loud sobbing sound and slowly realised that it came from herself.

She did not stop in the village, didn't stop until she came to Caherciveen and then only because it was nearly closing time. She needed something to give herself energy for the journey home and this would be her last chance.

The doorstep sandwich made by an obliging barmaid, after a quick look at Bea's white face and shaking hands, did a lot to comfort and calm her down. Two cups of sweet, scalding tea, insisted upon by the barmaid, restored her enough to go on.

"Feeling better?" The barmaid's round, genial face enquired without presuming. The bar was warm, bright and reassuringly noisy. Bea nodded, tried out a smile and found that her facial muscles worked.

"A lot better now, thanks," she said and paid. When she came out the petrol pumps reminded her to fill up the car. The woman did this for her too. She left before her kindness and the blessed normality of the place seduced her into staying.

The storm went on but the wind and rain were nothing as bad as they had been on the exposed hill of the headland. Bea turned on the car radio, got FM3 and a Chopin prelude, tried to catch its mellow mood. But images intruded: of Wally's painting, Spenser's eyes, the cottage in the storm, James's face. Music failed her as it had never failed her in the past.

It was the driving, eventually, which offered a sort of therapy. As mile after mile of road was eaten up by the car, as the events of the previous few hours were put further and further behind her, a sense of detachment came upon her and she managed, for a while, to look at her situation objectively. It didn't change anything but it did dull the sense of betrayal and anger she'd been feeling all day. These were soon replaced by another emotion.

"I've lost the gallery. All those years. It'll never survive."

She was not prepared for the sense of grief this brought to her, the desolation. The gallery had been the ballast in her life, her own creation, her security for nineteen years. Now it was gone, destroyed by the person who, by abandoning her, had driven her to set it up in the first place. She could not, would not, begin to think of life without it. Not tonight anyway.

This time she took the ring road at Limerick and when she reached the other side found that the worst of the storm had been left behind in the south-west. Almost unconsciously she began to plan. She would grab a few hours sleep then begin cancelling first thing in the morning. She could get to everyone by midday. God knows what Olivia had been up to in her absence. She must have guessed where Bea had gone but would have had no way of getting in touch with Wally to discover the outcome of the confrontation.

"No, only I was fool enough to risk the drive in that storm…" Bea thought bitterly. "And I am a fool." Fool or not, she was glad she had done it. At least now she knew everything.

At least she was a fool who had a daughter. Thank God for Sinéad. She was going to need her in the days and weeks ahead.

Resolve came somewhere around Naas. As she hurtled along the last stretch of motorway Bea felt the stirrings of feelings she was more used to. She had never in her life been defeated. She was not going to lie down now and have all that she'd worked for destroyed. Not by Wally and not by Olivia. Certainly not by an amoral shyster like Nigel Spenser. She would begin again, rebuild her own reputation and the gallery's.

She would do it if it took her the rest of her life.

It was after four in the morning when she drove into Dublin. Her plan of action involved being at the gallery first thing so she drove straight there now. Her body ached with tiredness as she wrapped herself in a blanket. Somehow, she managed a troubled three hours sleep. By seven o'clock she was on the phone, making the first calls.

When the caterers turned up a few hours later, she paid them and sent them away. When she gauged it was time for them to be in their offices she phoned the critics, the special "name" guests, her regular buyers. Slowly and painstakingly she went through everyone on her invitation list. She spoke personally, she left messages and with everyone she was brief.

"I'm sorry. The pictures are fraudulent. I'll be issuing a statement." By noon she had told everyone.

CHAPTER
TWENTY-NINE

B ea took the pictures down, one by one, deliberately. When she had stripped both exhibition rooms she stood for several minutes looking at her naked walls. This was it. This was how things would be in The Hennessy Gallery unless she worked, fought back. But she had done all she could do for now.

Staving off the still, empty hours of the afternoon ahead she began busily to make coffee. She ground more beans than she needed, overfilled the kettle, washed a mug which was perfectly clean. Once the coffee was made she sat sipping, glad of its black strength, waiting for the phone to start ringing. When Olivia arrived, she was an almost welcome respite.

Bea did not want to see her sister. She did not want to talk to her, face her betrayal. But it had to be done and perhaps now was the best time while, she was in the process of tearing down. There might never be a better occasion to dismantle the façade of friendship she and Olivia had pretended to for years.

So she looked up calmly as Olivia burst into the gallery. Her sister did not look well. The week at the health farm might have toned her body but her face showed its age in a way that Bea had not seen before. Its creamy freshness had gone and her skin looked stretched and strained. She was wearing red again, a Cerruti suit with short skirt and long, gilt-buttoned jacket. It was, Bea knew, a favourite item of Olivia's wardrobe. But today its vivid colour merely emphasised the pale, taut quality of her sister's skin.

"What the fuck have you done?" Olivia did not swear, as a rule. She usually controlled the strident tendency in her voice as well. "You've ruined everything..." Her voice rose as she spoke and ended almost in a squeal.

Bea, gripping the mug tightly, stood up from the desk and walked to the window. The naked hatred on her sister's face shocked her to the core. She'd had no idea, no idea at all, that Olivia hated her so much. But it explained everything. Simple greed had seemed such an inadequate explanation for what Olivia had done.

But hatred...hatred was so much more powerful, so much more capable of destruction. It had kept Jude alive for years after life had ceased to have any meaning for her. And Bea now felt sure it was hatred that had made it possible for Olivia to go along with Wally's scheming.

But Bea was not going to become part of a triumvirate. Let Olivia hate. Let her continue Jude's life. Being hated did not mean she had to hate in turn. She turned to face her sister.

"I suppose I *have* ruined everything, from your point of view. I prefer myself to think that I've set things to rights."

"The thing I hate most about you," Olivia's lips were a tight, red, barely moving line as she spewed out the words, "is your almighty and unbearable self-righteousness. You were always the same, even as a child..."

Something snapped in Bea. The shock, anger, desolation and sheer physical strain of the last twenty-four hours were more than she could take. Her sister's bile, itself the malignant result of their mother's own hatred of and disgust at her children, was the last straw this morning. Still holding the mug of by now lukewarm coffee she advanced on her sister and yelled loudly, with a great feeling of liberation:

"Shut up, Olivia! Just shut up and get out of here! I don't ever want to see you in this gallery again! Out! Out!" She brought her arm back in a wide arc and, with a sense of wild exhilaration, emptied the mug of coffee in one great, darkly staining splash over the glowing red of her sister's Cerruti ensemble.

Olivia's shock was complete. While Bea, close to hysteria, laughed uncontrollably, Olivia stared, disbelieving, at the ruin of her suit. She seemed dazed, as if unable to comprehend fully what had happened. The phone began to ring but Bea, almost crying now, didn't hear it. Its shrill pealing jolted Olivia into action. "What am I going to do?" Her wail was the distraught cry of a child who has lost a toy. "I can't go out like this! I don't even have the car with me..."

Bea, calmer now but no less resolute, stepped past her sister and opened the door.

"Well, you can't stay here."

Holding the door open, she tried to stop herself shaking. She became aware of the phone ringing, then stopping. It began to ring again, almost immediately. She ignored it. She very much wanted to be alone, certainly did not want Olivia around any longer. Bea knew her sister to be incapable of fully comprehending the evil of what she had done, selfish, immoral creature that she was. There was no use in arguing, no point she could make that Olivia would see or care about anyway. She did care, very much, about the pictures being down and the cancelling of the exhibition. Those things meant the end of her dream of lotsamoney. And she cared deeply about facing the street, being seen in one of Dublin's main thoroughfares in a coffee-stained suit.

Bea watched while Olivia made matters worse by rubbing frantically. She was not normally vengeful but would at that moment have gleefully thrown a second mug of coffee, if she'd had one to hand.

"I won't go," Olivia sai. "I'm staying here until I get a taxi."

"Oh no, your're not! You can hail one in the street. Or you can walk, run, stand bloody still out there. Do whatever you like. I don't care. But you are *not* staying here!" She wedged the door open and moved, determinedly, on her sister.

Olivia, at last conscious of the steely purpose facing her, whimpered and backed away. Instinct told her that Bea had been pushed far enough. Any further and the chances were that she, Olivia, would be propelled, head first, into the street. That was an indignity she could not risk. If anyone were to witness it her reputation would be ruined; as it was there were too many people around town willing to pull her down. As things stood she might, be able to salvage something from this débâcle with a lot of work and some luck.

"I'm going, I'm going."

She edged around Bea's grimly poised figure. Once in the street she tottered blindly, head down and bag clutched in front of her, in the direction of the nearest hotel.

Bea watched her for several moments from the window before making her way through the still, empty gallery rooms to her office. The phone was ringing again. Too tired to think and too drained to talk to anyone, she removed the handset, cut off the male voice which had begun to speak, and sat listening to its empty purr. Her hands, she noticed, were trembling uncontrollably. She became aware too of a throbbing headache and at the same time, to her surprise, of tears streaming down her face.

Too weary to care, she allowed them to run as she looked at the stacked pictures, trying to banish thoughts of betrayal and her own stupidity. She sobbed quietly for a long time. When it seemed at last that she could cry no more, would never have tears to cry again, she put her head on her arms, bent over the desk and fell into an exhausted sleep.

A hand on her shoulder, gently but insistently shaking, woke her. She had no idea, as she looked at Sinéad's worried face, how long she'd been asleep. There were sounds from the gallery. Oisín lay asleep in a carry-cot on the floor.

"You okay?" Sinéad gently brushed a strand of hair from Bea's forehead as her mother unsteadily stood up.

"I'm fine." She tried a smile, found it helped. "Really fine." The words helped too so she said them again. "Really, really fine..."

"Good," said Sinéad. "Because we've decided that a little celebration is in order."

As she spoke she closed the door firmly on the gallery, cleared the desk and placed a large suitcase on top. Out of it she produced a complete change of clothing for Bea. She had been to the flat and chosen well from her mother's wardrobe. There was nothing defeatist about the chocolate-coloured suede skirt and paler, toning, linen tunic. Nor about the shoes, high enough to give Bea a dominating elegance. Sinéad spoke quickly, full of no-nonsense cheer. "You don't need to explain a thing. I *know* what's happened. Olivia freaked out yesterday and Mark began a bit of detective work. We couldn't get you, of course, and only pieced things together late last night. When Olivia came up with some information. God, mother, that was *such* a stupid thing to do—I mean going off to Kerry! I was out of my mind with worry." She gave the dazed Bea a quick, fierce hug before turning her towards the shower room. "I got your message on the ansaphone this morning but haven't been able to get through to you since then. We decided, Mark, Daniel and I, that a celebration of your timely discovery of the fraud would be *just* the thing."

Propelling Bea quickly along, she finished talking only when she'd closed the door and was satisfied her mother had turned on the shower. "All you have to do is make yourself presentable."

As the streaming water cleansed her and brought her fully awake, Bea reflected wryly that Sinéad's approach was probably as valid as any. Why not a party? Why not celebrate discovery and exposure?

Twenty minutes later, after a few whispered words to the sleeping Oisín, Bea opened the office door on a gallery transformed. From somewhere a table had been procured. It had been covered with long-stemmed glasses, fresh salmon and a dizzy display of hors d'oeuvres. There was champagne too and a great many smiling faces. Amongst them, Bea saw James, Daniel, Mark, Stephanie and even, she noted with intense gratitude, a few of her regular buyers.

"Oh, God." Her throat constricted. There was nothing to be said. Sinéad gently took her arm and led her forward as everyone raised their glasses.

"To Bea," James said and put an arm tightly around her. As the gallery rang with the unfamiliar and raucous sound of "For She's a Jolly Good Fellow" Bea, for the second time in a few hours, felt tears on her face. She had thought them all spent—but these tears were different. As she lowered her head towards her glass one dropped with a small splash into the champagne. The sparkle went on tickling her nose. Life, she knew, would go on like that too. Her betrayal would, in time, become nothing more than a small forgotten splash. She raised her own glass. "To The Hennessy Gallery!"

CHAPTER THIRTY

The rain and wind had spread across the country from the south-west to the south-east. With the wind behind it, the black Volvo, with English registration, was making good time in its feverish rush to catch the car-ferry from Rosslare.

Just outside New Ross, on the last lap of its journey, the Volvo passed a high truck coming in the opposite direction. The truck swayed in the wind, and, exactly as it had done earlier, one of the boxes of vegetables it was carrying fell off and burst open on the road. The truck driver hadn't noticed them. He was unaware now too, when a second carton became dislodged and fell, narrowly missing the black car. He shrugged when the Volvo's horn blared at him. English drivers never knew how to handle Irish roads.

The Volvo hurtled on, the driver intent and alone in the front. In the back his three passengers slept. The road widened and the Volvo accelerated. When the road narrowed again it did not lessen speed. The windscreen wipers, working flat out, were barely managing to clear the glass.

The driver could not have stopped even if he had seen the vegetables strewn on the road. He went straight into them and the car went into a spin, wildly and with a malodorous scorching of tyres. It did not stop until it had ploughed through a low wall and smashed into a heavy tree on the other side of the road.

The horn, blaring into the wind and silence which followed the sickening sound of impact, alerted the occupants of a nearby house.

An ambulance, quickly on the scene, removed the dead body of the driver, a dark-haired man in his early forties. The occupants of the back seat were found to be in a state of severe shock but otherwise unharmed.

CHAPTER
THIRTY-ONE

W ally was buried, on a day of rare autumn beauty, in Dean's Grange Cemetery. Bea had seen to it that he would be buried there. She had seen to everything since, in the end, Wally had had no one else. To have him rest close to his son, in peace at last she hoped, had seemed somehow the right thing to do.

The funeral was a lonely affair. Nigel Spenser, shaken and subdued, had been there. He and Bea did not speak. A brother of Wally's, whom Bea had never met, came too. He was a sour, bitter man, a lot older than Wally. Meeting him gave Bea some inkling of why Wally had cut himself off so completely from his family. There had been no meeting of minds between him and Bea, not even a feeling of shared grief. Bea doubted they would ever meet again. She felt immeasurably sad.

Sinéad stood by Bea and wept, more for what might have been than out of sorrow for a father she had never known. Olivia was there. She seemed quite anguished and had to be supported by Albert and Mark. Bea was shocked to see how like Jude she was becoming. James sent his condolences but, at Bea's request, did not attend. James was for another day.

Bea drove straight to Inverskena after it was over.

Inverskena seemed to her the only place she could gather her thoughts, make some sense of everything that had happened in the last year.

Charles and Jake were waiting for her when she drew up. Jake growled, deep in his throat, as she got out of the car. "Oh, shut up," Bea spoke with infinite tiredness and Jake, without even a bark, walked away.

"Was it very grim?" Charles gave her a quick hug and wrenched her bag from the car.

"Not too bad. All over now anyway."

They sat for a long time by the drawing room fire, quietly, not talking much. There was not a lot left to say. Tomorrow, maybe Bea would start forgetting. When she began to feel the peace of the old house creep over her, and knew she would sleep, she said goodnight and went to bed.

But sleep did not oblige. She lay, listening to the night sounds in the house, images of Wally shuffling through her mind. Wally as he had been twenty years ago, full of life and love and good sex. Wally full of bravado and smiling lies as he had been at Christmas, less than ten months ago. And then Wally as she had last seen him, paintbrush in hand and filled with despair. Just one week ago.

She did not weep. She would weep no more for Wally, nor for herself.

Sometime in the night a sort of peace came to her and, with it, sleep.

Before it claimed her, a thought, grim but satisfactory, occurred to her. Wally's death had given her more than her freedom. After twenty years of living without a husband, twenty years of being neither a divorced nor single woman, she at last had a status recognised by the

State. She was a widow.

She slept until noon. She would have slept longer except that Jake, returning from a walk with Charles, began frenziedly barking at a crow.

"He's doing it on purpose," Bea groaned as she slipped out of bed. She stood for a while at the window, seeing how the trees were already becoming bare, their gold turning brown and falling. In the distance the church spire pierced a clear blue sky.

"Tomorrow is here."

She spoke softly. And now that it was, she knew she should never forget. She would simply find a resting place in her thoughts, maybe even in time in her heart, for Wally and for what they had once had together.

Downstairs, Charles had a brunch waiting for her. "When you've eaten I've got something to show you," he said. His eagerness was obvious and Bea obliged him and didn't dawdle.

"The picture you were working on at Easter?"

"The same." Charles insisted they both take a glass of claret before he led the way to his studio.

When she saw the picture Bea was glad of the wine. This was one to toast; Charles had at last struck gold. The murky canvas had been transformed into a pastoral scene bursting with life, colour and vitality. Bea, recognising the work of a celebrated nineteenth-century artist, lifted her glass to Charles.

"You've done it," she smiled.

"I have, haven't I?" Charles raised his glass to hers.

"A toast," she said, "to pictures, life—and whatever's to come."

Shaken & Stirred
by
COLETTE CADDLE

Businessman Doug Hamilton had everything under control – but he didn't have a heart attack on his agenda.

When it happens, his is not the only life shaken up.

Pamela, his ambitious wife, lives in a perfect world. It is thrown into chaos when his illness stirs up new emotions and leads him to question his life and their future.

Gina Barrett gets that promotion. Life could be bliss – if she could find a man who understood the meaning of the word "commitment".

Susie Clarke is over the moon when she lands the job of her dreams – except that she's nineteen, pregnant with the father fast becoming a distant memory.

**SHAKEN AND STIRRED –
CAN THEIR LIVES EVER SETTLE AGAIN?**

Shaken & Stirred, available from
Poolbeg, The *Irish* for bestsellers

ISBN 1 85371 9587

£6.99

Too Little, Too Late
by
COLETTE CADDLE

Stephanie West is fed up.

She has a job in a successful restaurant that she
loves but a boss she hates. The only answer seems
to be to leave.

Amazingly, an opportunity arises to buy him out
and she jumps at it.

So when her boyfriend Sean lands a job with a
software company in Phoenix Arizona and wants
her to go with him, Stephanie is clear about where
her loyalties lie . . .

But ghosts from the past have influenced her
decision. Can she come to terms with them? And if
she does, will it be too little, too late?

Too Little, Too Late, available from Poolbeg,
the *Irish* for bestsellers

ISBN 1 84371 693 6

£6.99

A Taste For It
by
MONICA MCINERNEY

A trip to Ireland to promote Australian food and wine –
Maura Carmody can't wait to get going.

A week promoting wine, then three weeks as guest
chef in a top cooking school – she is confident she
can put Lorikeet Hill, her South Australian
restaurant-winery, on the map.

The wine's been shipped, the menus tested –
everything has been planned to the last detail.

But Maura has not planned for the whirlwind of
mishaps, misunderstandings, rivals and revelations that
awaits her in Ireland.

And she's forgotten to cater for love

A Taste For It, available from
Poolbeg, the *Irish* for bestsellers

ISBN 1 84223 043 3

£6.99

Dancing Days
by
ANNE MARIE FORREST

Ana: a little girl intently dressing up in her old friend Celia's jewels . . . a young woman walking alone to church in her bridal gown . . . a loving wife who suffers tragic loss but survives to travel to Africa and fall in love . . . an ageing woman who still has an eye for form and likes to take a risk, ride pillion on a motor-bike, sing in a woodland glade with a handsome gardener . . .

Ana: who always depends on life's unexpectedness . . .

When such a woman at last comes to retire, do we believe for a moment that her dancing days are over?

AN UPBEAT, HILARIOUS AND TENDER NOVEL FROM THE AUTHOR OF THE BESTSELLING

Who Will Love Polly Odlum?

***Dancing Days**,* available from Poolbeg, the *Irish* for bestsellers

ISBN 1 84223 045 X

£6.99

Three Times A Lady
by
SARAH WEBB

Meet three very different women

Sally's back from the Caribbean where she has been
working on a luxury yacht.
She eats men for breakfast and now she has a certain
man in mind!

Eve is an accountant, a solitary control freak who
has chosen career over love and lived to regret it.

Ashling is a journalist, bringing up a six-year-old son
on her own. The only man she trusts is hundreds of
miles away . . .

Three women with one thing in common:
Mark Mulhearne.

And now he's back for a certain school reunion.
Maybe, just maybe, he can be persuaded to stay
for good.

Three Times A Lady, available from Poolbeg,
the *Irish* for bestsellers

ISBN 1 84223 042 5

£6.99

Take 2
by
MARIAN MURPHY

*Clare looked around her apartment one last time,
took a deep breath and left. The click of the door behind
her had a satisfying finality.*

*Now all she had to do was find a life she
might want to live*

Clare needs to escape – from the city, from a
humdrum career, from the aftermath of a
disastrous love affair. And for Clare "escape"
means only one thing: her little cottage in
Connemara, in the West of Ireland.

There she finds herself converting the cottage
outbuildings into holiday homes and though her
blueprint does not include a new man in her life,
relationships too have a way of developing . . .

Second chances, new beginnings and the courage
it takes to turn your back on the past and get on
with your life.

Take 2, available from Poolbeg,
the *Irish* for bestsellers

ISBN 1 85371 918 8

£6.99